PRAISE FO

A ...

"Great dialogue, a w........ story line, and, not one, but two very romantic couples! What more could a reader ask for? Don't miss this latest novel by Nicole Byrd."
—*Romance Reviews Today*

"A fun historical romance starring likable sisters and the hunk cousins who fall in love with them . . . readers will enjoy this jocular tale."
—*Midwest Book Review*

Seducing Sir Oliver

"Charming and delicious—*Seducing Sir Oliver* will seduce anyone who loves witty, adventurous romance!"
—Celeste Bradley, author of
Desperately Seeking a Duke

"Superb."
—*Midwest Book Review*

Gilding the Lady

"A riveting read."
—*Romance Reviews Today*

"Another awesome book by Nicole Byrd, and I look forward to reading more from such a wonderful author."
—*Romance Junkies*

continued . . .

Vision in Blue

"A superb and compelling Regency historical that will keep the reader riveted to the page . . . A wonderful, richly detailed reading experience. Complex, humorous, and sensual, *Vision in Blue* will delight historical fans."

—*The Romance Readers Connection*

"Ms. Byrd does a fantastic job . . . I look forward to the next book in this intriguing, well-written series."

—*The Best Reviews*

Beauty in Black

"The social whirl of Britain's Regency era springs to vivid life." —*Publishers Weekly*

"Another delightful tale by the multitalented Nicole Byrd . . . Heartwarming, humorous at times . . . a well-written page-turner." —*Romance Reviews Today*

Widow in Scarlet

"Nicole Byrd scores again with her latest Regency historical . . . with touches of suspense, sensuality, and the exotic."

—*The Romance Readers Connection*

"A superb Regency tale you won't want to miss."

—*Romance Reviews Today*

Lady in Waiting

"Byrd's unpretentious writing style and sense of humor render this a delicious read."
—*Publishers Weekly*

"Byrd sifts a measure of intrigue and danger into her latest historical confection, which should prove to be irresistible to readers with a taste for deliciously witty, delightfully clever romances."
—*Booklist*

"A prime example of a Regency-set romance done well, with personable characters, intrigue, and a lovely secondary romance adding spice to the mix."
—*The Romance Reader*

Dear Impostor

"Madcap fun with a touch of romantic intrigue . . . A stylish Regency-era romp . . . satisfying to the last word."
—Cathy Maxwell, *New York Times* bestselling author of *Bedding the Heiress*

"A charming tale . . . Great characters, a plot that keeps the pages turning, and a smile-inducing ending make this a must-read. Delightful, charming, and refreshingly different . . . Don't miss *Dear Impostor*."
—Patricia Potter, *USA Today* bestselling author of *Beloved Warrior*

"*Dear Impostor* is the real thing—a story filled with passion, adventure, and the heart-stirring emotion that is the essence of romance."
—Susan Wiggs, *New York Times* bestselling author of *Dockside*

Enticing
the Earl

Nicole Byrd

B

BERKLEY SENSATION, NEW YORK

THE BERKLEY PUBLISHING GROUP
Published by the Penguin Group
Penguin Group (USA) Inc.
375 Hudson Street, New York, New York 10014, USA
Penguin Group (Canada), 90 Eglinton Avenue East, Suite 700, Toronto, Ontario M4P 2Y3, Canada
(a division of Pearson Penguin Canada Inc.)
Penguin Books Ltd., 80 Strand, London WC2R 0RL, England
Penguin Group Ireland, 25 St. Stephen's Green, Dublin 2, Ireland (a division of Penguin Books Ltd.)
Penguin Group (Australia), 250 Camberwell Road, Camberwell, Victoria 3124, Australia
(a division of Pearson Australia Group Pty. Ltd.)
Penguin Books India Pvt. Ltd., 11 Community Centre, Panchsheel Park, New Delhi—110 017, India
Penguin Group (NZ), 67 Apollo Drive, Rosedale, North Shore 0632, New Zealand
(a division of Pearson New Zealand Ltd.)
Penguin Books (South Africa) (Pty.) Ltd., 24 Sturdee Avenue, Rosebank, Johannesburg 2196,
South Africa

Penguin Books Ltd., Registered Offices: 80 Strand, London WC2R 0RL, England

This is a work of fiction. Names, characters, places, and incidents either are the product of the author's imagination or are used fictitiously, and any resemblance to actual persons, living or dead, business establishments, events, or locales is entirely coincidental. The publisher does not have any control over and does not assume any responsibility for author or third-party websites or their content.

ENTICING THE EARL

A Berkley Sensation Book / published by arrangement with the author

PRINTING HISTORY
Berkley Sensation mass-market edition / April 2008

Copyright © 2008 by Cheryl Zach.
Cover art by Lesley Peck.
Cover design by George Long.
Hand lettering by Ron Zinn.

All rights reserved.
No part of this book may be reproduced, scanned, or distributed in any printed or electronic form without permission. Please do not participate in or encourage piracy of copyrighted materials in violation of the author's rights. Purchase only authorized editions.
For information, address: The Berkley Publishing Group,
a division of Penguin Group (USA) Inc.,
375 Hudson Street, New York, New York 10014.

ISBN: 978-0-425-22097-9

BERKLEY® SENSATION
Berkley Sensation Books are published by The Berkley Publishing Group,
a division of Penguin Group (USA) Inc.,
375 Hudson Street, New York, New York 10014.
BERKLEY SENSATION and the "B" design are trademarks belonging to Penguin Group (USA) Inc.

PRINTED IN THE UNITED STATES OF AMERICA

10 9 8 7 6 5 4 3 2 1

If you purchased this book without a cover, you should be aware that this book is stolen property. It was reported as "unsold and destroyed" to the publisher, and neither the author nor the publisher has received any payment for this "stripped book."

Once again, as ever,
For Sid

One

"*They do say he's desperate handsome,*" the first hotel maid said as she scrubbed the door panel. "And a wild man in bed!"

"Tell me some'um I ain't 'eard," the second maid jeered. "The earl's famous for 'is way wid the ladies. And I 'ear 'e's dumped the 'igh-priced ladybird 'e's been supportin' in such style. She'll 'ave to find some'un else to pay for 'er 'igh perch carriages and diamond-studded boots. Wish I 'ad a chance to take over her post, and she could 'ave this 'ere mop!"

Grinning at this fantasy involving the Quality's love lives, she sloshed her mop about on the staircase landing, splattering drops of dirty water. Thick with muscle, her arms wielded the handle with ease.

"Ha!" The first servant snorted. "You and me and half of London's females, besides. He's probably built her a castle—and–and—God knows! Who wouldn't want to be mollycoddled with jewels and pretty clothes, and made love to night and day?"

"It'd jolly me just to spend a few 'ours alone wid a man like that!" The other maid groaned in mock ecstasy, and both servants dissolved into fits of giggles.

Who indeed?

Seated on the stairs a flight above them, Lauryn Applegate Harris wrapped her arms about her knees, feet drawn up beneath her, and wondered if she would ever meet such a man. It didn't seem likely.

She had been in London for six weeks, and this—eavesdropping on the hotel maids as they worked—was as close as she had come to any social life. Not that Lauryn had clothes suitable for entering Society, anyhow. She was still wearing the rusty black gowns she had dyed for her unexpected widowhood last year, and now she lacked the money to replace them. Just this morning she had found a hole in her last pair of good stockings. Being poor was enough to make a saint curse.

And she was no saint—just a young widow who was acutely weary of always making do with too little and forever covering up her own sadness as she tried to help her father-in-law, the squire, cope with his. He had taken the loss of his only son so hard that she'd feared more than once for his sanity. And the only comfort that might have assuaged his misery was beyond her power to offer. If only she had given her late husband an heir. . . .

Then Squire Harris would have had something to console him and take his mind off the terrible deprivation they both felt. And she would have had some part of her husband to hold on to, and a child to love.

She pushed away the guilt that rode as constant companion with her lingering grief. She had to look forward, not back, as her four sisters reminded her in their letters.

"If you will not come home, if you are determined to stay and aid the squire, please try not to dwell on the past," her older sister Madeline had written. "You know we love you, Lauryn. I write this for your own good."

Everyone had advice. Easy for Madeline to say, Lauryn thought, as her sister cuddled her own firstborn, with a husband beside her to offer his strength and support. But Lauryn knew the counsel was sincere. Early on, she had made herself ill with grief, and at some point, she'd realized she could bear no more tears and sleepless nights. None of it would bring Robert back. Now if she could just hear a little laughter again, once in a while enjoy an outing and a pretty dress—was she terribly selfish to think such thoughts?

She'd had few enough such entertainments to enjoy even before Robert's death. Sighing, she glanced at the sewing basket beside her and the abandoned stocking she'd been trying to darn.

Wedding her childhood sweetheart when both were quite young, Lauryn had expected to live an agreeable life with her husband, bearing many children, with long, happy years to enjoy them together. But the babies had not come, and as the years passed, Robert had seemed to accept their childless marriage.

Their first flush of postwedding passion had drifted into occasional lovemaking and pleasant companionship, and her husband had amused himself instead with hunting and shooting and the details of running their small estate. Perhaps more aware of time's relentless passage, Robert's father, the squire, had appeared more concerned about the lack of an heir—the next male in the Harris family line was a distant cousin whom the squire detested—and Lauryn herself had felt the guilty burden of her barren state.

Then Robert had been struck down by a sudden illness. Now, at the age of nine and twenty, Lauryn found herself a widow, doomed to a life of sitting on the sidelines, wearing her widow's weeds and her matron's cap, and watching other young ladies dance—if, indeed, she ever had the chance to attend a ball again, which didn't seem probable.

And now—

A new, brightly colored dress, nothing black or gray or even violet . . . a handsome man with eyes only for her . . . a man who made her blood quicken once again, a man who made her feel alive, not in the grave with her poor, struck-down-too-soon young husband . . .

Oh, was she a terrible person to allow such wistful reflections to dwell in the farthest reaches of her mind?

Despite herself, Lauryn's reflections turned to the scandalous Earl of Sutton. What did he look like, this much talked about lord? What would it be like, to be the lady he sought out? For a moment, her pulse quickened, then the fantasy faded. Turning back to her basket, she picked up the wooden darning egg, which she thrust into the heel of her stocking. She'd better darn that hole, unless she wished for cold feet, as she and licentious earls were most unlikely to meet!

Hours later, when her father-in-law returned at long last, his face appeared gray with fatigue. He had looked weary before, but this was worse. His eyes had seemed lifeless ever since Robert had died, but now—now, the light inside them had retreated even farther.

Lauryn opened the door to their rooms. Observing his slumped shoulders, she swallowed hard. "Are you all right, sir?"

"I've lost it all, Lauryn. All. I'm an old fool."

Her first feeling was one of relief. Perhaps now he would return to Yorkshire and give up this reckless behavior, drinking too much, gambling with men with deeper pockets. The squire had never spent so much time in the city before. Normally, he was content in his own shire, on his own acres, but after losing Robert, it seemed as if he could not stand the sight of his own land, not without the son who should have inherited it.

Without an heir . . . Guilt moved once more inside her, and she tried to push it back.

"Do you have enough left to pay the hotel's charges? We can return to Yorkshire—"

"You're not attending, child. There's nothing to go back to." He rubbed his hand across his face.

"What?" She felt the first stirring of panic.

The squire's voice shook a little, and she could smell the drink thick on his breath. That had likely not helped his skill at cards, but she would not remark on it. It did little good to offer censure after the fact.

"I don't know how I shall pay the hotel, or how we shall

eat. The pot had gotten so large, and I was in so deep—it was all I had left to cover my losses. I thought with just one more good hand, I might redeem it all—"

He named a figure that made her blanch and reach for the support of the back of a chair to keep her legs from folding.

"And then I lost again. Now the land is gone, the estate in Yorkshire, and the worst of it is, I don't think the earl even wants it. He was making jokes about moth-eaten sheep to the rest of the table when I took my leave. I've already written him out a deed—best to get the thing over with, don't you know—but he'll like as not toss it away or throw it into another card game."

The squire dropped down onto the side of the bed as if his legs would not hold him. He buried his face in his hands.

She patted his shoulder, but her stomach roiled, and she thought she might be ill. The squire's land—the land that had been in his family for generations—the land that should have been Robert's some day—gone in a game of cards? The squire wouldn't survive this!

"Who is it—to whom did you lose it?" she asked, when she could make her voice work. Could she call on some of her brothers-in-law to come together and as a group loan the squire enough to get his land back? Would his pride endure such a lowering blow? She doubted she could get his permission to even ask.

"The Earl of Sutton," he told her, his tone grim. "It might as well be the devil himself . . . he has the devil's luck at cards, I can tell you."

Lauryn was glad her father-in-law was lost in his own misery and not watching her face as he lay back on the bed. She had gone quite rigid.

Sutton? The notorious rake the hotel maids loved to gossip about? He was the one who now possessed the squire's deed and other vowels? Good heavens!

Was the earl a cruel man? Had the gossip about him ignored that side of him—was this an aspect she had not realized as she'd painted him in her daydreams? Or were the eternal card games that the men played just ignorant of all real life outside of the patter of cards and the skill or the luck that determined who came out on top?

And if the squire had been lost in the deepening circle of his despair, would someone else, if not the earl, have been bound to have won. . . . Should she blame the earl for being the winner or was it just fate?

Yet why should she let the earl off the hook? She didn't even know the man! It was the squire who was suffering, who would suffer. . . . Was there anything she could do to help?

That land had been in the Harris family for more than a hundred years. Even though not formally entailed, it was meant to stay in their family. She had not dreamed of anything else, and she knew the squire hadn't, either, so she could not think what momentary madness had led him to offer it up as collateral.

Could Lauryn do anything? Although Madeline had been the "little mother," Lauryn had always been there to offer help, the gentle middle child who looked out for her younger sisters, who assisted around the house when her mother had died too young, who had made her father smile by being mature beyond her years—it was second nature.

And to be truthful, if aiding the squire now brought her into contact with a handsome, dissolute lord who might bring some excitement into her subdued, even bleak existence—she felt a small thrill deep inside, and she was aware that the idea didn't exactly displease her.

Feeling guilty at once, she pushed the feeling back. She had to think first of the squire. She went back to check on him and found him dropping off to sleep.

Lauren pulled a blanket up over her father-in-law as he shut his eyes and fell into a troubled slumber, muttering and tossing about now and then. She went into the next small room and paced up and down as she tried to think.

Despite the lateness of the hour, she was suddenly wide awake. She went to the window and opened the pane, leaning out to look and listen. The street was still busy with elegant carriages returning from evening engagements.

Lauryn thought of the affluent, perhaps titled personages inside, with their fancy clothes and rich and privileged lives. That was the existence the Earl of Sutton must lead. What would he want with the squire's small Yorkshire estate, and how could she convince him to release it? If she told him how devastated the squire was and why—no, no, it would be unfair to strip away all her father-in-law's dignity. Plus, if he should find out, he would never forgive her.

Men were stubborn, as well, about gambling winnings—it could become an affair of honor if she were not careful. Then both men's hands would be tied as to what they could do.

Sighing, Lauryn rubbed her temples, which all at once threatened to ache. One would think she must have something of worth to give the earl in return, in order to get the squire's estate back, but imagining what was near impossible. She looked down at her empty hands. She had nothing of value to give. She had no jewelry, except a few trinkets of sentimental value that Robert had given her. She had had no real dowry; her own family was not wealthy.

For some time her thoughts flew from one impractical scheme to another. And then the obvious answer came to her.

She had only herself. . . .

Lauryn blinked. What about—no, no, that was unthinkable. Was it?

Jumping up, she ran across to the small looking glass on the wall. She strained to see her reflection in the faint light now coming from the window as the sun fought to rise over London's horizon, its weak rays pushing valiantly through the haze of coal dust from countless chimneys.

In her girlhood Lauryn had been called pretty by swains in her shire. She made out a familiar pale, heart-shaped face, with large green eyes, delicate features, and long hair of a golden hue with reddish highlights, just now pulled back behind her head. No longer the girl she had been, but not totally repellant, surely. Was it enough to satisfy an earl known for his discerning taste in women? If she went to him and pledged to serve as a–a courtesan, would he engage her?

How did such a woman work?

Her heart dropped. She had no clothes! How could one look alluring in faded black mourning gowns?

Still, perhaps she could ask for a wardrobe as one of her terms of engagement, Lauryn told herself. That would solve the problem quickly.

Was that typical of courtesans? She wished she knew more of such women. But really, how could she be expected to? Ladies were never informed about that side of life. Lauryn bit her lip. The earl must not know her background, or he might not retain her—even the notorious Earl of Sutton might have some scruples.

She would just have to hope for the best. She balled her hands into fists, wondering if she had the nerve to carry through with such an outrageous, highly improper scheme.

If anyone found out, she would be ruined for life. Still, it wasn't as if she expected to ever have the chance to marry again; she had no money to attract another husband, and she expected her first husband's property, even if they should get it back, would stay with his family line. It would be different if she had borne him children, but—

What would her father, her sisters, say?

Perhaps they would not have to know.

Even if the earl agreed to such an arrangement, he would surely tire of her quickly. She had a dim idea that men like that did, and didn't the maids' gossip bear that out? Then she could return to her real life. And courtesans did not go into company with ladies of quality. Lauryn knew that much!

She would use an assumed name, staying away from anyone who knew her, and no one in London did know her, as she had not been out in company, not having the clothes or the money to do so.

And she was not an innocent young thing, virginal and untouched. She was a married woman, or at least, a widow now, but the main thing was she had experience in the marriage bed. She would not be shocked, Lauryn told herself, and she could—she hoped—keep him interested for a few weeks, at least, enough to make their bargain valid.

She paced up and down again for several hours, trying to think of possible loopholes, likely weaknesses in her scheme. Was there any better way to save the squire's home? She could think of none.

Finally, she stared into the looking glass again and observed the look of determination on her face. She tucked a few straying locks into place before she picked up her simple bonnet trimmed with black ribbon.

If she were going to do such a thing, she had to do it now before she lost her nerve, Lauryn told herself. She checked on the squire, who still slept, his breathing heavy with the aftermath of too much drink.

She hesitated for a moment at the door to the hall. Was she really going to go through with this insane idea? It was madness.

But a thrill of excitement moved inside her at the thought of living with a handsome lord, of being indiscreet, of kissing and romancing an experienced lover—surely she deserved a few weeks of being wicked after spending most of her life obediently toeing propriety's line.

After Robert had died, she had ached for him, and their bed had seemed so painfully lonely. She had been so agonizingly aware of how much her body had craved a man's touch. . . .

Could she not be wicked just briefly, just once? Surely a man who had sought out so many women must know how to please a lady . . . or any woman at all!

And it would be for a greater good, if she could retrieve the squire's land. She couldn't bring back Robert, but she could give his father back his home.

Taking a deep breath, Lauryn headed down the stairs.

At the bottom of the landing, she almost bumped into the hotel owner's daughter, a quiet, rather shy young woman, who must be a year or two older than Lauryn herself. They had chatted a few times since Lauryn and the squire had taken up residence here.

"Are you all right, Mrs. Harris?" Miss Mallard asked.

"Yes, I just—I wasn't looking where I was going, forgive

me." Lauryn paused for a moment and gave the other a brief
smile. "I may be going out of town for a time if I—if I get a
post with a—ah—noble family. Would you—could you keep
an eye on the squire for me? Sometimes he doesn't think
about ordering dinner when he gets into a despondent mood."

"Oh, the poor man misses his son, I'm sure." Miss Mallard
shook her head. "And it will be worse with you not here. I will
try to make sure he remembers his meals, without being too
intrusive. You take care."

"Thank you," Lauryn told her. And then, feeling that she
had done what she could, she pushed open the outer door and
stepped into the courtyard.

Sutton was halfway through a stack of letters, most of it
business and all of it, sadly, demanding his personal attention,
when his butler coughed from the doorway.

It was the *your attention is needed, truly needed, my lord,
or I would not interrupt you* cough, so he reluctantly raised his
head.

"There is a young lady to see you, my lord. She says the
matter is urgent."

"At this time of day?" Sutton knew his tone was skeptical,
but most young ladies of the Ton were still abed at nine in the
morning, or at the most out riding in Hyde Park, where they
could be seen by other fashionable ladies or admired by young
sprigs of fashion.

He had been up late himself, playing cards at a smoky
gaming hell in a disreputable part of town, but he never indulged himself by sleeping late when he had business to be
seen to, and besides, he hoped to leave London by tomorrow.

His half brother Carter was at the Lincolnshire estate, and
if left to himself, was sure to get into trouble.

And what the hell did she want of him?

"Did you make my excuses?" The butler was usually good
about shielding him from those kindly souls collecting for good
works or from matchmaking mamas foolishly endeavoring to

introduce him to giddy daughters. "I am in no mood for charity seekers."

"I did, my lord, but she is quite—ah—persistent," Parker said, his usually bland expression covering some emotion Sutton could not quite read.

The earl was aware of a flicker of curiosity.

"Very well, show her in, but warn her I have time for only a short interview." He put the paper, a ship's bill of lading, back on his desk.

At first glance, the female who entered his study did not seem particularly prepossessing. Of medium height, dressed in shapeless, drab black garments, her figure was obscured, and beneath a bonnet that had seen better days even before it had developed a fatal droop, her face was hard to make out.

But when, standing, he motioned to a chair in front of his desk, she sat down and loosened the hat, removing it so that he got his first good look at her, his interest quickened. She had the face of a classical beauty, pale skin and delicate features, with hair of a pale reddish gold. She met his gaze with her chin up and a defiant intelligence burning in her clear green eyes, and that stirred his curiosity even more.

"How may I help you, Miss—?"

"Smith, Mrs. Smith," she said quickly. "I—I have come to you seeking employment, my lord."

"Indeed." He paused, not sure how to go on. She might be poverty-stricken. Indeed, she looked it in a genteel kind of way, as a country parson's daughter might, but she was, in her speech and her deportment, also obviously a lady, so how on earth she could expect to serve in his household, he could not think. She could not mistakenly think he was married with children, and be looking for a post as a governess? It was about the only situation in which indigent ladies could earn a respectable income. He opened his mouth to disabuse her of the notion, when she spoke again.

"I realize–I realize this is unexpected, but–but I have need of a position, and I–I have reason to think that you have a vacancy—that is, that is I have heard gossip—I mean, I have heard comment—"

She stopped again, her face flushing as she seemed to search for words. She was not looking for a post as governess, he decided.

Fascinated, Sutton gave up trying to guess. This was too entertaining, even though he knew it was too bad of him to be amused by her discomfort.

"I wish to obtain a post as–as a courtesan," she blurted.

Sutton knew that his eyes must have bulged. "What?"

"Yes," she said, looking relieved that the word was out. "That's it. I realize I have no recommendations—"

The earl had to hold his breath to keep from whooping—he wanted to laugh so badly he had to ball his fists and stiffen his whole body. "I see. That is a problem," he managed to say.

She stared at him anxiously. "But I do have experience, my lord, and I assure you that you would not regret taking me on."

With a surge of heightened awareness flooding his whole body, he had a sudden image of tipping her over the desk and "taking her on," then and there. He drew a deep breath.

Perhaps she also realized how the term could be construed. Blushing, she turned her gaze toward the marble surround of the fireplace.

"Indeed," he said, his tone neutral.

Oh, God, he thought, wondering that he had been so bored this morning that he had longed to walk out on the desk full of business and social correspondence. Now he wanted to roar with laughter and—and more. He wanted to tilt up that heart-shaped face and try out those "experienced" lips and see just how much of a hoax this all was!

What in hell was she playing at?

"And what kind of wages are you expecting, may I ask?" he inquired, his tone very polite.

"Oh, the–the usual," she said, her voice airy. She waved one hand. "A–a new wardrobe, of course."

He nodded. "Of course." He would burn that black gown she currently wore with absolute pleasure, he thought. It made her look like a pudding insufficiently cooked. But her slim hands and the well-shaped ankles he had had a glimpse of when she had sat down suggested that her figure deserved much better.

She glanced at him, as if to gauge his response. "You may—you may shower me with jewels, if you like," she suggested.

Sutton swallowed another shout of laughter, managing with some effort to keep a straight face. "I will consider it," he said instead.

Had she been reading the worst of the scandal sheets? This must have to do with his recent "retirement" of his poorly chosen and short-lived—ah—*courtesan*, as this surprising guest chose to call it; *harpy* would have served for his last companion, *greedy*, *scheming*, *selfish*, and *untrustworthy* were a few other terms that came to mind.

"But the main thing," she went on, and this time he saw the effort it cost her to keep her voice level and her expression calm, "the main thing is—I should like a small estate."

"Really?" Watching her, he narrowed his brows. "That is quite a costly proposition, Miss—Mrs. Smith."

"It does not have to be close to London," she added quickly. "So it does not have to be quite so costly, my lord. In fact, it can be a good deal farther away, perhaps in the North Country, somewhere like Yorkshire. . . ."

So that was it, the earl thought grimly. Had Squire Harris sent this innocent to get back what he'd lost? If the man had done this in cold blood—what was she, young wife, daughter, what?

His face must have shown his disgust, because the young lady in front of him looked alarmed. Sutton tried to smooth out his expression.

"Yorkshire, you say?"

Still watching him anxiously, she nodded.

"It seems to me I might have recently won a small estate such as that in a card game. I will turn out the contents of my pockets and peruse my winnings. Then I will give some thought to your proposition. But now it is your turn."

"My turn?" She stared at him as if he had turned into a bear from the circus.

"I must see a sample of the wares if I am to consider buying," he told her, his tone pleasant and noncommittal. "That is a reasonable request, as you know."

Her eyes widened, and she looked as if she might slide off the chair. But she pulled herself together quickly.

"Oh, oh, of course, my lord," she stuttered. "What do you wish me to do?"

"Take off your gown," he ordered.

Two

*W*ondering if her ears had heard the words correctly, Lauryn stared at him. Take off her clothing, here and now? Had the man no shame?

"I–I can't!" The words burst out without conscious mandate from her brain. If her plan was to work, yes, of course he would have to see her unclothed, but—in his study in the middle of the morning? Without even the pretense of wooing? How cold-blooded could any man be?

"Of course, you need help with your buttons," the earl said calmly. He stood up and came around the desk toward her.

Lauryn jumped to her feet in alarm and just stopped herself from backing up and running out the door. If she did that, she knew she would never be able to come back, and her precious plan would be for naught.

But she thought she couldn't breathe. Without seeming to notice her panic, the earl went behind her and slipped a button through its hole at the back of her well-worn black gown. She felt his fingers, warm on her skin, even through the fabric.

And he was so tall that he seemed to tower above her; his breath stirred her hair—why had she been moved to take off her bonnet? Robert had stood only ten inches above five feet, a decent enough height for a man, but the earl was so tall that—

She couldn't think. She felt her dress loosen as he continued to slip the buttons free of their confinement, and the bodice sagged. She grabbed it before it could fall. She couldn't really take it off, could she? Could she go through with this?

Did she have a choice?

Not if she wished to follow through on her outrageous plot. . . .

The earl walked back around to lean against his wide mahogany desk and observe her, his expression so impersonal that she felt an urge to kick him. "You may remove your gown any time you are ready, Mrs. Smith. Unless you are having second thoughts. Perhaps you have reconsidered your offer?"

Was he deliberately taunting her? Did he suspect something? He must not!

Spurred on, she slipped one arm out of its sleeve, holding on to the prim neckline of her day gown in order to hold it high, then slowly withdrew the other arm, still gripping the bodice so that not an inch of her cleavage was revealed. She watched him as she did so and could not help but see a change in his eyes, no matter how hard he tried to maintain a dispassionate countenance.

She'd show him second thoughts!

Now she lowered the gown slowly, very slowly, so that a curve of pale skin was exposed. Then the thin creamy muslin of her shift and her light corset were revealed, the curves of her breasts showing clearly above the restraints of the corset as she allowed her day dress to puddle at her feet.

He blinked and appeared to take a deep breath.

"Ah, I fear we shall have to go to a deeper level," he pointed out, and his voice sounded a bit husky. "We have really not scratched the surface of the matter, so to speak."

Show him her naked self? Here and now? In a pig's eye!

"But first," she retorted, having regained her balance, "I might ask the same of you, my lord?"

"What do you mean?" he asked, his glance wary.

"You may also remove your clothes," she noted, her tone demure. "Do I not have the right to also examine how sound is the compact I am making?"

He opened his lips, but nothing came out.

Expression calm, Lauryn waited. It was a totally spurious argument, of course. The man had such wide shoulders, such a trim waist, and such an obviously well-made body—no padded tights or creaking corsets necessary for the earl—that a closer look was unnecessary. Add his well-built body to his ruggedly handsome face, with its dark eyes, dark hair, slashing brows, strong nose and chin, and he would have had no—and she knew he had never had—problems attracting women of any class or status.

"Ah, I see your point," he murmured.

But instead of backing down, as she had expected, his next actions gave her a jolt of surprise and shock.

He put his hands to his carefully arranged neckcloth and pulled it loose, then unwound it unhurriedly from about his neck. He allowed it to fall to the desk, draping it unheeded across the piles of paper.

Surely he wasn't going to undress!

Lauryn knew her lips had fallen open, and she hoped she had not gasped aloud. No, no—this was not what she had meant to occur. Oh, dear lord!

One part of her mind spoke coldly—*It will have to happen sooner or later, you ninny*! But the other side said, *Not yet, not yet, we have to build up to it*—if he has an ounce of sensitivity in him—but perhaps men who felt any sensitivity were not men who hired courtesans.

Now he was tugging off his tightly fitting, exquisitely tailored jacket. Oh, heavens, oh, heavens, what was she to do now?

And all the time he watched her, observing her reaction. Lauryn tried to stay calm, tried to maintain her air of business as usual—wasn't that what a woman of the world would do? It was her best guess, anyhow. But she feared she must have gone pale. At any rate, her hands felt cold and she knew her heart was beating fast.

His waistcoat came next; he unbuttoned the silver buttons with alarming speed. And now the earl's hands dropped to his white linen shirt. Just how far was he going to undress? And what would happen then?

Lauryn's hands might still be cold, but other parts of her body were becoming strangely warm and quivery.

He lowered his hands to pull his shirt over his head—

The door to the study opened, and the butler stood in the doorway.

Lauryn gasped, and the earl abruptly dropped the tails of his shirt back into place.

"Yes, Parker?" he snapped.

"Ah, beg pardon, your lordship, but your agent is here—"

"Put him in the book room, and tell him I will be with him presently," the earl said, his tone still curt.

Withdrawing in some haste, the butler shut the door behind him.

Lauryn fought a dreadful desire to giggle hysterically. Worse, she thought that the earl—who glared at her suspiciously—knew precisely why she bit her lip and almost dared not breathe. If she laughed, she feared he might become quite angry. And he had not yet agreed to the bargain, she told herself. That cured her of the desire to laugh.

"As you can see, I have business to attend to," the earl pointed out, his tone austere.

"Of course, your lordship," she said, keeping her own voice meek. "I would not wish to take up too much of your time. So, do you feel I should be suitable for the post?"

What he thought, Sutton told himself, was that she was a minx—and he still wasn't sure who had put her up to this, or why. Was it possible she was really doing this on her own? Or was the squire—it had to be he—forcing her into a disgraceful situation?

It mattered, because if she were someone's cat's-paw, he could not allow her to be treated so badly. If, on the other hand, she had chosen to engage in this mad venture on her own, then–then–then he knew just what he might chose to do to those luscious lips and curving breasts—

He shook his head to clear his thoughts—

"You don't think so?" she said, her voice distressed. "But I had hoped that we might be well suited, my lord." She began to dress and gathered her things.

He realized she had taken the motion for an answer.

"Ah, no, that is, I mean, yes, we will suit nicely, I should think." He realized he was making little sense, but at least the panic in her eyes had eased, and she had unclenched her hands.

She blinked at him. "You mean you will? Employ me?"

"Yes, at least, I have decided to give you a trial engagement," he told her, keeping his expression bland. "We'll say two weeks, and if both sides are amenable, and all is satisfactory, two weeks more, and then we shall be open for possible extensions."

He had a sudden vision of the horrible scene that had ended his last affair, and he said quickly, "But keep in mind, this is a purely business arrangement. There will be no talk of love or lasting commitment, no suggestion of anything more between us than mutual pleasure and physical enjoyment."

She nodded slowly. "Of course. I would expect nothing more."

He added, speaking more gently, as he remembered her first stipulation, "I'm planning to leave London tomorrow, so we'd better make our plans quickly, don't you think? If you will wait in the small room just down the hall, I will send for my valet, whose name is Boxel. He will accompany you to a good dressmaker to have your measurements taken."

She stared at him.

"For new gowns," he reminded her.

His newly acquired paramour dropped her bedraggled bonnet on the floor as she impulsively clasped her hands together, then she blushed again, even more deeply than before. "Oh," she said. "I mean, yes, of course. Thank you, my lord."

He nodded.

Retrieving her bonnet, she left the room with a bemused expression on her face, and Sutton told the footman to ask his valet to come down to speak to him, wondering what on earth the man would say when he was told his errand. Boxel had been with his master since long before Sutton had achieved his title, and he never hesitated to speak his mind.

Nor did he now.

"She don't look like no light o'love to me, yer lordship," the servant told him. "I took a peek at 'er in the anteroom. Yer sure ye know what yer doing? This is likely to end up costing ye dear, and I don't mean just in coin."

"It is not your place to suggest to me that I might be an idiot, Boxel," the earl said, his tone stern, thinking that none of the other staff would dare to intimate such a thing.

Sadly, the stout servant with the balding head looked unimpressed.

The earl's frown deepened. "Just see to it that she orders a reasonable amount of clothing and have it sent on to the country. I plan to leave town tomorrow."

The servant rolled his eyes, but he turned toward the hall. "Don't say as 'ow I didn't warn ye," he muttered, going out the hall door, although his expression showed only the proper mixture of respectful obedience.

Sutton grimaced at his back. If this woman turned out to be trouble, Boxel would never let him hear the end of it. He should probably just send her away and be done with it. What did he care about the squire's pitiful estate, anyhow?

But the earl pictured the way that fine-textured gold hair curled at the base of her long neck, where a strand or two came loose from her severe updo at the back of her head, and he thought of how it would be to shake free the whole contraption and release the mane of hair, free it from all restraint and let it fall in silken waves down her back, lying easily on her smooth skin—upon a naked body free of any corset or shift or other "proper" cover-up that would prevent him from seeing every inch of that enticing ivory skinned body . . .

Just thinking of the possibilities made him ache.

He had been relieved to see, when she had slipped out of her dowdy black dress and he had observed her more closely, that she was not a girl in her first season. Somehow that made it more likely that she was not being pushed into offering herself at someone else's bidding. He had noted the subtle signs of maturity around her eyes and mouth, the more ample breasts—he felt another surge of desire at the memory—of a woman, not just of a girl barely out of the schoolroom, and thus he could believe she understood what she was doing with this offer.

No, he didn't wish to send her away. He would risk the consequences, dammit all! He was no faint heart, afraid to take the first fence, afraid of what lay beyond—

When he picked up the bill of lading, he stared at it for a good five minutes before he realized he had no idea what he was seeing.

The valet was an older man who wore an expression of unqualified disapproval. Lauryn thought his haughty politeness was much more alarming than his master's. The carriage ride made her tense with nerves, and she was relieved when she could step down at last and enter the couturier's shop. But then she found she had wasted the ride worrying about Boxel when she should have spent it thinking what she would say to the dressmaker. How did one explain that one had taken up a life of disrepute? Did the dressmaker have some code word for expressing that fact without excessive embarrassment to all concerned?

A young shop assistant was the first to greet them. "Yes?" Her glance at Lauryn's shabby black dress made her expression doubtful, as if they did not appear to merit an enthusiastic welcome. "Perhaps you are seeking the shop next door?"

Lauryn blushed, still not sure how to explain, but she had not allowed for the sheer efficiency, disapproval or not, of her escort.

Boxel fixed his stern stare on the shop assistant. "This lady is the companion of the Earl of Sutton. I believe Madame duPree will be pleased to assist her? Or should we take our business elsewhere, to the Austrian couturier on Bond Street, mayhap?"

"Oh, oh, no, indeed, sir," the assistant stammered. "You

don't want to go nowhere else. Indeed, she will wish you to stay. If you'll just step into the fitting room here, ma'am."

Boxel was left with a glass of wine, sitting in a gilt chair that looked too fragile for his sturdy frame, and Lauryn was soon measured up, down, sideways, and every other way she could imagine, and shown fabrics of the most delightful hues and textures by Madame duPree herself, as well as not one but two assistants, including the first, formerly supercilious one who now oozed nothing but politeness.

When Madame heard that they were leaving at once for the country, and speed was highly desirable, she was helpfulness itself. "Fortunately, Madame Smith," she said, waving her measuring tape as if it were a magic wand. "I have several gowns almost done for customers who are, unlike yourself, not in such a 'urry. The dresses are near your size, and in pleasing colors that will suit your complexion. They can be made over for you with very minor inconvenience, and you will 'ave a few costumes ready to take with you, and then the rest will be sent out for you within a few days, as soon as they can be completed."

"That's very kind," Lauryn said, a bit taken aback. "But will not your other customers object to—ah—"

"Not at all, they will be delighted to be of service," Madame duPree predicted with complete lack of guilt.

And one of the assistants added, in a conspiratorial whisper. "Don't worry. They won't know. The earl pays very well, you see!"

Obviously, the earl had done business here before, Lauryn realized, trying not to blush. With which one of his many conquests? Oh, well, best not to dwell on that. Think instead about the wonderful new gowns she could enjoy. And the ladies she was depriving of their gowns—they would get their dresses, just a bit more slowly, she told herself, as she submitted to having a creamy silk dinner gown dropped over her head and the waist adjusted to her own measurements, while a gold-thread trim was loosened to allow for her more ample bosom.

Next came an azure ball gown—there would likely be no balls in the country, but she was too dazzled by the beauty of the dress to object, and another dinner dress, then two day dresses. Last, a handsome navy traveling outfit that—"So fortunate!" the dressmaker proclaimed—could be made ready to go with only an adjustment to the bodice and a slight change made to the waist.

Lauryn found herself almost dizzy with happiness at the thought of putting aside her faded black garments, worn for so many months. "I shall have to visit a hatmaker," she thought aloud, "and, oh, undergarments, and I suppose shoes . . ."

"No, indeed," Madame duPree corrected, frowning. "They will come to you, Madame Smith. When we are done, the artiste from the next street will be here to check your sizes."

And so he was, leading a line of young assistants almost invisible behind the stacks of hatboxes they carried. And what a joy to choose among so many pretty bonnets! The afternoon passed quickly, and by the time she was sufficiently outfitted— amazed by the number of outfits and accessories that were considered necessary for a few weeks in the country—she found herself quite weary.

But the only time she had dared to object that she might not need so many, Boxel, who had looked in now and then to see how the fittings were coming, had at once frowned her down.

"Would you disgrace the earl by a poor display, madame?"

"Oh, no–no, of course not," she'd stuttered, flushing.

So she reminded herself now that she could not disgrace the earl, as she did not dare to incur Boxel's censure yet again.

When at last the shopping was complete, and most of the her purchases sent on to the earl's residence, with only a few kept by her, Boxel had fixed her with his stern look. "I suppose you are coming back to the earl's residence?"

"No," she blurted without even thinking about it. "I will join you in the morning."

"I see. Then I shall escort you home in the carriage." He looked somewhat suspicious. "What address shall I give the driver?"

Ah, where indeed? If she went back to the hotel, the squire would demand to know where she was going, and she didn't wish to explain in person, not wanting an argument, and she certainly didn't want the earl's servant to find out she had any possible link to the squire. Lauryn thought rapidly, then named the street.

She was silent on the ride, and when the carriage stopped again, even Boxel looked surprised when he looked out at their destination. "You are staying at a church?"

"At the rectory," she said, her tone pleasant. "The vicar never gives up on seeking to reclaim souls." Giving the valet a sweet smile, she stepped down from the carriage, took her bundles of purchases from inside the vehicle, and turned to walk up the pathway to the rectory building.

And hoped God would not strike her dead on the spot!

To her disapproval, the carriage lingered until the door to the rectory opened, but the housekeeper knew her and admitted her readily, and at last the vehicle pulled away.

"'Ow are you, Mrs. 'Arris," the placid woman said. "Where is the squire? Is 'e not with you?"

"He's a bit under the weather," Lauryn said, thanking heaven for the good-natured but rather slow-witted servant. "So I left him at the hotel. Is my sister in?"

"I'm afraid not, ma'am, but the vicar is 'ere. 'E's in the sitting room if you'd like to go through," the housekeeper said. "I'll make up a nice pot of fresh tea for ye."

"Thank you," Lauryn said. She left her packages on the side of the front hall—the phlegmatic housekeeper might not have wondered at Lauryn's unusual whirlwind of shopping but her more sharp-eyed employer might. Then she went on into the sitting room, where she found not just her good-looking brother-in-law, but a small, sweet-faced toddler with a strong resemblance to her mother.

"Juliette, how are you?" Lauryn said, as the little girl exclaimed in delight and immediately barreled into her legs.

"Mind your manners, little ruffian," her father admonished, his tone good-natured, but he shook his head as he scooped up his daughter.

"It is very nice to see you, Lauryn. Ophelia has gone down to the theater for a few hours to observe a rehearsal, but she will back shortly. Is Squire Harris out gaming again, or could he be thinking of at last returning north? Not that we wish to say good-bye to you, but I know his behavior since you've come to London has greatly troubled you."

"No, but perhaps now he will have to." Without mentioning her own wild plan, Lauryn told the vicar quickly about her father-in-law's losses at the gaming table. "If you could visit him with enough to pay for the hotel fees, and urge him to return home, Giles, I would be much obliged. He will not ask you for help himself, I know."

"And you?" He was entirely too perceptive. "What are you planning, Lauryn? I sense that you have something up your sleeve, as well."

Her small niece was reaching for her, and Lauryn took the little girl into her arms and threw her up in the air to make her giggle. It made it easier to evade the vicar's kind, but searching gaze. "I have accepted a—a post with a titled family for a few weeks to earn some money on my own." It was—more or less—the truth.

"Ah, and you think that will shame the squire into settling down? Perhaps it will work. It's time he ceased his tumultuous behavior and accepted his son's death, as deeply painful as I know it was. But Robert would not wish to see his father destroyed, or you."

She could not look Giles in the face, and if her own complexion reddened, she hoped he would think it was from the exertion of tossing about his small daughter.

"You're very kind," she murmured.

"We care about you. Don't stay too long, and don't stay at all if you are unhappy with the family, Lauryn," he told her as she continued her lively play with Juliette, who looked as delicate as a fairy child but was, in fact, as tough as ever her mother had been. "You know you are always welcome with us, or indeed with any one of your sisters."

That made her eyes dampen, and she blinked.

"I hope the children you care for are not as rambunctious

as this harum-scarum," her father said as he reclaimed tiny Juliette. "Enough, little one. Allow your aunt to go up and wash for dinner. Your mother will be home soon."

And how would she evade her sister's sharp eyes when she told her tale again? Oh, dear. Lauryn smiled her thanks and retreated while she could. She retrieved her packages from the hall and went up to the guest room upstairs where she could shut the door and bathe her flushed face with cool water. How did deception grow so quickly complicated?

Fortunately, when Ophelia returned from the theater, she was full of tales of the new play she had penned that was almost ready to open, and although ready to commiserate with her older sister over the predicament that the squire had gotten them both into, she was not as inquisitive as she might otherwise have been.

"I do think you need not hire yourself out, however, Lauryn. You cannot be making that much for a few weeks. Stay here with us, instead, if the squire has become irksome, and you wish for a change of scene. Children can be very wearying, let me tell you!"

Young Juliette was upstairs asleep in the nursery by this time, but Juliette's mother shook her head at the veracity of this statement.

Lauryn laughed, but she assured her sister she was determined to carry out her plan. "I have given my word."

"At least, do be sure to leave us your direction," the vicar said, his tone firm.

"I will," Lauryn said, meekly, though she wondered just how she was to do that without giving away the falsehoods she had wrapped her mustard seed of truth within.

She went up to bed early and slept little. When daybreak came, she woke and sat up in bed, looking out to see the flowerbeds beside the rectory, and the handsome spire that rose from the nearby church. She felt a wave of guilt at the course she was about to take.

How could she leave a vicarage and the good people who slept here and go out to assume a life as a courtesan? It was unheard of. And yet, if she did not, the squire would not get his estate back, and what was he to do? He would have to be persuaded just to take a loan to pay off the hotel charges; he would never take the amount needed to redeem his gambling debts, even if Giles could afford that large a loan, which Lauren doubted.

No, she would go, as promised.

And when she unwrapped the brown paper that had hidden the new traveling costume, so handsome in its navy broadcloth, with gold trim and shining buttons, but still neat and ladylike, she could claim no altruistic motives but the simple pleasure of donning a new outfit. It fit her well after the last-minute alternations, and she looked so much nicer than she had in ages. And the simple but nicely made hat with the navy trim, and the new gloves and stockings—oh, they all made her heart lift.

It was ridiculous how a female heart could sing when one felt well dressed. Yet she felt at once more prepared to face the world, even with the uncertain future that lay ahead of her.

And as for her promise to leave a direction—she sat down at the small table in her room and wrote:

> Dear Ophelia,
> Open this only if I do not return in four weeks, or fail to send you word that all is well.

And inside a second sheet of paper, she wrote:

> I have gone to the Lincolnshire estate of the Earl of Sutton.

And she sealed one paper with sealing wax, put it inside the other, and then sealed the other again.

She wrote one more short note to be sent to the squire, which she would post later, telling him she had taken a position for a few weeks with a "good family" and her sister Ophelia had the location, then she packed the rest of her belongings rapidly, took her carpetbag and hatbox, and stood listening at the top of the stairs. The house seemed quiet around her. She tiptoed down the stairs and at the bottom, almost jumped out of her new traveling clothes.

Still in her nightgown, Juliette sat on the bottom step playing with a ginger-colored kitten.

"'Lo, Aunt Lauryn," the child said cheerfully.

"What are you doing up so early?" Lauryn whispered. "You should go back to bed."

"Dat's what Nurse always says," her niece agreed. "But I like mornings. So does Snap."

That epithet seemed to apply to the kitten, who now curled up in Juliette's lap and purred contentedly as she rubbed its ears.

"That's good," Lauryn said. "Listen, my dear. I have a note for your mother. Can you remember to give it to her, and no one else?"

The little girl nodded and accept the small folded paper. "Are you going? Don't you want tea first? And a bun?"

"No, I must leave." The vicar had given her enough coin for a hackney, and she had no inhibitions about hailing one. She leaned to kiss her niece on the forehead and then picked up her bags again. "Go back to the nursery, my love, and don't forget the note. Give it to your mother."

Juliette nodded, making her uncombed blonde curls fly about her head. She watched her aunt let herself out the front door. Then she stood up. When she did, the kitten jumped down and ran around the back of the stairs, disappearing into a small hole beneath the stairwell.

"No!" Juliette objected. "Stay with me, Gin'ersnap!" She hurried after the kitten, dropped to her knees, and tried to squeeze her hand into the hole. She could barely fit her five fingers into it. "Come back! I'll gif' you my cream from breakfast."

But the kitten didn't seem impressed. It had disappeared into the darkness.

Sighing, she pulled out her fingers and looked at both of her empty hands, one now very dusty. Snap was gone, and Nurse would scold, Juliette thought woefully, wiping her fingers on her nightgown as best she could as she climbed the stairs toward the nursery.

Three

The earl had been distinctly disappointed when Mrs. "Smith" had not returned for the evening. Had she changed her mind? Lost her nerve?

For her sake, he should hope so. If, as he suspected, she had no illicit connections in her past, he should discourage this highly improper decision she had made.

Of course, she would certainly not be the first woman to be driven to prostitution by pure need, if that were the case, though he still suspected it had to do with the squire's lost estate. It happened more often to working-class women, but he felt sure that it was not unknown in the upper classes as well.

He should, but truth be told, he wanted her back. . . .

He kept remembering the curve of her neck where it met her shoulder, and how her hair had smelled of lavender when he had stood behind her, and how he had wanted to pull the strands out of their pins and allow it all to fall free down her back. . . .

And that wistful expression he had glimpsed in her eyes . . . how long had it been since someone had made her truly happy?

He tried to put her out of his mind. Dammit all, her problems were none of his affair . . . why could he not forget her?

But he had slept restlessly last night, waking often, and his body had made him aware of its needs—yet the thought of finding another woman to solace him was not appealing. He didn't want any other woman.

And that was a truly alarming thought. He had only seen her once; she could hardly have made such an impression upon him.

"You are not a green lad, ready to fall for a pretty face and a sad look, Sutton," he muttered to himself. "Get a grip on yourself, man."

But when he dressed, it took him much longer than usual to arrange his stock. When the earl tied his neckcloth—he always did his own—it twisted in his hands and refused to fold neatly. He ruined three pieces of immaculately pressed linen before finally getting one right. His expression impassive, Boxel stood behind him, holding out yet another long strip of white linen, his silence a reproach while his master swore and indulged his bad temper.

Marcus frowned into the looking glass. "You should have insisted she return here for the night."

"She wished to go elsewhere," the valet told him, not for the first time, his expression still impenetrable. "Ye din't tell me she was a prisoner."

"Of course she's not—she wasn't a prisoner, it's just—"

What if she didn't return? Marcus drew a long breath. Was it his fault? Had he scared her away? Was he so alarming?

Next Boxel couldn't seem to find the right jacket—Marcus shook his head at two, at last settling for a plain forest green, then slid his arms into the coat, shrugged once to settle it on his shoulders, and turned and hurried to the stairs. He wanted to go down and see—no, no, he only wished for his breakfast, that was all.

But when he reached the dining room and sat down alone at the long table, he found the tea was too bitter and his toast too cool, and the new cook couldn't seem to make porridge without making it too thin or too thick.

After only two bites, the earl dropped the silver spoon back into his bowl, pushing the whole thing away from him. He stood. He had no appetite at all. Everything was tasteless. Who would wish to live here, he asked himself. He couldn't even keep a decent cook, and besides—

Looking up, he saw Parker in the doorway, and hope flared inside him.

"Yes?"

"Ah, the young lady—"

"Yes?" the earl repeated, interrupting, then drew a deep breath and with a palatable effort pressed his lips together as he saw the look of surprise cross the butler's face.

"The young lady who was here yesterday—she has returned, my lord. I have put her in the book room."

"Why the hell did you do that, Parker?" Marcus demanded. "Show her in and invite her to have some breakfast. And bring me some of the ham and steak and take away this bloody porridge; it's an insult to man or beast. I wouldn't feed it to my dogs."

He suddenly felt hungry, after all.

He remained standing until he heard light footsteps in the hall, and then she appeared in the doorway, still looking somewhat abashed. But her appearance, in a navy traveling outfit, smartly trimmed with gold thread, was so much improved over the shapeless black gown of yesterday, that she looked like a different lady. Her color was a little high, but she held her chin up and her eyes were bright, and her radiant beauty sent a surge of awareness through his body as if he were that green lad and made him glad he was standing behind a solidly build chair.

"Please come and have something to break your fast," he told her. "I am happy to see you again."

She smiled shyly and allowed the footman to pull out a chair for her at the side of the table. She sat and waited for the servant to bring her a steaming cup of tea.

The earl sat back down, too, and did not speak again until she had a plate piled high with meat and eggs and bread.

His guest looked almost startled at such largess, but she took a bite of the ham and nodded her thanks.

"I'm afraid I arrived rather early," she said in a few moments, after she had swallowed her first bites. "I waited outside until the housemaid came out to sweep the front steps." She colored a little to make the confession, but he only found it charming.

"I am happy to see you back," he said again. "Besides, being prompt is an excellent habit. We can now make an early start for the country."

"Yes, I thought you might wish to do that," she agreed, looking down at her plate.

He let her eat. Now that he knew that she had not abandoned him, he could give his attention to his own food, which tasted much more savory. And although he wanted to reach out and stroke the small hollow at the base of her neck, or twist a loose curl of her shining hair about his finger, he knew he would alarm her, and there were servants all about . . . So he told himself he would have to be patient.

Soon enough, he thought, soon enough . . . but this would be an endless day before he would have the chance to get Mrs. Smith alone!

As soon as she had finished her meal, he ordered the carriage made ready, and her few pieces of luggage were added to his own and secured to the back or the top of the vehicle.

"You have no lady's maid?" he asked. His own faithful Boxel was ready to accompany him, as usual.

She shook her head.

"We will have to see about finding you someone," he told her as they walked out to the chaise. "Perhaps one of the housemaids at the estate, or someone from the village."

As always, Marcus himself would ride. One of the grooms had brought up his big rangy gray from the stable and stood holding the gelding, who shook its head and snorted with impatience, ready for a run. He would have to hold the horse to a short rein until they were out of the city.

He could have spent the journey in the carriage with his new paramour, of course, but in his experience, a cramped and jolting interior was hardly the best place to pursue passion, and certainly not with a new and perhaps inexperienced lover, even if his own servant had been exiled to an outside seat, which Boxel hated. No, Marcus wanted a more comfortable and convenient—and more private—setting than that!

So he kissed her hand before he helped Mrs. Smith—he wondered how long it would be before she told him her real name—into the carriage, then Boxel scrambled in after her, and Marcus mounted his steed and led them out into the London traffic, ready to leave the city behind.

Lauryn climbed into the carriage and sat demurely in the corner. She was aware of a distinct feeling of relief that the earl was not sitting beside her, but riding instead. She could postpone yet awhile any private time between them—not that it would have been private with the morose valet sitting opposite.

What would the earl say if he found out she was using an assumed name, she wondered uneasily. Would he be very angry, indeed? Feeling guilty, she gripped her hands in her lap and drew a deep breath, trying to ease the tightness in her shoulders.

At least Boxel was not inclined to chat. He gazed out the carriage's glazed windows, and she turned her head and did the same to the other side of the vehicle. They left behind the quiet square where the earl's residence was located, passed through the crowded streets of London's shopping distinct and past poorer residences, more crowded and with houses more close together than the West End. But Lauryn had seen the other side of London, so these lanes came as no surprise.

In time the coachman steered his team through narrower streets filled with drays and oxen pulling carts piled high with coal and turnips and other wares that kept the great city's shops and kitchens employed. Sometimes they slowed, and drivers shouted at each other, "Give way there!" or "Mind the carriage, ye lackwit!" but somehow, they always slipped through the narrow openings without the crash that seemed inevitable.

By and by the houses grew less frequent and meadows appeared, with cows and sheep grazing, and then fields dotted with farmers at work, and then the coachman cracked his whip above the horses' heads. The team could stretch their legs and settle into a faster gait, and the wheels hummed as the carriage rolled along the roadway.

After her restless night, Lauryn found her eyelids growing heavy. She dozed, her head falling back against the smooth leather squabs. So for her, the morning passed swiftly, and when the carriage slowed, she woke with a start.

Looking around, she asked in some confusion, "Are we there?"

"Naw," Boxel said. "We're only stopping at an inn for some refreshment; the earl must think you need a pick-me-up." He sounded a bit scornful. "And to change horses, a' course."

"Oh," Lauryn said. She had felt a stab of guilt. The valet had made it sound for a moment as if she were being a burden on their journey. Did Boxel think she was an imposition? But surely the earl, the much gossiped about rake, had had ladies—well, women—accompany him to his estate in the country before?

She pushed some straying hairs back beneath her hat and tried to straighten the jacket of her traveling suit, hoping she did not looked totally wrinkled already after sleeping in the corner for several hours. Then the door to the carriage opened, and it was the earl himself who looked in.

"Would you care for a light luncheon and a chance to stretch your legs, Mrs. Smith?" he asked politely.

"That's very kind of you," she told him, smiling shyly. She accepted his hand and his help to guide her out of the carriage.

Now she could see that they were indeed stopped at a handsome inn, with flowers blooming in boxes hanging from windows and its doorstep brushed clean. Ostlers ran about, changing the team, holding horses and lacing harness quickly back into place. She vowed to eat just as quickly so as not to hold them up. But she also became aware of a pressing need to use the necessary and was glad that they had made a stop.

The earl escorted her up the second flight of stairs and into a private parlor. He held a chair for her, but then turned aside to speak to their host, who was being most agreeable to his important patron, bowing and smiling as he showed off a bottle of his best wine.

"This here is our most mellow claret, me lord, and, you there"—he turned aside to say to his waiter—"bring up the roast turkey and that ham we had smoked, the big one, now, right away!"

Lauryn thought that this was not really her idea of a light luncheon, but no matter—she found that even after a hearty breakfast, she was, improbable as it might be, hungry again. After weeks of eating meagerly while the squire's funds had sunk lower and lower, it was a relief to not have to worry about where the money for one's next meal was coming from.

But first—calling over a maidservant who was pouring the uncorked wine into the glasses, she made a whispered query and excused herself briefly. When she returned, she found the table filled with enough food for a small army, and she shook her head at the earl's idea of a light refreshment.

She wasted no time in partaking of the bounty, and fortunately her host did not seem to expect her to make conversation. He only offered her, now and then, another particularly pleasing treat.

"Try the jellied apricots," he said once. "They go very nicely with the ham, which I will admit our host does know how to smoke properly."

So she did, smiling her thanks. And when Boxel disappeared, apparently to check on the progress of the team, and reappeared to report that the carriage was now ready, she at once pushed her plate back and prepared to stand.

But the earl shook his head. "We are in no rush," he said, his tone firm. "We have not even sampled the sweetmeats. And I have a particular fondness for the apple tarts the inn's cook prepares."

Sinking back into the chair, Lauryn brightened. Their cook at home made a wonderful apple tart. She was more than happy to try this one and see how it compared, so when the earl offered her a sample, she accepted.

Only after another half hour did they rise from the table and return to the carriage, and she was so replete from the excellent meal that Lauryn was sure she would be dozing again once the hum of the carriage wheels lulled her into somnolence with their rhythmic drone.

"Thank you for the excellent luncheon," she told the earl as he helped her once more into the carriage.

"You are more than welcome," he said, smiling at her, his usually stern eyes unexpectedly tender, with a light in them that made her blush. And again, he kissed her hand.

As she settled herself in the vehicle's interior, she felt a warmth inside her that had nothing to do with her full stomach. And when she gazed out at the green meadows, she was thinking, instead, of what she might see and experience tonight, at the earl's residence, and a growing excitement simmered in her veins. But as the wheels turned, the valet on the other side of the carriage was just as loquacious as he had been during the morning, and again her eyelids grew heavy, and soon she dozed.

When the carriage slowed once more, she sat up quickly. But this time there was no shouting or clatter of wheels on cobblestones as there had been at the innyard. Where were they?

She looked out and saw that the earl had ridden up to the carriage. He dismounted, and the groom had hurriedly jumped from the carriage and come to hold his master's mount so that the earl could open the door for her.

"I wanted you to see this," the earl called to her. "Your first look at the Fens."

Bending her head, Lauryn made her way out of the carriage. When she could look up, she gazed in astonishment at the landscape before her.

The land stretched out as flat and green as a billiard table. Waving fields of some type of grain moved in the constant breeze that made her glad for her warm navy jacket and, even then, she wrapped her arms about her body.

And the sunlight—the sky was so amazingly blue and the light so clear and brilliant that she narrowed her eyes. After a moment she realized that the usual dulling coal smoke that always clouded London's skies was absent, and the land was so flat, lacking the hills and dales of Yorkshire most familiar to her, that the sky seemed a bowl, surrounding them with an aura of pure sunlight. The light was clear and golden, slanting toward sunset but not yet turning rosy, and she thought she could hear a skylark faintly trilling with exuberant notes high above them in some distant corner of the sky. Dazed, she thought she might, like the bird, break into song.

Looking much less forbidding than usual, Sutton smiled. With a slight shock, she realized that he loved his home shire.

"It's beautiful," she said slowly. "Yet . . ."

"Yet?"

"I've always heard . . ."

She hesitated again, and he waited.

"I've always heard how dismal the Fens are," she said, daring to be honest.

"Oh, they often are, offering gray dank days in winter when the winds howl, or even perilous when the spring floods come and overflow the canals built to drain the natural lowlands." He nodded toward the flat lands around them. "But the land is very rich." He leaned over and picked up a handful of soil, letting her see the deep black sod that he crumbled within his fingers before allowing it to fall back to earth. "It rewards the farmers, if you know how to treat it, how to humor its moods. And the land has its own beauty."

She could not dispute that, looking at the undulating grain and the flat land that stretched as far as she could see, though now she could also see ribbons of water stretching through the vegetation, and streaks of black earth showing beneath what she decided must be growing barley.

She shivered as the wind gusted, and he motioned her back to the carriage. "Come, we're quite close now to home," he told her.

Back in the shelter of the carriage, she leaned to look out the window as the team broke once more into a trot, and the vehicle jolted back into motion. If she lived here, would she ever get used to the flatness, after growing up in Yorkshire?

What a strange thought—she was only staying a few weeks!

Shaking her head at herself, she shivered again and wondered what the earl's seat would look like.

Within the hour, her questions were answered.

The great house was built on a slight rise, like a small island amid the flat land that surrounded it. Probably built in the seventeenth century, she thought, a large house with wings reaching out to each side, and a central building with columns rising on either side of its massive doors.

Horses' hooves and wheels crunching on the gravel drive, the carriage pulled up in front of the great house, and Lauryn was eager to get out and stretch her limbs. She was conscious of the weariness caused by the long drive and of cramped muscles brought on by sitting for so long in the tight space.

As footmen came out to untie the luggage and bring it in, the earl had already dismounted. A groom hurried up from behind the house, and Sutton tossed him the reins so that the servant might take the steed, now tossing its head wearily, away to the stables.

"Give him an extra ration of oats, Wilson," the earl said. "He has had a long ride."

Then the earl turned back and offered her his arm.

Stern he might be, but he did not lack for manners, Lauryn thought, accepting with a grateful smile.

"You must be fatigued," he noted, not waiting for her to agree. "I will have a maid show you up to your room, where you can rest until dinner is served."

And thoughtful, she added to her list of his virtues, even if a bit peremptory in manner. But then, he was an earl; he must be accustomed to ordering people—as well as horses—about.

At any rate, she nodded and walked in at his side while the servants hurried about, following his commands.

Was that what she would be expected to do? Lauryn had a moment of doubt about her role here, but she pushed it back, not ready to examine the thought just yet. She wanted a few moments to admire the great hall.

A pair of marble columns inside the tall outer doors echoed the columns on the outside, and the high ceilings were gilded and crisscrossed with plaster moldings. Niches in the walls held classical statuary, and the floors were of hardwood and shone from years of polishing. It was like entering a museum or great cathedral. How did one live in such a building?

Feeling completely unworthy, Lauryn held on to the earl's arm and was glad that he didn't seem to expect her to comment on his home—her mouth seemed as dry as the Fens were damp—and they passed through the wide entrance hall and on to the staircase.

They climbed the wide staircase side by side, but she became aware of an unusual amount of sound spilling over from the next level, and the fact that the earl had tensed and a deep frown now masked his handsome face.

They reached the top of the stairs and turned toward the double doors of what must be the drawing room; music could be heard, and the sounds of quite a number of people talking and laughing. The earl's frown grew even deeper, and Lauryn braced herself, thinking he was about to shout.

But just as he seemed ready to explode, one of the doors opened, and a young man, with a superficial resemblance to the earl, but more slightly built and with lighter hair and eyes, came out into the hall.

"Oh, there you are, Marcus," the younger man said, his tone blithe. "About time you arrived."

"So it would seem," the earl said. "What in bloody hell are you doing, Carter, having a damn house party without consulting me first?" He did not raise his voice at all, but the coldness of his tone would have frozen a braver man than the calfling who stood before them.

However, to Lauryn's private surprise, the young man did not quail as she'd expected. He might have blinked a time or two, but on the whole, he seemed to hold his ground.

"Oh, come now, Brother," he said, trying to smile as heartily as he had on first seeing them. "You'll make this lovely young lady think you're a grumpy old bear."

"I'm Carter Sutton, the earl's half brother, don't you know," he added for her benefit.

"How do you do?" Lauryn's lips were suddenly dry; she tried to lick them, and could barely swallow. How did one greet a member of the family when one was a not quite respectable—but she had no time to even finish the thought.

"I am," the earl snapped. "And that's neither here nor there. But I had no plans for a houseful of guests, Carter—"

"Yes, but—"

"So you can give whatever friends you have conjured up their marching orders," Sutton told him, his tone curt. "At once! I'm in no mood to play nursemaid to a bunch of squalling tulips of fashion."

"Here now, no need to insult a fellow," Carter said. "Anyhow, most of these are your friends, don't you know? Viscount Tweed is on his way, should be here any time, he's most certainly not in my crowd, and the Contessa d'Ellaye is—ah"— he glanced at Lauryn, who felt a tremor of unease—"ah, anyhow, they're not all my friends, by any means."

"Tweed is hardly a close friend. We do business together, that's all. What made you think I wanted any of these people as long-term guests? And the fact remains, you are the one who seems to have invited them," the earl retorted. "I had no mind to have a house full of people just now, Carter."

"Oh, really?" Carter took a long look at Lauryn, who felt herself flush. "Just a private week in the country, eh? Well, I'm afraid I wasn't made aware of your plans, brother mine. And speaking of the contessa—"

He paused as another person emerged from the drawing room. Although she glided quietly enough through the open doorway, allowing only a burst of laughter and chatter to bubble around her, Lauryn felt it would have been more apt if there had been a blowing of trumpets to herald her emergence.

This woman was stunningly beautiful, with quantities of dark hair held up by a silver comb, Spanish-style, and drawn into a half knot on the back of her head, then allowed to cascade down her neck. Her wine-colored evening dress had a deep neckline, revealing more cleavage and olive-toned skin than most English ladies usually permitted, but this did not seem to abash the contessa in the slightest. Her dark eyes sparkled nearly as much as the red-colored stones in the necklace about her neck—stones which Lauryn suspected were quite real. Everything about her was a little extravagant and a little overblown and very eye-catching. Lauryn couldn't imagine how any other woman in the room would ever be noticed after the contessa entered.

She herself felt at once as plain as yesterday's stale bread, and very, very tired. Why had Lauryn thought she could do this? She should simply go back to Yorkshire here and now, take back her old black gowns and her place in the corner of her father-in-law's sitting room. But with great effort she held herself erect, kept her chin up and a polite smile on her face. She would not reveal her sinking heart, no matter how much she wanted to turn and slink away.

"Darlink' Marcuz," the contessa was saying in heavily accented English, putting out both her hands to the earl. "How lovely it is to zee you again."

"Indeed," Sutton said, his tone less enthused, nodding but seeming not to see the lady's outstretched wine-colored glove-clad hands. He kept a firm hold on Lauryn's arm, instead.

"Ah, you have brought along a little friend, how agreeable. Veel you not introduce uz?"

The earl looked pained, but he turned to Lauryn and said, "Mrs. Smith, may I present the Contessa d'Ellaye. We are old—"

"*Belle amies*," the contessa finished for him, her smile dazzling.

"Acquaintances," the earl corrected, his tone firm.

Lauryn smiled, too, and gave the most graceful curtsy she could manage. Perhaps she would not steal away just yet, she told herself.

"Come and join uz in ze drawing room, Marcuz. We are enjoying your vine, it is quite decent," the Contessa told him.

"No doubt." The earl gave his brother a look that made the younger man grin sheepishly.

"Now, now, old man, it's a celebration, remember."

"So you said. I have yet to hear what we are celebrating," Sutton told him. "If you will excuse us, Mrs. Smith would like to rest before dinner, and I—"

"Oh, right. No wonder you're still looking so grim." Carter

brightened. "Though that is your normal—I mean—not to worry, Marcus. I shall buy you a whole new wine cellar! They've found the *Brave Lassie*!"

This statement made no sense at all to Lauryn, but the earl, who had already turned toward the staircase, halted almost in midstep.

"What did you say?" he demanded of his half brother.

Carter beamed as he repeated, "You heard me—they've located the *Brave Lassie*! And most of her cargo is intact!"

Four

*L*auryn *waited for the earl to answer, and when the pause* stretched too long, she glanced up at him. She blinked to see that although his expression was controlled—perhaps too controlled—he could not command his complexion, which had paled.

"Are you sure—absolutely sure?" The harshness of his tone made his half brother take a step back. "This is not some drunken sailor's cup-tale?"

"No, Sutton, I swear, they are sure of it. We're lucky twice over, that it's found and that it's found by one of our own ships—well, ours and Tweed's, or it could have been claimed as salvage. And the majority of the cargo is there, I have it on the best of authority. The teas and the silks have rotted away long since, of course, but the rest—"

"What could have zurvived zo long under the zeas?" the contessa asked brightly.

The earl ignored her question, or was concentrating so hard he perhaps genuinely did not hear her. "Where did they find her, when, and how?"

"The wreck seemed to have shifted and washed up into the lagoon at Far Point where the ships used to weather the storms when the typhoons blew. I'm thinking the *Brave Lassie* was sheltering from a bad blow when it sank there. . . . we were never sure, of course, of exactly how it came to grief."

"Didn't we look there at the time? I thought we combed the islands for her." The earl's tone was so severe that Lauryn almost shivered, but his brother seemed to have more backbone than his flippant appearance indicated, as he didn't appear to quell at the interrogation.

"Of course we did, but the wreck has since been washed up to shore. Another ship from the viscount's fleet had stopped to get fresh water, and they saw a few timbers that led them to search farther down the beach. One storm took it from us, and another restored it. Although not the crew, of course, poor wretches." Carter shivered.

The earl still frowned.

"And they have retrieved the cargo? What has survived?"

"Oh, yes, the ship holding it should be docking at Yarmouth within days, and then it will be sent on to Skegness. Then you can see it with your own eyes, Doubting Thomas," the younger man grinned.

Sutton's lips stretched, but there was little humor in the grimace. "Let's not bring theology into it, Carter. I doubt either of us would measure up to the analogy."

Lauryn had a dozen questions on her lips, but she kept them firmly closed. In good time, she told herself, in good time. She was a stranger. The earl did not seem disposed to talk of these matters in front of just anyone.

The contessa however, had not given up. "Zuch romance, the boat zinking and being found again," she purred. "And vat did you zay waz in thiz valuable cargo?"

Again, no one seemed disposed to enlighten her. Carter flashed her a brief smile, but turned at once back to his brother.

"When it arrives, then—then I will believe it," Sutton said.

"We've had a king's ransom rise up out of the sea, riches we thought were lost, Sutton, can't you show a grain of elation?" His brother waved his wineglass in the air, almost splashing them both.

"We've had a long day's travel. Let us rest and change, and perhaps we will be more in the mood for frivolity, Carter," Sutton replied, his tone still cold. "And as for illusionary ghost ships—when I see it, nay, touch it, then, as I said, I will celebrate."

He turned back toward the stairs, and Lauryn wheeled with him, leaving his brother, looking distinctly disappointed, in their wake.

As they walked away, Lauryn could hear the contessa appear to be consoling him.

"Do not think of it, darlink, tell me of this vonderful boat and the treasures it 'olds, xee? Me, I zo much like treasurez."

Her voice trailed off behind them as they climbed the steps to the next level, where the hallway was still broad, but not quite as wide as the spacious corridors below. Here the earl showed her to a large chamber where her carpetbags and hatboxes had been taken, and where she found a maidservant awaiting her command.

"I suppose I will have to go down and see who is making merry in my house, even if without my invitation," the earl told her, his tone still grim.

Lauryn thought she detected an implied question underlying his words, and she answered that instead of what he had said. "I will change my costume and make ready as quickly as possible, my lord."

She noted distinct approval in his glance. "If you are not too weary, I would value your presence at my side," he said. "Just send word when you are ready."

Flushing that he cared if she was beside him or not, Lauryn vowed that she would, indeed, be swift. On the other hand, it was even more important that she look good, especially now that she had witnessed the contessa's amazing beauty. Lauryn was prepared for the earl to tire of her soon enough. But now that she had seen him, felt the power of his nearness, she didn't want it to be *too* soon!

She curtsied gracefully to him as he nodded a farewell, then, as soon as the door was shut behind him, whirled and spoke to the maidservant. "We must make haste! Is there water in the ewer?"

"Yes, ma'am," the servant said. She was a pleasant-looking young woman who, Lauryn was pleased to see, seemed able to move rapidly but adeptly to unbutton the back of Lauryn's navy traveling suit after Lauryn removed the jacket. So Lauryn was able to change her outfit much more speedily than she would have done on her own.

She was able to wash off some of the dust of the trip, and take down and comb out her hair, deciding how to make the most of her own strengths—she did not have blue black tresses like the contessa, she had pale reddish gold instead, but her hair made a nice appearance when allowed to fall free—did she dare—

No, she was too old, Lauryn decided with a sigh, to go downstairs looking like a maiden just out. She didn't want to be judged mutton trying to pass as lamb! But she did tell the maid, whose name was Molly, to loosen the knot at the back of her head so that the hairdo was not so severe. This time a softer knot swept up the golden curve of her hair, and she looked less like a prim governess. The smoother, softer line seemed more sensual, she hoped, and more inviting.

And when the maid had shaken out the wrinkles and pressed one of her new dresses, Lauryn allowed the girl to drop the gown over her head, delighting in the lightness of the silk, relishing the feel of it against her skin, where the thin corset and chemise didn't keep the silk from touching her.

And thank heavens she had a dress with some color, so that her fair complexion would no longer be washed out by the severe black of her abandoned mourning gowns. Dressed again with the aid of the servant—the whole process was so much more efficient with someone to help—she glanced once more into the tall looking glass. She was not totally displeased.

"Do you know who is downstairs, Molly?" she asked.

"Oh, some of the younger Mr. Elton's friends, very dashing they are," the maid told her as she helped her pull on evening gloves. "Several of 'is lordship's neighbors. And then there are friends of 'is lordship's from Lond'un, some of 'em have titles, some not."

"I suppose there are ladies in the party, too?" Lauryn could not keep herself from asking.

"Oh, yes, ma'am," Molly told her. "And the ladies are somethin' to see, with bright-colored gowns like yourn, real beauties most of 'em are, too." Her voice was reverent.

Lauryn's stomach felt hollow. "I see."

"But not to worry, yer just as pretty as any lady 'ere, ma'am," Molly predicted. She inclined her head to look at Lauryn's reflection. "And more—that color brings out yer eyes real nice!"

Lauryn grinned ruefully. She could not be so a faint of heart! To sit here trying to draw courage from a maidservant's reassurances was a paltry thing. But she did feel better.

"Thank you," she told her. "And thank you for your help."

Molly looked at her in surprise. "Yer most welcome, ma'am. I 'ope ye stay longer than the last—um—"

"Than the earl's last lady friend?" Lauryn supplied, matter-of-factly.

Not meeting her eyes, Molly looked away as she folded the damp linen towel. "Um, yes, ma'am."

"Yes," Lauryn murmured. That was not really her plan, but—well, they would see, would they not? The earl would no doubt tire of her, too. And she would love to know just why he had sent away his last mistress, but there was a limit to what she felt she could gossip about with the servants. Anyhow, she couldn't quite bring herself to ask Molly such a bald-faced question.

"If you would inform the earl that I am ready," she told the maid.

Molly dropped her a curtsy. "I will tell Boxel, ma'am," she said. "'E won't let me speak to the earl direct, but 'e'll pass on yer message."

Lauryn nodded her thanks, and careful not to wrinkle her beautiful new gown, sat down on the edge of an upholstered chair.

Within a couple of minutes, a low knock sounded at her door. When she stood to answer it, she found the earl himself standing outside.

There was a moment of silence when she opened the door, then he smiled slowly.

"You look ravishing," he told her. "That color suits you very well, much better than the black."

Blushing, she sent profuse if silent thanks to the London couturier.

"Thank you," she said, her voice low.

"Shall we go down, then?" He offered his arm.

He did have lovely manners, Lauryn told herself as she smiled up at him and accepted. He never made her feel as if she were—as if she were what she was in fact being, a kept woman, his hired paramour . . . and that really was greatly to his credit.

On that note, they walked down to the drawing room.

Marcus found her arm tense in his hold. Was she frightened of facing the crowd in the front rooms? If she only knew it, she had every excuse to be, he thought, his humor still bleak. If Carter had invited them, they would be a motley crew.

And he had hoped to have the big house mostly to themselves. He really was not in the mood to be a pleasant host, offering entertainment and constant attention to a houseful of guests. Why in the hell must Carter pull a stunt like this? This rumor about the *Brave Lassie* would likely prove to be mere scrimshaw, nothing except the dirty windblown bubbles that formed atop restless waves . . . and as hard to grasp.

Truth be told, he'd wanted to take his new prize straight up to bed as soon as they arrived. Marcus ached for her right now, especially after he'd seen how lovely she looked in her pale blue green dinner dress, her green eyes seeming endlessly deep and clear in the pale light as the many candles reflected back from the crystal chandeliers above them—much like a sunset colored the endless hues of the Fens' sky. Her golden red hair seemed to glow, as well, and she seemed as ethereal as a faery queen and as graceful, floating into the big room on his arm.

He shook his head at the footman waiting at the door to announce them—he wouldn't bother with that. If his own guests didn't know him, they didn't belong in his house, and if they didn't know the name of his new paramour, all the better. He'd rather keep her to himself, like holding a good hand of cards close to his chest, so no one else in the game could steal a look at his queen of hearts.

Of course heads were turning, anyhow, dammit. How could anyone not get a glimpse of Mrs. Smith's gossamer beauty and not look again, and again.

Carter came up, the contessa clinging to his half brother's arm. "There you are, at last."

"You must break yourself of this new insatiable appetite for my presence, Brother," Marcus told his sibling.

Carter flushed. "You know it's not that. Only—"

"And no talk of private matters in front of our guests," the earl warned swiftly. "That would be highly impolite."

"Oh, well, if you say so." Carter looked frustrated at the ban. "But—"

"I mean it," Marcus warned. "You will start rumors that will cause fluctuations in our company's stock on the Exchange."

"I wouldn't do that," his brother argued, but he looked guiltily down at the hardwood floor as he said it.

"You vill not allow him to explain to me about the treasure ship?" The contessa spoke at almost the same moment, and several men nearby turned their heads.

"Carter!" the earl said, his tone grimmer than ever.

"I didn't mean to!" his brother protested. "She has a way of getting around a fellow, don't you know?"

"He knows." The contessa smiled sweetly and nodded toward the back of the big room where musicians were almost hidden in one of the large alcoves. "Ve have music and dancing. If you vould dance vith me, Marcuz, for ol' timez, you could tell me all about it, yez?"

Lauryn, who felt that she had shrunk to the size of a field mouse, unnoticed by all in this conversation, felt her mouth go dry. If the contessa turned the full strength of her beautiful dark brown eyes on a man, could any resist her?

Apparently there was hope.

"Thank you, no," the earl told her, his voice firm. "I am engaged to dance with Mrs. Smith. And I'm sure that my brother would be devastated to lose the pleasure of your company."

"Er, right," Carter said at once, under the pressure of his brother's glance. "If you would allow me the privilege?"

The contessa gave in with good grace. She accepted Carter's hand and allowed him to lead her toward the dance floor.

"You don't have to dance unless you wish it," Lauryn muttered, meanwhile, as the earl led her in the same direction.

"I have every intention of dancing with you, Mrs. Smith," her escort said, his tone even. "Do you object to dancing?"

"No, no," she said, flustered at once. "I mean, I only thought—"

Instead of a formal set, where she stood up in a line of females while he took his place with the gentlemen, he pulled her into his arms, taking one of her hands in his, and putting his other hand on her waist.

To her alarm, she saw that it was that most fast and frivolous of all dances, the waltz.

He must have seen her confusion because he raised his brows.

Keeping her voice low, she said quickly, "I have only practiced this dance a few times, and never in company!"

She thought her face must have flushed, or else gone quite pale. She could feel her pulse jumping—he was so much pure male and the heat of his hand on her waist, the subtle odor of soap and clean linen and his own unique male scent teased her senses, and she was so aware of his nearness—

But they were supposed to be dancing and surely everyone was looking—

What if she made a muddle of it in front of all his guests? He would be angry, and she would be mortified!

"Don't concern yourself, it's not that taxing," he answered

her, also in a quiet voice. "Just take a deep breath and follow my lead."

And then the notes flowed from the musicians' instruments, and they were off. With one hand on her waist, the other gripping her hand, and with his firm guidance, and the lilting melody of the music to observe, Lauryn found she was not as lost as she'd feared she would be. In fact, she forgot to think at all; she simply allowed her body to float across the floor, swaying with the earl, who was remarkably light on his feet for such a tall man.

With his hand at her waist, his firm pressure gave her warning when they were about to turn, or step forward or back. With this help, she soon caught the rhythm of the dance. She felt almost as if she were flying across the dance floor, and she forgot to be afraid of disgracing herself or him and only delighted in the pleasure of the graceful and rhythmic movement.

When the music faded to an end, she was conscious of a distinct disappointment. The earl spun her once more, then they came to a halt.

The earl looked down at her sparkling eyes and slightly parted lips. He wanted to kiss her so badly it was a physical pain, made so much worse by having to hold himself back. He became aware that she was speaking.

"You are a very fine dancer," she said, smiling up at him. "Thank you for guiding me so well through my first waltz, my lord."

"You are more than welcome, my dear," he told her. "You dance very well, indeed. It was my pleasure."

He thought of all the other activities he wanted to guide her through, for the first time, or almost the first time, he rather thought that it might be. He ached to find out! And how long would this damn party last? When could he send these yammering guests upstairs to bed?

Releasing her with the greatest reluctance, he wiped a drop of perspiration off his forehead and knew it did not come from the effort of the dance.

The next tune denoted a country dance, and they had to move several paces apart as they flowed in step with the parallel lines of ladies and gentlemen. Lauryn smiled at him from a few paces away, and he smiled back, forgetting the rest of the dancers and almost missing the hand of the woman he had to circle.

The dance continued, and Marcus had to focus hard to remember the steps, and that was unheard of because Mrs. Smith was quite right: he was a good dancer. But tonight he was in no mood for any dance except the ultimate one of two bare bodies engaged in delightful coupling. His body tingled with the thought, and he had to wrench his speculations away yet again. How many more minutes would this torture continue?

He was obsessed, he thought. How long had it been since he had felt this way about a woman? Had he ever felt this intently? One thing he knew for certain—if he did not get her alone soon—He should not have even come down. He should have pretended not to be in the residence, his "guests" would likely not have known he had come in—if he had told Carter to keep his mouth shut—a pity his half brother could not keep a confidence!

As if his thought had conjured him up, when this dance ended, his brother popped up again, and again the contessa was there at his elbow, both unflaggingly cheerful.

"Now may I ask the lady for the pleasure of a dance?" Carter demanded.

Marcus glared at his brother, and he must have looked murderous because his sibling took a step back. But he didn't retreat totally, only lowered his voice and continued, "Now look, old man, people are going to talk if you don't allow her to dance and talk to others. You can't keep her to yourself all night—might as put her in a golden cage. They'll have you committed to Bedlam, don't you know?"

The earl clenched his jaw, wanting to argue but knowing that Carter, who knew social niceties if nothing else, was right. And he did not want to make her the subject of more talk than she already would be, simply by being here.

So with grudging agreement, he nodded when his companion said, her voice firm, "I should be happy to dance with you, Mr. Elton."

"Happy to hear it," Carter said, offering his arm. The two walked off toward the dance floor.

Marcus watched them go, and didn't care if his frown deepened. For one heart-wrenching moment he thought the musicians were striking up a waltz. He would kill Carter if he had told them to play another waltz so soon! If his brother touched her waist and pulled her close, he was a dead man!

No, no, the melody was not right; it was only a country dance.

The earl let out his pent-up breath. The contessa was watching him. "Are you not going to ask me to dance, Marcuz? Ve make a good partnership, too, you must remember!"

"Not just now, forgive me. I have something I must do," he told her, his tone vague. And despite the fact that now she was the one frowning, he walked rapidly away. He would warn the musicians that on no account, until he expressly ordered them differently, were they to play another waltz!

Lauryn found Carter also a good dancer, though she suspected he might not be quite as strong at leading as his older half brother. But he was also light on his feet, and in the line dances she knew what she was doing, only once finding an unfamiliar pattern, and she was able to follow the lead of the lady in front of her and avoid making a mistake.

After two dances, he took her—most correctly—back to her first partner, the earl. Sutton was still standing where they had left him, and had not danced with anyone else, to Lauryn's surprise but private relief.

They did not dance again, however, but stood at the side of the big room and chatted with others in the chamber. Lauryn met neighbors of the earl and deflected their veiled curiosity as much as she could.

"You are not from the Fens, I take it," one matron pointed out. "Your accent is not that of southern England."

"No," Lauryn agreed, taking a sip of wine that a servant had procured for her.

Her expression expectant, the matron waited, but Lauren smiled sweetly without supplying more information.

"But you do not sound as if you are a native Londoner,

either," a second lady pointed out, her tone shrewd, "and, unlike some of the earl's—ah—previous guests, you do sound like a lady born."

This made Lauryn narrow her eyes, but she took another sip of wine and hoped that she had bent her head in time to hide her reaction. Denial would likely only provoke more argument, however. "Of course," she said in a moment. "Why should I not?"

This left her circle of interrogators at a quandary; they were standing too close to the earl to be deliberately rude to his current "guest."

Who but the earl would so ignore social protocol as to host events and invite his courtesans and his neighbors? No, the party was Carter's idea this time, she told herself.

"I do find the Fens intriguing," Lauryn added. "I had not visited this part of the countryside before. Have the canals ended the threat of flooding? If so, it must be a great boon for you."

She already knew the answer from the earl's earlier comments, but it seemed a good way to turn the topic of the conversation away from herself. She felt like a lone kernel of corn surrounded by a flock of hungry, sharp-beaked chickens.

"Oh, gracious no," the first neighbor said. "If you had been here last spring—I thought several times I should have to climb onto my own roof." She narrated a harrowing tale of the dangers she and her family had survived, and then it seemed that all of the women had stories to relate, as well.

"Oh, that was nothing. If you had been at our house . . ." an older woman spoke up, waving her fan for emphasis.

Lauryn listened closely and made appropriate comments at the right times, glad to have, for the moment at least, diverted their attention.

The evening seemed to pass very slowly, and Lauryn was aware that she was weary from the long ride in the carriage, and that in some ways, the party itself—had she longed for parties?—was taking as much of a toll on her energy as the long trip had. The curious stares of the women, the sometimes openly licentious ogles of the men—trying not to blush, she stood up straight and was very glad that the earl stayed close by her all evening.

At last the butler appeared to announce that a light supper was served in the dining room. The musicians allowed their music to fade, and the crowd of guests surged toward the hallway. Of course, Carter had returned and cajoled his brother into sitting with him at supper, and to Lauryn's private chagrin, Carter's partner was the omnipresent contessa, who still seemed more determined to attract the earl's attention than Carter's, whom she seemed to treat as only second best.

The meal was set up on a long sideboard where one could pick and choose before sitting down; the array of edibles was quite amazing. She filled her plate with meats and cold salads and some delightful sweets, little cakes and ices and gelatos in the Italian style, and returned to sit beside the earl.

He stood as she was seated, and then a servant came to speak quietly in his ear.

"Please excuse me. I shall be back in a moment," he told her, then bowed and left the table.

"Of course," she said, as he left.

Carter was absent, perhaps still at the buffet table, and Lauryn found herself alone with the contessa.

"It seems you 'ave quite enthralled ze earl. My compliments, Miz Smith," the contessa said, flashing her brilliant smile.

Lauryn looked the contessa in the eye. "My feeling is that you would like to be the one doing the enthralling," she said, her tone courteous.

"But of course," the other woman shot back, her smile widening. "The earl iz a 'andsome man—and a rich one. Both desirable qualitites, yez?"

Her frankness was disarming.

"I suppose so," Lauryn agreed, grinning despite herself. "But there is more to him than that."

"Oh, yez, he iz a magnificent lover, *aussi*." The contessa licked a spot of butter off her finger, her tongue lingering for a moment on the tip.

Lauryn found herself flushing. "I—" She couldn't find words to finish the sentence.

"Ah, you 'ave not yet made *l'amour*? You vill find it most gratifying. He understands 'ow to please a woman." The contessa sighed. "Few men have been so inspiring. But it appears I shall 'ave to find another lover this time. *Pauvre moi*!"

Lauryn found her mouth was open and shut it hastily. The contessa might be conniving but not–not duplicitous, she thought, a trifle wildly.

"Yes, no, I mean, yes," she murmured. Since she had no intention of giving up the earl to another woman, yes, the contessa should look elsewhere.

She wasn't sure the contessa had heard, but when she looked up again, she saw the contessa's wry look, and she thought that they understood each other.

"I vill warn you of one thing, *jeune fille*," the other woman said.

"Yes?" Lauryn answered, wary.

"*C'est vrai*. It is best to be candid in dealings vith him. He vill not stand for lies." The contessa's glance was shrewd, and her tone seemed sincere.

"Oh," Lauryn said, for a moment unable to meet the other woman's eyes. Here she stood using a fictitious name—how could she answer that? "I–I will remember."

When supper was announced, the earl could tell by Parker's strained expression not to expect a great deal. And when he saw what was offered, he winced. Carter must not have given the house chef much notice—it was a relatively bare spread. So much for the Sutton reputation for gracious hospitality! But nothing he could do about it now, except, the first chance he got, shake his damned brother by the collar till his bones rattled!

At least it marked the passing of time—this bloody evening seemed to be stretching on forever, when all he wanted was to whisk his woman upstairs and strip her naked and—

He groaned inside and again tried to push back his highly improper and wonderfully pleasurable thoughts.

A footman came and leaned over to speak softly to him.

"Viscount Tweed has arrived, my lord, and wishes a word with you before he comes into the company."

Now he was in for it. Marcus excused himself to his companion and strode rapidly toward the hall.

In the doorway, the viscount waited, his mud-splashed boots showing how hard he had ridden to get here as fast as he could.

"Is it true, then?" Marcus asked before the new arrival could speak.

Tweed was older than Marcus by a decade, and Tweed's grimly clenched jaw revealed his agitation as he nodded. "It was her, the *Brave Lassie*, true enough. They even found a few planks showing part of the name. And we have the cargo, or at least the most valuable part, looking mostly still intact and apparently undamaged, worth even more now than when it went down eight years ago. We'll get a better look when it arrives at Yarmouth."

They stared at each other bleakly.

His mind a jumble of conjecture, the earl was silent. But the other man didn't appear to have the patience for him to work out his tangled thoughts.

"So what the bloody hell do we do now?" the viscount demanded.

Five

*S*omewhat daunted by the contessa, who was so much bigger than life that Lauryn wasn't yet sure how to deal with her, Lauryn couldn't help looking away from her supper companion. Glancing discreetly toward the door, she saw the two men talking quietly, and more important, since she was too far away to make out their words, she saw that both frowned.

Why would they be displeased that valuable cargo, once lost, had been reclaimed?

It made no sense.

Of course, it also was not her affair, and she would do well to remember it, Lauryn told herself. Right now, she had enough trouble fending off the cheerfully unrepentant prying of the contessa.

"The magnificent earl is your first patron, *n'est ce pas*?" the other woman asked now, between bites of what appeared to be a particularly delicious gateau, from the way she licked her fingers.

Lauryn was pulled abruptly out from her musings about the mystery ship. "What would make you think that?" she asked, her voice sharp.

The contessa shrugged. "*Comme ça*, you are such *l'enfant, n'est-ce pas?*"

"I hardly think that is the case," Lauryn said, her tone dry.

"Ah, I can zee that you are past the first blush," the contessa agreed, reaching for her wineglass and taking a hearty gulp. "But in the milieu of *l'amour*, I am not zo certain, *que'que c'est?*"

Frustrated again, Lauryn glared at her. "I am sure that I understand the world of love, both in the drawing room and in the bedroom," she said boldly.

Her dark eyes sparkling, the contessa grinned. "We shall zee, *ma petite*. Remember, the earl is a man of experience. He vill know, more than anyone, just how skilled you are, and if you are a voman who is able to hold his attention."

She looked back at her plate and took a spoonful of a vanilla-flavored ice while Lauryn repressed a shiver of apprehension.

What if she was *not* skilled enough at lovemaking?

She found her appetite for the delicious foods had quite vanished. Was the contessa deliberately trying to make her lose her confidence? She tried to think more hopefully, but it was hard to find her courage with the contessa flashing her jewels and her smile so close by.

Lauryn nibbled at the sweetmeats on her plate and smiled until she knew the corners of her mouth were going to freeze in place. How long until they could leave this dratted assembly? Could she say as much to her host or would he think her unbearably fast? Were courtesans allowed this privilege? It seemed the least they could do, given their purpose.

When the earl returned to the table, however, his expression was preoccupied, and although he spoke politely to her, his thoughts seemed far away. Lauryn was mystified; what had the new arrival had to say that had made such a change in her host?

After trying a few comments about the evening's entertainment and the guests that crowded the big rooms, and getting very disjointed replies, she decided to go to what was perhaps the heart of his abstraction.

"Is Viscount Tweed not joining the party?" she said as Sutton picked at his plate, eating only lightly of the savories that covered it.

"He has elected to ride to Yarmouth to get the earliest possible look at the cargo recovered from the *Brave Lassie*, so we can see what is true about this news and what may be only rumor."

"You still doubt that it is really your ship that was found? Or do you question that the cargo did survive?" Trying to understand his strange reaction to the news, she stared at him.

He shrugged. "We wish to be certain, that's all. We are not all as gullible as my stripling of a half brother." He reached for a piece of lobster tail from his plate.

A man sitting further down the table called out to the earl, giving news about one of his mares who had been bred to Sutton's champion sprinter. "Dropped her foal and a sound little fellow he is!"

A lively discussion about racing ensued, so she did not feel she could pursue the subject further.

When the supper ended, the crowd flowed back toward the big drawing rooms, and she could hear the musicians striking up another tune.

The earl seemed in no hurry to rise, however. Even Carter and the contessa eventually stood to rejoin the others. The younger man grinned.

"Come along, Marcus, you're becoming a laggard in your old age. Someone has to be there to play host," he pointed out.

"Since you're the one who invited them all, you're just the man to play the part," the earl answered, his tone composed.

Carter blinked, but kept his easy smile. "Just so."

The contessa rolled her eyes. "Oh, Marcus, darlink, you are zo practical." But she followed the younger man, and when the other couple had reached the doorway, the earl turned back to smile at Lauryn.

She met his smile with her own. "Do you not wish to dance again, my lord?"

His eyes had a warmth that sparked an answering glow within her. She realized that dancing was not what was on his mind. Soon he would know—they would both know—if she could live up to the role she had taken on. As she thought this, she swallowed too quickly on the last sip of her wine and almost choked.

He reached over and rubbed her back while she coughed, his hand warm on the smooth silk of her gown. "Are you all right?"

Knowing that she must be as flushed as an overheated pastry chef, Lauryn cursed herself silently and hid her face for a moment behind her napkin.

Nodding until she was able to say, more or less normally, "Yes, thank you," she tried to ignore the nervous quivers in her stomach. Or perhaps they were not *all* from nervousness as he took her hand and she felt the warmth and strength of his grip.

Around them, the dining room was almost empty. Silver platters clattered now and then as servants cleared away, wiping up crumbs and the occasional spill.

The earl rose, and she followed his example as he ignored the servants and led her into the hall and toward the staircase. Without looking in any way self-conscious, he held her hand, and they proceeded up the flight of stairs to the next landing. Instead of turning toward the big rooms where the party was still underway, as was easily perceived by the music and chatter escaping past the double doors, they continued on up the next flight of steps.

Her stomach knotted even more.

The time of decision was upon her.

This time when they reached the landing, he did not turn toward the guest chamber she had been given. Lauryn had naively expected that he would allow her to go to her own room to change into a nightgown and wait for her to prepare herself for bed. But apparently that was not how it worked.

She wished she knew more just how it did work!

Was she supposed to be overcome with anticipation of the big moment, moaning with passion before they even reached his bedchamber? She glanced doubtfully up at him from the corner of her eye. Somehow she could not quite bring herself to put on such a charade, nor could she see the earl believing that sort of obsequious display. He was too discerning to be taken in by such tomfoolery, and besides—what had the contessa said—he disliked above all things being lied to.

She shivered despite herself.

Sutton looked down at her. "Are you chilled, my dear?"

"No, no," she said quickly.

"Because I will see to it soon that you are warm," he promised, with a half smile showing on his lips.

A small shiver went through her again, of a quite different nature, and her own lips parted.

And thinking what he might mean by that, she found that they approached what must be his chamber. The earl pushed open the door and paused to allow her to walk through the doorway.

Heart beating fast, she stepped over the threshold. His bedroom was large and sumptiously appointed, just what one would expect for the master of the house. Full of furnishings of polished dark wood and deep blues and reds, it seemed very masculine. Candles had been lit, and the room overall offered a welcoming aspect. She glanced around, noting the large fireplace with a fire leaping behind the gleaming brass fireguard—no, she was in no danger of feeling chilly here—and the fur rug spread out before it. Two large chairs sat before the hearth, as well, and a desk and chair and chests and other furniture occupied other corners of the room.

And the bed—the bed was large, too, with deep blue hangings pulled back to show the high mattress arrayed with smooth linens and other coverings. Afraid that her face was flushing, Lauryn looked swiftly away again.

She felt his fingers at the base of her neck and jumped.

"Are you a little—apprehensive—perhaps, my dear Mrs. Smith?"

His voice was as smooth as much rubbed leather. She tried to pull herself together. She was supposed to be a courtesan, someone who did this by trade, she reminded herself hastily. She must not act like a green girl. She had asked to be here, remember!

"No, no," she replied. "That is, I am honored to be your—your amour, your grace, that is, my lord."

"You honor me a bit too highly," he said, his voice amused, "but, yes, we will agree that we are mutually honored to be here together."

His fingers moved, and she realized he was once again—as he had the first time they had met, when she had petitioned him for a position as his lover—undoing her buttons.

Why did she need a lady's maid, she thought, when she could have an earl to help her out of her clothes? She felt a little dizzy.

She must have swayed slightly because he paused. "Are you sure you're all right?"

"Yes, of course, your—my lord," she said quickly. "I just—you are—you have a powerful effect on me."

"That's good, I hope," he said, his tone hard to read.

"Of course it is," she told him. How could she explain that the heat in his fingertips burned her skin and seemed to sizzle its way through her, blazing inside her like lightning in a summer storm? She could not remember feeling this way even with her husband, but perhaps she had only forgotten, it had been so long since Robert had—since the early days of their passion . . .

No, no, she could not think about Robert just now—it sent flashes of disloyalty through her and turned the lovely feelings of passion that had begun to rise inside her into sour notes of betrayal, instead.

She tried not to think of anything at all, only to feel. The earl's fingers on her back, the rustle as her gown at last fell away, slipping past her corset and petticoat as the earl helped push it to the floor. The petticoat followed almost at once.

"Why do women wear these confounded things, anyhow?" he muttered into her ear, half laughing, half swearing as he unlaced the corset with an amazingly rapid touch.

"To look good for our menfolk, of course," she replied without even thinking, not trying to stoke his vanity, only murmuring the absolute truth. Though, also, she could not imagine getting into a ball gown without first donning the proper undergarments—one would look like a lumpy sack of potatoes.

"I will tell you a great secret, my dear," he whispered into her ear, the slight breath making goose bumps rise on her skin. "Men would prefer that you wear nothing at all!"

She laughed a trifle hysterically, imagining a line of naked women doing a reel on the ball room floor, to the delight of their still clothed partners, then decided fair was fair, when he leaned over to kiss her—even though she was eager for the kiss, she slid out from beneath his touch.

"In due time, my lord," she told him, her tone demure. "It is your turn to be—ah—denuded."

She smiled up at him as she gave her attention to his carefully tied neckcloth, pulling it out of its twist and then unwinding it gingerly, then more rapidly as he cocked his brows at her in whimsical acceptance.

"You could be a trifle faster," he suggested. "You'll note that I, at least, wasted no time in my disrobing of your lovely body."

"True, I will try to hurry the process," she agreed. When she tossed the neckcloth aside, she pulled off his evening coat and took off his waistcoat, then lifted his shirt for him to peel off. The pantaloons made her pause, and she saw him smile.

"At any rate, I have us more or less equal, dress wise," she pointed out. She was down to a loose and almost transparent shift and drawers and stockings, and he was close to an equal layer of undress. And she wasn't at all sure about attacking those pantaloons, or what she would find beneath; her husband had rarely worn full evening dress.

At least he was naked above the waist, and at last she could touch those well-shaped arms and chest—she had longed to reach out and caress such amazingly sculpted limbs. She ran her hands over his upper arms and felt the hardness of his muscle beneath the skin. She skimmed his shoulders and down to his chest, and he made a small groan, deep in his throat.

"Would you tease me, my dear? I must have the same privilege." And he, too, ran his hands lightly over her shoulders, but as the thin fabric of the shift was in his way, he moved swiftly to lift it over her head and, as she gasped, pulled it off to toss casually aside. Before she could protest he pulled her closer and allowed her naked upper body to meet his own.

The shock of bare skin touching bare skin sent waves of sensation through her as her softer malleable breasts pressed against the firmness of his chest. For a moment Lauryn stared wide-eyed at him. She didn't know whether to protest or—no, how could she protest? This is why you are here, you ninny, she told herself.

And anyhow, it felt so delicious. She shut her eyes for a moment and delighted in the touch of his solid body against her own, then opened them again when yet another incredible sensation shot spasms of delight through her. He had bent to kiss the tender skin of her neck, just where it met her shoulder, and she trembled from the joy of it.

"Oh, it's heaven," she whispered. She shook from the intensity of the feelings until he had to hold her steady, his hands on both her shoulders. He kissed her again, his lips warm against the sensitive skin, while she stroked his shoulders and back, pulling him as close to her as she could, not wanting to lose any contact, any moment of this wonderful closeness. Already, she was longing for more, for anything, for everything that they could possibly share.

"Do you really want all these damned clothes?" he paused long enough to mutter into her ear. She shook her head. Otherwise, only an incoherent sound answered him—words were fleeing rapidly from her mind, only sensations and raw hunger seemed to be left.

It had been so long. . . .

She reached down to untie the drawstring at her waist and pushed down the cotton drawers, letting them fall to the floor and kicking them out of the way.

To her relief, as she really didn't know how they fastened, she saw that while she did so, he had slipped out of his pantaloons and now was drawing off the rest of his garments. She looked about her for a chair so that she could take off her stockings, the only bit of her clothing that remained.

"No, no, allow me," he said, flashing a roguish grin.

He led her to a chaise longue and she sat, then put up one leg, and he ran his fingers along the calf until she shivered from the light touch. Then he untied the blue garter and unrolled the stocking, inch by inch, kissing each square of skin as it was revealed. It was an exquisite sort of torture, and Lauryn caught her breath, sitting still with great difficulty. She wanted to move as he kissed her legs, and now she did want to moan, genuine heartfelt moans, and she had to bite her lip to hold them back. When he reached her toes, taking each one between his lips to tease it with his tongue, she didn't know whether to giggle or moan—such amazing feelings he could induce! It had never occurred to her that one's feet could have sensitive feelings.

Already she was ripe for lovemaking—*hell*, Lauryn thought. How long had it been—how many months had it been since she had had a man in her bed?

The earl could have swung a dead cat at her, and she would have been ready!

He was starting the same routine on her other leg, and this time Lauryn knew she was hardly going to be able to maintain any sort of ladylike pretense. Of course, he did not think her a lady, so did it matter?

"Oh, my lord," she murmured, as he kissed her calf, hardly halfway down. "I must have you!"

"Patience, my lamb," he murmured back. "We have so many delightful games to play. I would not cheat you out of your delights by rushing you into bed."

"You are not cheating me!" she assured him. It hardly helped that he was now naked, and she could observe what a fine specimen of manhood he was, and that he was plainly ready for the main event, himself. He had remarkable patience, she thought. Well, just now, she had not!

The fact that she ached, longed, pined for him, that she had waited so long for completion that she was almost mad with longing was something she could not explain, so how—

She couldn't bear it!

With an ache inside her so intense it was like a pain, Lauryn watched as the earl slipped off her second stocking and lifted her foot to his mouth. No, toes were not enough. She pulled her foot back, and saw his look of surprise.

"It's my turn, my lord," she told him.

Taking his hand—as well as advantage of his moment of surprise—she pulled him toward her and put her arm around his neck, drawing his mouth to hers. She kissed him as hard and as long as she could, all the while dragging him toward her and twisting both their bodies back against the chaise lounge.

Using his heavier weight to her advantage, they fell backwards together. Since they were both naked, she was able to push herself against his torso until she found the right position and could slide down upon his firm, erect shaft.

Gasping at the new/old feeling, she felt his whole body stiffen for a moment, then his hands gripped her shoulders once more and he pulled her even closer.

"You little vixen!" he said against her mouth, and then they were pounding flesh to flesh, and the glorious rhythm that she had been so long absent from encompassed her. He was a large man, and he filled her so wonderfully, gloriously. And he knew what to do with what he had. He shifted position just slightly, put his hands on her hips and allowed her to sit up a bit. And he rubbed her tender folds just in front of where he entered her, and the resulting wave of pleasure startled her so with its intensity that she almost lost her grip. Good heavens!

She had never felt such delight!

He paused for a moment.

"Should I stop?"

"No, no," she said, her voice wobbling. "No, indeed."

Dark eyes twinkling, he grinned. She rolled her hips and eased again into the pounding rhythm of the greatest game of all, slowly at first, and then, as waves of pleasure swept through her—and judging by the expression of his face, also through the earl—more rapidly. The joy was so strong—how had she forgotten how good it could be?

She and her husband—no, don't think of Robert just now! But she had never made love in this position before, and she was astonished at how deep he could go when she sat atop him.

The pleasure was so deep and so real. He seemed to reach so far inside her that with each pounding stroke he went farther and farther into her deepest core, and each stroke brought a greater pleasure, an ecstacy so deep and so high it was almost pain, yet at the same time never painful. It was joy at its highest and most pure, and she had never felt this before in her life.

And that brought a shadow with it she could not examine now—she pushed it aside so that the moment was not darkened and tried to focus only on feeling, not thinking, never thinking. The feelings were so deep, so joyous, and it went on and on and, dear God, if they could only do this forever.

The sensations were everything, reaching inside her to her deepest core, then turning her inside out and spiraling up and up into spinning circles of pure joy, lifting her outward, spilling them both into rising fountains of pleasure, dropping them when she spasmed with him into an ocean of delight. Surely he must feel it, too.

And at last she spun into breathless completion, making wordless sounds that she did not recognize, as she had not recognized so much about this journey, this shocking journey into new and uncharted territory, all of which she had been so complacently sure she would know.

Still sitting atop the earl, Lauryn wavered and might have fallen if he had not pulled her down into his arms. She lay for a moment with her eyes shut. She was exhausted, and also a little abashed to look him in the eyes—was he angry at her most unladylike performance?

She was both surprised and relieved when she felt a light kiss on her forehead. She blinked and opened her eyes to see him regarding her with a smile.

"Shall I always expect to be attacked on the chaise longue?" His tone was mild.

She could not keep from blushing. "No, no indeed, my lord. It was just—"

"Yes?" He watched her, and she could not think of anything that would serve, except perhaps the truth.

"It had been a long time," she said simply, then thought belatedly to add, "and you are a most handsome man."

He laughed aloud, and she wished she had said the last part first. But when he looked back at her, his dark eyes were still merry.

"I have no complaints, my dear. You may attack me, anytime."

She smiled back, although she suspected her color was still high.

He put one hand gently to cup her cheek, and she felt a sudden strong sense of déjà vu. A searing wave of guilt and betrayal cut through her, as painful as a rusty sword.

Without any warning, she sat up.

He looked at her in surprise. "Is anything wrong?"

She shook her head, but she could not meet his eyes. "No, not at all—it was all most wonderful." But she heard the formality of her tone. "But I think–I think I will go back to my own room, now, if you do not mind."

His smile had faded, and he gazed up at her with a penetrating gaze. "Did I offend you in some way, Mrs. Smith?"

"Of course not, it was a most felicitous encounter," she said, but still she could not meet his too candid stare. "But it has been a long day, and I am most fatigued."

"A few minutes ago, I would never have guessed," he said, his tone dry. "But I will not keep you if you wish to retire."

"Thank you, my lord," she said, hearing the formal words come out of her mouth as if she were some other person, some prim governess, and she herself, the real Lauryn, were far away, in a distant corner, weeping away the pain.

Why had her brief intense happiness flown? She could not think about it here, or she would weep for real, and he would see—

She pulled her wildly spinning thoughts back to the moment so that she could stand up, pull her shift over her head, try to get into her gown, and achieve enough of a respectable appearance to get down the hall in case any of the servants, or—worse, one of the other guests—should see her.

The earl rose and helped her dress hastily and then she dropped him a brief curtsy, gave a murmured good-night, the formalities absurd after their tumultuous love scene, and then hurried from the room.

To her intense gratitude, she saw no one in the hallway. She almost ran to her own chamber, which also, mercifully, revealed no maidservant waiting—perhaps they had not expected her to return here tonight? At any rate, she was only partially done up, and she would manage to undress herself, though she had to pull loose a couple of buttons to do it, and she had not bothered to put her corset back on just to traverse the hallway.

When she had shed her lovely new dress and pulled on a nightgown, she snuffed the candles and crawled into bed, wanting the darkness to hide her so that at last she could allow the tears to fall unchecked.

What kind of awful person was she?

She had made love to a virtual stranger.

She had known, of course, that this would be a big part of the deal she had made when she decided to pose as a courtesan. It was to redeem the squire's lost land, she reminded herself—that virtuous goal seemed made long long ago. And she had thought, then, that allowing herself to be wild and wicked for a time would not be so awful, when she had been virtuous and proper all her life. But still—

She had not expected to enjoy it so *much*!

Love with the Earl of Sutton had been joyous, had been heaven, had been beyond–beyond anything she had known before with her sweet, boyish, dead husband.

And admitting that made her feel so very guilty . . . so very disloyal.

So the tears came, as she wondered why—how she could be such a dreadful person—and Lauryn beat the linen counterpane and the down pillows with her fist and wept even harder.

She slept little that night. The next morning, she woke to hear a light tap on the door. She opened one eye and found she had a pounding headache.

"Who is it?" she called, her voice hoarse.

"I have your 'ot water, ma'am, with tea and some breakfast, if ye do't wish to come down."

"I'm not hungry, go away," Lauryn said, and shut her eyes again.

She dozed again, but presently through her sleepy stupor intruded the sound of louder knocking, more determined this time. Lauryn groaned. The thumping did not help her painful headache.

"I said to go away!"

"It is *moi*, not the servants, and I do not go the vay, so you may as vell open ze door," came a voice unmistakably the contessa's.

Oh, hell. She would probably stand there and make noise all day, Lauryn thought. What in heaven did she want?

With immense reluctance, Lauryn pushed herself up from the bed, blinked against the sunlight slipping past the drawn curtains, and stumbled over to the door, turning the lock and allowing the woman to come in.

Lauryn herself turned and went back to the bed, and pulling the covers back to her chin.

The contessa marched into the chamber as if it were her own, folded her arms, and stared critically down at Lauryn. Meanwhile, a timid-looking maid came in also, carrying a tray which she sat on a nearby table.

"Sacre bleu, you look most dreadful," the contessa offered helpfully. "Your eyelids are the zize of melons. You"—she turned to the maid—"go and bring us cold compresses and a sliced cucumber from the earl's 'ot 'ouses, at once."

"Yes, my lady," the servant said, dropping a terrified curtsy. "Do you wish that soaked in vinegar?"

"Vinegar?" the contessa had swung toward Lauryn, who was trying to disappear beneath the covers, but she paused. "I do not make a zalad! No vinegar. I vish to put them on Miz. Smith's eyelids; she 'as 'ad a restless night. The cucumber iz good for reducing puffiness."

"Oh, yes, my lady." The servant seemed impressed at this bit of wisdom. She curtsied again and went out, shutting the door behind her.

"Now then," the contessa said, her voice stern. "Enough of thiz. If the earl iz un'appy with you, there is always the next time. I varned you that 'e vas a man of the vorld. I can teach you some little tricks, *ma petite*—"

"He is not unhappy with me!" Lauryn pushed back the cover enough to almost shriek. "Why do you assume you're the only woman in the world who knows how to make love!"

"Then thiz is good, but do not shout, that iz very much not like the lady," the contessa told her, apparently not in the least discomposed. "And it 'urts my ears. Then if you did not disappoint him, what iz the problem? I cannot believe that 'e disappointed you? Not Marcuz!"

"No, he did not—he did not disappoint me," Lauryn said slowly, trying not to blush. "He is indeed an incredible lover."

"As I have reason to know," the contessa said, with a gusty sigh. "So why do I find you 'ere crying out ze eyes?"

"And anyhow," Lauryn broke in, trying to turn aside these very private inquiries, "why do you wish to help me? I should rather expect you to be downstairs in my absence flirting with the earl and trying to insinuate yourself into my position."

The contessa came and sat down on the other side of the bed. "I make the good try," she admitted with her usual devastating candor. "'Is zilly brother is not down for breakfast; 'e drank too much last night—the poor boy 'as no stomach. So this morning I talk and laugh and smile vith the earl. But, alas, poor Marcuz 'as the thought only for you, are you ill, what is your vorries? Why did you not let in the zervant vith your breakfast? Zo until 'e is over this infatuation—"

Lauryn had been feeling a sudden warmth, but the word *infatuation* deflated that feeling as quickly as it had come. "Oh, so you think it will pass quickly?"

"Of course it vill. Marcuz iz not a man for lasting passions; look at me!" The contessa drew a silk fan out of her sleeve and flipped it open to fan herself vehemently. "Ve vere a vonderful couple!"

Lauryn would not have dared to dispute that assertion, so she said nothing.

"The only thing I could do to make 'im smile was to zay I

vould come and check on you, so 'ere I am," the contessa said, flashing her wide smile. "Zo, ve must get you together, *ma petite*."

Lauryn thought about pointing out she was barely half an inch shorter than the contessa, but it didn't seem worth the effort.

"Ve vill put the cucumber on the eyes, and you vill 'ave the cup of tea, and you vill feel better, yes?"

No, Lauryn thought.

The contessa regarded her sternly. "If you do not come down to dinner, I vill tell 'im you are 'aving your courses."

"And what will I say when I do have them?" Lauryn demanded.

"Oh, ve vill think of something." The contessa waved her fan in the air, unabashed. "Now, drink zome tea before it iz all cold and tell me what iz vith the tears?"

She left the bed to pour a cup of tea and brought it back, taking her seat again on the edge of the mattress.

Lauryn took the teacup the contessa held out, if only to keep it from being dumped into her lap, and as it was overfull, it seemed better to sip a little of the lukewarm brew. "It's—rather—private, if you don't mind."

"Vould you rather tell ze earl?"

"No, certainly not!"

"Then, talk to me, *oui*? It is better than zitting and crying out the eyes," the contessa pointed out. "And then you vill not 'ave the eyelids like melons. Ah, I 'ear the maid coming at last."

The servant had made good time, actually, and she had a plate of sliced cucumber and a cold compress. After the contessa had shooed the servant away, she directed Lauryn to lie back in bed and placed cucumber slices over her eyes and positioned the cold, wet cloth on top.

It did feel quite nice on her swollen eyelids.

"Zo, vhat is it that makes you veep all over the nice sheets?" The contessa would not let go of the most private part of the conversation—at least it was all private, but that consideration seemed to abash her not at all.

"That's really not your—I mean, I'd rather not discuss it," Lauryn said stiffly, but the contessa waved her hand as if brushing away a buzzing fly and plunged ahead.

"You are 'ere with the earl, who iz a most considerate man. If you 'ave changed your mind and vish to leave, 'e vill not hold you back. Did 'e pay you in advance?"

Despite the chill of the cloth over part of her face, Lauryn felt herself flush. "No, indeed."

"Zo, you are not bound to 'im. Nothing iz keeping you."

The contessa was always cheerful of mien, but she sounded quite eager, as indeed she had already admitted she was, eager to take Lauryn's place in the earl's bed. Lauryn was startled at the ripple of jealousy she felt over a man she hardly knew—at this rate, she fumed, she would turn her cold compress into a steaming heap of linen.

"I don't wish to leave!"

"Then vhat iz the matter?"

"I don't—I'm not—it's hard to explain. It's my husband," Lauryn said before she could stop herself. There—it had slipped out. She had not meant to share her deepest emotions with a woman like—like what? At least the contessa was honest, whereas Lauryn herself was here hiding behind an assumed name, and behaving like—well, best not to even think about that, for the moment, she thought miserably. The thought made more tears squeeze out of the corner of her eyes.

"No, no, do not start again," the other woman said hastily. "Now ve are making ze progress. It is your 'usband, *oui*. 'E has forced you to come 'ere? 'E will beat you if you do not please the earl? 'E vill take all the money that your patron gives you? Zuch is not unknown, *c'est vrai*."

"Of course not!" Lauryn almost laughed at such a ridiculous idea.

"*Non?* Then, what, 'e beats you even if you do please the earl?" Looking mystified, the contessa wrinkled her well-shaped if rather long nose at Lauryn.

"No, indeed. My husband never beat me. He was a kind-hearted, dear man." Now she had to blink hard against more tears.

The contessa pulled a clean handkerchief from her sleeve and pushed it into Lauryn's hand. "Non, non. You vill veep us off the bed. Your 'usband is a zaint, we agree. You are zick for 'ome, is that it? As I zaid, if you miss your 'usband, you can leave and rejoin 'im at your vill. So what keeps you?"

"My husband is dead!" Lauryn almost shouted, raising her voice for the second time. "Unless I wish to cut my throat, I can't join him."

This time the contessa did not admonish her. Instead, she stared at her for a moment. "Ah, now I understand, a little. You mourn the good dead 'usband. 'E died this week, this month?"

Lauryn shook her head.

"When vas it that 'e died?"

Lauryn told her, and the contessa again looked mystified. "But, *ma petite*, you cannot mourn the man, even the good man, the rest of your life."

"I loved him," Lauryn told her, exasperated in her turn. "Don't you know how it feels to love a man?"

"I vas married for eight years. It vas a buzinezz arrangement; 'e had a good family name, a zatisfactory estate," the contessa said, her tone matter-of-fact. "Ve got along quite vell. When 'e died, I mourned him dutifully for zeveral months. Then I made the decisions I must to continue my life. You must remember the words of the priest, ma petite, when 'e makes the wedding vows: 'until death do uz part.' The good 'usband has died. The marriage is over."

It sounded so harsh, put like that. Yet in her mind, Lauryn knew that the contessa was right. It was in her heart that she felt she was being disloyal to Robert . . . especially . . .

"There is more, oui?" The contessa was still watching her face, where her sisters had always told Lauryn her thoughts were too easily read.

Lauryn tried to wipe her countenance clean. "What do you mean?"

"It iz not that last night waz not good. It iz that last night waz too good. That iz what troubles you zo."

"I didn't say that!" Lauryn turned away from this too

inquisitive, too discerning stranger, but the contessa would not be ignored.

"Of course, thiz iz the whole nutshell," she said, nodding wisely. "If the lovemaking 'ad not been good, or only a little good, your conscience vould 'ave been easy. But Marcuz never makez love that is not exquizite. So now your 'eart iz smote—you vorry that the good dead 'usband vill look poorly in comparison."

"I do not!" Lauryn tried to interrupt, her cheeks surely flaming, but the other woman ignored her.

"Do not be foolish, Madame Smith. Every man is different. Iz not necessary to judge better or good or not so good, just different. Zo, let it go and be eazy. And rest the eyes with the cucumbers, and come down for dinner, for if you do not—"

The contessa rose and glided toward the door, pausing with one hand on the door handle to say, "If you do not, I vill tell the earl that you are contemplating taking vows to become a nun, and 'e might as vell take me back as lover in your place."

And smiling brilliantly, she pulled the door hastily shut before the handful of cucumber slices that Lauryn sent sailing her way splattered against it.

Even after the contessa had departed, Lauryn lay there for a time and fumed. Yes, she had been lying in bed overcome with guilt, it was quite true. The fact that what she had felt with the Earl of Sutton last night had taken her to such heights of passion—the very first time they had come together, too— how could it be possible, and what did it say about her years of lovemaking with her own husband?

She felt disloyal to the extreme. It was all very well, what the contessa had said, but she couldn't just turn her feelings off and on, like placing a candlesnuffer upon a candle's tiny flame when one was ready to kill the blaze. Her marriage may have ended at the moment life had been extinguished in her husband when he had succumbed to his illness, but feelings took much longer to fade.

Lauryn wished the contessa were not so skilled at putting her finger on the crux of the problem. It was quite true that if their lovemaking had not been so wonderful, she would not feel so guilty. Groaning, she put the cold cloth back over her eyes. She hoped that her swollen eyelids would be less noticeable by dinnertime, as she'd be damned if she would have the contessa telling spurious tales about nunneries while Lauryn lingered upstairs.

So she spent the afternoon in her room, wondering occasionally what the earl was doing, and how energetically the contessa was trying to cut her out of his activities. When the maid came up to help her dress before dinner, Lauryn was more than ready to get up and see people again. She choose another attractive dress from her collection of new gowns, this one a deep forest green, and with the servant's help, prepared for the evening.

When the knock came at her door, she recognized the hand and hurried to open it.

The earl's expression was hard to read. "I hope you are feeling better?"

"Yes, thank you," she said, trying to smile naturally.

"Good," he said, and to her relief, did not question her about the nature of her indisposition. He only offered her his arm. They walked downstairs to the dining room, where again a large party of guests was assembling.

She did not, of course, sit by the earl; her seat was at the other end, in the place of honor at the hostess's position, where she sat above even the higher-ranked ladies, which must annoy many of them, Lauryn thought. She was careful not to appear to relish the fact. No need to make enemies; one never knew what the future would bring. She had hoped not to meet any of the Ton in this persona, but schemes could go awry, and this one had already strayed far from the course that she had intended it to take.

The fact that the contessa was seated near the earl didn't bother her overmuch. The contessa would do what she could to insinuate herself with the earl, but the woman was so honest about it that Lauryn found her less of an annoyance than she would otherwise have been. And really, how many of the other women here would do the same, if they could? Either the earl wanted Lauryn, or he didn't, and what the other females did or didn't do would not change that, so Lauryn wasted no time trying to watch her lover for telltale signs of an altered interest. She kept her eyes on her own partners, as was proper, and smiled and chatted as any well brought up lady should.

Lauryn kept her dinner conversation polite and trivial, and deflected questions about her own past and personal life with light answers and smiling jests.

The gentleman to her left said, "But how have I not met you before, Mrs. Smith? Such beauty could not be easily hidden."

She smiled archly, like the worst kind of society maven, and said, "I'm sure I was under your nose the whole time, Colonel Archwell."

And when the elderly baron on her right insisted he had sat just behind her at the opera two weeks past, she only smiled and allowed him to treat her as an old acquaintance. Mostly she sipped her wine and ate her dinner and kept her chat easy and inconsequential, feeling that she was picking her way barefoot through a nettle patch.

The strain of keeping up a flow of light and unrevealing conversation left her with little appetite, and then there was the knowledge that she would be the one to lead the ladies out when dinner ended. She had not counted on serving in the position of the lady of the manor when she took on this role, and probably, neither had the earl. It was his brother, by inviting this large house party, who had thrust them into this imbroglio. She had expected her only significant position would be in the earl's bed!

That thought almost made her blush, which would never do—they would all wonder what she was thinking, so she hastily turned her thoughts back to the boring talk about hunting and horses in which her dinner partners were deeply engaged. She kept her thoughts under strict control for the rest of the meal, and when the many covers had been consumed and the delicate pastries and hearty meats and well-stirred sauces and finally, the delicious desserts had all been sampled, she looked around the table to gather the attention of the ladies, then stood.

The other females followed her example, and the men stood as well while she turned to lead the feminine half of the dinner party away. At the other end of the table the earl inclined his head and gave her a brief smile. She thought she read approval in his glance and even a glint of admiration, and she smiled back, trying not to blush again.

If he approved of her performance—she was conscious of a warm glow inside. That carried her down the hall and up the broad staircase and into the drawing room, where she selected the best and most comfortable chair—she was giving pride of place to no one, not as long as she was playing hostess!—and sat down, arranging her skirt gracefully around her. Now the inquisition would really begin.

As the other women came in and settled in chairs and settees around the hearth and around her, she tried to draw their names from her memory—she had met so many people last night. But tonight most of the neighbors were back at their own tables. The guests still here were the ones staying as houseguests, the ones that the earl's brother had invited to come from London to stay. Her gaze skimmed over them lightly as she made an inventory in her mind.

This lady in the purple plumes was the plump baronet's wife and those two were his daughters; she rather thought Lady Roberts was hoping for a husband from if not the earl, who was rather out of her social sphere, at least his brother. From the wary way Carter eyed the two girls, who seemed silly and giggled too much, Lauryn thought the odds were against this matchmaking mama. But their father was one of the earl's hunting friends, so they had been invited.

The two fashionably dressed young matrons chatting to each other were wives of two former university friends of Carter's; these two ladies eyed Lauryn with open speculation. Another two even younger women were also dressed in high fashion and could barely be told from the demimonde themselves, but she thought they were teetering on the edge of respectability—and she couldn't remember if they were someone's wives, or not.

And of course, the most fashionable, the most beautiful, if not the youngest, was always the contessa, who seated herself on the other side of the hearth from Lauryn herself. Dressed tonight in gold satin, she shone like a statue carved from precious metal.

"I am happy to see you so improved, Madame Smith," she told Lauryn. "I see my visit, it was encouraging, yes?" She grinned.

"Thank you," Lauryn said. "And yes, your advice was most helpful." And she could not help smiling back.

The contessa's openness was refreshing. Too bad the English ladies were more veiled in their methods.

"You must tell us how you met the earl, Mrs. Smith," one of the matrons said, as if to demonstrate Lauryn's thought. "I'm sure it is a memorable story."

"Oh, no," she answered, giving the other her best smile. "Quite boring, in fact. It was just another social encounter." And wouldn't they love to know the truth, she thought. They would drag her over hot coals, first. . . .

"So you are saying he was so smitten by your grace and charm, he immediately swept you off to his estate to get to know you better?" Mrs. Roberts suggested. The two nitwitted offspring giggled at their mother's drollness.

"I would never submit anything so vain," Lauryn replied, smiling. "You are the one who suggests it, not me."

"Ah, the English, they do not demonstrate," the contessa broke in. "Now, when the earl was courting me, he was much more useful with the imagination." She swept on with a long story about the number of flowers he sent, and how generous he was in the matter of jewels, and how often he came to call. The other females glared at her, which seemed not to bother the contessa at all, and only made Lauryn want to giggle.

This caused a lull in the conversation, which bothered Lauryn not at all. But the women around her exchanged glances, and she could feel them gathering their barbs for the next assault.

"And where did you say your family is from?" The other matron asked. "My cousin is married to a Smith from Devonshire, whose family is extensive. Perhaps you are related?"

This was a potential trap in more ways than one. If she claimed kinship, they could track down the link and prove it untrue, and if she did not, they would dig for another family connection. The others were silent, waiting for her to answer.

Oh, for the wisdom of Solomon, Lauryn thought, feeling the muscles of her neck tighten. "Devonshire, I don't believe so," she said. "But then, tracing one's family tree is such a boring exercise, don't you think?"

Since this was a common exercise for members of the Ton, the lady who had been about to follow up her first question with more demands for information paused with high spots of color showing on her cheeks, and the whole roomful of women gasped at such effrontery.

Lauryn pretended not to notice.

"Why should one have to—ah—trace it?" the contessa added, her tone innocent. "Is it not already known?"

"For *most* of us, it is!" another lady snapped.

"I suppose," the lady's friend put in, while the first still fought to control her outrage, "that you are expecting an offer from the earl anytime?" She smiled, looking as congenial as any tiger in an eastern jungle ready to spring upon some helpless prey.

Lauryn laughed aloud. Her amusement was so obviously unfeigned that the rest of the room stared at her.

"I think not," she said. Continuing to smile, she turned to the first Roberts daughter. "What about you, Miss Roberts? I suppose you have many admirers?"

The young lady blushed and made a disclaimer, but she seemed to enjoy the attention. She twirled a lock of her hair and traded teasing comments with her sister for several minutes.

And then, to Lauryn's relief, the men joined them, and she could leave it to the earl to take over management of the guests. Carter and some of the younger of the company soon wandered off into the billiard room, where presently occasional shouts of glee suggested lively games were being pursued, whether on the green felt tables or other more vigorous types of diversion, Lauryn wasn't sure she wanted to know.

Meanwhile, in the drawing room, Mrs. Roberts volunteered her daughters to play upon the pianoforte for the entertainment of the guests. This meant the occasional wrong note or off-key assault upon their ears, but at least it got that threesome out of their way, as Mama and the other sister had to go and turn pages and look over the first sister's shoulder as she played.

And it drove the contessa, who had first stayed to be near the earl but appeared to have real musical taste, off to rejoin his brother and the younger party.

The earl came to stand beside Lauryn as a servant passed around glasses of wine on a silver tray.

"I see you have survived the gauntlet unscathed."

"Oh, I have endured a few bites, but the blood loss is minimal," she told him, keeping her voice as low as his own.

His grin was mischievous. "I cannot imagine any of my neighbors, and certainly any of Carter's friends, getting the best of you, Mrs. Smith."

For a moment, she felt a warm surge of answering feeling, that he should think her capable, that he should seem to think them a team, set against his neighbors or his half brother's silly group of friends . . . and then she looked away from his admiring glance. She was making too much of a few joking words. She must not imagine more here than was really the case.

She had not come here to get her heart broken.

Six

*A*lthough the earl's demeanor was polite and attentive to his other guests, she felt his impatience, and even shared it. The conversation in the drawing room was less than diverting, the music certainly less than entertaining, and just having him stand by her side was a gentle torture. His nearness made her long for the time when they could be once more alone together.

What was wrong with her that she could so hunger for his touch? The man was like laudanum, she wanted him so badly. She tried to listen to one of the other men talk about a new hunter he had bought, but her thought kept drifting back to their time together last night, how his hands on her body had inflamed her—she pulled her thoughts away with the greatest difficulty, afraid her color was rising.

Was he breathing too quickly, as well? She was sure it was not over the fine points of the nice little roan that the colonel was describing with such precise language. "Her sire is an Irish hunter from north of Dublin, excellent bottom."

She glanced up at the earl, and he met her eye and smiled,

and her pulse leaped. Soon, soon, they could escape the others and come together once more. . . .

A crash of keys from the pianoforte made her jump. It was the end to yet another tune, and she turned to clap politely. Miss Roberts beamed at the praise and at once turned the pages of the sheet music to find another tune.

"Would you like to play for us, Mrs. Smith?" the earl asked, leaning closer to ask. The soft touch of his breath against her cheek made her draw in a deep breath, even as she shook her head at his question.

"No, indeed. I'm afraid I've had little training at the pianoforte," she told him, her tone candid. "I would not wish to perform before company."

"I hardly think you could do worse," he muttered, keeping his voice low as he nodded toward the young ladies sitting at the instrument on the other side of the room, who had now decided to favor the remaining guests with a duet. At least they seemed to be driving many of the remaining company up to bed.

Lauryn tried not to laugh. "Be that as it may," she said, "I would not wish to display my own lack of skill, trust me."

"Always," he told her.

Lauryn looked up, and for a moment, their gazes met. She felt breathless, and once again everything inside her was melting like wax left too close to a fire. And yet, she also felt the urge to run away and hide—it was too much, too soon. For all of her brave words, she felt as if this masquerade were almost out of control—her body had reacted so strongly to his powerful masculinity that she felt barely in command of her own actions.

But she had no choice—she could hardly back out now.

When he put one strong hand on the small of her back, she quivered.

He bent to speak into her ear. "Shall we go up?"

Was it polite for a host to retire with a few guests still downstairs? She supposed he was leaving his brother to bid the last guests a final good-night.

So she nodded. Her throat seemed closed. His nearness spoke to her in so many ways, it was hard to maintain a ladylike facade; all her years of training in propriety and ladylike behavior, and now, now it seemed to strip away. She wanted to put her arms about him and pull him to the floor and tear his clothes aside and attack him as she had done last night.

And, no, she must not do that again! He would think her demented, insane, without any scruples whatsoever.

So steeling herself to keep her raging hungers under control, Lauryn pressed her lips together and, chin held high, walked up the staircase to the earl's bedchamber, with the bearing of some tragic French aristocrat going to face the guillotine, instead of a lover going to a delightful tryst.

His room was as welcoming as it had been the night before, a fire burning on the hearth, the bed turned down, the curtains drawn over the windows against the dark outside. With difficulty, she tore her gaze away from the bed, hesitated for one moment on the threshold, then stepped over and went instead toward the fireside, warming her hands for a moment before the flames. For some reason, she felt cold, despite the heat that coursed through her. Why did her emotions change so quickly moment to moment?

She wished he would come and sweep her up and throw her upon the bed, and be the one tonight to rip off her clothes . . . and yet, she could not meet his eye, and something held her back, even as she longed for the feel of his hands on her body, for more than his hands, for all of him against her, inside her. . . .

She could feel him watching her, but for a long minute, the earl was silent. Then he walked across to the bureau, and to her surprise, she heard a tune play. She turned to see.

He had lifted the lid of a small gold-embossed box, and a swan circled as a fragment of music played over and over. It was a music box, she realized. Lauryn came close to look as he held it out for her to see.

"It was my mother's," Sutton told her. "One of her favorite possessions, and I keep it to remember the pleasure it gave her. You wind it up at the back with a key, and the music plays and the swan circles when the lid to the box is raised. It has clockwork mechanisms inside it. You may have seen the like."

She nodded. "It's lovely."

"Yes," he agreed, "it's a well-made piece." They both watched as the swan slowed and the music ran down, then he closed the lid and placed the music box once more onto the top of his bureau.

"Mrs. Smith," he said, running one finger over the top of the delicately crafted box before he turned to face her, "I do realize that you are a living being, you know, not a clockwork piece, to be wound up and run on order."

"What?" She looked at him in surprise.

"I just wanted you to know"—now he looked at her, and his dark eyes were serious—"you are a beautiful woman, and, of course, I desire you. But you seem—conflicted. I simply want you to know that if you feel unwell, if you have other reflections on your mind—despite our—our arrangement, you do not have to come to my bed every night. You are a person with thoughts and opinions, and I will respect that. I'm not a monster."

"Oh!" she said, blinking hard for an instant. It was more consideration than she suspected many "patrons" would have shown, in such cases as theirs. "You are indeed an honorable man, my lord."

He shook his head. "Only thinking what is best for both of us, in the long term. I would not have you come to hate me, my dear."

Surely he didn't think there would be any "long term" for them? Lauryn pushed the thought away as too far-fetched and almost missed his next comment.

"Shall I walk you back to your own chamber and leave you to rest tonight?"

He would do it, too, she thought, marveling, even though she could tell that he was holding himself back, that he wanted to reach out and touch her, that he was controlling his natural inclinations.

What did she want? She hungered for him, and yet, the memories of her husband, the lingering feelings of guilt—it was easy for the contessa to say to put those reflections behind her—but it was all so confusing . . .

Impulsively, she put one hand on the earl's arm.

It was like touching liquid fire.

The sensual need that he had contained ran through her and released her own need, and suddenly she was aware of him, twice fold, his dark hair, the lock that fell over his forehead and the sun-bronzed skin, the strong nose, the intense dark eyes that looked into her own and seemed to see all the way to her soul. His arms corded with muscle that could lift her into bed and caress her with such strength and command and gather her close to him—and yes, yes, that was what she wanted.

She looked up at him now, and without a word, told him what *she* wanted. He bent over her and pulled her to him with a grip that was almost savage—as if they had both waited overlong, and now restraint had melted away and, almost, civility with it.

Lauryn didn't care. She met his kiss as forcefully as he gave it, pushing back against his lips, meeting the hard thrust of his tongue with joyous abandon, her own hands pushing his tight-fitting evening jacket back and off his shoulders even as he did the same for her low-cut gown. She heard buttons pop in the back—he had not taken the time to undo them properly—they were both too impatient—and there was still the damned corset but later, later—the fevered kiss grew harder and deeper.

Lauryn was barely aware of anything except his hands and his lips and his tongue, and all the places he could use them to such aching and delicious advantage.

She was filled with heat, and his hands were hot on her skin . . . touching her neck, his lips kissing the underside of her jaw, where the skin was so tender and so sensitive that she felt her heart leap, the blood pulse inside her, and again her need surged, always to a higher level, and she pulled him closer . . . she pushed her skirt down, and the petticoat followed. . . .

Presently she found herself clad only in her corset, breasts peeping out atop where he could nibble the delicate skin and tantalize as much of the sensitive area as he could reach, while she sat once more atop him, moving vigorously as he held her hips so that he could position himself to reach high inside her, thrusting deeply and sending her gasping and rising with him in wonderful rhythm.

The pleasure was exquisite . . . mindless, all encompassing, it rolled through her body, flashing in waves across her skin, wringing her inside out, releasing her from any thought, any grip of remorse . . . no thoughts now, no memories . . . don't think, she commanded her innermost self, don't, don't, just feel, just be . . .

When he spasmed and pulled her even closer to him, she allowed herself to float into joyful release. Nothing had ever been so perfect, she thought. But again, the joy of the moment almost at the same instant curled back on itself into guilt and shadowed her pleasure.

Oh, God, why could she not simply take the good and let the other darker reflections fade away? The contessa could live for the moment, why could Lauryn not do the same?

Yes, but the contessa had not loved her husband, Lauryn thought, a trifle bitterly.

She became aware that Sutton was watching her, his gaze disquieted. "My dear, tell me what concerns you."

"This was wondrous," she said instead, her tone low. "You are a marvelous lover, my lord, truly."

But she could not meet his glance, and instead of lying back inside his arms, she scrambled up from the bed.

"Do you not want to lie together for awhile?" He didn't try to stop her, but he frowned, pushing himself up on one elbow as she hastily gathered up her discarded clothing.

"Forgive me, not tonight," she muttered. Again, she could not look him in the eye. With only a quick look first to check the hallway, she ran to her own bedroom, locked the door, and threw herself upon the bed.

Tonight, she was dry eyed, at least, but her heart was still heavy, and she did not know what to think, what to feel.

"I am not married," she told herself, like a child trying to learn a lesson by rote. "I am no longer married. Any vicar would say so, even if he would not sanction exactly what I *am* doing. But I am not being unfaithful to my husband."

So why did she still feel that she was? Why did it feel so wrong when the earl made her so happy?

It wasn't as if she would have this chance forever! Why could she not enjoy it? She was being a fool to chastise herself for disloyalty, but even knowing it did not seem to release her. She felt like some fairy-tale princess trying to find the right words to undo a wicked spell.

Just to feel in her heart what she knew in her head—that by sharing this incredible, amazing lovemaking with the earl, she was not harming her husband's memory . . . why was that so hard to believe?

She had to find the key to freedom from her senseless guilt, and soon, or even the earl, as forbearing as he had shown himself, would lose patience and show her to the door.

He should have slept. His body was sated, but his mind was not. Marcus lay awake for a time and watched the fire burn itself into coals. Why would she not lie beside him? What was holding her back? He had seen women pretend oft enough, even though he seldom had reluctant lovers, and he would bet his whole inheritance that she genuinely lusted for him—the fervor that she showed when they came together was not assumed, or she was a better actress than any he had seen tread the boards in London or Paris.

No, he was sure that she brought a genuine passion into his arms. He would never have forced her into bed; he hoped that his eponymous Mrs. Smith believed what he had said to her about that. But he wanted it to be of her own free will, and always of her own choosing. He thought of the small noises she made as her passion rose, of the faint color in her cheeks as she grew excited, and how her body arched as she came into her climax, and he found his manhood hardening once more, just thinking about her delightful qualities—

"No, you fool, she's not even here," he told himself. "Would you wake her from her sleep?" Perhaps *sated*, then, was not the right term. He'd be happy to start again. She was a woman one could make love to again and again, and never tire of. . . . And yet it was even more than that. He wanted to know her as a person, get past this silly masquerade, find out what she thought, who she was beneath the surface, who she was— good lord, if she was the squire's wife, he would be in a pickle!

A coal popped on the hearth, and the room seemed darker than usual for a long moment. He blinked against the darkness.

And why was that, you fool?

He paused in his line of thought, feeling a sudden cold wash over him. Surely, he wasn't thinking of marrying a woman who had walked into his home and offered herself as a prostitute? No, of course not, that was preposterous. . . .

Except that was not who she was, he was certain of it. Yes, she had a capacity for deep passion at her core, but she was not practiced at it, he had known that at once—she was too surprised and delighted by what she had found with him . . . and every night brought her new experiences to marvel over— it was easy enough to tell. He felt it with every ounce of his body, saw it and felt it in every reaction she gave him when they came together.

She was always genuine in her open-natured and generous responses to him, never holding back, never pretending. Sometimes he saw her eyes widen in surprise or pleasure, and he tried every night to find new ways to please her; it was becoming his particular joy. He did not recall ever enjoying sharing love with anyone else as much as he did with this lady.

Nor did he have any doubts that she was, indeed, well born, truly a lady.

Why would she not tell him the truth? And how could he persuade her to do so? And why in the bloody hell was she not curled up against him in his bed now, instead of spending the night alone in another bedroom?

With an inarticulate growl, he tossed a pillow against the far wall of his bedroom so hard that a handful of feathers spilled into the air.

When a maid tapped on her door, Lauryn blinked and rubbed her eyes. It seemed very early. Yawning, she stumbled out of bed and went to unlock the door. If the maid wondered that Lauryn had turned the lock on the door, the servant didn't remark upon it.

The girl placed the breakfast tray on the table, then went back outside to bring in an ewer of warm water. "The earl has ordered your bags to be made ready, ma'am. 'E wants to go see about one of 'is ships. 'E says you should be ready to leave in an 'our."

"What?" Still half asleep, Lauryn tried to make sense of this. "Where are we going?"

The maid repeated her comment, pouring a cup of tea as she did so. Lauryn sat down and ate some toast and marmalade and drank some tea while she tried to get her thoughts in order.

Had the earl decided he must inspect the salvaged cargo, too? What was the great mystery about this ship, Lauryn wondered, while the maid packed a carpetbag for her.

"Which gowns would you wish to take, ma'am?" the servant asked.

As she had only a couple more new gowns on hand, that was easy to decide. Perhaps by the time she returned, the rest of the dressmaker's assortment would arrive, she thought.

The maid picked up the dress she had worn last night to hang up in the clothespress and shook her head. "You've pulled out some buttons in the back, ma'am," she said. "I'll sew these back for you."

"Thank you, that would be appreciated," Lauryn told her.

While the maid packed her things, she washed and dressed quickly in her new travel suit, glad that the maids had brushed it out for her and hung it neatly in the clothespress. She brushed her hair and put it up into a simple knot at the back of her head, put her bonnet on top, and was ready by the time she heard the earl's usual quiet knock at her door. Her bag had already been taken down.

She opened the door herself.

"Good morning," he said. Looking as strikingly handsome as always, today he wore riding clothes, and his expression was stern. Was he concerned about the ship, or could he be unhappy about her conduct last night?

Lauryn curtsied and tried to give a polite smile. He hadn't exactly given her a choice about going along on this trip, but in fact, she was not unhappy about leaving the houseguests behind for a time.

"How far are we going, my lord?" She asked as they walked together down the hall and descended the great stairwell.

Lauryn wondered if the contessa knew that they were slipping away, or if his half brother Carter had been told. They encountered no one else in the hallway, and they did not stop in the dining room to chat with any early risers.

"We should be in Skegness by early evening," he told her, holding her hand and helping her himself into the carriage, which waited outside the front entrance. This time, he did not seem to be taking his valet with him.

She settled into the comfortable seat and looked out the window of the vehicle. They had not bothered to say good-bye to anyone. Of course, Carter was rarely up early. The earl did not seem to consider anyone else's opinions overmuch when he made up his mind to a course of action.

The coachman slapped the reins and the carriage lurched into motion. The gentle swing of the vehicle was soothing, as long as the road was good, and Lauryn found her eyelids wanting to close. After watching for a time as the earl rode slightly in front of the carriage, she allowed herself to doze.

When she woke, they seemed to have made little progress. The flat countryside of the Fens had little variety to catch one's eye. Mile after mile of flat green marshland, the occasional canal, a few birds soaring in the endless blue sky— Lauryn watched it move around them, and at times wondered if they had made any progress at all, or perhaps they were caught in one of those glass balls made for children, where small figures were caught forever frozen in midstep. Then she would nod off again.

At midday, they came through a village and stopped at an inn to change horses and have food and drink themselves. The earl ordered a private parlor, and she was shown up to a room on an upper floor.

The day was warm and the air heavy, so she was glad to remove her cape and wash her face and hands. Then she returned and sat down with the earl. The meal was simple but well cooked, and just to have the privacy of sitting alone with him, with no other guests to observe them, no one to gossip or guess at their motives, was a delight.

He lifted her hand and kissed one finger, then another. "What makes your eyes sparkle so, Mrs. Smith? I refuse to believe it is merely the strawberry tart and clotted cream, excellently made though it is."

She laughed. "No, although it is delicious. I admit I was thinking that it is refreshing to have this time with just the two of us."

He smiled at her, and his glance also seemed very telling. "I agree, utterly and completely." He lifted her hand to kiss it lightly, then surrendered it, but only, he told her, to allow her to eat the strawberry tart.

Laughing, she complied, offering him a bite of the dessert from her spoon, and kissing a trace of the cream off his lips. He kissed her back very warmly. It was with some regret that eventually she allowed him to escort her back to the carriage.

The afternoon was much the same as the morning: a long uneventful drive, again with little to see except miles of green, flat land, expanses of blue sky, occasionally farmers in the marshy fields bending over to harvest whatever it was that they grew there—she would have to ask the earl.

By the time the sun was dropping like a great golden ball to the west, Lauryn was conscious of considerable fatigue, simply from the jostling of the carriage, which did eventually wear upon one.

But instead of driving into a town, they turned into a side road, and the next time the carriage stopped, she found that they had come to a tall stone wall surrounding a small house set in a copse of trees on a windy heath, with a distant view of the coast. The coachman blew his horn, and a servant came out of the house and opened the gate to let them in.

Alone in the carriage, Lauryn had no one to ask, but she wondered where they were as the coachman clucked to the team and the carriage lurched into motion once more. They pulled through and up the drive.

When they stopped again, and the earl came to help her down, she looked at him in inquiry.

"This is one of my hunting lodges," he told her. "Very private, very quiet. We are only a short distance from the coast and Skegness, where I will make inquiries about the cargo, but I thought you might like the—ah—intimacy of the setting, as opposed to a busy hotel in a port town."

Looking around at the lovely little house, Lauryn thought that it was quite charming. A woman in a white cap and a maid and manservant had come out to make their bows to the earl and his guest.

"My housekeeper, Mrs. Piggott, who will take good care of you, Mrs. Smith." The older lady beamed and made a deep curtsy.

Sutton added to the servant, "A simple meal when you can, and warm water for my guest and for me to wash, if you please."

"Yes, my lord," the housekeeper told him. "And we have the beds aired and your room turned out for you, just as you like."

Lauryn realized that the staff had had advance notice, so this journey was not as spur-of-the-moment as it had seemed. The lodge was well maintained, with climbing roses growing up the outside wall. The inside hallway smelled of lemon wax, and the polished floor reflected their passage.

The housekeeper, a smiling woman of mature years, her hair gray beneath her white cap, led Lauryn up to her bedchamber. This room had pink flowered hangings and was just as clean smelling and airy as the downstairs.

"If you need anything at all, Mrs. Smith, just pull the bell rope for the maid."

"Thank you, Mrs. Piggott. I'm sure I will enjoy my stay here," Lauryn told her.

She went into her room and took off her hat, washing off some of the dust of the journey before going back down to re-join the earl in the small dining room. The servants were already laying what seemed to be a very ample meal.

The earl was standing before a small fire in the hearth at the end of the room. She joined him there. "I have an appointment tomorrow morning with the Harbor Master," he told her. "Tweed will likely have already seen him, but I wish to hear the report with my own ears."

"Do you not trust the viscount?" she asked, keeping her voice low, even though the servants were unlikely to know to whom she referred.

He gave her a twisted grin. "Oh, I trust him, mostly. But it's always just as well to double-check."

Not sure what that meant, she simply nodded. He looked past her toward the table and said, "I believe we may sit down now, if you are ready?"

She took her place at the table, and when one of the servants had seated her, the earl sat down at the head of the table, and a manservant offered them ham and roast beef and other foodstuffs.

For a few minutes they ate, without trying to keep up a conversation, and the silence was soothing after the clamor of the crowded table back at the earl's estate. Lauryn wondered what Carter and the contessa and the others would think of their absence, but found that she didn't really care.

After the dessert had been served, the earl dismissed the servants. "I will call you when we wish the table cleared," he said.

While he ate an apple dumpling, Lauryn toyed with a plate of berries and cream, thinking about the ship and its mysterious cargo. But as one appetite was sated, she grew more conscious of the call of another, and the presence of the man sitting so close became more and more imperative.

Neither of them had changed for dinner. The earl, in his riding clothes, the navy jacket that showed off his broad shoulders, the tight-fitting buckskin breeches that empha-sized his powerful thighs—nothing could have showed him to better advantage. She discovered that she was thinking most unladylike thoughts, and looking down, saw that she was licking her spoon with long slow motions even though it was quite empty.

The earl watched her with an unreadable expression.

"I have had the feeling . . ." he began, his tone abrupt.

"Yes?" she said, when he paused, her voice a bit breath-less.

"That is," he said, taking a deep breath. "I feel that you have been—that you have perhaps felt the need to hold back. And I thought that if we had a greater privacy, with fewer peo-ple around us who knew who we were, you might feel freer to enjoy our coming together and to express your own feelings."

Not sure that she wanted to confess everything that had been holding her back, she simply muttered, "I see."

He waited a moment for her to comment, but she could not think what to say, and she did not meet his eyes. She thought he might have frowned.

"Would you like anything else?" he asked politely, nod-ding toward the table.

Oh, yes, but not from the table, she thought, but she didn't have the nerve to say her thought aloud. How can I say that I crave your body, your attention, when I cannot be honest about my emotions? And you are entirely too perceptive about my responses! Had he always been this penetrating in his in-sights? For a man who was so forceful in most of his dealings, so commanding in his public persona, it was surprising to find that he could also be so sensitive to others and read her so well.

Lauryn remembered the contessa's warning that it was a risk to lie to the earl. She thought that he would surely detect a falsehood. She didn't think she would dare try—well, no more than she already had.

It might be best if she ended this whole arrangement. He was not a cruel man; she did not think he would try to hold her to their agreement if she wished to leave. Yet the thought of walking away made her ache with need for him. The only direction she wished to go was toward his arms—

As if guessing her thoughts, the earl was rising from the table. "Shall we retire? I will have the table cleared away, then the servants will leave us."

She looked up at him in surprise, and he explained, "The housekeeper and footman have cottages on the grounds, and the maids and other servants live in the village, a mile down the road."

She raised her brows. So they would be quite alone in this small, elegant house. He had meant what he said about providing privacy. Yet, how lovely it would be not to have so many people around them.

He did not bother with sitting alone at the dinner table, having, as he told Lauryn, no interest in any solitary absorption in his port. Or perhaps he was more interested in other— not solitary—pursuits, Lauryn thought, taking out her fan to cover her grin.

While the dining room was given over to the servants, she and the earl ascended the stairs. The maids had left ewers of warm water in the bedrooms.

"Since we have sent the maids away, before I leave you," Sutton told her, "allow me to undo the buttons, so you can easily get out of your traveling costume."

"That would be helpful," Lauryn agreed. She slipped off her cape and turned so that he could reach the line of buttons that stretched down her back. She tried not to think about the feel of his strong fingers—later, she would enjoy his touch, very soon, very soon—no need to get goose bumps already!

Did he know that she was reacting to his nearness? As he unfastened the pesky buttons, he leaned closer to kiss her neck very lightly. Yes, he could tell, how could he not? She sighed in pleasure as she pushed down the skirt and tossed the bodice aside, allowing them to fall unnoticed to the floor.

"Now I will unlace your corset and make myself scarce, or your bathing water will grow cold," he pointed out, although his hands seemed to want to linger. Since she enjoyed having them explore their way over her body, she had no complaint.

They continued to stroke her skin, smoothing her as if she were a cat, and if she were feline, she would purr with contentment, Lauryn thought, and stretch and ripple her muscles just as cats were wont to do.

Not having so supple a body, she had to contend herself with a telling glance and a smile. Still he ran his hands over her shoulders, lightly massaging muscles sore from the ride, then abruptly reached down to pull her shift over her head. She threw her arms about his neck while he bent, putting his mouth to her neck and allowing his lips to linger, as if tasting her skin.

She felt a shiver of response. But after a long delightful moment, he raised his head again.

"But as I said, your bathwater will grow cold."

"I suppose so," she said, hearing the huskiness in her voice and knowing how reluctant she was to let him leave her side.

"Of course"—he glanced back—they had shut the bedroom door behind them, and surely the servants had left by now, as ordered—"perhaps I can render you some small assistance?"

While she shivered again in delicious anticipation, Lauryn was still not totally sure what he intended. But if the earl had a hand in it, she was sure it would be pleasurable. So with his assistance, she pushed off the rest of her clothing as quickly as possible, and he lifted her easily into his arms, with three easy strides carrying her to the dressing table where the china bowl and ewer of warm water, the lavender-scented soap, and bathing sponge had been set out for her use.

He draped a large linen towel over the stool and lowered her carefully down, then, grinning, shed his own clothes.

Watching him with appreciation, she did what she could to help, pushing his jacket back off his shoulders and tugging at the tight-fitting riding boots when they proved hard to remove.

"Boxel warned me of dire consequences when I told him he would be left behind," the earl confided. "But this shooting box is so small, I told him I would make do with the footman to help me, if I needed aid. My poor valet may never recover from the slight, of course."

She grinned.

When he, too, was naked, he turned to the large silver ewer and poured warm water into the clean china bowl, taking her sponge and dipping it into the water.

"Now, where do you prefer to start?" he asked, his tone polite.

"I suppose one should start at the top and work one's way down?" she suggested, just as gravely.

"A logical progression," he agreed. He brushed her face very gently with the soft sponge, the warm water teasing her cheeks, dripping a little as it ran down her neck, tickling as it continued over her naked breasts . . .

He leaned to kiss away one of the drops. "I fear I have not yet perfected my technique," he noted.

Lauryn tried not to giggle, wishing he would put his whole mouth there, but then again, this was too exciting, waiting to see what he would do next. "Then continue, my lord," she commanded. "I have never been bathed by anyone so high born or so exquisitely male."

"Yes, my dear," he agreed meekly. He picked up the scented soap and worked up a slight lather, rubbing the soapy bubbles over her neck and chest with his bare hands, easing down over her breasts and under her arms till she giggled, then back down her breasts till she gasped from an entirely different sensation.

"Do you think we have covered this ground sufficiently?" he murmured into her ear.

"Perhaps," she whispered back. "We can't be too careful." He nibbled on one earlobe, then wrung out the sponge and dipped it again into the warm water and followed the path of his soapy hands. The touch of the soft, warm sponge was incredibly provocative when he held it against her skin—and when he followed its sleek touch with kisses pressed against her damp flesh, she gasped again and raised her body to push more closely against him.

He repeated the process, warm water, soap, damp sponge, kisses, his lips and his tongue against her skin, her breasts, the tender and so sensitive nipples—she might be the cleanest lady in the kingdom, Lauryn thought, and certainly the most distracted! The delightful waves of sensation ran over her skin and through her whole body—she felt overcome with rippling tides of pleasure that only made her ache for more.

The earl put both his hands to hold her by the waist, then he took the soap and repeated the exercise on her thighs and calves, which created more elegant torture. Lauryn tried to sit still on the delicate stool, tried not to moan deep in her throat, barely holding herself still as he laved her with the warm sponge. His hands were so strong and felt so delightful as they grasped her legs, holding them, lifting them as he wielded the sponge, running his hands along their length.

"No one will hear, sweetling," he reminded her. "You may make any noise you wish!"

She nodded, almost beyond words already, reveling in the sensations that he flooded her with, over and over.

And next he stretched her feet and massaged her toes as he washed them—it was total hedonism, she thought, sighing. It was so relaxing that she thought she might fall off the damned stool—at least until he ran the sponge, still warm and soft, lightly between her legs.

This time she did jump. His eyes were wicked in their inner laughter.

"Did I startle you, my dear Mrs. Smith?"

She found she was breathing quickly. "I think I deserve equal time, my lord."

"If you wish."

Despite her rapidly rising desire, she reached for the sponge and, pushing the stool away, dropped to her knees and pushed him back so that he sat easily on the rug, as well. Now she could dip the sponge into the basin and try her hand at washing his incredibly muscled and well-made body.

It was as if she had at last taken a long-desired toy down from a shelf. She could run her hands along his solidly built shoulders and down his strong arms, enjoying the feel of the finely made male animal. She dipped the sponge into the water and scrubbed his arms and chest, rinsed and then reached farther down for his hard stomach and firm thighs, hearing him gasp as she reached closer and closer to the dark curling hair—and as for the rest—she smiled and allowed her fingers to wander teasingly close, then retreat, from the potency where her final delight awaited.

She grasped his firm shaft, touching it and marveling at the firmness, running the sponge lightly over it, then stroking it lightly, then more firmly with both her hands until he groaned.

But she had not the patience to make him wait with the same infinite care as he had tantalized her. No, her hunger was too overpowering . . . she leaned closer to feel the slight scratchy touch of his chin, to kiss his lips, and allowed him to pull her into his arms, not caring how or in what manner they came together, as long as this fever was soothed.

"I want you!" she muttered, without trying to disguise her hunger.

He did not seem to be shocked. He pulled her down with him, stretched her body out on the thick rug, and, holding her lightly, arms out from her body, kissed her open lips, his own mouth firm and as hungry as her own, his tongue probing.

From her mouth, he lowered himself far enough to kiss her breasts, and she groaned with pleasure, gripping his dark hair with both her hands and pulling him even closer.

Moaning again, she arched against him, and when he pushed himself inside her, she allowed herself to fall at once into his rhythm. Already, they seemed to know how to fit their bodies together, how to reach for the best positions. He knew to touch her *there*, and *there*, where the most delicate spots sent exquisite circles of pleasure flowing up through her whole body while she exclaimed with soft sounds of pleasure.

And as he rose and fell above her, she moved with him, meeting him as he pushed, pulling back as he did, and when he moved faster and faster, his breath coming quickly, she was ready with him, till he pulled her so close that their low sounds of passion mingled, and she felt his heartbeat thunder against her own and his hips spasm as she pushed with all her might, delighting in his strength and his passion.

Then when they reached the height of passion together, he wrapped his arms about her and held her tightly, and only later did Lauryn realize that he had effectively prevented her usual retirement from the bedroom. Tonight it was her bedroom and not even her bed. The floor was hard beneath the rug, but she felt too limp and replete to consider complaining, and it was too easy to lie inside his arms to contemplate withdrawal.

And her usual ration of guilt—well, it hovered outside the circle of the earl's embrace, waiting to descend upon her. Just for a few moments, she shut her eyes and enjoyed the illusion of closeness that this posture allowed her, as if Sutton might care for her, as if they might really share feelings, emotions, love—if she dared say the name.

And it did not occur to her to open her eyes and observe the expression upon the earl's face. Perhaps she was afraid to.

Only after she felt his heartbeat slow to normal, and she could feel him lift his head to gaze at her face, did she school her features into a civil banality that she hoped gave nothing away. Then, only, did she open her eyes.

But the earl was frowning, and she felt her heart drop. Had she still not pleased him?

"What is his name?" he demanded.

Seven

"*What?*" *Lauryn stared at him.*

"You still do not give yourself to me, your whole self," the earl told her, his tone accusing. "Who is the other man you think of, Mrs. Smith, when we lie together?"

She could not think what to answer. They lay so close, and yet there seemed to be an immense chasm separating them. She felt as if a cold wind swept through the room, howling through the gulf between them, and she shivered.

Feeling suddenly abashed to be lying here naked, she sat up. For an instant, she thought he would reach to pull her back—he half extended his hand—but he lowered his arm instead. She turned and reached for a blanket lying across the end of the bed and wrapped it around her.

His lips were pressed together in a tight line. "I am being nonsensical." He stood up in one economical movement, ignoring his nakedness and walking across to a table on the far wall where a silver tray held a carafe of wine and several glasses. He poured two goblets of wine and offered her one.

She started to shake her head, then realized how dry her mouth was. She accepted the wine with a murmur of thanks.

After taking a sip, Lauryn drew a calming breath and said, "What do you mean, my lord?"

What had she done, or not done, that he objected to? She had armored herself to undertake this role of lover for hire. She had tried to bring him pleasure. He had forbidden her to speak of love. Had he changed his mind? Surely not!

What did he want from her now—perhaps it was simply true that she had not been, would never be good enough at the art of love for such a practiced lover? Lauryn hugged the blanket closer to hide her naked body and looked away, refusing to meet the earl's stare. . . . She should have known she would never be able to pull off such a charade.

Marcus gulped his wine, a sad abuse of a good vintage. He was acting like a fool. He had asked—made a business arrangement—for her company, for the pleasure of her beautiful body. When had he ever before expected a lady of the evening to offer him her total devotion? Oh, they pretended, of course; his mistresses often spouted words of extravagant affection, but it was only a token display, and both parties knew it. He would be only asking for trouble.

Except that nothing about this pairing was as usual; for one thing, she was not really a woman of the evening, and he had known that from the beginning, although she still did not know that he knew. And she did seem starved for physical affection, and he had almost at once come to crave her touch. The delicate beauty of her face, her body, her fair hair and unusual green eyes which revealed so much intelligence and spirit and sensitivity—and so much emotion that she couldn't seem to completely hide . . . it awoke an answering hunger inside him, and he wanted to see her respond fully, he wanted to see her smile, dammit, and allow her eyes to open candidly to his, not slide away from his gaze to veil themselves beneath lowered lids.

Yet, he knew had no right to ask it—how could he?

But he did.

Anger simmered inside him at the injustice. He knew he was behaving irrationally—he had not contracted for her total devotion—he had no right to expect it. He wanted so much that made no real sense.

'*Ware your heart, Marcus*, he told himself, swallowing the rest of the wine with one gulp. You are no green lad to wear it on your sleeve. Recollect the last "lady" you tossed back into the street—she was greedy and lascivious enough to please a king's regiment.

And just to consider his former mistress and Mrs. Smith— he wished to hell he knew her real name—in the same breath was to do the latter an enormous injustice!

But nonetheless, he glanced at her—still curled up on the rug, pulling the blanket around her, as she watched him uncertainly. Had he frightened her? No, she met his glance with her chin up; she had courage enough. Her gaze was wary, however, and he tried to soften his expression. The smooth white shoulder with its lack of covering, the wisp of red gold hair that fell over her bare neck—already desire was rising once more inside him. Damn, the effect this lady had on him was unparalleled.

She was like the drug that kept a opium-crazed man asleep for days in an opium den, lost to the world. He couldn't get enough of her. Almost despite himself, he moved closer, bent to kiss that soft, tender skin, and he felt her shiver with response.

But to his surprise, she stood and drew her blanket around her, unsmiling as she met his eyes. "If I am not satisfying you, my lord, perhaps we should reconsider our arrangement."

Let her go? When adders sang and pigs could fly!

He put one arm around her shoulders and pulled her closer. "Do I satisfy you, my dear Mrs. Smith?"

She looked at him in surprise. "Of course."

"Then why should you suppose that you should not satisfy me?"

"I—" She flushed. "I–I suspect I lack your experience in the art of lovemaking, your lordship."

"You have a natural zest that makes up for any possible deficit of well-practiced technique, not that I find you in any way lacking. If I did, that is an expertise we should devise together," he told her, allowing his hand to slide beneath her cloaking blanket and cup the soft skin of her breast. She quivered with response, and he felt his body react to hers with a hunger that surged through his whole consciousness. He held himself in check, careful not to reveal the effort his self-control demanded. "And besides, perhaps I simply prefer you the way you are."

Blinking in apparent surprise, she looked up into his eyes.

"There is no one else I would rather have in my bed tonight," he told her, his tone very gentle.

Her lovely green eyes widened, and then for the barest moment, he saw it—that shadow that passed across her face at inauspicious times. Then she looked away again. And this time he could not leave it alone.

"And who do you think of now?" he said, almost gritting his teeth, steeling himself to hear the answer. "Who is the man you would prefer to me? Who is it that comes between us?"

"No, no," she protested. "You misunderstand, my lord."

"Tell me who you are thinking of!" he demanded, his hands moving to grip her by the shoulders, his voice suddenly stern.

She gazed at him in alarm, but there was no denying that at this moment he had her undivided attention.

"Who is it?" he demanded.

"My husband," she said faintly.

A long moment of silence, and he felt his jaw go stiff. "You are not a widow?" Had he been taken in by a more clever ploy than he had suspected? Had he been completely mistaken in her? The hurt implicit in that thought sent cold icing through his whole being.

She paled. "No, no, my lord. I am indeed a widow," she protested. "That is the truth, I swear on my sacred oath!"

His relief was palpable, and it took several moments—and the look of pain in her face—before he realized he was gripping her shoulders much too tightly. He loosened his grip, though he did not let her go completely—*he could not let her go!* Something inside him echoed the words again and again.

This woman was meant to be his. She belonged to him, whatever her name, whatever her marital status; but thank all the gods she did not have a living husband. And yet, still—

He tried to think what this complication meant to him, to them both.

"So I must compete with a dead man," he said, his voice low.

Eyes wide, she chewed on her lower lip and did not answer.

Of course she was not experienced, or she would have better hidden the truth, he thought. She would not have allowed him to glimpse her abstraction. And he was a madman that he cared. Her husband was buried, dust, fed to the worms; why should it concern him if her thoughts still turned to her late spouse?

Because it did. Because her heart must still be there. Because he wanted her heart, dammit.

He wanted her attention, her total concentration. Perhaps it made no sense, what he felt about this woman who had walked into his life, but that hardly mattered. He desired her beautiful body, but it was so much more than that; he discovered that with every passing day he wanted more and more from her—far more than their "business arrangement." He did—he would not, could not let her go.

And he did not dare tell her so now. He feared he would frighten her away.

So he pressed his lips together and reined in his regenerating passion. She watched him with a touch of distrust that he could not allow to build.

"You must be tired," he said instead. "Would you like more wine?" He held out the carafe, but she shook her head. Her goblet was still half full.

"Shall I leave you to your rest?"

He hoped she would refuse and offer to share her bed with him instead, even if they did not make love again. Lately, he had been too aware of how empty his own bed was when she left it. He had never had that feeling before, when his mistress of the moment had turned away. In fact, he had usually been ready to be alone.

To his disappointment, she smiled at him, but did not dispute his suggestion.

"I am weary," she agreed. "And you are a most considerate lover, my lord."

Keeping his expression courteous, refusing to reveal any negative emotion, he stood and bowed as gravely as if he were fully dressed.

"I shall see you in the morning," he told her. "The servants will return to see to our breakfast. Then we shall ride into the harbor town to see what I can learn about the *Brave Lassie*'s cargo."

Lauryn nodded, remembering the real reason they had come to the area. It was not, of course, just to make love in the privacy of this lovely little hunting box. When the earl had shut the bedroom door behind him, she rose and put on a nightgown and finished making herself ready for the night.

She really was tired, and the jumble of emotions inside her made her feel even more drained.

Why had the earl demanded to know about her husband? Why did he want to know her private feelings—why on earth did he care?

She'd never heard that a courtesan was supposed to have emotions—oh, just say it—was supposed to love the man she served. And he had said there was to be no thought of emotions between them. She must have misunderstood his meaning tonight.

Snuffing the candle beside her bed, Lauryn pulled the covers up and lay back, trying to still the thoughts tumbling around in her mind so that she could sleep. Tonight, even past the usual guilt that dogged her, she was puzzled by the earl's behavior. It would not help that she did not understand his reactions—she didn't even understand her own! Sighing, she changed position again as she tried to push the mishmash in her mind aside. Eventually, she slept.

When she woke to hear the first birds singing outside her window, she blinked and yawned and found herself little refreshed. When she rose and glanced in the looking glass, she saw she had dark circles under her eyes, the sign of a restless night.

A maidservant soon brought up a tray and warm water and was there to help her dress.

Lauryn was glad to sip the hot tea and sample the fresh-made bread, still warm from the oven, and the other equally tasty foodstuffs that filled the tray. Shaking her head at her reflection, she washed and dressed and did what she could to disguise her wan complexion. When the earl sent word, she was ready to join him downstairs.

She found him pacing restlessly in the hall. He was dressed for riding. Expecting to once again be left alone in the carriage, she was startled by his first words.

"I should have asked earlier, but do you ride, Mrs. Smith?"

He saw the answering flicker of anticipation that lit up her eyes before she mastered her expression.

"After I married, I learned to ride and enjoy it very much," she said slowly. "But I'm afraid I do not have any riding clothes with me."

He could hear the disappointment in her voice.

"We will not be stopped by such a small thing as that," he said, smiling. "It's a beautiful day, and I have a nice little mare in my stable here that I think you would enjoy. There are several riding habits upstairs in the clothespress." He did not have to look at her hips and waist and the sweet curves of her breasts to judge their size—he remembered them well from having them encased delightfully inside his palms. "I'm sure you can find something that fits well enough."

She brightened at once. "I will be swift," she promised, turning to ascend the stairs.

She was true to her word, and when she returned, he escorted her outside, where the groom had brought two horses to await them. One was the earl's usual steed, the other a mare of medium height, an attractive chestnut with bright eyes and long mane.

Lauryn exclaimed, "Oh, what a beauty!"

Marcus smiled. It pleased him to see her excitement about her chance to ride. He motioned the groom away and helped her up into the saddle himself, watching her settle herself easily into place.

He mounted his own horse, and nodded to his companion. "The harbor is not far; we will have only a short ride."

It was almost a shame that the distance was not longer. The sky was blue, the breeze light and off the sea, and they had a good road so they could canter side by side.

He was happy to see his companion's eyes sparkle and her manner freer than he had so far observed. Her diffidence was not in evidence today, and he relished the easy laughter that greeted his attempts at humor as they rode through the countryside.

Watching her open countenance, her bright eyes, her unguarded mien, for once he could picture her as she was surely meant to be—the genuine person, Marcus thought, beneath the counterfeit. He only wished he could observe this side of her more often. How could he convince her that he could be trusted?

As they neared the town, they had to rein in their horses and proceed more slowly as they encountered other riders and vehicles on the roadway. And to his regret, Mrs. Smith reclaimed her facade of discretion, even as she slowed her steed to a more manageable gait.

The more crowded roadway also made them now unable to ride side by side, instead moving into a single file procession, so they could no longer talk, and they made their way down to the harbor without any more pleasantries being exchanged. When they came to the harbor, Marcus helped his companion dismount, then located the office of the official he needed to speak to. He found someone to look out for their mounts while they went inside.

The local official was ingratiating but hardly a fount of information. "Aye, me lord, the Viscount Tweed was on 'and almost before the '*Ampton Court* docked, the ship carrying the recovered cargo from the ship ye lost—what was it, the *Bonnie Lassie*? All the recovered cargo 'as been taken to the company's warehouse. We 'ad a look, and ye can see it there, as well. It all seems in order. Quite remarkable that such a quantity of it 'as survived. Amazing that it should turn up from the depths of the ocean, eh, yer lordship?"

"Yes, quite a surprise," Marcus agreed. He knew that his tone was dry, and that Mrs. Smith glanced at him from beneath her eyelids, but he didn't think that the Harbor Master detected anything singular in his tone.

"I'll write out an order giving ye permission to get past the guard and visit the warehouse, me lord."

"Thank you," Marcus said. He took the paperwork, and after a few more courtesies exchanged, they were bowed out of the office and could remount their steeds and proceed down the docks toward the warehouse where the remains of the recovered freight were stored. The air was redolent of dead fish and brine and filled with the noisy shouts of seamen busy as other ships at anchor nearby were emptied of their own hauls of barrels and boxes or else being resupplied as their crews prepared for new passages to faraway countries.

Mrs. Smith's eyes were wide as she watched the hustle and bustle. Once her mare danced to the side as a burly sailor came too close, his vision obstructed by the bulky crate whose weight he balanced on one shoulder. But she tightened the reins and pulled the horse back into line, avoiding the seaman and controlling her mount.

He nodded in approval, and she flushed slightly at his sign of praise.

Lauryn had been relieved that she still remembered how to sit a horse. They had been away from Yorkshire for some time, and she had not had the funds to ride while staying in London. It was a great pleasure to have the opportunity to ride today, and earning the earl's look of commendation gave her more private delight than she cared to admit.

They reached the warehouse without further incident and dismounted again. When the guard said, "No admittance, gov," the earl presented the Harbor Master's documents.

"Oh, sorry, me lord," the man said.

The big building stank of mildew and rot. Lauryn drew out her handkerchief and held it to her nose, but she followed the earl as he approached the stack of water-stained boxes and bins stacked unevenly at one side of the structure. He cautiously lifted the top of the nearest crate to inspect its contents.

Unable to contain her curiosity, Lauryn came closer to see what he found.

As he raised the lid, the wood—soft and rotted by its long exposure to water—came apart in his hand. What could have survived the years beneath the sea?

But it seemed what was inside the crates had indeed fared better than the rotten wood. When the earl pushed aside soggy sawdust, she saw beautiful sculptures of what appeared to be green or bluish stone. The next box held vases and urns of delicate china, in Oriental patterns of white and blue. She bit her lip, wondering if these were as precious as they appeared. He continued to check box after box, and although the crates were close to falling apart, the contents seemed in good condition.

So why did the earl frown?

She waited for him to speak, and when he did not, finally asked, "Are you not pleased that they are mostly undamaged? Are they costly?"

"Yes," he said. "They are most valuable, Ming vases and urns, and good quality jade sculpture of some age. But . . ."

"It's amazing that they are intact," she said when he paused, thinking of these delicate pieces tossed about in a storm, then sinking with the ship to the ocean's depths.

"They were packed in sawdust, and the vases had beeswax melted inside them, to help cushion them against the rolling of the waves," he pointed out, but his thoughts still seemed far away.

She saw that the vase that he lifted to inspect for cracks still had wax clinging to its lip, though someone seemed to have scraped it mostly clean. The earl tried to brush aside the wax that clung to his fingertips.

"How much of the original cargo survived?"

"I'm not sure, likely about half. I will have to see if Tweed has made a list of the salvaged goods and compared it to the original," the earl told her.

He glanced about them and seemed to be counting the boxes and barrels. She was silent, in order not to interfere with his concentration. They had worked their way back toward the entrance of the warehouse. The earl turned back toward the guard at the entrance.

"Do you know if Viscount Tweed made a list of the cargo?" he asked the man.

"I don't rightly know, me lord," the other man answered.

"How long was he here?" the earl asked.

The guard looked a bit harassed. "Not so long, yer lordship."

The earl gave up his questions. "I shall have to write to Tweed," he told Lauryn. "I believe he has gone back to London. I think we've done all we can do here. Let's get out and get some fresh air."

She nodded. The atmosphere was noisome with the heavy stink of the rotten wood and the mildewed sawdust and other strong scents; it was almost hard to breathe.

It was good to step out into the open air. She saw the earl dust off his trousers, which showed traces of black spots from the mildewed and rotten crates.

"I think we could use a nuncheon," the earl said, "after dealing with the dregs of Neptune's bounty. But first, there is one errand I would like to do."

"Whatever you like, my lord," she said.

He had noted a store with a window filled with lockets and jeweled necklaces, bracelets of gold, and silver chains. She gave it hardly a passing glance. He thought of the ribbon about her neck he had shredded when he had pulled off her clothes, and hesitated. He was no doubt asking for trouble, but still, fair was fair.

"Wait," he told her, as she looked about her, ready to cross the street at the safest and least littered path.

"Yes?" She turned back to him. "Is this the errand you wish to attend to?"

He nodded. "Since I accidentally ruined your ribbon last night, it seems only fair that I should replace it. We might take a look in here for a trinket to go about your neck." He motioned to her to go through the door first.

She raised her brows, and then, in a small gesture of independence that he found oddly alluring, her chin. "My lord, a ribbon is easily found at the notions counter of a ladies' shop. I think you are in the wrong emporium."

"We can always look," he repeated. Her lack of enthusiasm somehow strengthened his insistence. If she had jumped at the chance, he would have been sure that he had been wrong to suggest it—perhaps she was more canny than he knew—but no, he thought her reluctance was genuine. At any rate, he held the door for her until she relented and allowed him to usher her inside.

A clerk, no, more than a clerk—one of the partners himself, if Marcus didn't miss his bet—hurried forward, having taken a quick measure of the patrons who entered.

"Good day to you, sir, madam. How may I assist you?" he asked, giving them a deep bow.

"The lady would like to see something that would grace her lovely neck," Marcus suggested.

Mrs. Smith flashed him a look of indignation. He had given the jeweler much too big a rein, and the man was going to run with it.

Perhaps he simply wanted to see what she would do. He couldn't help remembering that remark when they had first met about having permission to smother her with jewels . . .

The man was already pulling out one of the gaudiest and, no doubt, most valuable pieces in the shop, a diamond and ruby necklace that was likely worth a prince's ransom.

"Now, this, madam, is something truly spectacular—"

"No, no." Mrs. Smith looked horrified. "You misunderstand. I wish only something small and simple."

The jeweler's smile faded. "Oh, very well, then. How—um—simple do you wish to go, madam?"

"Very simple," she said firmly, leading the way to the far end of the counter. "Now this is quite charming." *This* was a single gold chain with a gold locket at the end of it.

The jeweler followed her with much less spring to his step. "No doubt, no doubt, but let me show you another locket with diamonds set around it, which would augment your charms even more," he tried to tell her.

Marcus watched for the next few minutes, being no help at all as his companion fought back all the shopkeeper's efforts to talk up his more expensive wares. But she kept her gaze resolutely on the gold locket, and presently, they walked out of the shop with a paper-wrapped package and a slightly crest-fallen shopkeeper left behind them.

"You are most generous, my lord," she told him, smiling as if he had given her the crown jewels.

"I think I am a paltry fellow, actually, and you are a determined shopper," he said. "I salute you."

"Most of the other pieces were truly gaudy," she said. "And I do like this locket, so I am well pleased."

She smiled at him, looking satisfied with her small prize. He smiled back, and again wondered when she would tell more about who she really was.

He led them on to the small inn on a side street, which he had selected earlier.

"I think we can find a quiet meal here," he told her. They gave the horses to an ostler, and the earl asked the servant who met them for a private parlor and a meal to be sent up.

"If you don't mind going on up, Mrs. Smith," he said. "I just want to check on my mount; he seems to be favoring his left front foot. I want to be sure he's not picked up a stone."

"Of course," she said cheerfully.

The landlord himself came to greet her in the front hall, bowing and rubbing his hands on his apron.

"So happy to have ye. Mrs. Smith, is it?" he said, all smiles. "I've me kitchen working on your meal, and yer good man is in the stables, is he? He'll find all in good shape, there, too, though I don't fault him for seeing to his horses his own self. A good mount is worth a pretty penny, in't it?"

Trying not to smile at the idea of the Earl of Sutton being called her "good man," Lauryn managed not to giggle as she was escorted up the stairs. Chatting all the while, he showed her up to a small parlor, assured her that all would be seen to it just as she would wish it, and then left her to find the facilities and return to warm her hands at the fire in the hearth, all before the earl returned.

"How is your horse?" she asked when he came into the room.

"A small stone under the shoe, but I had it out before there was any real damage, I think," he told her. "Ah, this looks promising."

Servants brought in the first of the dishes, and the smells would certainly tempt anyone with a stomach as empty as hers, Lauryn thought. Soon they could sit and eat, and for a few minutes, they gave their attention to their meal.

Presently, their landlord returned to be sure that all was satisfactory.

"I 'ope your beef is to your liking, Mr. Smith," he said now, his smile broad. "We do our best to please, we do, for you and your good wife."

The earl paused for a moment, and Lauryn blinked, waiting for him to freeze out their host with a haughty look and to apprise him of the earl's correct rank and name. But after one slightly startled moment, the earl said nothing, only nodding in acknowledgment.

"You've taken good care of us," the earl agreed. "The dinner is excellent." Nor did he say anything to correct the man's mistaken assumption about their marital relationship.

Feeling her cheeks burn, she looked down at her napkin. In this small town, it was somehow comforting that they should assume that she was a proper married lady, not a woman of the evening, though she hoped that the earl did not guess the direction of her thoughts. He was often entirely too perceptive, however, and she did not dare glance in his direction.

"Have you been down to the docks?" the landlord was asking.

The earl nodded. "For a short time."

The man lowered his voice as one with a choice tale to relate. "Ye might want to make a longer stay. We 'ave a real excitin' tale of the sea in our town jest now, a ship what was lost in 'igh seas and then washed up on a far beach and its fabulous treasures reclaimed."

Looking surprised and not exactly pleased that the *Brave Lassie*'s fate was so well known, the earl raised his brows.

Knowing that their host was expecting a different reaction, Lauryn said quickly, to distract him from the earl's reaction, "Oh, my, that is an exciting story!"

Looking gratified, the landlord turned to her. "Aye, in't it? The whole town's abuzz, I can jest tell you."

"What is this treasure?" the earl put in, his tone now suitably interested. "Gold and silver doubloons from a pirate's hoard?"

"Ah, not quite that," the landlord told them, wrinkling his broad brow. "But jade artwork like what the lords and ladies put into their great 'ouses, and fancy china, and all that. Lucky, too, as that stuff don't rot away in the seawater, see?"

While the earl pursed his lips, Lauryn said, to keep the landlord talking, "Who owns the treasure now?"

"Ah, it belongs to a couple of lords and was only found again by a great stroke of luck." He leaned over to stir a sauce for them, and lift a cover on a plate of apple crumble. "If ye are willing to 'and over a small bribe to the guard at the ware'ouse, ye can get a look at all the treasure what's been found at the bottom of the ocean."

"Really?" the earl said, keeping his voice even with great self-control, Lauryn suspected, to find that his reclaimed cargo was being shown to all the curiosity seekers in the neighborhood willing to bribe the guard.

"Aye," their host told them.

Frowning, the earl was silent.

Their landlord seemed to expect a response, so Lauryn exclaimed, "My goodness, that is indeed a wondrous tale."

He beamed. "Jest what I said."

The earl looked grim. "Amazing indeed."

"And, I can tell ye what they're saying about the death of the ship's captain," the other man added, his expression smug.

"And what is that?" the earl asked, his voice sharpening.

The landlord's eyes narrowed, as if wondering if he had gone too far.

"I mean, is there some mystery involved?" Sutton smoothed his voice to simple curiosity. "I'm eager to hear it."

Lauryn put in, with a girlish simper, "Oh, this is too amazing! Do we have a local ghost story, as well? I do adore ghost stories!"

Their host guffawed. "I can't guarantee ye a 'aunting,

Missus, but they be saying 'e may 'ave come by a violent end. 'Is skeleton t'was found in the bowels of the ship wid 'is skull bashed in. Now that's a fine tale, don't ye think?"

"Indeed, it is," the earl muttered, while Lauryn rewarded the landlord with suitable squeals of horror.

When their talkative host at last seemed to have run out of rumors to share, he took his leave. After the door was shut safely behind him, Lauryn turned to the earl. She found that he was frowning once more.

"Amazing what plain Mr. Smith can learn, and the Earl of Sutton cannot," he said. "The Harbor Master told us nothing of this. My compliments, Mrs. Smith; you should be on the stage."

She smiled, then sobered quickly. "Not at all. I'm happy to help. But, my lord, do you think there is really something more than a ship going down in a storm, something sinister here?"

"We shall have to try to find out. And as for the so-easily corrupted guard"—the earl frowned—"I believe I shall have another conversation with him very shortly!"

Eight

*T*hey set out again for the warehouse in the early afternoon. This time two carriages waited outside, and it seemed that they had caught someone in the act of touring the warehouse.

The guard looked ashen with horror that Lord Sutton should return so soon. "Me–me lord, I weren't–weren't expecting to see you again," he stuttered.

"Obviously not," the earl said, his voice dry. "Who is inside?"

The guard blinked, as if trying to pretend he had not noticed the carriages with their bored-looking coachmen and teams. The horses pawed the gravel and shook their heads at flies that buzzed too close.

"Ah, well, a-as to that," he stuttered under Sutton's relentless stare.

It turned out to be a party of wealthy merchants and their wives. The earl sent the hapless guard inside to instruct the oglers that they would have to leave.

As he and Lauryn followed the man inside, Lauryn heard one of the women, a loud-voiced matron dressed in puce, arguing with her husband. She seemed to wish to bribe the guard to allow them to take away one of the jade statues.

"It's just a bit of colored stone," her husband said. "I don't wish to beggar myself just to indulge your whim, Wendella."

"But you can get it from him for half the price of the shops, I'll wager," his spouse shot back. "And you know that oriental is still all the crack. Look at the prince regent's pavilion . . ."

She lowered her voice to eye the newcomers with suspicion. And then the guard had reached them, his own voice low and quivering with nerves.

Lauryn glanced at the earl, who appeared grim.

"They are making your priceless artifacts into a village fair, available to the highest bidder," she said quietly, feeling a rush of indignation on his behalf.

The look he gave the trespassers should have curdled their enthusiasm for their illegal purchase, but the visitors looked more offended than embarrassed. Glaring at Lord Sutton, they swept out of the warehouse and made their way back to their carriages. Standing near the wide doorway to make sure that they left without any part of his belongings, Lauryn and the earl watched them go.

Lauryn listened to the couple still bickering as they entered their carriage, and the jingle of the team's harness, and the stamp of the horses' hooves as they at last moved away, the second carriage following close behind.

"What shall you do?" she asked quietly.

"I will have to make arrangements immediately for my own guards to take over security here," the earl told her. "It's apparent that the Harbor Master's men cannot be trusted."

"Indeed," she agreed. "Shall I stay here while you go to find men to take over for him, at least for the time? I know the objects inside are of immense value."

She could not interpret the look he gave her.

"Mrs. Smith, I would not leave you here alone and risk your safety for all the priceless cargos from all the seven seas in all the world," he told her. "Come along. We shall replace the guards with more dependable ones as expeditiously as we can."

He turned to say a few brisk words to the guard, who hung his head and appeared unable to put up any protest, but Lauryn didn't hear what was said. She felt as if the blood had rushed to her head, and her ears seemed to ring for an instant, his words to her had had such a strange effect.

Did he truly value her so? No, he was only a decent man, she thought, putting more value on an innocent life than on objects. He was a good person at heart, she knew that. It was not that he cared for her . . . was it?

He had only known her a few days. When he held her close, sometimes she wondered . . . No, he was merely a practiced lover, she knew that, had always known that. She could read too much into such gestures, and she must not . . . she could not leave her heart behind when he sent her away, as he invariably would.

Hadn't she sworn she would not allow this stint as a courtesan to ruin her life? She must not go away maimed forever. She had promised herself she would do what she could to protect her reputation and her heart.

She had to try to keep her own promise. She must.

So she allowed him to give her a foot up into her saddle, and then they rode away, and she did not allow her thoughts to linger on his words. But if she could not erase them from her heart, well, one could not *always* be logical.

They rode back to the small inn where they had taken their meal, and the earl asked to speak to the overly talkative innkeeper.

"I've a mind to find a man I've had recommended to me," he told their host. "A man who was a soldier in the French wars. I believe he's sold out by now, but he was a man of great honor during the wars, highly dependable—his word was his bond—and still in good health."

The innkeeper scratched his balding head. "You don't ken 'is name? That might be Colonel Swift; 'e sold out when 'e got the bullet in 'is left arm. 'E lost it below the elbow, but otherwise, 'e's still in fine form, I'm told, and has fathered three splendid sons since 'e came 'ome. Or mayhap Captain Bullsmore, though 'e's a bit long in the tooth and 'as gotten a bit fond of 'is drink of late."

"I think Colonel Swift may be the man I seek," the earl said, straight-faced. He got directions, and they set out.

"How do you know Colonel Swift?" Lauryn asked him when they were on the road again and had pulled up at a narrow bridge, waiting for a carriage to pass.

"I don't, but I needed someone to recommend men I can trust, as the local guards sent out from the harbor are obviously not reliable," he told her.

She gazed at him in admiration of his gall. "What if this man had not existed?"

"I took a chance that he did." He grinned at her.

When they reached the address of the retired officer, they were fortunate enough to find him in, and they were admitted without problem. This time the earl gave his true name and explained candidly why he needed to hire a team of trustworthy men.

The officer had an intelligent face and grasped the position almost at once. His left arm showed an empty sleeve, neatly tucked up, but he paid little attention to his old war wound.

"I had heard rumors about a sunken ship and the recovered cargo, but I paid little attention. So it's true, then. I appreciate your position, Lord Sutton. I'm sorry to hear your sad experience with the Harbor Master's men, but not really surprised."

Nodding, he went to his desk and picked up a quill. "I know just who you need," he told them. "There are plenty of ex-soldiers who are in need of honest labor, even today. I shall see to it at once, my lord. I'll be glad to see my men—for these were my men, once—given a chance for some work."

"I appreciate your assistance," the earl told him, giving him the location of the hunting lodge and making arrangement about fees and payment for the men. "We shall be in the area for several days until I know more about the situation."

They discussed the question of security for several more minutes, then, when the earl was satisfied, took their leave.

She wondered if they would make their way back to the earl's shooting box, but it seemed that he was not yet finished with his investigation.

They returned to the office of the Harbor Master, and the earl asked to see the body of the *Brave Lassie*'s captain.

The Harbor Master, who had looked distinctly surprised and not particularly happy to see them return, blinked at the unexpected nature of the earl's demand.

"The captain? T'weren't much left of the poor man, me lord. You understand the body had been trapped below decks for the whole time—"

"Of course I understand!" Sutton's voice was icy, although controlled, and his expression . . . Lauryn was glad she was not the man who had to confront him.

The Harbor Master gulped, and his brow showed fine beads of sweat, although the day was not particularly warm.

"Then you ken it t'were underwater, and the crabs and the t'other fishes, well, t'were mainly only the bones that remained, so—"

"So show me the bones!"

"I can't, me lord, they been a'buried." The more agitated he became, the stronger the man's accent also grew. He pulled out a lavender handkerchief and wiped his forehead, giving up any attempt to maintain a show of composure.

"If there were only bones left, what was the rush?" the earl inquired.

The other man looked aggrieved. "Viscount Tweed insisted it be done as soon as possible, me lord, as a sign of respect, 'e said. And it was done all decent and proper, with the vicar to read a service just as 'e ought. The viscount didn't ask no such questions about looking at nasty bits of bone, neither." He gave another wipe of the violently hued kerchief.

The earl drew a deep breath. "I see. Yes, that was very proper. May I ask where the captain and—I assume—the rest of the crew have been laid to rest?"

The Harbor Master looked suspiciously at him, but the earl's expression was bland.

"So that I, too, may go to pay my respects to men who died in my employ."

"Oh, of course, me lord." He gave them the location of the church, and then they made their farewells.

The Harbor Master tried to mask his relief, but he was obviously only too glad to see the door shut behind them.

"Why do you think he was so agitated?" Lauryn asked as they rode away from the harbor once more.

The earl was silent for a moment, then, as they rounded a lumbering coal wagon, he said, "If you find a company where the men are taking bribes and corruption is rampart, it usually starts at the top."

"Oh," Lauryn said, as the meaning of this sank in. "So you think the Harbor Master himself may be—"

"Not what he should be, yes. And he may well be the richer for a bribe connected with the recovered ship's cargo. The only question is, from whom did the money flow?"

She had no answer to that, though it was food for thought as they rode back to the warehouse one more time. It was a sign of Colonel Swift's military efficiency that already a different pair of guards stood smartly at attention at the doors of the big building by the time they arrived.

"Sorry, sir, no one is to be admitted," the first man, a burly, square-jawed fellow said without prompting.

"An excellent sentiment," Sutton told him. "However, I am the owner of the property inside, as Colonel Swift may have made known to you, and I am also, by the by, your current employer." He handed over the paperwork he had obtained earlier from the Harbor Master, which showed his name and title.

"Thank'ee, me lord, sorry, me lord," the guard said, after giving the papers a quick glance. "Colonel Swift did describe ye, but I were told to take no chances, ye see."

"Good man," the earl agreed. "I wish to take one quick look, and then we will be on our way."

Lauryn followed him inside, wondering why he wished to look at the boxes and their contents once more. He pulled the top off one more crate and touched the china urn, running his hand around the smooth interior, then absentmindedly rubbed his fingers together as he stared into space, apparently thinking hard. But he said nothing, and she did not want to interrupt his deliberations with idle questions.

In a moment, he turned and they left the warehouse and headed back into the countryside, this time with little conversation. The sun hung low over the western horizon, and the air had cooled, so Lauryn was happy when they reached the earl's shooting box.

She dismounted, aware that long unused muscles were protesting a day spent mostly in the saddle. She would be sore tomorrow!

But for now, she could go upstairs, wash, and change for dinner, and she certainly had a good appetite; it seemed long ago that they had eaten.

When she came downstairs again for dinner, she found that the earl had also changed, and he looked handsome and somewhat aloof in his evening dress.

The feeling of intimacy that she had had as they had pursued information together, ridden side by side together all day, seemed to have disappeared. He bowed to her, of course, and led her in to the dining room, but somehow he had resumed a formality that brought back the gulf between them.

What had happened to their easy interplay?

She wished intently for the return of their more natural, more easygoing manners of the day. Oh, where were Mr. and Mrs. Smith, who had eaten a simple meal at a small, second-rate inn while the landlord lingered to gossip?

Now they had returned to being the Earl of Sutton and his hired courtesan, no matter how civilly he might treat her—and it made her heart ache.

So the delicious sauces were as sawdust on her tongue, and she found she could eat little of the thin-sliced venison with raspberry glaze or the foie gras on toast.

Her spirit wanted sustenance, too, and the earl had somehow retreated from her—what had she done to be shut out like this?

Or perhaps she had only imagined that he had let her in, in the first place? The pain that suffused her made it hard to chew and swallow the exquisite dishes that kept coming up from the kitchen. She'd rather have bread and butter with a smiling Mr. Smith sitting beside her, at ease and friendly, than the elegant earl at the head of the table, his manner cool and his eyes somehow reserved.

She had been so happy to have been able to come away from the noisy, crowded house party back at his estate in Lincolnshire. She'd delighted in being alone together, private in this lovely spot. Now she felt that she might as well be marooned at the top of the world.

How could she bear being pushed away from him like this?

The meal seemed to stretch on for endless hours, but at last the final course had been served, she had played with a few pieces of fruit on her plate, and the earl glanced at her.

"Are you unhappy with your meal, Mrs. Smith? Is there something else you would like, instead? I can send word to the kitchen."

"No, no, of course not," she hastened to say. "Your cook is superb, and the dinner was delicious, all of it. I am simply replete."

He lifted his brows. "Very well. Shall we withdraw?"

She nodded. "Yes, if you please."

He stood, and as the servants had been dismissed from the dining room, came himself to pull back her chair. Conscious of his closeness, she allowed him to stand behind her, and wished she could pull him to her here and now. But she was afraid a footman might remain at the doorway, and they could not be caught in an embrace by the household staff!

He offered his arm and they returned to the sitting room. She could think of little to chat about. After offering her the instrument—she shook her head, her skill at the keyboard was limited—he sat down at the pianoforte and played a short interlude while she listened, admiring his proficiency. Then, when the clock struck ten, he looked at her, his expression still closed.

"I'm sure you are weary after our journeying today and would like to retire. Good-night, Mrs. Smith."

He bowed over her hand, and he was so near, and yet so far, encased in a veritable shield of icy correctness that she did not dare try to penetrate, that all Lauryn felt she could do was curtsy and take her leave.

But she climbed the stairs feeling heavy of heart. So there would be no lovemaking tonight? She felt a sense of abandonment, yet knew that she was being nonsensical. It had been a long day, with a lot of riding. Perhaps he was tired, too. And he had much on his mind.

Yet—was he tiring of her already?

In her room, she pulled the bell rope for a maid, and when the servant appeared with warm water, accepted her help in getting out of her clothes. After preparing for bed, Lauryn turned to climb into the big bed, and was conscious of a sense of anticlimax.

The bed seemed very empty, and she felt very alone.

She missed him.

She slept very ill that night and woke early, conscious of a sense of aloneness that she was only now aware of having escaped, during the last days with the earl.

Did he think of her? Had he missed her company? What would it be like to spend the whole night with him, to wake and find him sleeping beside her, or looking across at her with his first waking moment?

Sighing, she knew she should not tease herself with what she could not have. A few stolen moments of passion—she was lucky enough to have that pleasure with a wealthy, important, and highborn man. And if he were tiring of her company already—well, she had been fortunate in the few nights of pleasure they had shared. She would have to go cautiously forward and see what transpired—it was all she could do.

She sat up and almost groaned, finding that her day in the saddle, after months of not riding, had left its mark. She was decidedly sore. She got out of bed cautiously and prepared to dress.

When Marcus came down to breakfast, he looked at once to see if Mrs. Smith had yet risen, and when he saw that she was up apace, he wondered if that was a good sign or ill. Did she slept well because she had not been bothered by his advances, had not had to pretend to return his passion? But surely, gods, she had not been pretending—he would have bet his right hand that those nights of shared passion had been genuine!

Or could it be that she had waked early because she had not slept well, that she had missed his touch—God knew he had ached for hers! He looked at her closely, but she smiled as serenely as ever and bade him a good morning. He could see no sign of anything being amiss, dammit all. He answered her greeting, trying not to growl, and pushed back his plate too quickly.

"I'm going back today to find the church and the graveyard where the captain of the *Brave Lassie* is buried," he told her. "You may come if you like, or you may wish to stay here."

"What do you expect to find?" she asked.

A reasonable question, and he wished he had a better answer.

"I have no idea," he told her honestly. "It is simply the last stone to turn, and I feel I should make the effort."

She nodded. "Then I will come along, my lord. For luck." She gave him a small smile. He realized that she was once again clad in the riding habit, and she had obviously expected him to be once more at his search, whether it was reasonable or not.

She seemed to know him almost too well, already!

A footman appeared. "The horses await you, my lord."

Nodding, Marcus offered his arm to his companion, and she accepted it. They walked through the front doors and he helped her up and into the saddle. She seemed a bit stiffer settling into the saddle than yesterday, but he was thinking about how he should approach the churchman when they arrived at the parish church, and paid little heed.

He mounted his own horse quickly, and then turned him toward the coast once more. Lauryn nudged her mount with her knee, and they set off.

Today was warmer than yesterday, but they did not have to ride all the way into town, and the breeze from the sea cooled her cheeks and blew stray tendrils of hair back from her face. It was a good thing that her mount had an easy gait, Lauryn thought, as she was indeed sore from her hours in the saddle yesterday.

When they turned off from the main thoroughfare and followed a side road to the village, the earl found the small parish church that had been described to him. Lauryn drew up her mare behind his gelding as he paused and looked about him. The church was not over large, but it was a handsome building, in the Tudor style of wood and plaster but well maintained, and behind it was a graveyard also of some antiquity. Was this where the shipwrecked sailors' scant remains had been laid to rest?

The earl dismounted and helped Lauryn down, also, then tied the horses' reins to a convenient tree. They strolled into the church, but found it untenanted. The interior was handsome if a bit austere. The altar was bare except for a small arrangement of flowers, and a brass cross hung above it.

The windows to each side were of stained glass and showed biblical scenes. Lauryn stood at the back of the church and admired the tall windows and the scenes they depicted. She felt like an interloper. If ever there were a spot to be aware of one's sins . . .

She was roused from her more serious thoughts by the earl's return. He was frowning. "I can find no one," he told her. "Let us see if there is a vicarage nearby."

Nodding, she followed him outside the church building, where they saw a small house a short distance behind.

"Perhaps that is it," she noted, and the earl nodded.

"We shall see," he agreed.

They returned to their horses and untied them. But before they remounted, the earl hesitated. Now the graveyard was closer than the house. "Let us walk through the cemetery at least, on our way to the rectory," he suggested.

Aware of the same intense curiosity, Lauryn made no

demur. Leading their horses—it felt disrespectful to ride through the graveyard—they picked their way carefully through the old, sometimes leaning, headstones, looking for graves that appeared more recent. The marble and granite stones were old, many touched with moss or discolored by years of rain and sun and wind. Some leaned like drunken sailors on long-delayed shore leave.

But they all told their own tales, and the faint indentations spelled out names of the inhabitants buried beneath. Lauryn walked along the grave sites and looked for the men who had served aboard the *Brave Lassie*. After several rows of villagers, she spotted some graves where the dirt atop looked fresher.

"Here!" Lauryn called, feeling a sudden thrill run down her spine. She felt as if a cold finger had touched her. "I think these might be the ones." She bent over to see the names, which meant nothing to her, but the dates sounded right. She waited for the earl to catch up with her, and he, too, leaned to make out the inscriptions.

"Yes, you're right," he said slowly. "The bodies, or what was left of them, are indeed safely buried. Safe for someone, at least. There are not enough here to account for the entire crew, but I suppose it's understandable that not all of the crew might have been recovered. I wish . . ." But he did not finish the sentence.

"Let us see if we can find someone who did see the remains before they were put away from view."

They walked on to the rectory and knocked on the front door. A maid in a white apron answered their knock, but she told them that the vicar had been called away to give comfort to a farmer's wife confined to a sick bed in a farmhouse some distance away.

"I don't rightly know when 'e'll be back, sir," the servant said. "Can I take a message for ye?"

Sutton looked frustrated. "What I need to speak to the good vicar about is best said face-to-face, I'm afraid," he said. "I'll leave my card." He handed over a calling card, which impressed the servant so much that she regarded them both with widened eyes.

"May—may I offer you refreshment, me lord?" she stuttered. "I'm sure the vicar would wish it, if ye'd like to come in."

Lauryn thought the earl was about to refuse, but he glanced at her and seemed to change his mind. "We have had a long ride. Perhaps some tea would not be amiss."

She nodded, conscious of a dry throat, and the need to excuse herself.

So they went inside the rectory after all and were shown into a neat sitting room. Lauryn took care of her business, then washed the dust of the ride off her face and hands and felt much refreshed.

"Thank you," she told the maidservant, a fresh-faced girl who looked barely in her teens.

"Oh, no, me lady," the servant said, beaming. "It's lovely to 'ave such noble visitors. Our little church don't usually 'ave such exalted guests."

Lauryn thought of explaining that only the earl was the aristocrat here, but her heart sank at having to spell out her own rather doubtful particulars, so she simply didn't speak of it. She rejoined the earl in the sitting room, where the servant soon brought in a tea tray for them, with not only tea but sandwiches and half a cake and scones and jam.

"This looks lovely," she told the girl, who beamed once more. "We are indebted to the victor for his hospitality. You have represented him very well."

"Thank'ee, my lady." The little maid looked very pleased as she curtsied before leaving the room.

Lauryn blushed and cast a glance at the earl, but he smiled, so he did not seem to castigate her for the servant's mistaken assumption. He motioned to her to pour, and they sampled the tray's bounty.

"Do you think the vicar will have seen the bodies before they were buried?" Lauryn asked him, curious as to why Sutton was so determined to follow through with this part of his investigation.

"I don't know. I just wish to find out if that part of the gossip has any truth to it or not, if I can," the earl told her, grimacing as he ate a very fine scone.

She spread clotted cream on her own pastry, took a bite, and enjoyed every morsel, so she decided it must be his thoughts that worried him, not the taste of the food. They took their time with the tea and foodstuffs, but still the vicar did not return, and it seemed awkward to linger at the vicarage much longer.

Lauryn decided that she would try to see if she could get more information out of the young servant. On the pretext of getting a small tea stain out of her glove, she went back to the kitchen with the young girl and while the servant tried rinsing the riding glove with cold water, she spoke to her about their errand.

"The earl wished to pay his respects to the men who died aboard the sunken ship. They were in his employ, you see," she said, as if making conversation.

The maid was all agog. "Ooo, that's very kind of 'im, to be sure, me lady," she said, dabbing carefully at the glove. "I think this will lighten the spot."

"Good work," Lauryn said. "I should not have had it in my lap while I was drinking my tea." Since she had deliberately spotted the glove—which like the riding habit itself was a loan from the earl—to have any excuse for this conversation, she was just as glad to see the spot lighten.

"Did the vicar help lay out the bodies before they were buried?" she asked now, trying to keep her tone casual.

The maid shuddered. "Oh, me lady. 'Aving been under the sea, there weren't much left of the poor buggers, you know, only bits of bones."

"Oh, dear." Lauryn paused, not sure how to ask the next question. "It's just that we heard, in town—"

"What? I'll 'ave you know that the good vicar did all that was proper!" Her lips pressed together, the maid fired up at once in defense of her employer.

"Oh, I'm sure he did," Lauryn said quickly. "It's just—we heard a rumor about the captain's wounds, and we wondered if the vicar perhaps could have gotten some idea how the captain had died."

The maid's eyes widened. "I s'ppose 'e drowned, me lady,

'ow could 'e not? Going down on a sinking ship like that, poor man. And any'ow, t'was only bones left that they brought back, ye know. But . . ."

She hesitated.

Lauryn tried to look sympathetic. "Yes?"

"Well . . ." She looked around as if expecting someone to be crouched behind the big kitchen table, listening. "If you want someone who saw the remains . . ."

"Oh, we do!"

"If it won't get 'im in trouble, I might could tell ye who to speak to."

"We will not—the earl will not be be censorious, I assure you!" Lauryn told her.

"Then, if you're assured . . ." The maid twisted her apron in her hands and spoke very low into Lauryn's ear.

Lauryn took a shilling from her reticule to reward the maid and made her way back to the sitting room, eager to share her news. She threw the earl a meaningful look, and he stood. They offered their thanks to the servant and took their leave.

Outside, the earl turned to her.

"You look like the cat who emerges from the canary's cage, feathers dripping from his whiskers. What did you learn?"

She smiled at him. "I have found someone who viewed the bones of your unfortunate captain!"

He gave a low whistle, which made his horse toss its head. "You have all my admiration, Mrs. Smith. Who is it?"

"The vicar's cousin, James Hilber, is a medical student, and he helped arrange the bodies—well the bones—into the wooden caskets. It was necessary to straighten out just which went with what, so to speak." Lauryn wrinkled her nose—it was a distressing thought.

The earl looked thoughtful. "I see what you mean." He picked up his reins. "Did she tell you where can we find this gentleman?"

"Yes, indeed."

"Mrs. Smith, you are a marvel!"

Feeling warmed by his smile, she told him where they

should go, and then he helped her into her saddle. Was it her imagination or did he linger for a moment with his hands on her hips?

Her blood warmed to have his hands again on her body. Why did he stay away last night? Would he join her tonight or ignore her again?

Sighing, she settled herself comfortably—or as comfortably as her bruises from yesterday allowed—back on her mount.

The earl mounted his own horse, and they turned back toward the roadway. They urged their steeds onward. Traffic was heavier now, but within the hour they found the inn that the maidservant had described. Behind the counter a tall, thin young man studied a thick book while two workmen nursed their mugs of ale and talked in low voices. When they entered, the young man looked up quickly and marked his place in the volume.

"Like a drink, gov?"

"I'd like to talk to you, Mr. Hilber," the earl said, laying a guinea onto the well-scrubbed surface. "And I'm willing to pay for the privilege."

The young man's jaw dropped, and he gazed at the coin. "I–I—" He turned and yelled toward the kitchen. "Holly, come out here."

When a somewhat blowsy woman in a long apron emerged, he told her, "Watch the counter for a bit; I need to talk to this gentleman."

"But me bread's in the oven," she protested.

"I'll give you a half shilling for the extra work," he promised.

Seeing that the guinea had already disappeared from the top of the counter, Lauryn bit back a grin. He had scooped it smoothly off and into his pocket.

"Would you like a drink, sir?" he asked, turning back to the earl.

"An ale, if you please," Sutton said.

"Missus?" The young man asked.

"A cup of tea, perhaps," Lauryn murmured.

"Holly, bring us a cuppa tea, there's a good girl," he told the woman, who rolled her eyes. "Oh, come on, you got to check your loaves, anyhow."

He brought a tall mug of ale for the earl and emerged from behind the counter, motioning for them to follow. "There's a more private table in the corner, just there."

They sat at the scarred, slightly sticky table, and the young man slid into the chair across from them. He stared at them in the dim light. "How'd you know my name, and what is it that you want?"

"We've been to the rectory, and the servant there told us where to find you. I understand that you're a medical student?" the earl asked, his tone polite.

"Oh." The young man flushed. "When I get enough funds laid by to go back to school, I shall be, again," he told them. "I completed my first year of studies, but my money ran out. I have to make my own way. My parents died when I was young, and my father was only a poor cleric with little money of his own, so . . ."

He shrugged, and Lauryn felt a wave of sympathy for him. She knew well enough how difficult it was when money was scarce.

"We were also told that you saw the remains of the men who were found on the sunken ship, the *Brave Lassie*." The earl paused. "I am Lord Sutton, and that was my ship. I am understandably interested in the men who worked on my behalf, and in what led to their deaths."

The young man hesitated a moment, then he rose and went back to the bar, going behind it and bending to disappear from view for a moment. Holly came out of the kitchen with a cup of steaming tea just as he straightened. He took the tea and came back toward them, but he also had something tucked beneath one arm.

Putting the teacup in front of Lauryn, he sat down again on the other side of the table. He also put down a drawing tablet and opened it to a page that showed several sketches. Lauryn looked down at the pencil sketches and recognized several different views of what must be a human skull.

"This is one of the men, or his remains, found on the ship."

"We went to the graveyard," the earl interrupted. "There are not enough men buried there to account for all the crew."

"No, my lord." James Hilber sounded earnest as he met the earl's gaze. "I assume that the rest of the crew's remains may have drifted off or been swept away by the storm or the sea's currents. We buried what was found. This man had two fingers with joints missing from an old shipboard accident, which the Harbor Master said marked him as the captain; it was a man the Harbor Master knew. He was found belowdecks, the skeleton intact. I made sketches of his injury just as practice, since I get little chance to study, just now."

"I see," the earl said, looking over the drawings once again. "And if you had seen this skull in a class at university, what would you say had caused this injury?"

"If I had seen this at school," James said, hesitating for a moment, "I would have said he died from a blow to the head, my lord, from a thief in a dark alley seeking to steal his purse, perhaps. But I suppose, given the circumstance, that it must have been some kind of blow from a falling mast, or such like. I'm not a sailor, you understand, but I'm sure given a terrible storm, that some such could have happened."

Lauryn spoke up for the first time. "Were there other bodies around him?"

They both looked at her. "No, just the one," the young man said. "I'was said they found most of the others, what there were, closer to the upper decks."

"Just so," the earl muttered, staring at the drawing of the cracked skull, which James had so well depicted. "Was there anything else that stood out from these remains, anything else that seemed unusual?"

The young man shook his head. "No, my lord. They showed the kind of marking we would expect from their time in the seawater. That's all."

"I see." Sutton's tone was controlled. "Thank you for sharing your expertise." He put his hand inside his coat and removed several more coins, which changed hands.

James Hiber's expression brightened. His savings would be considerably enriched by this unexpected encounter, Lauryn thought as she sipped the mahogany-colored tea.

When the door to the tavern closed behind them, the earl handed a coin to the man who had held their horses, but they lingered for a moment before remounting, and Lauryn looked at the earl. "A mast cannot come down inside the ship, can it?"

He shook his head. "If so, we would have found evidence, and the whole ship might have broken up, which it did not."

"Why do you think the captain was found there?"

He frowned. "I can think of many places a captain might be during a hard gale, but the bottom of the ship is not one of them."

"If he had been injured from a flying piece of broken wood, he might have been taken below, with other wounded men, I suppose. But he was not." He looked at her with admiration, and she felt her cheeks warm. "That is why you asked if other bodies were found there. If he alone had been hurt, he would more likely have been taken to his cabin, so more mysteries here. Did someone wish the captain out of the way?"

She waited, as it seemed he had more to say, and sure enough, he continued, his expression grim. "We had a warning that something was wrong on the *Brave Lassie* even before the ship disappeared."

Lauryn knew her eyes had widened. "You did? From whom?"

"I don't know. But a letter came just after the ship had sailed. And two different ship's officers died in apparent accidents—at the time, it seemed trivial enough, but looking back . . ."

She nodded when he paused.

"Do you have any idea?"

"Speculations, but nothing that I can put solid evidence to. And I wish something tangible before I accuse anyone of serious crimes . . ."

His expression serious, he motioned to the horses. "Let us get started on the ride back to the shooting box; the sun is dropping in the sky."

She nodded and the earl was helping her remount when he suddenly stiffened.

"What is it?" Lauryn asked, keeping her tone low and trying to make out what had caught his attention.

"What the hell is he doing here?" Sutton muttered.

Nine

*H*e quickly gained the saddle of his own horse, tightened his hold on the reins, and moved forward, motioning to her to follow. Just as she caught a glimpse of two familiar faces and knew whom he had recognized, she turned her own away and urged her mount after him.

It was Carter, the earl's half brother, and the contessa, a parasol held over her head as they strolled along the pavement on the other side of the street. What were they doing in this small coastal town?

Fortunately, a high perch phaeton rolled past, blocking the newcomers' view. Lauryn and the earl had moved away by the time the carriage had passed them. Hopefully, the pair had not glimpsed them.

What were Carter and the contessa doing here? Were they searching for Sutton? The next time she was able to move her horse up parallel to the earl, Lauryn asked the question aloud.

"I don't know, but if he plans to move into the shooting box along with us, he is mightily mistaken," Sutton told her, frowning. "It is a small residence, and we came here to leave

Carter's house parties behind! I have no desire for more unwanted guests."

Lauryn bit her lip, aware that she was gratified by the earl's emphasis. Perhaps he was not yet totally tired of her company, after all. Perhaps she could hope for more shared evenings, then, before they parted.

Despite his indications of his desire for her company, the earl decided to stop and check on his newly acquired guards at the warehouse that held the recovered cargo.

This time two men stood where they should be, and they surprised no illicit visitors within the big building. The earl spoke briefly to the men on duty, and as it was becoming too dark inside to take a closer look at the cargo, told them that he would be back another day.

As Lauryn waited, she caught a movement at the corner of the building. A man on foot appeared briefly, then stepped back out of sight.

Was it because he saw someone at the door of the warehouse?

Probably it was nothing, she told herself, perhaps it had nothing to do with the guards or the fact that she and the earl were there. But although she'd had only the briefest glance— there had been something, something not right . . .

When Sutton returned, she decided she should mention it, even if she were being overly cautious.

He seemed to read her face. "What?"

"I saw a person come out of the alley," she told him. "It was a man on foot, and I had only an instant to glimpse him before he turned back into the shadows, but–but his face was not just as usual. I don't know how to explain—I did not have enough time to get a good look—but something about him was different, somehow."

About to mount his steed, the earl paused.

"Perhaps I only imagined it," Lauryn said, afraid she might be making too much of her perplexed moment. "And he might not have turned because we were here, but—"

"But perhaps he did, and perhaps you are not," the earl said. "Let me check out the alley. Wait for me here."

He swiftly gained his seat on his horse and nudged the beast forward. Lauryn bit her lip and watched him trot around the corner and turn into the dark alley. She waited impatiently until he reappeared, shaking his head.

"I see no sign of him, but he likely ran out the other side and disappeared down one of the back streets," he told her. "I doubt we can locate him now, however. We may as well call it a day."

They headed out of town, side by side, and continued to talk.

"I want to take a closer look at some of the crates of cargo," he told Lauryn as they rode away. "But it would be a waste of time this afternoon; the light is too far gone."

"Do you have more questions about what was found on the ship?" she asked.

"I am wondering if someone could have substituted fake Ming vases for the real thing," he told her. "It has to be something truly valuable to be worth killing for."

"You think that was why the captain died? Did he discover what the plot was?"

"Perhaps, if he was not part of it. Or if he was, he wanted a bigger share, or—there are numerous possibilities. We may never know the answer." The earl shook his head in frustration.

They turned toward the outskirts of town, and once the traffic on the road had lightened, were able to make better time. Lauryn was glad when they could urge their horses to more than a sedate trot and leave the town behind; it made the pressures of the earl's mystery seem less insistent.

Twilight fell as they rode back to the hunting lodge, and birds twittered in the trees around them, and insects sang. On the last part of the ride, they were alone on the road, and it heightened her feelings of intimacy. It was as if they rode through a golden garden, the light was so luminous, glinting on the growing grain as birdsong provided a lyrical accompaniment to their easy ride.

She could forget the sad puzzle of the sunken ship and the crew's death—it seemed far away, after all, and hardly touching

them. They would return to the lovely hunting lodge, enjoy another delicious dinner prepared by the earl's servants, and
tonight—tonight, hopefully, he would not be too tired or too
preoccupied with his concerns over the ship and its cargo to
wish to take her into his arms. They would share the kind of
magnificent lovemaking that they had already created together
several times. Just the thought made her smile.

They turned into the drive leading up to the hunting box,
and the horses tossed their heads, recognizing that they were
home. Stalls with oats and warm rubdowns awaited them in
the stable behind the house. Flambeaux had been lit outside
the front door, illuminating circles of light amid the growing
darkness so Lauryn and the earl could more easily see as they
reined in their horses.

As she pulled back on her reins and waited for the earl to
dismount and come to catch her as she slipped out of her saddle, Lauryn felt the same spark of anticipation—already this
lovely little house seemed like home.

The earl, too, smiled up at her as he helped her down. "It's
been a long day," he said. "We've barely time to change for
dinner. You must be hungry."

"Yes," she said, her voice low and husky. And as she
looked up at him, she saw something in his eyes that acknowledged what he saw in her own—that she hungered for more
than mere food.

Don't shut me out again, she thought. And she hoped she
saw understanding there.

But he said only, "We should go in."

So for the moment, she had to be content with that.

A groom appeared to take the horses around to the stables,
and they turned to enter the house. But when the door opened,
Lauryn felt her heart drop.

An unfamiliar hat and gloves sat on the hall table, and she
heard voices in the sitting room and a tinkle of melody.

"Oh, bloody hell," the earl swore briskly.

He exchanged glances with her, and then, his expression
stern, turned to face his obviously unwelcome guests.

They must have gotten ahead of them while she and the

earl had gone to check the warehouse, Lauryn thought. *Oh, damn, damn.* And the hunting box did not have that many bed-chambers. Where would they put them all? And it was a dark, moonless night—the carriage could not even travel this late, so the earl could not very well throw them out at this time of night, even if he wished it. They were stuck with them.

On this uncharitable thought, she took the earl's offered arm and they went into the sitting room.

Sure enough, Carter was leaning over the side of the pi-anoforte as the contessa ran her bejeweled fingers along the keys, producing a merry tune.

"Hello, brother," Carter said breezily. "We thought you might be in need of company."

"Did you?" the earl said, his tone dry. "How considerate of you."

The footman appeared in the doorway. "Shall we put off dinner, my lord?"

Raising his brows, Sutton turned to Lauryn.

She looked at the two unwelcome guests, who at least were already changed for dinner. "I can be ready in fifteen min-utes," she promised the earl, hoping it were true.

"Very well." He turned back to the servant. "Tell the cook fifteen minutes, if you will."

"Very good, my lord."

"We shall see you shortly," he told his brother. "Contessa, your servant." With a short bow to the newcomers, he offered Lauryn his arm again, and they left the room and headed for the stairwell.

"I do apologize, Mrs. Smith," he told her, keeping his voice low. "But I will not be able to send them away tonight. And I fear I will have to give them your room, just for to-night."

Having already worked this out, she nodded. "I under-stand."

There was no time to discuss the arrangements further, and anyhow, they had no choice. She hurried down to her bedchamber, which already had the contessa's baggage in-side. At least a maid was waiting to help Lauryn change out of her riding outfit and into a dinner gown, which she did in record time.

She didn't have enough leisure to comb out her hair. All she could do was have the maid brush out the worst of the tangles and pin up the tendrils that had escaped her braided coil.

She only went over her estimated time by five minutes or so, Lauryn figured. She pulled a clean handkerchief out of her bag to slip into her sleeve. Then she headed back down the stairs, to find the earl at the bottom, waiting to escort her into the dining room.

Carter and the contessa were still in the sitting room, but the footman announced dinner, and they came to join them. Lauryn was privately pleased to see that she still held the hostess's seat at the small table.

The food was as well prepared as ever, although the cook could not have had much notice that the number of diners for tonight had doubled. But then, they usually had such an abundance of dishes that it was simple enough to think that all would be easily fed.

As they ate, the contessa kept up a flow of small talk and anecdotes, mostly about acquaintances of the earl that Lauryn, of course, did not know. Lauryn simply smiled and gave no indication how annoying she found this. Carter, on her side, seemed rather quiet.

"Did the house party at the earl's estate come to an end?" she asked him politely when it seemed that he had nothing that he wished to contribute to the conversation.

"Since he ordered me to end it, yes," he told her.

"Oh, I see," she said, thinking it a good time to dip her fork into the broiled asparagus and change the topic of conversation. "The cook is very skillful, don't you think?"

"Yes, all my brother's cooks are good; he will not put up with anything less. As you may have noted, he doesn't settle for anyone except the best."

Lauryn wasn't sure if this was a veiled comment on her own skills or not, but she decided not to remark on it. She took another bite from her plate, not sure if Carter were antagonistic towards her—why?—but deciding to be cautious.

"I don't know why he's so all fired up about this missing ship," Carter said now, his voice lowered as he threw a searching glance toward his brother at the end of the table. "I mean, I thought he'd be happy about getting back such valuable cargo. But he seems put out about it. Doesn't make sense, does it?"

She murmured something indistinguishable, not about to tell Carter anything that his brother had said. If the earl wanted to share any facts or even opinions about the *Brave Lassie* or its cargo, he would tell his sibling himself. She would certainly not pass on any comments the earl had shared with her.

Carter gave her a shrewd look now, as if she might have said her thought aloud. "Not very forthcoming, are you?"

"What makes you think I should know anything?" she asked, keeping her tone pleasant.

He shrugged. "He's certainly not talking to me. He must have shared his thoughts with someone . . ."

She took another bite of her roasted potatoes and didn't answer.

Carter rolled his eyes and cut his roast beef with a bit too much vigor, almost overturning his glass of wine.

The contessa was laughing at a jest of her own, to which the earl gave a token smile. He seemed to be only in the barest good humor, which Lauryn was sorry to admit made her mood lighten. Despite the good food, the dinner seemed longer tonight than usual. At last, the courses ended, and she could finally catch the contessa's eye, even though she would have sworn the other woman tried to evade her glance as long as possible. But tonight the ladies would leave the table to the menfolk and retire to the sitting room as protocol demanded.

Marcus watched them go, glad to get the contessa out of his hair for a few minutes. God, how that woman could chatter on—he had almost forgotten. When the door was safely shut behind them, and the servants had cleared away the dishes and poured them more port, he turned to regard his brother.

"Now then, Carter," he said, his voice deep with annoyance. "What the bloody hell are you playing at?"

Carter shrugged. "What do you mean?"

"Don't play the innocent with me! I left my own home to get away from a crowd of people I had no desire to see, and here you are again—"

"Take care, Brother! You will have me thinking that I am one of the crowd you are trying to escape," Carter said, his tone dry.

"God forbid," Marcus shot back, his voice just as acerbic. "But leaving that aside, you must have gathered that I wished some privacy. So why the hell did you follow me?"

"Since you didn't bother to tell me where you were going, I didn't know that I *was* following you," Carter pointed out, his tone injured. "If you would honor me with more of your confidence, tell me what you were about, I wouldn't blunder into your private love nest! I simply thought that this would be a good place to come without incurring large hotel bills."

Marcus bit back a groan. "Don't tell me you're already overdrawn on your allowance?"

Carter looked slightly aggrieved. "I didn't say that."

"But it's true, nonetheless?" Marcus took a long swallow of the deep-colored wine in his goblet.

"No, but if I have to frank the contessa for very long— she's an expensive lady to entertain, let me tell you—"

"Not necessary, I have had the pleasure," Marcus said.

"So you know I speak the truth," Carter appealed to his brother. "So you might give me a little benefit of the doubt here."

Marcus's expression did soften just a little. "She is a costly *bon amie*, that is true. How did you end up entertaining such an elegant lady?"

"I didn't exactly plan it," Carter said, his tone plaintive now. "Honestly, I thought I was doing you a favor when I invited her to come—that's what she hinted, at least. She wants you back, I would swear, but since you're not falling into step with her plans, I think I'm her second-best choice."

"I'm not sure whether to congratulate you or commiserate with you." Marcus grinned reluctantly.

"I know." This time Carter took a long drink of his wine.

"I mean, she does have her–her appeal. She is handsome, intelligent, very charming."

"So far, I wouldn't know."

"Ah, in that case, I can't put you two in the same room, which means you're going to have to make do in the study. I'll have the footman put you up a camp bed."

When his half brother grimaced, he added, "You know there are only two bedrooms, Carter; do you expect Mrs. Smith and me to sleep on the floor? If you don't care for the cot, you can go out to the stables and sleep above the horses with the grooms."

Carter made another face and reached for the bottle to replenish his glass. "In that case, I definitely need more wine."

In the sitting room, the contessa had fixed Lauryn with her steely charm. "I zee that I am taking your bedchamber tonight, alaz. Have you quarreled with the earl that you are zeeping apart? *C'est dommage.*"

"Of course not," Lauryn said, her voice tranquil. She had expected this. "I simply enjoy ample space when I dress. But you are welcome to use the room."

"Ah, I zee. You are very kind, I think." The other woman fanned herself delicately. "If you are zure . . . Because if all is not well with the earl, if he begins to tire of you, or you of him, we could always make the exchange—"

"I'm afraid I don't understand," Lauryn said, her tone polite. "Exchange what?"

"I could zeep with the earl, à la the old times, and you could spend the night with his brother, Carter. He is an amiable gentleman; I am sure you would find him congenial."

Lauryn stared at the other woman, her lips falling open for a long moment, then she closed her mouth with an effort. "Are you mad? I don't bounce about among men like a rubber ball."

"It is always best to be zensible, I think," the contessa said. "And you are the professional, are you not? Zo you would not have a hard time taking on a new lover. I'm sure you do it all the time."

"No," Lauryn snapped, "You mistake yourself; I am not! And I do not!" Then belatedly, she realized that was exactly what she was supposed to be. Too late, and too bad. If the contessa thought she could jump into bed with just anyone, she refused to keep up that pretense. "Are you?" she asked, keeping her voice calm with great effort.

The contessa laughed, a tinkling sound that sounded quite natural. "Alaz, no, *ma cherie*. I am only an enthusiastic amateur. But *l'amour* is a game we all play whenever we can, *mais oui*? And if you decide to tozz the earl back into the pond, I will be 'appy to try my 'and at catching 'im again."

"I will keep that in mind," Lauryn agreed, wondering if the earl would be as pleased. "But I think the earl has a mind of his own, and tossing him anywhere he does not wish to be tossed might be a bit hard to do."

The contessa sighed gustily. "Ah, but for the pleasure to try."

Lauryn really couldn't blame her for the sentiment. She thought of the earl's intense sensuality, and how she herself felt when he touched her, and something inside her melted a little just at the reflection. And tonight they would be sharing a room—surely he would not ignore her again, would he?

She thought of asking the contessa how long she and the earl had been together—and she also wondered why had they parted. It didn't seem to be because the contessa had wanted them to separate. But it seemed undignified to ask, so she held her tongue. And anyhow, the men would reappear at any moment. She hardly wished to be caught gossiping about him—that would be enormously bad mannered.

So she let the other woman chatter on, commenting on the decor and every detail of the small but finely decorated hunting lodge. "But it could have been larger, *mais non*?" the contessa said. "What is the point of having all this lovely money if one does not make use of it?"

"I suppose," Lauryn said, hardly listening.

Now she heard male voices as the earl and his brother appeared in the doorway.

"Shall we have some cards, Sutton?" Carter suggested as they came into the room.

"If you like," the earl agreed without much enthusiasm.

"I am not much of a card player," Lauryn warned them.

The earl drew up a small table and they placed four chairs around it, and Carter found a deck of cards and dealt the first hand. As they played, Lauryn found herself an even worse player than usual, as the unexpected guests had distracted her from any hope of concentration. Once or twice she pulled out her handkerchief to dab her cheek—she was sitting too near the fire. Looking down, she realized that her handkerchief had the initials LAH embroidered neatly on one edge.

Oh, dear. She crumbled the fine square of linen quickly within her palm and stuffed it back into her sleeve before anyone else could see the revealing initials. She would have to be more careful! Now, she really could not concentrate on her cards.

In the end, it was the contessa and Carter who won most of the hands. At least they broke up the game early, to Lauryn's relief.

"I'm sorry," she said quietly to the earl. "I'm afraid I'm not much of a partner."

"That depends entirely on the game," he countered, giving her a mischievous grin.

Taking a deep breath, Lauryn tried not blush in front of the other couple. "Shall I call for some tea before we go up to bed?"

"That would be agreeable," the contessa agreed.

As Lauryn crossed the floor, she felt for the dratted handkerchief again and this time could not feel it. Oh, no. Had it slipped out of her sleeve?

She turned to scan the floor, but just then, the earl noticed the crumpled linen square on the rug, and reached toward it.

"Whose is this?" he asked.

Lauryn blinked in dismay.

But the contessa was faster. "Oh, that iz mine, thank you, my dear Zutton!" And she scooped it up before her host could grasp it.

Lauryn turned her back on the others for a moment as she went to the bellpull and hoped that the earl had not noted her disorder. She did not know how spies did it; she would never make a good dissembler!

Later, when they did go upstairs, she made an excuse to go back to her bedchamber. There she found the contessa, already in a lace-trimmed nightgown, having the maid brush out her dark hair.

"You may leave us," the other woman told the servant.

"Yes, my lady," the girl said, throwing a curious look toward Lauryn.

When the door shut behind her, the contessa took the handerchief out of a pocket and held it out to Lauryn. "Yours, I think?"

Lauryn blushed. "Yes. It was most good of you not to give me away."

The contessa examined her reflection in the looking glass. "I would have the earl, if I can, but I will fight fair, *ma petite.*"

Lauryn nodded, but she thought that she still did not understand this woman.

"What is it vith the name?" the contessa asked, her dark eyes bright with curiosity. "You do not 'ave another lover, or a 'usband still alive, coming to find you? You must not let 'im challenge the earl to a duel; I vould not have Zutton 'urt!"

"No, no, of course not," Lauryn said. "It is nothing like that." She was reminded that she must get back to the earl's bedroom before he became suspicious.

The contessa stared at her. "Just recall what I zay: Marcuz iz not a good man to lie to."

Lauryn met the other woman's eyes for a moment, then looked away. "I will remember."

She took a nightgown and a hairbrush out of the bureau, tried to think what to do with the handkerchief, then decided to just put it into the fire. She stood for a moment watching it blaze till it turned black, then made her way back to the bedroom on the other side of the stairwell.

The earl was already changed into his dark silk dressing

gown. He sat in a chair looking out of the window, but he rose when she entered the room.

"Shall I call for a maid to unbutton you, or shall I perform the chore?" he asked, his tone polite.

"I–I would not wish to inconvenience you," she said, not sure how to read his tone, nor his expression, which was veiled.

"I would hardly call that a chore," he said.

So she turned her back to him and allowed him to undo the back of her dinner gown, feeling prickles of sensation as his strong, supple fingers—fingers that could evoke so much magic when he chose—moved along her back, leaving her gown gaping open behind him. But so far, to her disappointment, he did not take advantage of his opportunity to touch or kiss the bare skin that presented itself to him.

Instead, she was left to step out of the skirt and pull off the bodice, and then he unlaced her stays, and throwing a quick look toward him—he barely seemed to be paying attention—she turned slightly away before she pulled the thin linen shift over her head.

It must be true. He must be tiring of her already. Lauryn felt tears rise behind her lids and tried desperately not to allow them to fall. He must not see how attached she had already become to him—she would not be an object of pity! Was this how it had happened when he and the contessa had been together? Perhaps she would throw pride to the wind and ask the other woman.

Right now Lauryn reached for the nightgown to pull it quickly over her head and cover her naked body. She would sleep on the edge of the bed and she would not reach out to him—he must not be allowed to think that she was begging for his touch!

Marcus held himself back only with the greatest of efforts. The sweetly curved buttocks that he glimpsed from the corner of his eye, the slim line of her back, the breasts that he knew fitted so well into his palms—he felt a slight sheen of perspiration break out on his forehead, and his body reacted in other ways as well. He was glad he had put on his robe, to hide the betraying signs his body would give.

But he was determined not to make love to her again, not until he was sure that she was focused on him with all her heart and mind. How could he be sure—and was he a fool to be doing this, when his body craved her like a dying man craves water?

Probably, probably, Marcus told himself, becoming more irritable with every passing moment. He felt as if heat were building inside him like a blocked boiler on a steam engine; how on earth was he going to get through a whole night having her so near and having sworn that he would not pull her into his arms?

This was madness!

And then—he had tried so hard not to look, not to see—he suddenly realized what he had also glimpsed in that half moment of seeing. Just as she climbed onto the bed and lay precariously on the edge of the mattress, pulling the blanket up to wrap around her, he whirled and pulled it off again so unexpectedly that she cried out in surprise and dismay.

"What?" Lauryn exclaimed.

But he had lifted her nightgown in a totally dispassionate fashion to gaze at the dark bruises covering her thighs and buttocks. "Why didn't you tell me? You must have been in agony today! You could have ridden in the carriage—or, better still, you could have stayed behind at the lodge when I went back into town!"

She was flushing, though from what cause, he wasn't sure.

"No, I do like to ride, as I said. Only it has been a while since I have ridden, so I am out of shape, hence the bruises from riding most of the day yesterday. They look worse then they are, truly. I did not want to stay behind today, nor ride in the carriage. After the first hour, I hardly felt them. I'm all right, just a little sore."

"A little sore?" He raised his dark brows and shook his head. "I will fetch the maids and have them fill a hip bath with warm water so you can soak your bruises."

"No, indeed. They've all gone back to the village by now," she protested. "And I would not trouble the housekeeper. I'm all right."

"I do not think—"

"Please! I don't want to make a fuss," she said, putting one hand on his arm.

He pressed his lips together, frustrated that she would not listen to sensible advice, that she seemed determined to consider the servants' feelings on a par with her own. He looked over the dark purpling bruises once again and shook his head.

Flushing, she pulled her nightgown down to hide the marks.

Some would-be poet's verse flashed through his mind— "My vision of paradise?" he murmured.

She blushed.

"Then if you will not allow me to soak you into more pliable comfort, at least"—he turned and considered, then walked across to a large chest on the far wall—"I think there might be something here that could help." He bent over a large chest and raised the lid, looking through a variety of feminine trinkets and cosmetics, left from former visitors, until he found what he sought. He came back to sit on the bed beside her, carrying a glass jar, and when he unscrewed its lid, it proved to hold a sweet-smelling cream.

"What is it?" she asked.

"Cream for your skin," he told her. "I'm going to rub your bruises to help them heal."

She looked doubtful. "Don't rub too hard," she suggested.

He nodded. "You may tell me if I am not gentle enough," he assured her. "But we must do something to assuage your bruises and your aches."

Or perhaps he simply ached for an excuse to get his hands on her? He refused to examine that thought too closely.

He took some of the scented cream in his palm and touched her thigh very softly. He felt the quiver of her response. He was sure she was very sore, so he stroked the cream on her skin with light, delicate strokes, down into the soft skin of her thigh and calf, kneading with a feather soft touch, one thigh, then the other.

He cupped her buttocks with both his hands, rubbing them with a light circular pattern, rolling her onto her stomach, so that he could knead her skin, still with a gentle touch, barely moving the skin. But he knew that she was very aware of his movements, that her cheeks had flushed, and that her fingers had curled slightly, almost into fists, and she made soft sounds deep in her throat. She moved her hips against the sheets, and he almost growled, too, at this sign of her wanting.

They were both breathing quickly. He felt his own response to her grow, and he allowed his hands to drop lower, his fingers to slip deeper, rubbing gently, teasing almost into the folds of her sweet inner lips where they would soon both be lost—

Now, she was quivering from more than just the soreness of her bruises. In another moment, neither of them would be able to stop—

Someone screamed.

Ten

*T*hey *broke apart, and Lauryn sat up. "What is it?"*
she exclaimed.

The earl had already jumped to his feet. Pulling his robe tighter around him, he picked up a candle from the table by the bed and strode for the door.

Tugging her nightgown down, she hurried after him. The only other woman in the house, since the servants slept outside the lodge itself, was the contessa. What could be wrong? Had someone broken in? Or perhaps it was only a nightmare. . . .

It was only a few steps down the hall to the other bedchamber. The earl beat his fist on the closed door. "Contessa?" he called. "Alexanderine, are you all right?"

For a moment, there was no answer, then Lauryn heard another scream.

The earl wrenched open the door. The room inside seemed very dark. Holding up his candle, he took a step inside. "What is amiss?"

Lauryn tried to make out what was wrong; the room was filled with shadows. "Are you all right, contessa?" she called, thinking that perhaps the room's inhabitant would wish to hear a feminine voice.

"There is a creature!" the contessa shrieked, her voice sounding muffled. She was in the bed, it appeared, although Lauryn could see nothing except a large lump beneath the covers—she seemed to have pulled all the bedclothes over her head. "Save me!"

"What?" Lauryn said. She could make out nothing moving except for the quivering mound that was the contessa in the middle of the bed.

But the earl uttered an exclamation perhaps not suited for ladies' ears, and she didn't ask him to repeat it. Was there a rat that had emerged from behind a wall? What had frightened the contessa? Lauryn looked nervously about her at the floor.

Then something moved, indeed, but it was a shadowy shape that flickered at the corner of a ceiling beam. Lauryn bit back a gasp, and the contessa screamed again, though how she had seen it from beneath her bundle of bedclothes, Lauryn could not have said.

The earl swore once more. "Hush," he said, "you're only exciting it."

"Is it a bird?" Lauryn asked, ducking as it swung past, its flight strangely erratic. "How did it get in?"

The contessa shrieked.

The earl held his candle higher as he tried to make out the thing. Then the long wingspan and uneven flight pattern clicked in her brain. Lauryn knew the truth even as the earl set down the candle on a table and looked around for something to marshal against the intruder.

"Oh, my God," she muttered. "It's a bat." Lauryn sat down rather suddenly in the chair beside the bed. There was a scarf lying on the arm of the chair; she grabbed it up to wrap about her hair. Her maid at home had always said that bats loved to tangle themselves in one's hair. Her sister Juliana's husband, an amateur zoologist who studied animals, said that was a folktale. But just now, Lauryn decided she didn't care to risk it. Let Juliana be the sample case if she preferred!

Marcus had found a long stick somewhere—no, it was a

parasol—he was waving it at the bat, who simply flew faster when harassed. That seemed to accomplish nothing except that the bat was weaving up and down and around through all parts of the bedchamber. The contessa was now shrieking almost without taking a breath, and Lauryn didn't feel too happy, herself. She crouched lower in the chair.

She looked around to see if there might be a more effective weapon than the parasol. The contessa had left pieces of her wardrobe lying here and there about the room. There was a rather formidable set of cagelike corsets, but the bat would simply fly out the top . . . no, that wouldn't do.

There was a thickly knitted shawl, however. Lauryn looked at the long piece of wool and swallowed hard, gathering her courage. They couldn't chase this beast all night, and the contessa was going to have a nervous spasm, or at least lose her voice—though that might not be all bad, as Lauryn's ears were ringing already—if this went on much longer.

With considerable reluctance, Lauryn gathered the ends of the shawl in her hands and climbed up to balance herself on the chair, watching the bat until it came her way again. The earl saw at once what she intended to do and tried to herd the bat toward her, but driving a bat was not exactly the easiest thing to do.

Twice he tried to send it flying toward her, and twice it zigged and zagged another way entirely. But finally, when he had waved it accidentally toward the other corner of the room, it took a sharp turn and then zoomed right into the shawl. Lauryn was able to pull it down, trapped in the folds of the thick woolen cloth.

"Careful, they have sharp teeth!" the earl warned.

"I know," Lauryn said, shivering as she quickly wrapped the shawl over and over the small animal, then held it out at arm's length. Sutton came just as swiftly to take the struggling bundle from her.

The door to the bedchamber suddenly opened once more. Yawning, Carter stood in the doorway and stared at them.

"What in blue blazes are you making all this racket about? Can't a fellow sleep in this house?"

"Now you finally wake? We could all be dead three times over!" Sutton told him. "Here, you get the task of taking this brute outside and letting it go—mind you go far enough so that it flies away, far away, and doesn't end up in the lodge again."

Carter drew back in alarm. "What the hell are you giving me?"

"Don't drop it! A perfectly bloodthirsty beast the size of a mouse, you goose," his brother said. "And mind you don't let it bite your fingers."

Looking suddenly pale, Carter took the well-wrapped bundle as gingerly if he had been handed an asp, holding it at arm's length.

Sutton sighed. "I'd best go with him," he said to Lauryn.

She was looking at the bed. The contessa had at last stopped shrieking, but judging from the sounds coming from beneath the heap of bedclothes, she was now sobbing.

"I think I should stay here," she said quietly. Remembering what they had been doing so pleasurably before the interruption, she said it reluctantly, but she didn't feel she could leave the contessa, who seemed truly disturbed by the invasion of wildlife.

He nodded. Lifting one of her hands, he kissed it gently, which made her flush with pleasure. Then he turned. "I will go with Carter, just to be sure that we have no more casualties tonight," he told her.

She smiled and nodded. When the men had departed and shut the door behind them, she went to the bed and cautiously pulled back the blankets. "Contessa? Are you all right? Did it bite you?"

The usually immaculately groomed aristocrat looked very strange with her hair mussed and her eyes swollen from weeping. "*Non*," she said, rubbing her eyes. "It iz is only that I do not like"—she shuddered—"I have the horror of zuch beasts. They are zo nasty, *oui*?"

"Yes, I know. But it's gone, now. The men have taken it away."

"*C'est vrai*?" She looked about the room as if she expected a few more bats to spring out of the woodwork. It would have been funny if the contessa had not been so sincerely frightened. Lauryn was not tempted to laugh. She sat down on the bed and put out her hand.

"It's gone, truly. We caught it in a shawl."

"My shawl?"

"I'm afraid so; it was the first thing I saw that was thick enough to wrap it in. But I will wash it for you when they bring it back."

The contessa shuddered. "*Non, non*, I never vant to touch it again if it 'as touched that creature! Put it in the fire!"

"Whatever you say," Lauryn agreed. "Why don't you try to sleep. Would you like me to get you a little wine?"

"*Oui*, or perhaps a brandy," the contessa said, her voice wan. "For the nerves."

It occurred to Lauryn that she should have made sure she knew where the wine was before offering—then she recalled there were bottles in the sideboard in the dining room. So she went back to find her slippers and wrapper and made her way downstairs to pour a glass for the contessa and bring it back up. And, indeed, when the contessa had sipped some brandy, she was more composed and agreed to lie back and try to sleep.

But the other woman still appeared very worried about the chance of another bat emerging from the shadows of the room, and not until Lauryn offered to lie down with her, like a mother with a fretful child, did she at last shut her eyes and fall into a troubled sleep.

Lauryn made herself comfortable on the other side of the bed and pulled the blankets up around her. It looked as if she were here for the night. And how unexpected that this cosmopolitan aristocrat, who was older than Lauryn and experienced in so many things, could still have such unexpected fears.

One never knew. *C'est la vie*, as the contessa herself would have said.

And even Lauryn jumped when the windows rattled in the breeze. "Nonsense," she muttered. The odds of another bat getting into the house tonight must be very long. She shut her eyes and, eventually, drifted off to sleep.

The next morning, everyone slept late and seemed to wake in a less than perfect mood. But at least the contessa seemed composed again, although she sniffed when she saw her own reflection in the looking glass. She sent the maid for a cold cloth—there were no hothouses here to grow cucumbers in—and had tea and toast in her bedchamber, then went back to bed with more cold compresses on her still swollen eyelids.

"I vill rise in ze good time," she told Lauryn. "When I look more presentable, *non*?"

"Whatever you say," Lauryn agreed. She herself dressed and went downstairs. She found the earl and his brother in the dining room, which was thankfully absent of any animal life.

"How is the contessa?" their host asked, his tone polite.

"Better," she told them. "Although she is not ready to come downstairs just yet."

"Ah, I see," the earl said, bringing Lauryn a cup of tea himself. "Do try the scones, the cook here has a very light hand with baked goods."

Carter watched this unusual show of favoritism with some surprise. "You told me not to eat you out of house and home, Marcus."

"So?" The earl sat down after Lauryn did, and turned back to his brother, looking totally unrepentant. "Not everyone eats like a starving ox, Carter. Besides, Mrs. Smith is the heroine of the hour. She actually caught the beast last night, throwing a shawl over the thing as it flew through the air."

"Really?" Looking impressed despite himself, Carter stared at her. "I say, good show."

"A clever idea, better than mine," Sutton said. "All I did was make the confounded creature more frantic."

Lauryn blushed. "It was a lucky guess, that's all. I have had experience with them before. They would sometimes fly into our attic at home and have to be chased out." At once, she realized she had wandered into dangerous territory.

Both of the men looked interested.

"And where is home, Mrs. Smith?" Carter asked, his tone only civil but his eyes revealing a spark of curiosity.

"Oh, the north of England," she said, and lowered her gaze

to her plate as she reached to take a scone, still warm from the oven, and a spoonful of jam and a knife's edge of butter for her pastry.

She applied herself to the excellent breakfast and said little more, hoping that no one would ask more questions. By the time she finished eating, Carter had risen from the table.

"At least," the earl said to him quietly, "the incident with the alarming wildlife will be a good excuse for you to take the contessa into a hotel in town."

"Yes, but—" his brother began, looking alarmed.

"Not to worry," Sutton told him. "I will see that you are not in need of funds."

"Oh, well, then," Carter grinned. "In that case, you are a trump, Sutton. You may call on me for any favor that you need."

"So I shall," the earl said, his tone dry.

Lauryn kept her gaze on her plate, not sure what she should comment on, or probably, better not to remark on this exchange at all. But when Carter had gone out, she ventured at last to glance up at the earl.

He caught her eye. "At least we will have our privacy back, soon," he said, his voice low.

She smiled at him. "Are we going back into town today?"

He shook his head. "You are going to stay inside and rest your overworked body; I think you should stay out of the saddle for at least one day. We could use the carriage, of course, but with bruises like those, I think perhaps even driving might be too much. One day should not make any difference in our quest for answers about the mysteries surrounding the ship and its cargo. And I will not abandon you to entertain our guests all on your own."

She grinned ruefully at him. "That is most kind."

"It would be a woeful way to repay you for your courage last night." Once more, he took her hand and lifted it to his lips, a simple gesture but one that made her heart seem to swell. She looked up into his eyes, and for a moment, they seemed as close as they had ever been. . . .

Why had he pushed her away, of late? What was it that she

was not doing, for what did she not satisfy him completely—
if he did not tell her, how was she to know!

Frustrated, she caught her lower lip between her teeth for a
moment and wondered if she should try to speak openly to
him, and yet—

A footman came into the room with more hot tea. The earl
put down her hand, and she looked back at her plate as the servant poured the steaming liquid into the earl's cup and then
into her own, and the moment was lost.

She sipped her tea and finished her breakfast. Then, when
the earl went out to the stables, Lauryn rose and went back upstairs to check on the contessa. She found her dozing, so she
did not disturb her.

She went back downstairs and found Carter in the sitting
room playing solitaire, and the earl still outside, apparently;
he was nowhere in sight. She had no great wish to sit and chat
with his brother, so after glancing over the bookshelf, Lauryn
looked out the window for a moment. The day looked to be a
fine one. She decided to go back upstairs to fetch her hat and
gloves and take a stroll outside; she had seen little of the
grounds.

Upstairs, the contessa was still dozing; she must have had
little sleep after her upsetting encounter with the bat last
night. Lauryn found what she needed and quietly shut the bedroom door behind her. Downstairs, she let herself out of the
front door and made her way around the side of the hunting
lodge.

A path led to the stables, and there she met the earl just
emerging. "Hello," he said, looking up at her with a smile.
"Would you like to say hello to the mount who gave you such
grievous bruises?"

"It wasn't the mare's fault," Lauryn pointed out, pausing,
finding that it was impossible not to smile back at him, "just
because I am out of the habit of riding regularly."

He led her inside the stable, stopping to lift a carrot from a
bin for her to offer her horse, whom she found in a stall
halfway down the stable row. The strong smells of horses,
feed, and the slight lingering odor of manure, even though the

stable was obviously well tended, met her as she entered. She could see motes of dust floating in the rays of sunlight that slanted through an upper window.

She looked into the roomy stall, and the mare moved across to see her, pushing her head against the hand that Lauryn held out to the animal as she rubbed her velvety muzzle gently.

"Hello," Lauryn said softly. "You remember me, do you? Good girl." She held out the carrot with her other hand, holding it on the flat of her palm so that she would not be accidently bitten by the mare's long front teeth. The horse took it neatly out of her hand and, crunching, made short work of the vegetable treat. Lauryn laughed and turned back to see the earl grinning at her.

"You have a way with horses as well as men," he noted, his voice low.

"Oh," Lauryn drew a deep breath. "As for that . . ." She hesitated, not sure what to say. The allure of pretending to be a practiced—and professional—lover was losing its charm.

Perhaps he saw something of her conundrum in her expression. "Mrs. Smith," the earl said, motioning to a bale of hay, "may I invite you to have a seat?"

She raised her brows but she sat down carefully on the prickly bale and waited to see what he was about to say. None of the grooms were within sight or apparently sound, so they had a modicum of privacy.

"We are driven out of my own house, for yet the second time," he said, with a trace of annoyance in his voice. "You see the many privileges that come with rank and wealth, not to mention the joy of having assorted and myriad relatives."

She grinned, as she thought she was meant to do. But then he added in a more serious vein, "Do you not think it's time to stop playing games?"

She felt her heart skip a beat. "I don't know what you mean."

"Mrs. Smith—a very common and pleasant name, but not, I think, really yours?"

He met her eyes so steadily that she could not seem to

break the contact, and she felt her cheeks burn. "Oh, I—" Her mouth felt very dry.

"I would be honored to be favored with your real name," he told her.

She opened her lips, and then shut them again, knowing that her color must be high. How did he know? Had she given herself away in some fashion? She must have looked haunted because he shook his head.

"You are not at fault; you are simply too much a lady to pretend otherwise. Oh, you have a delightful zest for lovemaking, and a body that is thoroughly responsive, to my own keen pleasure, I assure you. I take joy in every reaction you give, my dear. But to believe that you are really a woman of the street—even the most high-class courtesan—no, it stretches fantasy too far."

Feeling trapped, she bit her lip again. What reason could she possibly give for posing as a streetwalker then, if, as was obvious, he did not believe her masquerade? He would think her either mad or totally dissolute and without morals of any kind . . .

He was watching with those intelligent dark eyes, which always seemed to know too much, and she could think of nothing to say. "My name is Lauryn," she told him, her voice very low. "That is the truth."

He nodded, his tone grave. "Thank you."

"But I cannot tell you why . . ." Her voice faltered. Truly, she could not tell him. How would anyone believe such a convoluted story?

The silence stretched, and she heard one of the horses in the stalls paw the ground, and another of the big beasts whinny softly. She could think of nothing to add, and her throat ached with tension. Would he throw her out, without the means to get back to London or return to Yorkshire? Would she be stranded in a town where she knew no one, penniless and unprotected? Oh, and she had thought that they were getting along so well . . .

"Would it help," he said, his voice quiet, "if I told you that I have already instructed my solicitor to send the deed to his estate back to Squire Harris, with ownership suitably made over to him once more?"

Lauryn knew that her eyes were wide. "You knew! How did you know?"

His tone was patient. "You come to me asking for a small estate in the north of England, not twenty-four hours after I win the squire's birthright from him in a card game—a property I have not the slightest interest in, I must tell you. Yet I knew full well the man was too proud to consider taking it back from me if I had refused it, even if there was any way that I could turn down legitimate winnings . . . and you expect me not to connect the two events?"

She flushed. "Of course, I should have realized."

Again there was a moment of silence, and something hung in the air between them that she could not interpret.

"How," he asked, his tone guarded, "are you related to the squire?"

She gazed at him, but this time she could not read his expression. "He is my father-in-law."

"And your husband agreed to allow you to do this—come to another man's bed?" He stared at her, his eyes very dark.

"No, no, I am a widow, just as I told you," she tried to explain.

"Ah." The earl exhaled slowly, and some of the tension in his voice faded. "So you are Mrs. Lauryn Harris, and you styled yourself Mrs. Smith simply to avoid scandal?"

She nodded. "I hoped that not many people would know that I had done this, and my family back in Yorkshire would not learn of it."

"Understandable," he agreed. His tone was somehow much easier, and his eyes now seemed more apt to twinkle. "I hope the experience has not been too painful or distasteful for you, posing as a—ah—courtesan."

"Since it is with you, and only you," she told him with a toss of her head, "that I have carried out this outrageous masquerade, you should be able to judge just how I have responded to the reality of making love to a man who is not my husband!"

If he chose to chide her for these actions, he had the right to do so—she had certainly been in the wrong. But he would not suggest that she had been licentious with any other man, Lauryn thought, becoming angry at the tone of these questions. And if he thought that she was too rash—well, so be it!

She stood up, dusting her dress as she tried to rid herself of the bits of straw from the bales of hay on which she had been sitting. The she turned to go back to the house, but the earl moved, too, and reached to catch her hand.

"No, no, Mrs. Harris, Lauryn, my darling girl, that is not at all what I meant to suggest."

His voice was low and tender, and so different from his earlier tone that it was that more than the hand that held hers that kept her from trying to pull away.

"What?" She looked at him in surprise. To hear her Christian name on his lips sent a thrill through her just as vivid as those she received when he touched her bare skin or stroked her hair or–or other parts of her naked body. . . .

His other hand took hold of her chin and brought it closer to his own, so he could lean in to kiss her lips, gently at first and then more firmly. Despite the passion that always flared so easily between them, she mumbled a protest. Did he think she would forget his cavalier attitude so quickly? But her blood heated as quickly as his, and well, yes, perhaps she would. . . .

He pulled her into his embrace, and she put her arms about his neck. They melded together as closely as if they were one being. The kiss grew stronger and more demanding, and he pressed her back against a post that supported the upper level of the stable. She hardly noticed, she was too intent upon pressing against his hard torso and lean-muscled body and wondering if they could find a quiet place where the grooms would not chance upon them—

As if her thought had conjured him up, a whistling groom approached the stable from the pasture outside.

The earl broke away from their embrace, and Lauryn drew a deep breath, feeling as if she had been pulled out of a dream.

"Damnation!" the earl swore. "Are we to have no peace inside or out?"

She could have echoed his thought. Standing up straighter, she took Sutton's arm and without speaking, they walked back to the lodge.

"I suppose it is better, for the time, that you remain Mrs. Smith," he asked her. "So it shall be our secret, just now?"

"I would think so," she said, relieved not to be embarrassed in front of the other two people in the lodge.

When they entered the house, Carter still lounged in the sitting room, the cards in front of him. The contessa was not in evidence, so she was doubtless still upstairs in the bedchamber. Lauryn thought briefly, but with regret, of withdrawing to the other bedchamber, but they could not simply disappear into it in broad daylight. She could not be so brazen, with other people about the house.

She saw the earl glance at her as if reading her thoughts. "A plague on all my house," he muttered beneath his breath, mangling the Bard without compunction.

She grinned reluctantly.

"Since we cannot continue our—ah—chosen entertainment, if you will excuse me, I will go to my desk in the study to work on some papers for a time," he told her quietly.

"Of course." She nodded in understanding. She found it hard to keep her hands off him, as well. She went across to the small shelf of books at the side of the room, selected a book of poems by the newly fashionable poet Mr. Wordsworth, and came to sit down in a chair by the window and read.

Although she tried hard to lose herself in the sylvan glades depicted by the poet, today it was hard to immerse herself in the pages of a book. She kept hearing slaps as Carter threw down his cards, not to mention the tuneless humming he carried on under his breath.

She glanced up at him once to see him looking at her. "Did you say something?"

"No," she said. "But since you ask, are you winning?"

He grinned. "One way or the other, I suppose. Since I play alone, there is no one else to claim victory."

She chuckled. "As good a way as any to define it."

He yawned. "No aspersions on your company, Mrs. Smith, but I find the country dashed boring."

She grinned despite herself. "Then why did you come?"

"Oh, the contessa wanted to follow my brother; she hasn't quite given up on collecting him again, I think."

This was rather less amusing, but Lauryn simply nodded. Carter gave her a knowing look. "Don't be heartbroken if he doesn't make a lasting commitment. I mean, you seem like a better person than most of his inamorata, but his petticoat affairs tend to be abrupt and quickly ended, if you'll pardon me for passing on the warning. I mean it in the best of spirits, don't you know." He gazed at her somewhat anxiously, as if afraid she would take offense.

Lauryn lifted her brows but kept her expression for the most part serene. "I will not kill the messenger, sir."

He grinned. "That's good. I never cared to be one of those Greek fellows who runs the whole way and then collapses at the end after delivering the message—oh, I think I'm getting the stories mixed up, don't you know?" He gave her a quizzical look, and she laughed.

"Are you always the jokester?" she asked.

"Of course," he said. "Why should I not? My brother has the title and the lion's share of the money, since he had the great good fortune to be born first. Our father was also second born, but his elder brother died, so he had it both ways—money and the ability to enjoy himself. Marcus and I both suffer from some of our parent's weaknesses, though I suppose I suffer from an enjoyment of parties and good times more than my brother. I will say that Marcus does have a sense of responsibility, though."

"A good thing," Lauryn pointed out, interested in his brother's assessment of the earl, though she hoped they didn't get caught in this family dissection of his character.

"As long as you don't take it to extremes," Carter complained. "Every man must have time to play, now and then."

"True," Lauryn agreed, dropping her gaze to her lap as she thought of the lovemaking she and the earl had shared. That was surely play at its best!

"Why do you feel your brother is unlikely to settle down?" she asked, bringing the conversation back to its starting point. "Surely he will marry, from his own class, of course, at some point. I mean, he will need an heir."

"Don't know," Carter said, his tone cautious. "He threatens to leave that dreadful task to me, which really ain't in my line, either. I like the playing better than the paying, as the saying goes. But if he don't, it goes back to his mother, don't you know. She left, you see, when he was only five."

"Left?" Lauryn looked up in surprise. If they were both Suttons, but only half brothers, she had assumed different mothers, but she had thought the earl's mother must have died, perhaps in childbirth as too many women did. "What do you mean, she left?"

"Ran off with another man, and the old earl got a divorce, act of Parliament, the whole business. Right lot of gossip it was, at the time. So poor old Marcus doesn't trust women a whole lot, you see."

"Ah, I do see," she said, wondering that he had not thrown her out the door when the first flicker of doubt had emerged over her identify or her status. Good heavens.

"Mind you, our father was a hard man to live with, I think even Marcus would tell you that, a right tyrannical old despot, down to the end." Carter shook his head in memory.

"The two of you must have had a difficult childhood," she said. And here she had been thinking that, with wealth and a titled name behind them, they had had all that they needed. How wrong one could be!

He shrugged. "Others had worse. We grew up with nannies and tutors, that's all. My own mother was sweet, but so terrified of the old earl she could say little to dissuade him if he were on a tirade. But Marcus would stand up for me, if I had been really bad and our father wanted to have me whipped."

Lauryn shivered. "Oh, that was good of him!"

"I should say." Carter gave a rather mirthless laugh, but his eyes turned bleak, remembering. "He was a good brother, actually. I'd like to see him happy." He gazed back at her suddenly, and appeared a bit embarrassed to be caught in a genuine bit of emotion. "Not that he'd thank me for interfering or telling tales out of school, don't you know."

"Of course not," she smiled at him. "My lips are sealed."

He put his cards away and, with a bow to her, left the sitting room. Lauryn stared at her book, but instead of the poet's groves, she saw two young boys coping with an old and too strict father, a timid mother/stepmother, and the lonely childhood one had faced growing up with the knowledge that his own mother had gone away forever, with no thought to the son she had left behind.

Her heart ached for him. Was there any trace of that boy left in the sophisticated, amazingly adept lover she knew and yet did not know? He could be gentle and yet could freeze up on her in an instant. Perhaps she would never get to truly know him—he would likely send her away before he ever opened up to her, and they would probably never be on a truly level plane . . . and there was nothing she could do to change the playing field . . .

She walked over to the cabinet where Carter had put away his cards, and on a whim, took out the deck. She let the cards shuffle through her hands and looked at their printed faces: queen and jack, trey and six, wildly different values, just as in life.

Marcus knew for certain now what he had suspected all along: she was not truly a member of the demimonde, but she was also not an aristocrat, not on the same rung of society as he. They would never stand on the same playing field, so she could not dream of facing him as an equal. She was now as she had been at the beginning—she must not lose her heart, no matter how winning his lovemaking, how bold his kisses, or even how much she might think he needed someone to love . . . She had to remember that. She could not risk leaving her own heart behind.

When it came time to change for dinner, Lauryn decided she had also better check on the contessa. She found her sitting in bed reading a book one of the maids had brought her from the shelves downstairs.

"Are you still feeling ill?" Lauryn asked her.

"I am not at my best," the other lady told her. "Look at me. Yet, the circles under my eyes. My skin is pallid. Bah, I am a mess! I do not come out of the room till I am *tres belle* again."

"I see," Lauryn said, although she didn't really. The contessa was always a strikingly attractive woman. "Is there anything I can do to help?"

"*Merci*, thank you no, *ma petite*," the contessa said, smiling at her. "You have saved my life already. The servants vill bring me up ze tray of food."

So with the help of one of the maids, Lauryn changed her gown for dinner, then went downstairs to eat with the two gentlemen.

"I understand you must represent the feminine side all by yourself tonight," the earl said. Now in evening dress, he had reappeared, and looked much too handsome to be allowed out alone.

She blinked at him, and tried to focus her thoughts on dinner and other mundane topics. "Yes, the contessa is–is not quite up to her usual good health."

"Oh, you can be candid. She had a message sent down to me," Carter told them, grinning. " 'She waits to be restored to her usual standard of beauty,' was how she put it."

Lauryn tried not to laugh. "The contessa is a lady of, ah, unusual straightforwardness. And that is certainly much to her credit."

"Much," the earl agreed. "I'm sure we will miss her conversation tonight at dinner. We shall have to do our best to get along without her, however." His dark eyes twinkled as he offered his arm to Lauryn. They went into the dining room, where they enjoyed another excellent dinner.

This time, she had little worries about protocol; Carter had an endless supply of funny stories, and when he sometimes wandered into anecdotes about their time as children, or as young men before their father the late earl had died, Lauryn was especially interested. She noticed that Carter never mentioned his brother's mother, however. It appeared that some subjects were taboo, even to the irreverent younger brother.

She left them alone to savor their port, but they came in to join her almost at once, and they played silly child's games in the drawing room, which Lauryn found much less nerve-wracking than cards. True, Marcus beat them all even at spillikins, but she still preferred that to being humiliated at whist.

When the earl put his hand upon hers to show her how to balance the long straws used for the game, she felt a shiver of response go through her, and she wondered if they would be able to share a bed tonight. She tried not to show how her body responded to his slightest touch. But when she looked at him, she felt a hunger that dwarfed anything she had felt in the dining room. . . .

Perhaps that was one reason that the earl proclaimed it time to retire even before the clock had struck ten o'clock.

"Are you going to bed with the cows?" his brother protested.

"Country hours," the earl told him cooly. "While we are in the country, you must do as the local populace does."

"I know one doesn't stay up as late as in London, but really, Marcus, you don't have to take it to extremes," Carter grumbled. "I'm the one sleeping on a camp bed, if you remember, and without anyone beside me to make it more agreeable."

"I do weep for you," his brother told him, grinning.

"Oh, I can tell," Carter retorted. "Well, I'm taking the rest of the port to bed with me!"

Lauryn said good-night demurely, without getting into the argument, but her heart lightened as she climbed the staircase. She went into the other bedroom to check on the contessa, but all seemed well, and surely tonight, there would be no further midnight alarms.

After changing for bed, she slipped down the hall to the earl's bedroom, and found that he was waiting for her, his expression hard to read.

But he had already shed his clothes, and with his robe on, he sat in a deep chair next to the fireplace. The room was warm from the fire and comfortably dim.

"You look lovely tonight," he said softly. He held out one arm to her, and she walked close enough so that he could pull her to him.

The strength in his arms was reassuring. He lifted her lightly into his lap, and they sat together in the wide chair. She put her arms about his neck and curled up with him, pushing the lapels of his robe further apart to warm her hands on his chest, touching the light sprinkles of dark hair.

He murmured as she ran her fingers over his chest. "You're teasing me," he said.

"I would never do that." She lifted her brows, then leaned closer to kiss where her fingers had lightly traced.

It seemed an age since they had been together, instead of only a few nights ago. She felt her body's hunger for him, the touch of his warm skin, the slight clean male scent of him. He suddenly pulled her nightgown up and she lifted her arms so he could strip it over her head and toss it away. She wanted nothing more than for him to pull her even closer so that their bodies could touch, could meld once more into one.

He put his hands beneath her buttocks and lifted her up. She put her hands into his thick dark hair and allowed him to push his face into her breasts, find her nipples, and take them one after the other into his mouth with the kind of hunger that also grew inside her.

They were pushing back and forth with a kind of frantic urgency till she thought they would topple from the chair, but the desire only seemed to grow—she was damp with need, and she wanted him now, wanted to feel him inside her. Lauryn put both arms about his neck and pulled him closer to her—

"Now," she murmured, "now," stretching her naked body along his, showing him just how ready she was.

Somehow they were both sliding past the chair, down to the bear rug in front of the fire, and its thick fur felt like a warm caress on her naked body. But she felt it only in a far corner of her mind, because most of all she thought of his body, how it felt when he entered her hard and quick and lifted her with his hands so that he could continue the strokes and hit just the right places while she gasped and groaned with the pure pleasure of their coming together. She arched with him, matching his rhythm, her body meeting his with an audible impact that only added to the pleasure, the deep-seated satisfaction.

And when he moved one of his hands to her soft folds in front of his manhood and stroked the pleasure point there that always sent her wild, circles of joy raced across her whole skin and turned her inside out, as if she zoomed into the night sky, then down again like a shooting star. She arched up, almost unseating him but for his skillful and continued pulsating beat.

It seemed they climbed to the very top of the sky together, as he continued to pound, harder and harder, and she pushed with him, glorying in every beat, every cadence. And nothing else could touch her, could penetrate the golden glow of ecstasy that wrapped them together as if it were a gift from fate itself—her mind had stopped working long ago—it was only feeling—only touch—only emotion—only pure sensation—only joy—

And when he came, she allowed herself to fly into the universe, too, and the joy continued. He stroked lightly—softly—firmly—and she thought she might die of sheer pleasure—

A woman screamed.

Eleven

It was like breaking a golden egg.
Lauryn was wrenched from her joyous daze, and she had to catch hold of Marcus, trying to find her balance as she fought to stand up.

He was swearing. "If it's another bloody bat, I swear I'll . . ."

They both struggled to find clothes enough to be presentable, nightwear at least and robes, and then in a minute, were able to stumble down the hallway.

It was like replaying a bad dream. The darkness, the screams, the candlelight in the darkened room. Except this time there seemed to be nothing to see.

"I think she's having a nightmare," Lauryn muttered, shaking the woman in the bed. "Contessa, wake up, wake up, my dear. You're all right."

But the other woman, her face tear-stained, looked very far from all right. She was chattering frantically in a language Lauryn did not know, German, perhaps, or Polish?

She tried to calm her, then turned back to confer with the earl. "If you would bring some brandy, perhaps?"

"I will, and I will wake that damnably hard-sleeping brother of mine to come and sit with her," he suggested, his tone savage.

"I think—I think I will have to stay with her again," Lauryn told him, sighing. "I wanted to linger in your arms, but she is truly terrified, and I don't believe I can leave. She wants another woman with her, I think."

He swore. "I wanted a woman with me, as well," he admitted. "I wanted this woman, you—selfish, I know." He kissed her quickly. "But you are more charitable than I, I admit it. I will fetch the brandy."

Lauryn turned back to the bed and went to sit beside the contessa, trying to penetrate the nightmare-induced fog. "You're all right, I promise," she told her, taking one hand and pressing it.

By the time the earl returned with a glass of brandy, they were able to persuade the contessa to drink a little, and her frantic sobbing subsided, but even then, she did not wish to let go of Lauryn's hand, which she clung to like a lifeline, so there would be no return to wonderful lovemaking tonight.

Lauryn had to comfort herself with recollections of the quite amazing performance they had already enjoyed as she lay beside the contessa and coaxed her back into sleep.

She wondered if the earl did miss her, as he lay alone in his bedroom. She could hope so.

Lauryn slept lightly, waking several times when the contessa stirred in her sleep, murmuring in her native language, but Lauryn was able to speak to her and cajole her back to sleep without the other woman erupting into shrieks of dismay and waking the whole house again. Once when she woke, she heard the hard patter of rain hitting the roof, and wind shaking the shutters outside.

When the first rays of light crept past the draperies, the contessa finally fell into a deeper sleep, and Lauryn also dozed again. When she woke the next time, her bedmate still slept, but Lauryn thought it high time she herself was up.

Would the earl return to town today? She thought it likely, so she dressed rapidly in her borrowed riding habit and descended the staircase.

She found the earl coming up.

"I was just about to leave you a note," he said, scanning her face. "Did you sleep at all?"

"Yes, quite tolerably," she told him. "Has something occurred?"

"The guards at the warehouse have been attacked. I have a note from the colonel. I'm going into town at once. But you need not accompany me, especially if you are still tired or need more time to recover—"

"No, no, I wish to see what is unfolding," she told him, having no desire to be stuck at the hunting lodge with the contessa and Carter as her only companions. Besides, the earl might wish her beside him, a thought which gave her a small thrill of pleasure.

"Are you sure?" he glanced at her thighs, as if he could see beneath her clothes. "We could take the carriage to spare you—"

"No, no, I am quite restored, and riding will be swifter." She smiled at him, and he returned it with the easy smile she had come to love.

"I shall order the horses made ready at once," he told her, turning on his heel. She went to the dining room to take advantage of the brief time to get a cup of tea and a piece of toast.

She had both, and a coddled egg, too, before they set out.

"Did he say anything else?" she asked, after the earl gave her a hand up. She settled into the saddle with a feeling of joy. Her bruises were considerably improved, although her thigh muscles protested a little as they stretched and tightened.

"Not much, but I mean to visit Colonel Swift first of all. We will see if he has anything new to add since he penned the note."

She nodded, and they urged the horses on to their best speed. The sky was dotted with tall gray clouds, and she hoped they were not rained on before the day was done. So far, the air was cool and the wind brisk, but the freshening breeze felt good upon her face. She tightened her reins and nudged her mare to ride around the biggest puddles in the roadway.

When they reached town, they maneuvered through the traffic-filled streets until they came to the colonel's house. The earl helped her down from her horse, and they walked up to his door. After knocking, they waited, and the door was soon opened by a footman.

The colonel welcomed them into his sitting room. "I find this very strange," Colonel Swift told them, without preamble. "I got word early this morning, when a street vendor taking out his cart discovered two of our men, the ones on duty last night, one injured, one dead."

"Good heavens," Lauryn muttered.

The earl's expression tightened. "That is indeed regrettable."

"They had been soldiers; they understood the risks," the colonel said gruffly. A maid brought a tea tray into the room and poured out tea for them, and their host passed the cups around.

Lauryn took a cup and sipped. It felt good on her parched throat after the ride.

"How much is missing from the warehouse?" Marcus asked.

The colonel lowered his cup of tea and dropped it abruptly back into its saucer. The china rattled. "That's the strangest part of all," he said, his voice overloud. "I had instructed them to take a count of the boxes and barrels in the warehouse." He walked across to his desk, bent over it, and found a paper which he unrolled and brought back with him. He handed it to the earl. "Here it is, and I hope it matches your official bill of lading as to the number recovered from the sunken ship. But the thing is, after we took the injured man away to see to his wounds, and had the dead man removed to be decently interred, I replaced them with a new and increased team, and we counted what remained in the warehouse. And nothing seems to be missing."

"What?" Lauryn had not meant to interrupt, but she spoke before she could help herself.

The earl was gazing at their host, looking quizzical, as well. "Did they look into the boxes and crates?"

"Aye, and as far as we can see—mind you, we don't know exactly what they held in the beginning, of course—they're still full." The colonel shook his head. "How could someone want to get into the building so badly they would kill to get in, and then take nothing away?"

There was a moment of silence as they all pondered this question.

"Unless the intruders were searching for something that they did not find, we are simply not seeing something," Marcus spoke slowly. "First, however, I mean to look carefully at the warehouse, myself."

"Yes, I was hoping that you would," the colonel agreed. "I will ride over with you. I want to check on the guards again and make sure that all is as it should be."

He sent a maid to tell his groom to saddle his own horse, and as soon as it was ready, the earl and Lauryn returned to their mounts, then led the way back to the warehouse that contained the recovered cargo from the sunken ship.

When they rode up to the large structure, Lauryn saw that now no less than half a dozen men guarded the doors, lined up with military precision and bristling with weapons. They appeared ready to fight a small war. The colonel was taking no chances this time.

They snapped to with even more exactitude when they saw the colonel. "Sir!"

"At ease," he said. "This is the earl, whose property you are protecting. We are going to examine the cargo inside."

"Yes, my lord," the man who seemed to be in charge said.

The earl acknowledged him. "Good man." They went inside the building.

Lauryn blinked in the dimmer light, and they walked across to the stacks of boxes and barrels.

"They've all been counted and recounted most carefully. The numbers have been accounted for," the colonel assured them.

"If you've done it already, I will not waste my time counting them," the earl told him. "I trust your efficiency."

The colonel nodded, as if in appreciation of the compliment. "So next, I suppose we must check inside the boxes."

This was going to be both time consuming and exhausting, Lauryn thought, meeting Marcus's wry glance. But there was nothing for it but to plunge in.

The earl removed his coat and rolled up his sleeves, and Lauryn did the same with the jacket of her riding habit. Then Marcus pried open the top of the nearest box—the lid didn't shatter or fall apart in his hands—and they began the task of checking what was inside each one.

Packed among the soggy sawdust, which reeked of rot and mildew, they found the same jade artwork and ancient Chinese urns and vases that Lauryn had glimpsed earlier. The earl looked over them carefully, trying to detect possible substitutions, as he explained to Lauryn and the colonel. But the contents seemed to be the originals, and he could make out no changes.

Nor did there seem to be any empty spots in the packing that could have marked where some of the statues or Ming vases had been taken away. Some of the boxes' contents seemed a bit shaken about, but whether that was from having been rearranged or simply from being tossed about during a sea voyage, it was impossible to say.

"This makes no sense," the earl said, after several hours had passed, and nothing had been accomplished except that they were all much dirtier and becoming short tempered and weary. "Why put up a terrific battle to get in and then take away none of these quite valuable treasures?"

"Perhaps they were ordinary street thugs and they didn't know what they had?" the colonel suggested. "Although that does stretch belief." He shook his head.

"Could there be any other reason for breaking in?" Lauryn asked.

"Like what?" Marcus turned to look at her.

"Oh, I don't know," she said. "I'm just wracking my brain for some reason that would explain what happened."

He nodded. "I know. When one can't think of anything that makes sense, we try for the nonsensical."

When they walked back toward the doors, Lauryn could see how covered with dust and grime they all were. She took out her handkerchief and tried to wipe off some of the dust from her hands, then her face. She could just see a black stain that had somehow ended up on the end of her nose. She tried to rub it, but her handkerchief was itself so black, she suspected she had accomplished little.

Colonel Swift was inviting them to his house for dinner. To her relief, the earl politely declined.

"I think we are hardly in shape to grace your dining table," Sutton told him, looking ruefully down at his own trousers, covered with specks of grime, and trying to dust off his hands. "Thank you, another time, perhaps."

They walked toward their steeds. Lauryn looked toward the far corner of the long building where she had glimpsed the mysterious figure of the man the last time she had been here.

A figure appeared, only for a moment, and then slipped out of sight around the corner of the building.

It was him!

She exclaimed, and when the earl turned, she cried, "He's back!"

The earl turned and looked toward where she motioned. "The same man?"

When she nodded, he said, "Stay here with the colonel." Marcus jumped on his horse and made for the corner of the building.

The alley was narrow and would barely allow for passage of his steed, but in the hope of making better time and running down the mysterious onlooker, Marcus decided to stay astride. So although he slowed his pace, he retained his seat in the saddle.

He saw no sign of anyone in the alley; it was littered with pools of dirty water from the recent rains and smelled of the refuse that usually cluttered such passageways. He came out of the other end and pulled up his horse to glance around him, trying to decide which way to go.

A glimpse of movement caught his eye and he turned to the left. There, disappearing behind a large wagon full of coal—he'd barely had time to register the figure before it had slipped out of his view, but just as Lauryn had said, a momentary impression of something different about him made the brief glimpse stand out. So even though other figures were also moving along the street, men in coats and trousers holding on their hats against the brisk wind, women in spencers and pelisses and bonnets tied securely against the same breeze, servants pushing prams with their young charges bundled up against the unseasonably cool day, still this one shape had seemed alien, exotic. His brain had hardly had time to register just why that was, but he'd had a distinct feeling of something different about the man, and he trusted his impression.

So, although he scanned both sides of the street, left and right, he saw nothing else that raised his hackles as did that one fleeting suspicion. He pressed his heels into his horse's sides and ignored the street vendor who called up to him, "Hot pies, gov'nor, savory meat pies, pipin' hot, they are, just two shillings!"

The smell of hot meat and grease might have tempted him if he had been a hungry young apprentice, but Marcus shook his head and hurried on.

Past the coal wagon he hurried, past two more shops, one with a window full of fat geese and hens, hanging by their feet and waiting to be plucked and roasted, another with barrels of root vegetables for goodwives to search through at their leisure. But still he could not seem to catch up with the man with the out-of-place appearance. Had he doubled back and outsmarted his pursuer? Was there somewhere he could have lost him?

But Marcus had been following very rapidly on horseback; how could the fugitive have gotten far enough ahead to have had the chance to evade him? He told himself he would search two more blocks before turning back to double-check the route he had already covered.

The next stores again showed no sign of anything unusual. From his stance on horseback, Marcus could look over the heads of most of the crowd and look through the shop windows, and he could see most of the people who thronged into the stores and small shops.

He kept his horse to a slow walk, and tried to make out a face amid the crowds that filled the sidewalks and the stores. The townspeople seemed to be a mostly law-abiding bunch. He thought he made out a pickpocket or two amid the shoppers, but he saw no evidence of any major criminal activity. Of course, just because he saw no indication of a crime in plain daylight did not mean that it was not stirring somewhere else, he reminded himself, remembering what he was seeking.

And speaking of that—now he passed a shop window with a few bits of china merchandise shown off behind the glass panes. Something was written in oriental characters alongside the words *Shop, Elegant Gifts*. Behind the glass, he saw a roundish hat turned down to hide the face of the person wearing it.

Curious, he thought, and very handy, if one did not wish his face to be seen. And perhaps it would be a good idea to check out how much these elegant gifts would cost.

He pulled up his horse and dismounted. Several street urchins ran up, yelling for the privilege of holding his steed.

"Me, me, gov'ner, I can do h'it!"

Marcus looked them over and selected the one who looked the strongest and most steady. "What's your name?"

"Tom, sir."

"Very well, Tom. A shilling if when I return, my horse is calm and unbothered. If anyone has mucked about with him, however, you'll be very very sorry."

"Don't worry, gov," Tom said, grinning. "He'll still be in prime shape."

Marcus opened the door and walked in. A few shelves of china bowls and plates could be seen in the front of the shop, and he could smell unfamiliar spices in the air. Wondering if he should rap on the counter, he waited for a moment, then someone emerged from the dimness beyond the curtain that separated the front from the rear of the building.

It was an older woman with graying dark hair, wearing a curious getup of a long-sleeved tuniclike top and long skirt.

She had strangely small feet and walked with shuffling steps. She had almond-shaped dark eyes and skin of a different hue than the average Englishwoman, and her accent bespoke her Asian birth.

"'Allo, sir. You like to buy?"

"Perhaps I will, another day," Marcus said politely. "I am just looking at your handsome china. Is this a family-owned shop? I thought a gentleman was here the other day?"

"Ah, yes, I have large and honorable family. And velly handsome china." She bobbed her head, and he bowed back, not sure what was the custom of her people.

"Then I am sure I will return," he told her. It was unlikely he would get anyone else to come out of the back to speak to him and allow themselves to be seen, though he much wanted to check out the men who worked here, to be sure this was where his missing man had gone to earth. How could he do that?

As he walked back outside, he tried to think of a stratagem.

Sure enough, he found his gelding waiting, shaking his mane at a large fly buzzing about his ears but otherwise quite untroubled. Marcus paid young Tom as promised, adding another shilling. The boy grinned widely at this largess, and the coins disappeared at once into an inside pocket.

"Would you like to earn more?" Marcus asked the urchin.

The youngster eyed him warily. "Doing wacher?"

"Walk a little with me," he said, keeping his tone low. Holding the reins of the horse, he strode ahead down the street, the boy beside him. When they were several shops down from the store he had walked out of, he paused.

"I'd like to see the men who work in the back of the shop I was in. I want them to come out, so that I don't have to go in, because I imagine they outnumber me, and I don't want to get into a row with them. I'd like to cause some kind of commotion, a small one, not a real disaster—I don't want to burn down the building or anything totally rash—just enough to make them come outside for a minute or two. Got any ideas?"

"Cor, what ye up to, gov?" the street lad asked, eyeing him with interest.

"That's my business," Marcus told him firmly.

The urchin screwed up his mouth and gave the question some thought. "I could shinny up to the roof and stop up one of them chimneys. That'd bring 'em out fast enough."

"What will they think did it?" Fascinated, Marcus considered him.

Tom shrugged. "Ah, they'll bet a bunch of swallows' nests spilt into the flues. 'Appens all the time."

"It won't burn down the house?"

"Naw." He shook his head, long dirty hair flying about his face.

Mentally crossing his fingers, Marcus agreed to the scheme. This time Tom demanded his pay in advance. Not sure whether to be amused or annoyed, Marcus handed over a half crown, and watched the lad buy a few handfuls of straw from a nearby stable. Tom sat down on the side of the street and wove the straw together loosely to form something that looked like the bottom of a basket except not as solid or as strong.

"They won't realize this was made by human hands?"

"Naw, after it's blacked in the smoke and 'alf burned by sparks from the fire," his partner in crime said. "After it's knocked about, they'll think it's part of them bird nests, like I said."

"Ah, done this before, have you?" Marcus noted, politely.

Tom grinned.

"All right. Go to it. I'll meet you at the inn down the street when you are finished."

Tucking his creation under his shirt, the stripling headed for the alley behind the shops and almost at once disappeared from view.

This time Marcus paid the stable to house his horse for a brief spell, then walked back to find a vantage point where he could observe the shop and not be seen himself. The street made a bend just below the building he was observing, and there was a pub with a bow window. He paid for an ale and found a seat by the window, where he should have a good view, and he could nurse the drink for awhile. He wasn't sure how long it would take the stopped up chimney to take effect.

As it turned out, he was wrong to doubt his young colleague. Before he'd had more than half a dozen swigs of the ale, he could see smoke billow out of the small windows of the gift shop, and several people, all of Asian descent, also poured out into the side yard, which he could see from his vantage point.

There were three men, one was too old, one too short. The last one might be the man from the alley, the one who seemed to be keeping watch over the warehouse.

"Turn around," Marcus muttered to himself. "Turn so that I can see your face!"

Then he almost rose from his seat.

The urchin, young Tom, walked calmly into the side court. Had he been caught at his tampering with the chimney? No, surely not, he seemed perfectly self-possessed. He spoke to the older man, bowed with ostensibly perfect manners, and then went toward the back of the house. Someone got him a ladder—oh, that was rich, they were helping him up to the roof, which the imp had already been up to on his own power—had he managed to get them to pay him to knock down the obstruction he had just put up? It appeared so.

At last, the third man turned to face the inn and Marcus got a better look at him. Yes, he was reasonably certain this was the same man.

He wondered if there was any way he could bring Lauryn to see him. If they sat here in the inn, she should not be in any danger, he thought. Although that would mean finding a way to get the man out of the building again. He doubted he could use the same scheme a second time—they would grow suspicious of blocked chimneys if it happened yet again!

Now they were returning to the building, so the smoke must be clearing, Marcus decided. Sure enough, presently Tom appeared in the doorway of the tavern, smelling a bit strongly of smoke, but grinning broadly.

He saw the earl and sauntered over.

"And how much did you make this time?" Marcus asked, his tone polite.

Tom smirked. "Not saying, gov. But it was thirsty work,

knocking them birds' nests down out of all that smoke. You could buy me a drink to wet me throat."

"I think you could buy me a drink, you've earned so much today."

The lad opened his mouth to protest, and Marcus waved his remonstrances aside. "Only a small jest. I will get you a half pint, and I predict you will end up as mayor, my boy."

Tom looked surprised but gratified at this vision of his future.

Marcus finished his own ale and paid the barman for them both, then took his leave. He reclaimed his horse and made his way back to the warehouse, hoping that Lauryn and the colonel had not grown too anxious about his long absence.

And in fact, when he reached the warehouse again, he found only the guards still there. Perhaps, he told himself, Lauryn and the colonel had repaired for some tea and light refreshment. There was no need for them to stand around and wait so long for him here, after all. But he felt a flicker of anxiety, nonetheless.

When he rode closer to the guards, the leader recognized him, and, straightening his shoulders smartly, saluted.

"My lord!"

"As you were," he said. "Where are Colonel Swift and the lady who was with me earlier?"

"Ah, the lady had a turn, my lord. The colonel called a hackney and took her back to his house so he could call a physician, if need be."

"What?" Marcus felt a cold wave of alarm run over him. Lauryn was ill? Had she done too much? Why had he allowed her to come back? It was his fault, dammit!

He turned his horse without another word and pressed his heels into the animal's flanks. The gelding sprang forward into the street. He made as good time as possible given the traffic and as he pushed his horse to edge past a slow-moving wagon filled with lumber and then avoid a large pothole in the street that no one had filled, Marcus felt the keenest anxiety pull at his nerves and tighten his throat. Surely it would be nothing serious, surely, surely . . .

But he would only feel better when he saw her sitting up, smiling, speaking to him as usual.

It seemed to take hours until he reached Colonel Swift's house, but at last the modest residence came into view. Marcus slipped down from the saddle, tied his reins to the post in front of the house, and hurried up to rap on the door.

He seethed with impatience, as it seemed another eternity until a footman pulled open the door.

"Lord Sutton," Marcus said, his tone brusque. "I am here to see the colonel."

Before the footman could speak, Marcus heard the colonel himself call, "Come in, my lord, I have been waiting for you to return. We are up on the next floor."

Brushing past the startled servant, Marcus took the stairs almost at a run, so anxious was he to find out Lauryn's condition. Colonel Swift stood on the landing of the stairs; he looked alert but not like a man with dire news to tell, so Marcus could try to calm his increased pulse.

"What has occurred?" he demanded. "The guard said—"

"Yes, after you left to follow the stranger, Mrs. Smith suddenly became ill. It seemed best to bring her back to my home so that we could call a physician."

"Of course, thank you for looking out for her. How is she?"

"You may see; she is considerably improved. The doctor says he thinks it is nothing serious, and she will soon be recovered."

The colonel turned to lead the way up. "She does not like to hear it," he said, lowering his voice. "But females are the more sensitive of the sexes, you know. Perhaps the excitement and the exertion have simply been too much."

He led the way to the next landing and on to what appeared to be a guest chamber. Lauryn lay atop the bedclothes, still in her riding habit, but with a blanket over her legs. She looked very pale but composed, and her eyes were open, her expression a bit wary.

"Laur—Mrs. Smith, how are you?" Marcus went quickly to her side and picked up one hand, feeling an immense need to touch her, make sure that he could feel the warmth of her skin, the rhythm of her pulse beating, just to be certain that she was alive. The immensity of his relief was almost shocking: his knees had gone weak. He felt as if he could fold up like a paper toy that the sidewalk conjurers made for children. Fortunately there was a chair beside the bed he could sink into, else he might have fallen, and God knows what they would have thought of him. If the colonel thought females were weak . . .

But she was speaking, and he wrenched his attention back.

"I don't know what happened, my lord." She was being very formal in front of Colonel Swift, but he saw from the quick glance she threw the colonel's way that she did not care for the current theory. "I would swear that it was not fatigue or the heat of the day because I was not overtired and I was not too warm, no matter what the doctor may say—he seemed to think that females are fragile vessels, indeed."

She grimaced, and Marcus swallowed a grin. He suspected that the doctor's visit had not been, perhaps, a totally felicitous experience for all concerned.

"But I suddenly found my mind—well, it's hard to explain, but it seemed to go strangely blank, and I felt as if I were floating away, and I saw almost a vision, similar to the images on the china in the ship's boxes we had been viewing inside, but these seemed to move as if they were alive . . ." She shivered. "I know it makes no sense."

The colonel shook his head. "We had eaten some meat pies from a street vendor while we waited for you, my lord. Perhaps Mrs. Smith got a bad pie and the meat disagreed with her. At any rate, she collapsed, and we could not wake her for several minutes, not until we bathed her forehead with cold water, and even then, she was not really awake."

Marcus felt a coldness sweep through him. This did not sound like heat exhaustion to him. "Were you—pardon me—sweating profusely?"

She looked at him in surprise, but she shook her head.

"Was your skin very hot?"

"No, chilled, if anything," the colonel volunteered. "I felt her forehead, and really, I feared for her for a time."

"It was not warm in the warehouse," she said.

"The physician advised—" Colonel Swift began, as one duty bound to pass on the expert's advice.

"I am not going to take to my bed for two weeks!" Lauryn snapped. For a moment, she looked quite her old self, and Marcus felt more encouraged by her spark of spirit than he had since he had entered the house. "Nor do I choose to be bled for three days running."

"We'll see," he murmured, but he gave her a wink while the colonel shook his head in doubt.

"I think we've done enough for today, at any rate. And I think we should return to my lodge."

He spoke to the colonel about setting up one of their men, in shifts, to watch the shop where he had tracked the Asian they had seen spying on the warehouse, and Swift agreed to assign someone to covertly take over this watch.

Then the colonel insisted on lending them the use of his small gig. That Marcus was happy to accept, and although Lauryn looked mutinous again, she had to admit she was still weak and perhaps not yet up to riding back to the hunting box. Slipping out of the saddle would not help her argument to be admitted back at the earl's side in the hunt for the answer to the mysteries of the recovered cargo.

So they tied the mare to the back of the gig, one of the colonel's grooms drove the vehicle, and Marcus rode his own mount just behind as they made their way out of town and back to his lodge. There he gave the groom a suitable beneficence for his assistance, and the man turned the gig around and started home.

Marcus's own groom took his two horses back to the stables, and Marcus offered Lauryn his arm as they went into the house.

"It was something else, you know, not just fatigue," she told him. "And I don't really think it was the meat pie. It seems to me that would have turned my stomach if it were bad, not given me awful dreams!"

He observed the blanched hue of her skin and the effort it was taking for her to walk with a normal gait, not drag her feet. "I believe you. Something affected you, and it must have been something in the warehouse. I'm not asking you to stay in bed for weeks, just until you feel that you have regained your strength. I do want you to stay out of the warehouse, however."

She opened her lips to argue, and he added quickly, "At least till we know more about what we are dealing with."

Sighing as the footman opened the door to admit them, she went inside and took off her hat and gloves, both dusty from the time they had spent in the warehouse. She sneezed as she pulled off one glove, then another, and then for a moment, she swayed.

Alarmed, he reached to steady her, afraid she would crumple at his feet.

"I'm all right," she murmured, but she allowed him to hold her shoulders until she drew another deep breath and seemed more stable.

"I'll see you up to—ah, which room?" he muttered. "Damn. Do you think our other guest will manage all right without you tonight? Surely she will. I think it's time you should be coddled, Mrs. Smith, instead of the contessa. And I'll have the maid bring you up a dinner tray."

"If it's not too much trouble for the servants, I would love a bath first," she said. "I do feel very grimy after digging through so many of those boxes and barrels. They were so covered in dirt and mildew and God knows what else."

God knew, indeed. "That would likely be a very good idea," he said, his tone low. He saw her into his own bedroom and resting on one of the chairs, then called a maid and gave orders to fill a a hip bath, which they set up behind a screen at one end of the room.

Then he went down to find his half brother, whom he finally located in the stable. There he gave him a brief account of their day and told him, in no uncertain terms, that he was responsible for the contessa tonight.

"If she has nightmares, you will have to calm her. If she is frightened, you will soothe her. If she is angry, you will appease her. I don't care what is wrong with the woman, you will take care of her, dammit. You brought her here, and Mrs. Smith will be sacrificed for her no longer."

"Don't feel a bit strong about that, do you, Brother?" Carter asked, his tone sardonic.

"She's ill, dammit, and she can't even think about herself for worrying about others." Marcus glared at his sibling. "So you take care of the contessa; I've had enough, and I will not have Lau–Mrs. Smith bothered. So do it." He wheeled and went back to the house, meaning to bathe, too, after Lauryn had been seen to.

Lauryn found the warm water and scented soap a splendid treat. If she did not feel so terribly listless, it would have brought thoughts of other pursuits, she was quite sure. But just now, it was enough to get the sour scents of the warehouse out of her hair and skin. When she had scrubbed and rinsed and rubbed herself dry, she lay on the chaise on the other side of the bedroom and enjoyed the luxury of feeling clean again. The maid pulled back the screen so that the footmen could carry the bath out, then back again, and Marcus took his turn.

My heavens, she thought. He'd dismissed the servants and had not bothered to put up the screen again, so she had an unfettered view. What a body the man had.

She watched him dunk his dark hair into the warm water and rub soap into it, then dunk it again. As he poured warm water over his shoulders and arms she watched the muscles ripple as he scrubbed each arm in turn, then did his stomach and thighs.

Sighing, she leaned back and wished she did not feel as washed out as last week's laundry. What on earth had induced her sinking spell?

Even now, she felt barely connected to the earth, and it was easy to doze off for minutes at a time. If she did not concentrate, she could almost close her eyes again and drift into a dream that was not quite—

Why did that jolt something in her memory?

As she pondered that idea, she felt someone sit down on the chaise beside her, and she looked up to see the earl bending low over her. She smiled at him.

He wore only his robe. His dark hair was still damp, and

his skin glistened with an occasional drop where he had hastily toweled dry.

"You smell like lavender, quite lovely," he said, kissing her very gently. "And you taste even better." His lips were warm, and she wanted him to linger, but after another moment he pulled away. "But you need to rest."

She grimaced but could not disagree. "Better than the smells of the warehouse, at least. I'm not sure if I will ever get the odors out of the riding habit you were gracious enough to lend me, though I will do my best."

"It doesn't matter," he told her. "We will have a new one made to order for you."

She smiled but shook her head a little at his extravagance. "And I will, at the very least, burn my handkerchief. It has a very odd stench."

"Really?" He looked across to the pile of discarded clothes that the maid had not yet taken away, and to her surprise he stood and looked through the mound, finding the crumpled square of linen and picking it up to sniff for a moment.

His expression changed.

"What is it?" Lauryn demanded.

"The smell—I just realized where I have smelled that odor before, in the warehouse, and on you. I think you got it on your handkerchief when you wiped your hands earlier after digging through the boxes," Marcus told her. "I believe I know what caused your illness!"

Twelve

"*What was it?*" *Lauryn demanded. "It is a very* unpleasant feeling, I must tell you!"

His expression strange, the earl stared down at her, then spoke one word only. "Opium."

Lauryn was so startled that she sat straight up. "What!"

"The strange dreamlike visions you had, the sleepiness, yes, it all fits," he told her.

"But–but—" That was what she had been trying to remember—*opium dreams*! She had heard the term. She felt soiled, and she swallowed hard, suddenly nauseated at the very idea of having consumed such a strong drug. "Will I be all right?"

He nodded, taking her hand in reassurance. "The worst is likely past. Your hands were black from handling the cargo and boxes, and even though you tried to wipe them off on your handkerchief, when you ate the hot pie outside the warehouse, I think you ingested a bit of opium without realizing it.

"That caused the 'opium dreams' you suffered. You may have some discomfort as it goes out of your body, but hopefully it will not be too bad. I would call a doctor for you once more except I don't believe there's anything that he could do."

Lauryn held fast to his hand. She felt as if she might float away again, partly from shock, partly from the still present aftereffects of the drug. "Where did it come from?"

"I'm much afraid . . ." he hesitated, and then sat down beside her on the chaise; she drew up her legs to give him room. "I'm afraid it was present on the ship, my ship." His tone had sharpened; she heard the effort it cost him to say the words.

"But—surely that must be illegal?" She stared at his face; his lips had flattened and his eyes—his eyes would have made her shiver, if she had been the person who had earned the enmity she saw there.

"Of course it is. But someone was smuggling opium into England on my ship, and I must find out who."

"Is that what caused the ship to wreck?" Lauryn felt as if her head were spinning as she tried to put all the pieces together.

"No, I don't think that had anything to do with the ship-wreck; that came from the storm," he said. "The last thing they wanted was the ship to go down—so that they would lose their valuable cargo."

"But what about the captain?" she pointed out. "Why was he killed?"

"Yes, we've got that," Marcus admitted, running his hands through his still damp hair. She resisted the urge to reach up and push those dark locks into place. "Perhaps he found the opium—I'd like to think he wasn't involved. I knew the captain. He was a good man. Let's consider it that way, anyhow. He somehow came across the opium, was very angry, demanded of someone to know what was happening, perhaps, or else, simply started to jettison the drug, throw it overboard—"

"And he was killed!" Lauryn knew her eyes had widened as she imagined the dreadful scene.

"Yes. And perhaps then when the storm came, they were in need of his leadership and his sailing skills. Perhaps that is one reason the ship floundered, and the crew was drowned. A fearful irony, if so."

"But why, if there are still traces of the opium in the

warehouse, did it not all wash away under the ocean when the ship sank?" Lauryn asked reasonably.

"More than traces, if that is why the guards were attacked. If someone who knew it was there came to retrieve it!" the earl pointed out. He jumped to his feet to pace up and down as he spoke, working it out. "Do you remember that I told you the vases were filled with sawdust and sealed with wax to protect them from breaking?"

"Oh!" Lauryn saw it, too. "What if it were not sawdust inside them!"

"Yes," he said, turning to smile at her. "Exactly."

"When you came out of the warehouse, you had black tarry spots on your trousers," she said. "Just as on my handkerchief, and that smell—"

"Precisely."

Lauryn shuddered. "Oh, heavens. What a vile thing. Why do people take this drug, Marcus? I can't imagine doing it on purpose."

"It's an escape, I suppose. I've been told that in the East it's an old man's drug, for someone who has nothing left to do with his life except sleep it away, dreaming instead of doing. In the West, the wealthy and bored sometimes do it for a lark, then find their body craves it again and again, and they can't get away from it."

She shivered once more. "How horrible, like carrying your prison around with you."

He came back to sit beside her and put his arms about her, holding her tightly. "I have arranged with Colonel Swift to assign one of our men to watch the shop I discovered when I followed the man you noticed observing the warehouse. We will see if this brings us any other information."

She nodded into his chest.

"But just now, I only want you to recover," he told her, kissing her ear, and her cheek, and the corner of her eye, and any other part of her face that presented itself. She turned her head so she could receive a proper kiss, and that one lingered pleasantly, but to her disappointment, he did not pursue it with more loverly activities.

"Rest," he told her firmly, scooping her up from the chaise and carrying her across to the bed. He lay her down and pulled the covers up to arrange them comfortably. "I must dress and go downstairs for dinner, but I'll be back to join you soon."

Lauryn had to admit that, in her enervated state, it was pleasant not to have to make the effort to dress and go downstairs. She still felt as if she were made of melting butter and barely able to stand. It was rare for her to be ill, but to have someone ready and willing to take over, willing to take care of her, was a heady sensation. It had been a long time since someone had been there for her—it was usually she who was tending to others.

She lay back in bed and tried to focus on the mystery of the opium smuggling. Who could have been doing it under the earl's nose and without his knowledge? It had to be someone who knew the schedule of the ships coming and going. Perhaps the earl was wrong about the ship's captain. Did the captain really not know about the opium in his cargo hold? Or was he in on the scheme after all, and had he and his fellow plotters fallen out, perhaps over the division of the profits? But—oh, it was too hard for her to think right now. Her thoughts all seemed to float away into nothingness . . .

Fighting the drug-induced lassitude, she shook her head, which still seemed not to function normally. Determined not to give in, she took up a book of poetry from the table beside the bed. She would read until her dinner tray came up.

Dinner was a masculine affair. The contessa asked for a tray to be sent up to her, as well, so it was only Marcus and his half brother at the table.

"She is not yet '*tres belle*' enough to leave her room," Carter reported, as he took a bite of his lamb. "Honestly, Marcus, how did you put up with this lady; she's a bit, ah—"

"Eccentric?" Marcus suggested, grinning. "Her mind is sharp, her knowledge and interests varied, and she has other charms as well."

"I think I'll take your word for it," his brother grumbled. He took another bite of his dinner and appeared to concentrate on his food.

Marcus looked at his sibling. "Carter."

"Hmmm?" Mouth full, his brother seemed more interested in a plate of sweetmeats the footman held out for his inspection.

The earl waited for the footman to finish serving and then dismissed him with a nod. When they were alone, he waited a heartbeat or two, then tried again. "Carter, have you ever taken opium?"

His brother almost dropped the goblet he had raised halfway to his mouth. "What? Do you take me for a totally brainless jackanapes?"

"I think your brain is quite adequate, but that's not an answer to my question," Marcus said quietly.

Carter had flushed, and he didn't quite meet his older sibling's eye. "I—I—I suppose you question my common sense, then, or my moral compass?"

"Carter?"

"Oh, hell's bells, Marcus." He wiped his suddenly damp face with his linen napkin, and the words poured out. "My first season on the town, some fellows I thought were all the crack took me down to see a hideaway they said had something quite new. I didn't know what they were taking me to see!

"Turned out to be this rather dismal place, much of it underground, with fellows sleeping in camp beds and clouds of odd-smelling smoke in the air. I saw these strange pipes with clay bowls, and they told us we would try smoking opium like the sleeping chaps had done . . . well, I'd never heard of the stuff. They dared me to try it."

"And you did, of course." Marcus sighed.

"I was a green'un, don't you know," Carter said, looking self-conscious, as if his current five and twenty years should be a mark of sterling maturity.

"And—"

"And it made my head hurt and gave me ghastly dreams, and cost me twenty quid, dreadful waste, considering it was only the middle of the quarter! I was sick as a dog the next day," Carter told him, shaking his head at the memory. "Left me feeling off color for days, actually, if not weeks."

"Why didn't you tell me?"

"And have you cut off my allowance for six months?" Carter gave a harsh laugh. "Send me to the country to twiddle my thumbs while I 'learned my lesson thoroughly'?"

Marcus started to reply, but paused, keeping his expression mild.

Carter eyed him reproachfully, but still Marcus judged it wiser not to speak.

"It's true. You used to come down hard on me, y'know, in case you don't remember!" But Carter's repressed bitterness seemed to have ebbed a bit. "I recall, anyhow."

"You often deserved it," Marcus pointed out, refusing to back down too far. "I was trying to do my duty as an elder brother, since our father had passed away and you had no one else to guide you. I may have been too hard on you, Carter, but I meant it only for your good because I cared about you."

The silence stretched a moment, and then at last Carter shrugged.

"Perhaps. I suppose I was a grimy little branchlet, at that age."

Marcus was careful not to allow his private amusement over Carter's jaded conviction that he was so much more mature now to show.

"But the opium—did you do it again?" Marcus asked carefully.

"Do I *look* mad?"

Marcus considered him. Carter sounded sincere. And he met his brother's gaze, at least briefly, before looking back at his plate and continuing to pile in forkfuls of food. And perhaps it was true, perhaps he had matured a good deal since the naive lad who had been led guileless into the opium den. But nonetheless . . .

Could his brother have gotten involved, willingly or not, in smuggling opium? If someone had blackmailed him over his earlier, youthful indiscretion, threatened to tell Sutton what Carter obviously didn't want him to know?

Somewhat grimly, Marcus considered the possibilities, then put down his fork and knife. Somehow, his appetite had gone.

After dinner, they had a glass of port and then went into the sitting room and played a few rounds of dice, for stakes Carter complained were insultingly low. But as Marcus pointed out that he didn't intend to take advantage of his own brother and he damn well didn't mean to allow his younger brother to fleece him, Carter was stuck with the penny points.

And since Carter claimed to be insulted by the low stakes, it gave Marcus a good excuse to end the game early and go up to bed, which he had intended to do all along. Lauryn, even if she did not feel inclined toward lovemaking, was still more enticing company than his half brother on his best night.

He didn't share this sentiment with Carter. Carter seemed to nose this out on his own, however.

"I suppose you just want to go upstairs and dally with your current lady of the evening," he grumbled.

"Careful, Carter," Marcus snapped. "Mind your manner when you speak of Mrs. Smith. She is a lady."

"Since when did you start dallying with ladies?" Carter looked at him in surprise.

"It's a long story," Marcus told him.

"I've got time; all I have ahead of me is a damned camp bed in the study," his brother pointed out.

"That doesn't mean that I am ready to tell it to you," Marcus noted. "Go read a good book; improve your mind. Your university stint did little for you. All I recall you doing is looking up all the willing barmaids in every inn near the university, before they finally tossed you out."

Carter made a rude noise with his tongue, but Marcus ignored him and headed up the staircase, taking the steps two at a time.

When he reached the landing, he turned toward his own bedroom. He opened the door to the bedchamber gently and went in as quietly as he could, in case she was asleep. There were candles lit around the bed, but Lauryn lay back against the feather pillows, an open book abandoned on her chest, which rose and fell with her slow breaths. Her eyelids were closed, and her breathing even.

Her color was still a bit pallid, and the veins in her temples seemed to stand out against the paleness of her skin. She looked so vulnerable that he felt his heart contract.

The opium she had accidentally ingested must still be affecting her. Perhaps he should have called a physician; however, he had a poor opinion of most doctors. He didn't trust them; mainly, they simply wanted to spill your blood, and as with his own father, were apt to bleed you until you died. Either illness would kill you, or the physicians would.

He pulled up a chair and sat down beside her, doing his best not to wake her. Probably rest, sleep, quiet to allow the body to heal itself was the best remedy, he told himself, trying to believe it. She was young and strong, nothing like his father in his last illness.

Still, there were at least two reasons it cut him to the bone to see her like this. First, it was his fault—he should not have allowed her to come this close to danger. He should not have taken her into the warehouse; he should have been more aware that the cargo could have held hidden perils. What had he been thinking, or worse, not thinking?

Most overwhelming of all, he could not even consider being without her . . .

How he had come to this point—gradually, quickly, in days or hours or minutes—he was not quite sure. Only that, from the moment she had walked into his study with her fantastical, sweet, and totally selfless proposition, it had seemed destined that he would end up here—looking down upon her face on the pillow with an overwhelming need to protect her, to possess her, to cherish her, and to know that she would stay with him for the rest of his natural life.

But as always, a question echoed in the back of his mind:

Could he depend on her to stay? He had no clue if she really cared for him, beyond the bounds of their fragile and highly mutable agreement, an agreement fast running out of time. Oh, she seemed to enjoy making love, responded joyously to his touch, gave back freely and with selfless and generous abandon. But did she love him? Could she stand to be with him for years, for decades, God willing they should have so long?

He didn't know, and he didn't know how to be sure.

He didn't know how to trust people anymore, and he sure as hell didn't trust Fate, that capricious and inconstant jokester.

Oh, dear God, Marcus thought, feeling a trickle of sweat run down his brow, even though the room was somewhat cool as the fire died down on the hearth. He needed her, with every inch of his body and soul, with every breath he took. He was a miserable wretch, he had no pride, no conscience, maybe he would simply throw himself on her mercy . . .

No, he could not; she would despise him. He could not keep her tied to him out of pity; what kind of man would he be to try to bind her to him in that way?

He wiped his forehead and paced up and down before the hearth before turning back to sit down once more by the bed. Get a grip on yourself, man, he told himself fiercely. You will have to wait and see. Either she cares for you or she doesn't. The fact that his stomach twisted just at the thought that she might not, that she might turn away, might leave . . .

He would have to wait and see.

If she left, he thought he might die. . . .

No, you will go about your life, he told himself through gritted teeth. You will be—outwardly, at least—just as you were before. And perhaps no one may guess that you will be merely the hollow husk of a man.

But at least for now she was still here. His gaze glided over her form on the bed, and he reached to pull the blanket up to cover her more fully, careful again not to wake her.

She sighed, and the book slipped down. He took it and closed it and put it on the table beside the bed, then sat back to feast his eyes on her, to imprint her sweetness on the back on his eyelids while he could.

He would cherish every moment they were together, just in case there were a finite number ahead.

A slight sound alerted him, and he lifted his head. For a moment he wondered if he had imagined it, then he heard it again, a faint knock at the door.

What the hell?

He stood. Taking long strides, he reached the door and opened it quickly, not wanting to risk Lauryn being disturbed.

Wearing a lace-trimmed peignoir, her hair in artful disarray about her face, the contessa stood with her hand raised to tap on the door again.

"Is something wrong?" Marcus asked.

"*Non, mon ami*," she said, her voice soft. "I came *seulement* to inquire about Mrs. Smith."

Knowing the lady too well to take anything she said at face value, he studied her for a moment before replying slowly, "I think she will be all right, but she is still not very well."

"Ah, *quelle pitie*," she said, shaking her head and looking past him at the still form on the bed. "I vill zit with her for a time if you desire to zeep, *cheri*."

She sounded quite sincere, and he felt ashamed of himself for an instant that he had doubted her motives. "Thank you, but I'm fine."

"Are you?" Raising her brows in a gesture he remembered well, she met his gaze with a searching one of her one. "Is there anything I can do for you, *cheri*?" She let the pause go on just an instant too long, and added, even more softly, "For old time's zake?"

Her eyes were knowing, and her lips gave a small half smile. He could not be angry at her; she was who she was, with rather, um, continental values, but apart from that, not at all a bad person, capable of real kindnesses and generosity. She was a practiced lover, with a well-shaped body, which, although he had not seen it in some time, was doubtless still appealing.

But he found he had no inclination to bring his knowledge up-to-date. Only one woman moved him now. Tonight or anytime, he was not in the mood to pursue amorous sports with anyone else. Lauryn lay ill, and he wanted to lie beside her and cherish her, hold her next to him until she was well again, and that was all he had on his mind. He could find no other desire inside him.

Not that he intended to explain all of this to the contessa. But, glancing from the sleeping form on the bed back to the woman standing next to him, he saw from the slight change in her expression that he had no need to.

"Ah, you are truly in love, then," she said, shaking her head just a little. "I thought it might be zo, *mon ami*."

"Yes," he said simply.

She patted his arm, as if he were suffering from an incurable malady. "You vill either be *tres* happy or terribly distraught. I vill hope for the first for you, Marcus. She is a remarkable female, I think, and she 'as 'eart. I like her. Does she share your zentiments?"

"I don't know!" he confessed. "I don't know how to know. And I fear what I will learn. If she does not love me, I will be much more than distraught. I will be devastated. If she does, well, people I love tend to leave, whether from their own volition or when they are snatched away."

He hadn't meant to say that, but here in the shadowy dimness, with only a couple of candles burning, and the dancing lights of the fire to light the room, talking to someone with whom he had once been friends, if not ever in love, the words tumbled out without his meaning them to.

She nodded slowly. "Your father's death when you vere only a lad vas hard on you, and 'e vas the only parent you had left. I remember you telling the story of it, Marcuz. But you must trust in zomeone."

"It becomes harder and harder," he said, running his hands through his hair and turning once more to look at Lauryn, as if she might have changed, grown more ill if he took his gaze away for too long.

"You need zomeone to teach you . . . And I vas never able to do it, although I tried." She shrugged again, looking resigned, then gave him a sudden smile. "Perhaps she vill be the one. For your zake, *cheri,* I 'ope zo. I vill still be 'appy to zit with 'er—you must not exhaust yourself. If you need me, call me."

"Thank you," he murmured.

She pulled the door closed after her, and he felt relieved to see her go. He returned to the bed and lay down beside Lauryn, curling up beside her, putting one arm lightly about her shoulders, wanting to protect her from the whole world, if only he could.

They lay that way for some time, and he dozed a little. When Lauryn moved, he woke at once. He looked down at her and saw that her clear green eyes were open, and he could see the firelight glinting off them.

"How do you feel?" he asked her, his voice quiet.

"My throat is dry," she told him, her voice raspy.

He sat up and poured wine from the carafe on the table. She sipped it cautiously.

"Would you like a cup of tea? Or some broth?" he asked. "If so, I will go down to the kitchen and see to it for you." He felt fairly sure he could manage to brew a cup of tea. The broth was a bit more problematic, but he would go out to the servant's cottages and wake the housekeeper if he had to.

She smiled at him. "This is fine."

He pushed a strand of hair back from her face. Her skin was cool—the air was cooling as the fire died down, but at least she had no fever. She still seemed pale, but not as wan as she had been, and a little of his fear for her eased.

"Was someone here?" she asked him.

"The contessa came and offered to sit with you if I wanted to rest," he told her. "Did she disturb you? We tried to talk softly."

Lauryn shook her head just slightly. "No, it wasn't that. I can smell her perfume in the air. Was that all she offered to do?" Her tone was wry.

He grinned. "She has no other services that I am interested in. And as you see, I preferred to stay with you myself."

She lay her head against his arm, and he bent to kiss her gently on her forehead.

She grimaced. "I'm afraid I am not living up to my contract. You must be feeling cheated. I'm sorry I am not up to performing the usual—"

"Do not be sorry for anything," he told her firmly. "I will be the judge of what is expected. And I wish you to rest and feel better."

She sighed. "I admit, I feel as limp as an unstarched cravat."

"Just get well," he repeated. "I have not a thing to complain about."

"I don't see why not," she muttered, but she lay against the curve of his arm, and he held her carefully, as he would something very precious. He watched her close her eyes again and drift into sleep.

The rest of the night was uneventful. Marcus rose early and went downstairs to breakfast, but he returned soon to see how Lauryn was.

He was pleased to see that she was able to consume a little dry toast, though she still felt weak and nauseated.

"It will take some time to get over," he told her. "I've known sailors with these habits, and they cannot be cured quickly, even though you had a small and accidental dose."

"But how long do you mean by 'some time'?" Lauryn asked, looking alarmed.

"Give it another day or two or maybe three at least," he told her, trying to sound soothing.

"This is dreadful stuff, opium," she grumbled. "I'm already tired of being in bed. At least"—she eyed the maid who had come to take away her breakfast tray—"tired of being in bed . . . alone," she finished when the servant had left the room.

Marcus came closer and kissed her hand. "My dear, I do sympathize."

"But you do not intend to do anything to relieve my tedium?" she suggested.

"I doubt that you are really up to any vigorous amusements."

Lauryn seemed to consider, then sighed and shook her head. "Since I feel half the time as if I'm about to lose my few bites of breakfast, no, I suspect I'd better not try. That would tend to destroy the mood," she suggested.

He laughed. If she could joke, then surely she was starting to recover. He kissed both her hands this time. "I'm going to make a quick trip to London, my darling Lauryn. I wish you to stay in bed and allow your body to heal. Carter will be here to keep you secure and look after you, as well as the contessa and the servants, of course."

"Of course," she said politely, adding with a touch of anxiety she could not completely hide, "will you be back soon?"

"Tomorrow or at least the day after, if there are no problems. I have a couple of business errands I need to do, and then I will return as speedily as possible," he told her, knowing he was being vague but choosing not to go into too much detail just as yet. "The weather looks to be fair, and I hope to make good time."

He squeezed her hands, leaned over to kiss her quickly on the lips, then, afraid to stay and be tempted any further, strode away.

By hard riding and changing horses when necessary, he made it to London before nightfall and had the felicity of sleeping in his own bed. The next morning, he took care of his primary business first, then hailed a hackney, not easy as many other Londoners also sought cabs. The wind was freshening and the once blue sky had been replaced by a layer of thick clouds. He hoped he had not been mistaken in the weather, Marcus thought, frowning as he was driven to Viscount Tweed's impressive new London home.

To his annoyance, the footman clad in highly trimmed purple livery who answered the door announced that his master was at his club and he "couldn't say" when he would return. He seemed about to shut the door in Marcus's face.

Annoyed—he could remember when Tweed had lived in rooms above a second-rate tavern—Marcus put up one hand to stop him. "You may tell him that the Earl of Sutton called," he said distinctly. "I need to talk to him, and he will wish to see me."

The footman had the grace to look abashed. "Oh, beg pardon, your lordship. I will tell him that you called. Do you wish to leave a card?" He stepped back to obtain a silver tray to hold out to receive the card that Marcus gave him, as he should have done in the first place.

Tweed needed to see to better training for his servants, not just fancy liveries, Marcus thought as he turned on his heel. He glanced up at the near obscured sun and shook his head. This was a waste of time. He knew Tweed's clubs; he could go by White's and see if he could catch him there.

But when he walked into the men's club and sent a servant there to see if the viscount was in attendance, he sat down long enough to accept a glass of wine and to remember that he himself had sponsored the man. He'd been a likeable if somewhat rough about the edges youth, and Marcus had tried to help him along. Tweed had been ecstatic to be voted a member.

He'd come a long way from the young man who'd started out with risky shares in a trading ship or two, scrabbling hard to make his fortune. When he'd inherited the title unexpectedly from an uncle, when two cousins as well as their father had died during an influenza epidemic on the Border, his life had changed a great deal. Now here he was wooing a young lady just out, and he seemed to be on the verge of a comfortable and settled existence.

The footman interrupted this reverie to report that the viscount had just departed.

"Dammit," Marcus muttered. He seemed to be one step behind Tweed everywhere in London. He sent the footman to hail yet another cab, and when eventually one was obtained, put down his glass and set out once more.

It was back to the viscount's house, hoping that this was where he had returned. This time Marcus greeted the same footman, who at least was more courteous, but again, the news was not good.

"I'm sorry, your lordship. He has departed the city."

"What?" Marcus stared at the man in disbelief. "Did you give him my card?"

"Yes, my lord. I did."

"Didn't you tell him I was here, in London, and I wanted to see him?"

"Yes, my lord."

"Why didn't he wait?"

"I do not know, my lord. He said he must go at once."

Marcus almost demanded to be allowed inside to inspect the house himself. He could hardly believe that Tweed had packed and departed in such a short time, and why, for the love of all that was holy?

How had he not understood that Marcus was here, now?

And then, to top everything, the heavens opened, and rain fell in heavy sheets—well, he hoped that Tweed had a sodden and miserable ride, Marcus thought, still angry.

He turned and stepped back into his hackney and directed it to his own address, where he dashed inside. As much as he wanted to set out himself, it would be utter folly. The rain fell so heavily that it was hard to see. Thunder rumbled outside, and thick gray clouds obscured the sun. The roads would be thick with mud by nightfall.

He gritted his teeth. Lauryn was there, and he wished to see her with his own eyes, be sure that she was continuing to mend. He wanted to hold her, feel her warmth and her sweetness. But as dearly as he wanted to depart, he would have to wait.

If he were a superstitious man, Marcus would have said that someone had set a gypsy's curse against him, as one of his old nannies had used to fear. It rained heavily for the next three days. By the time the rain let up, his self-control was showing signs of serious strain.

Even then, he debated over whether to take one of his carriages—he might need it if the rains returned. On the other hand, a horse might get through muddy roads where a carriage's wheels would be mired. He decided to take the horse, even if he could face the danger of being drenched to the skin if the rain deepened again.

So, with only a change of clothes and a few necessities in the bags behind his saddle, Marcus set out again to ride north.

The roads were still in wretched condition; the water had had little time to drain off, and the mud was still deep. He had to go slowly, allowing his horse to pick its way through much of the sticky mess.

Worse, when he was barely a third of the way into his journey, he was met with bad news. The river Ouse was out of its banks, and the bridge and roadway flooded. There was no way across.

Swearing, he knew there was no answer but to retrace his steps. He turned his tired horse and started back the way he had come, trailed by two other riders and a mud-stained gig with a father and his young son, and a farmer with a cart full of turnips.

But they had all trudged little more than a mile before an even sadder sight presented itself. A carriage had slipped into the ditch at the side of the road. The horses were still struggling in the traces, neighing and snorting in a panic, and he could hear shrieks of dismay from inside the vehicle, as well.

Sighing, Marcus knew he had no choice but to stop and do what he could to help. He pulled his gelding to a stop and slid off the animal's back, tying him to a nearby tree.

Where was the coachman?

"Ach," one of the other horsemen shook his head. "Poor man. He got caught under the team when they fell, I would say." He motioned to a figure lying very still at the side of the ditch. Marcus grimaced. He went down to check, just in case, but found there was nothing they could do, so he pulled the long cape out from beneath the quiet form and spread it over the body to cover him decently. Next, he went quickly to the carriage and looked inside.

He saw a woman with a trickle of blood on her cheek, and two children, who huddled against her. The boy was very pale, and his leg seemed to be bent at an odd angle.

"Are you hurt?" Marcus called.

"Mostly cuts and bruises, except for my son. I fear his leg may be broken," the woman said. She sounded tremulous.

"Try to hold him steady; we must see to the horses first, or they may overturn the carriage," he called to her.

Then Marcus went back to the front, where the farmer from the cart was already trying to catch the near horse's head, but the beast was frightened and hard to control.

"They're in a panic," Marcus said quietly. "Do you have any cloth with you, that we can tie over their eyes?"

"Aye, I've some empty feed sacks," the man said. He went back to his wagon and returned in a few minutes with coarse bags, which Marcus ripped into strips. Of course, he still had to catch the animal's head and hold it still.

Marcus came up from behind the near horse, while the farmer took the animal on the other side. "Here now," Marcus spoke quietly to the horse, who danced within his tangled leads, whinnying with fear. The animal had a gash on his right rear hind leg, but didn't seem to be badly injured. "Here now, it will be all right."

The horse half reared once more, then shook its head and seemed to listen to the calm tone of his voice. With a smooth motion, he slipped the band around its nose and up over its eyes. Unable to see, the horse stood suddenly still. Marcus rubbed its head and neck for another minute, speaking quietly, then he leaned over and, with the knife he'd borrowed from the farmer, cut the tangled leads where they threatened to trip up its legs, so that they could lead the horse away presently.

On the other side, the farmer had settled the other rear horse in a similar fashion.

Of the two horses in the lead, one was on its side, too badly injured to be able to get to its feet. One of the other men, who said he was a courier, had a pistol with him; when the third horse had been separated from its mate and led away along with the other two, he brought his gun and put the poor beast out of its misery.

The gun blast sounded loud in the quiet countryside. Marcus walked back to reassure the people still waiting inside the carriage.

"Is it one of the team?" the lady inside asked.

He nodded. "The right front lead. It was too badly injured to save," he told her.

She nodded. "And my coachman?"

He shook his head, and she paled. "Let's see about getting you out."

"My son, first," she told him.

With help from one of the other men, they propped the carriage door open and reached in to lift the boy out as gently as they could. The lad gasped when they jarred his wounded limb, and before they were able to set him down on the muddy ground, he had gone so white Marcus thought he might pass out.

The little girl came next, and then, with their assistance, the woman climbed out. She hastened to see about her son. "I need to get him to a surgeon," she said, observing his wan face with a worried appearance of her own.

"If I may," Marcus told her. "I think we should set his leg and make a splint to support it before he is bounced about any further. Otherwise, the journey will only cause more damage to his injury."

She hesitated, then nodded. "Do you have any experience?" she asked, twisting her bloodstained handkerchief, which she had been using to wipe her children's cuts, nervously between her hands.

"I have set my servants' limbs, and those of my troop, when I served in the army," he told her.

He knelt down beside the child, who clutched his mother's arm when she hurried to him, the little girl on her other side. Marcus took out his penknife and ripped the cloth of the boy's trousers so he could check the wound as gently as he could, although the child still shivered. Marcus was relieved to see that it appeared to be a clean break.

He sent one of the others to find two straight tree limbs; when the man returned with cut saplings of suitable length, the farmer stripped the bark off with a small hatchet from his wagon.

Marcus turned back to the youngster. "All right now. What's your name, my lad?"

The boy looked at him with some misgivings. "Richard."

"This is going to hurt, Richard, but I need you to be brave. We want your leg to grow straight when the bone heals itself, do we not? So you will be able to walk again and not limp forever?"

"Yes!" said, the lad who looked about six years old. "I don't want to be a bent over cripple. I will be brave."

"It will be one bad pain, and we will not mind if you wish to yell," Marcus told him. "Sometimes men even need to cry; it is no disgrace."

"I will not cry!" Richard said, his tone stubborn.

The child blinked hard as Marcus took hold of his leg, and when he pulled hard on the bone, the boy grunted more than yelled. He had gone very pale, and then he had to wipe his eyes, but he said at once, "I didn't cry!"

"Of course you didn't," Marcus agreed. "You were very brave, indeed."

"Indeed," Richard's mother told him, blinking hard herself and touching his cheek, while his younger sister looked on in awe.

Meanwhile Marcus worked rapidly to tie the pieces of wood on each side of the leg, to keep the bone from slipping out of place again.

He conferred with the other travelers. The gig was very short on space, but the wagon had no springs. In the end, they decided that putting the mother and boy in the gig was perhaps the best bet.

"How far do you need to travel back to your home?" Marcus asked Richard's mother.

"I have a sister whose house is outside the next village," she told them. "I can stop there; she can get word to my husband, who will see about the carriage and"—she gestured toward the silent body beside the road—"our poor servant."

One of her horses was tame enough to allow the gig's owner and his son and her daughter to ride astride and follow behind the gig so he could reclaim his vehicle when they were safely delivered to her sister's house.

After she had thanked them all profusely, Marcus saw them off. Then he and the rest of the travelers continued on their way, as he circumvented the flooded out highway and continued on his own journey.

By now, however, he had lost so much daylight, he knew he would have to spend the night at the next village, along with many of the other travelers. And when he and several others arrived, the only inn was sold out of beds. There was no hope of a private room as the inn was so crowded, but Marcus thought it just as well. Looking at the state of the tavern, he thought that he'd likely have left with a good selection of bedbugs.

He was able to buy an ale and a dish of stew for himself, but the public room was heavy with smoke, full of the scent of unwashed bodies and the bedlam of many voices talking, snatches of an argument here and a drunken song there.

When he finished his meal, Marcus went out to the stable to see to his horse, not trusting the local ostler. When he finished, he wrapped his cloak around him and sat down, leaning against a bale of reasonably clean straw, and shut his eyes. At least the stable was fairly quiet, as opposed to the taproom.

The next morning he set out again, and by late afternoon he finally approached his own hunting lodge. He was relieved to see that here the rain had apparently not been as heavy, and there was no sign of flooding. His hunting box was built on higher ground, and they had never had water threaten them here.

He urged his horse on and rode quickly up the drive, jumping off and hurrying to the door. A servant opened it at his knock, and came out to take his horse around.

"Good to see you back, my lord."

"How is Mrs. Smith?" Marcus asked.

"Doing well, my lord," the footman said cheerfully. "She came to dinner last night."

"Excellent," Marcus said. He felt better already. "Where is my brother?"

"Ah, I don't rightly know, your lordship."

About to head straight for the stairs, Marcus paused and looked back. "What? What do you mean, you don't know?"

"He went into town, my lord," the footman said. "He hasn't as yet come back."

"Carter, you imbecile," Marcus muttered beneath his breath, "is this how you protect the ladies?"

Thirteen

*M*arcus *hesitated, not sure whether to head at once into* town to find his idiot brother—no, first he had to see Lauryn, to see for himself that she was better, and just see her.

He strode into the house and up the stairs, pausing to look into the sitting room. He had not really expected to find her there, but to his surprise, he found both ladies sitting demurely on the sofa drinking cups of tea.

Lauryn glanced up, and her expression showed both pleasure and some concern.

"My lord, are you all right?"

He came inside the room and leaned over to kiss her, caring not at all that the contessa stared at them both. "Of course," he said, "why should I not be?" Only then did he remember what a sight he was. Streaked with mud from his exertions at the carriage accident, he also still had bits of straw clinging to him from his night spent with the horses.

Belatedly, he bowed to them both.

"Do forgive me. I spent last night sleeping in a stable. Before that, the road was washed out from flooding and I had to travel the long way around. On the way, I came upon a family who had suffered a carriage accident and did what I could to aid them. So as you can see, I had numerous delays getting back to you, and I am not as neat as I would like to be when presenting myself to two ladies." He looked down at himself and shook his head.

"I think you have ample reason to be forgiven," Lauryn told him, and the contessa laughed aloud.

"My *pauvre* Zutton, you are always the hero," she said, raising her brows and giving him a mischievous smile.

"Nonsense," he said, but he glanced back at Lauryn. She smiled, too. "I'm glad you're back in one piece," she told him. "It sounds like a most harrowing journey, my lord."

"I am more concerned that my feckless brother is not here, when I expressly gave him charge over you," he told them, feeling angry again. "I will change and go into town and see if I can run him down."

"But, that makes not the logic at all," the contessa pointed out. "You leave uz alone to go to rebuke *pauvre* Carter because 'e 'as left uz alone?"

"It's almost dinnertime, he should return at any time," Lauryn added. "And you must be tired, my lord."

He wanted to tell her that she didn't have to "my lord" him, but he knew that in public, she wouldn't call him by his Christian name. Which made him ache to get her into more private circumstances, for that and other even more pertinent reasons.

Perhaps they were both right, and he should wait to chastise Carter. He was tired and hungry, and he wanted to hold Lauryn, feel his arms about her once again. Damn his brother anyhow, couldn't he do what he was told just once in his life?

Marcus turned and walked across to the window. No, he had enough daylight left to ride into town and check the largest hotels and inns—there were only a couple—and he wanted to find Carter in the act—as it were—before his brother came riding home with another excuse for his irresponsible acts, as he always did.

Then Marcus could ride back and celebrate a proper reunion with Lauryn, who looked delightfully healthy once more, finally with a little color in her cheeks. He turned back to smile at her, hoping to convey a promise.

"I am going into town, but I will make it a short trip," he told them. "I think I know where to find my errant brother. Tell the servants I will return in time for dinner."

Looking resigned, Lauryn nodded.

The contessa made a clucking noise with her tongue. "Be on your guard, Zutton."

"Of course." He bowed to them again and headed back outside.

He had a fresh horse saddled in the stable, then rode for town. He made no effort to put aside his irritation, and with every mile closer, his anger only grew. If Carter had just listened—just because he'd been cut off from his drinking friends, his gaming, blast him—what excuse could he give this time?

When Marcus rode into the area near the harbor, he kept a close eye on the faces around him, knowing he was near his brother's usual haunts. He pulled up his horse near the hotel by the harbor. It was the best place to stay, and also had the best tavern in which to drink and gamble. If Carter were not here, there were only a couple of other likely places to check; it was not a very big town.

Marcus tossed his reins to a groom, and started inside the doors of the hotel, when a familiar profile made him stop so short he almost stumbled.

It was not his brother's face, which he had expected to see.

"Tweed!" he said, startled.

The other man, who was shorter and stockier, turned and frowned at him. He had been about to walk out of the hotel, but now he turned back and faced the earl.

"What did you expect?" his sometime business partner snapped. "You've been sending me letters and notes demanding that I come, haven't you? Well, here I damn well am! I've been down to the warehouse twice, and your bloody guards won't even let me in, so what the hell do you think I'm going to do to support you?"

Marcus couldn't help it. He leaned back against the hotel's doorframe and laughed out loud.

Tweed balled his hands into fists and his plain face flushed an ugly shade of red. "Damn you, Sutton, are you making sport of me? I finally find the girl I want to marry, and I had to leave her in London open to all the damn young twigs of fashion who are trying to steal her out from beneath my eye, just so I can come up here to help you go through moldy boxes of china. God knows what the hell good that's going to do, and you have the nerve to laugh in my face!"

"No, no!" Marcus said hastily. "It's not that. But I was in London, man. I came all that way, and you didn't wait to see me. I told your footman—why the bloody hell didn't you stay put and wait for me to return to your house?"

"What?" Tweed stared at him. "I thought"—he slowly relaxed his hands—"Oh, hell's bells. What a mess. Serves you right for locking me out of my own warehouse. Come on, let's have a drink."

"A fast one," Marcus told him. "I need to find my brother. And we do need to talk at length, but it will have to be tomorrow."

"Tomorrow?" Tweed looked outraged. "I need to get back to London. I have to—"

"I know, I know, you have courting to do," Marcus nodded. "I do sympathize with the pangs of a man in love."

Eyes narrowed in suspicion, Tweed stared at him.

"No, I'm serious, but still, you owe me at least a day, considering the trek you put me through," Marcus told him. "Come on, I'm buying."

He slapped the viscount on the back; the man felt stiff with his wounded feelings. Tweed had always found it hard to unbend. They walked inside and on to the bar where Marcus asked for two ales.

"Make mine a Scotch," Tweed said. "Now, why the damned brigade at the warehouse, and why would they not let me in to inspect the—"

"Moldy boxes?" Marcus finished for him. "Because we have had a break-in, and a guard killed earlier this week."

"Killed?" Tweed stared at him. "What on earth did they think was inside that was so valuable? The thieves must have been disappointed. How much did they take away?"

"Nothing that we could tell, that was the strange thing," Marcus told him.

Tweed shrugged and picked up his glass. After he swallowed a mouthful, he said, "Not so strange, they found nothing they expected to find. They swore a lot and got out before they were caught, that was all."

Marcus stared at the shorter man, who was looking into his glass. "Mayhap. But it still seems singular to me."

"What else?" Tweed demanded. "You said you wanted a long talk."

"I do, but I don't have time to go into it now. You know we had a suggestion of trouble on that ship before she even set sail, and then when she was reported missing—well, she seemed to carry her own curse, didn't she?" Marcus shook his head. "I'll be back early tomorrow, and we'll get you back on your way to London and your chosen lassie as soon as we may."

Tweed made a sour face, but he didn't protest again.

Marcus left him getting another drink, and, since there was no sign of Carter, left the bar to seek out another tavern. Where the hell was his brother?

He decided to leave his horse at the hotel and walked the two blocks to another tavern, but when he ducked his head to enter the low doorway and blinked at the dim light and smoky air, he made out a dozen or so patrons drinking, talking, gathered in boisterous groups at short-legged tables. But once again, he saw no sign of Carter.

Now what?

He had been sure that he would find his brother at one of these drinking spots. Unless he had found a willing barmaid, in which case, heaven only knew where an assignation was taking place as Marcus stood here, frowning at the thought . . .

Suddenly, he remembered the tavern on Two Hen Street where the odd little china shop stood, where he had traced the Asian to, the shop he was having watched. It was a small tavern, but perhaps worth checking out. He would have to go carefully; he didn't wish his face to be too well known on that street, but if he approached the tavern cautiously, he didn't have to be seen from the shop itself.

He strode off, walking quickly, thinking it more prudent and less obvious to come near the tavern on foot than by horseback, and it was only a few streets away. The sun was lower in the sky, and the temperature dropping, but he heeded it not at all.

This tavern, and this street, was somewhat less reputable, but in his present mud-stained condition, Marcus fit right in. In fact, he thought as he peeled off another clinging bit of straw from his jacket, just now he doubted that anyone would have claimed him as a gentleman, much less a lord.

He went into the tavern and, buying another ale, looked around at the dimly lit taproom. At this late hour, the pub was full of working men stopping on their way home for their brews, and it was noisy, too, and full of smoke. But although it took him a few minutes to check out all the faces, once more he came up with no answers. Where the bloody hell was his misbegotten younger brother?

And where was their man who should be watching the shop? Marcus looked covertly about him. Perhaps it was the quiet man with the scar on his face who sat at the side of the window, nursing an ale. Marcus did not try to speak to him, but noted his face for future reference.

However, Marcus took the dark brew over to the other side of the window where an empty stool presented itself as a carpenter, by the look of his sawdust-covered apron, got up and walked with slightly unsteady steps toward the door.

"Best get home," he told his mates. "Wife'll have the poker after me head, else!"

Jeers and laughter met this attempt at high comedy, but Marcus paid little heed. He was staring at the china shop up the street. The sun had dropped so low that the first blush of color was streaking the sky; he knew he should head back to the hotel and reclaim his horse. He should ride for home before darkness descended. He needed a bath and his dinner, and he certainly wanted Lauryn in his arms.

But he had a clear view of the shop where the mysterious lurker had returned to, and to Marcus's dismay, he saw someone come out of the door of the shop, a face and a frame that he knew all too well.

Carter!

What the bloody hell was Carter doing in the Asian's shop? Marcus forgot to be gratified that he had finally run his brother to earth in his dismay at where he had found him.

Was Carter—could it be that Carter was connected to the mystery man? Could he be working the group smuggling opium?

Marcus felt cold inside. His harum-scarum half brother . . . It was true that Carter had been in trouble often enough, boyish mischief, for the most part, petticoat problems, lack of applying himself, his father had said. After their father had died, Marcus had continued to pull him out of his scrapes, when he could. But he'd worried that Carter was never going to grow up, would always be irresponsible.

Could Carter be capable of true criminal behavior? Marcus had never contemplated such a possibility. But Carter was always about; he could have picked up information about Marcus's shipping, enough to manage to get the opium on his trading ships, enough to manage to send intelligence to his confederates in a smuggling ring.

Smuggling, murder . . .

It made his blood run cold to think of his baby brother up to his neck in such affairs . . .

Marcus found he had lost his taste for the ale. He put his glass—which he had brought up to his lips—slowly back down.

Carter was walking down the street, right past the tavern. He wore a satisfied smile on his lips.

Marcus had to turn his face away from the window. He could not decide whether to confront his brother right now, or wait. What was he to say?

Did he wait to see if Carter admitted going to the shop? Was there any chance there could be an innocent explanation? If so, Marcus could not think of it. His mind seemed to have stalled, like a spinning waterwheel with no water to push it.

He sat there a few moments more, then rose and went out of the pub, turned, and followed his brother's back down the street. Carter was going back toward the harbor. He returned to the same hotel where Tweed was staying. He headed toward the stable, perhaps on the same errand that Marcus would shortly perform. Yes, in a moment, a groom came out with his brother's horse. Carter handed over some coins, put his leg up, and mounted his steed.

Marcus let him go—he was surely headed for home—and then went to retrieve his own mount. As he retraced the familiar road home, he did not try to catch his brother up. For one thing, he wanted the time to think, and he had not yet decided how to handle this situation. He would certainly have something to say about leaving the women alone with only the servants to watch over them. But there was also the even bigger mystery of Carter's presence at the shop where the Asians were present. How did Carter know of it, how deeply was he involved, if he was involved at all . . .

Marcus felt as tense as if he were riding into battle, and his stomach roiled. His brother—how could this be?

By the time the sun, a huge glorious burning ball, had fallen over the western horizon, its last rays fading slowly behind it and twilight spread across the lavender sky, with crickets crying loudly into the growing darkness, Marcus saw the torches of the hunting box ahead.

He rode his horse around to the stable and put it away himself, still putting off the moment when he would have to decide how to handle his painful discovery. Then, at last, he strode toward the house.

When he knocked, the footman answered at once. "My lord," he said, swinging the door open wide.

Marcus strode inside and up to the next landing, where he found everyone gathered in the sitting room.

The two women had already changed for dinner. Carter was still in his riding clothes, and he greeted his brother with an easy grin. "I see I just beat you home," he said. "A hard trip to London, Brother?"

"Indeed," Marcus agreed. "And why did I find you not at

home where I had asked you to stay, Carter?" His voice sounded even grimmer than he had meant it to, but all his emotion was hard to control. And Carter would, of course, have already learned from the ladies that his elder brother had discovered that he had been away. He did not know, as far as Marcus knew, that his brother knew just where he had gone.

"I thought I would do a little detection on your behalf, since you had to be away in London," Carter told him, looking triumphant.

That answer, he had not been expecting.

"And what did you learn?" he asked slowly.

"*Non, non*," the contessa said. "You are a great mess, Zutton. You must change, or ve vill never have our dinner. Then Carter can tell uz his tale."

And the delay would give his brother more time to concoct his tale, if he needed to, Marcus thought. But he certainly could not sit down to a civilized table in his condition. Nodding to the ladies, he withdrew, going up the steps to the next level two at a time.

In his bedroom, he was pleased to see that the servants had brought up warm water for his bath. He lathered and rinsed to finally get off the mud and dirt of several days, then dressed in clean dinner clothes and felt much better. When he finished, he hurried back down, knowing they would not announce dinner until he had returned.

Sure enough, as soon as he came back into the sitting room, the footman ushered them to the dining room, and Marcus offered his arm to Lauryn.

She took it at once, and he found her touch both stimulating and delightful. "I have missed you," he murmured into her ear as they headed toward the dining room.

"And I you," she breathed back, pressing his arm. "So much!"

Smiling as he felt his body respond to her light touch, he took her to her seat at the table, thinking that hungry as he was, there were other, deeper hungers that plagued him even more.

"Now, Carter," the contessa commanded when they were

all seated, as if she were queen and this her court, "tell uz all about your mystery zolving."

Marcus looked up from the piece of savory roast beef he had been about to take a bite of. "Oh yes, we certainly want to hear this," he agreed, his tone dry.

"Ah," his brother said, beaming. "I do think I deserve some praise this time, Brother mine. I discovered that someone was watching our warehouse."

"Our warehouse?" Marcus muttered beneath his breath. Already, he had a bad feeling about this tale of adventure.

Carter continued to look triumphant. "I went round just to check that all was well, having heard the story of the murdered guards, don't you know?"

The ladies stared, and the contessa squealed. "*Alors*, thiz itz too bad!"

"So I wanted to check out the warehouse, since Marcus was gone, and be sure all was shipshape," his brother continued, still sounding very pleased with himself. "Since we have many valuables stored inside."

Marcus felt a surge of annoyance, but tried to control his expression. He glanced at Lauryn, who was eating her soup, and thought how much more valuable were the contents of this house, and this was where Carter had been supposed to stay!

"And by God, I found this strange man, some foreigner, not even an Englishman, lurking in the alley nearby, watching the warehouse. So I followed him back to a shop half a dozen streets away."

"And you went into the shop? So he knows your face?" Marcus interjected.

"Ah, yes," Carter admitted. "What was wrong with that? I wanted to see what kind of place it was. And it was selling chinaware, too, though not as valuable as the stuff we have in our warehouse, so it just goes to show, don't you think he might have been involved with the burglary attempt?"

Or much more, Marcus thought, feeling Lauryn's gaze on his face.

"A valid assumption," he said, and Carter grinned broadly

once more. "But better not to have trailed him back, as he probably knew he was being followed."

"I was careful," Carter protested. "I don't think he was aware that I was behind him."

Marcus raised his brows. His younger brother had all the subtlety of a drunken sailor, but he would not embarrass him in front of the ladies by voicing that thought aloud.

"It appears you vere quite the sleuth today, Carter," the contessa remarked. "I did not know you had it in you."

Carter preened and took a sip of his wine. "I can do more than some people"—he glanced at his brother—"give me credit for."

Marcus ignored the comment and concentrated on his dinner. He was enormously hungry after the long trip and several missed meals. The aromas of beef and fresh bread wafting across the table made him appreciate the skills of his cook even more after the privations of the journey.

"I'm sure you do many things well," Lauryn said politely. For the most part, however, she said little during dinner.

Once Marcus saw a worried look cross her face. She saw the dangers, too, he suspected, now that his heedless younger brother had likely alerted the smugglers that they were being watched.

When the ladies withdrew to the sitting room, there was silence for a minute or two as the footman brought them a bottle of port. Marcus poured some into his glass and passed the bottle to Carter.

"How did you hear?" he asked, suddenly.

His brother jumped. "What?"

"How did you hear about the murdered guard?"

Carter turned to frown at him. "Since you didn't bother to tell me, you mean? From a gossiping barmaid, if you must know. You can't expect a crime like that not to be whispered about all over town. But why didn't you tell me, Marcus? Why must you insist on treating me as if I'm so bloody undependable that you cannot trust me with any important fact or errand?"

"I gave you the most important task," Marcus interrupted, not caring to hear a litany of self-pity. "I asked you to keep watch over the two females, who can hardly be expected to protect themselves. We've already seen that the gang we are up against will not stop at spilling blood. Yet I come home to find that you have left the women on their own, with only a handful of servants around them."

He met his brother's startled gaze with a hard look of his own.

"You didn't tell me that!"

"I should not have to explain everything. Can you not take me at my word?"

"You don't explain anything! If you treated me like a man, instead of forever like a ten-year-old, dammit all—" Carter gulped down a mouthful of port and then slammed the glass down on the table and pushed back his chair. He stalked out of the room, not looking back.

It didn't appear to occur to him that he most often acted like an angry child, Marcus thought, running his hands through his hair and leaning his elbows on the table, his face in his hands.

He felt very weary.

Was he being unfair to his brother?

Even worse, was Carter putting on a show of wounded feelings to cover up darker motives?

How could Marcus tell?

Lauryn sat in the sitting room and made polite conversa-tion with the contessa, but she had to hide the fact that she was watching the clock on the mantel from the corner of her eye. She had missed the earl so intently that she couldn't bear for him to be out of her sight. She could hardly wait for it to be time to retire, so they could have privacy, could embrace, so she could be in his arms again at long last.

When she heard footsteps, she turned eagerly to see Marcus in the doorway. Slightly to her surprise, however, he was alone.

"Your brother is not vith you?" the contessa said, sounding surprised.

"I thought he was here," the earl said. "Perhaps he is tired after his long day and has gone up to bed."

There was nothing to say to that except to nod and pretend that healthy young men often retired early. Lauryn saw that Marcus had a crease in his forehead and his voice seemed overly controlled. Had the two brothers quarreled?

Perhaps the earl felt that his brother's actions today had not been the wisest. Still, they could not discuss it just now. Perhaps it would not be advisable to discuss it at all, she told herself. The contessa went to the small pianoforte at the end of the sitting room and sat down before it.

"Vould you like zome music, Marcus?" she asked.

"Of course, if you feel up to playing," he said politely.

The lady arranged some sheet music on the stand and moved her hands gracefully over the keys, and the notes flowed smoothly. They could not, in civility, talk, but Lauryn was content just to have the earl sit beside her on the settee and to revel in his nearness, after the wasteland of his absence.

It reminded her much too painfully of how it would be when they were parted for good. How would she stand it?

That was too grievous to consider; she pushed the thought away from her.

After some time, the contessa rose and returned to sit with them.

"That was beautifully played," Lauryn told her.

"Merci," the other woman said. "I try to keep myzelf in practize."

They talked awhile about music and a display of paintings that the contessa and the earl had visited, separately, in London. Presently the footman brought in a tea tray, and they had a last cup of tea. Then, at last, they could go up to bed.

Lauryn felt her spirits lift as she walked demurely up the staircase. But with the contessa on her own, alone in the other bedchamber, it would be very poor form to skip up the stairs, laughing aloud because she could at last be once more alone with Marcus.

Nonetheless, stealing one glance at the earl, who walked

beside her and could look back with his eyes twinkling, she knew he understood and shared her feelings. So she had to fight to hold her smiles inside.

When the door closed behind them, she turned and threw her arms about the earl's neck. "Oh, I have missed you so," she exclaimed, pulling him as close as she could and burying her face in the clean-smelling linen that covered his chest.

Marcus kissed the top of her head, and for a moment he was simply content to hold her, surfeit with the feel of her warm, healthy body in his arms. She was here, she was his—life was good.

She laid her cheek against his chest and they stood there for several long minutes. Then she sighed, and he looked down at her.

"What's wrong?"

"Nothing," she said quickly. "Everything is right; you are here."

He felt a surge of happiness.

"Tell me about your trip; it must have been very difficult, with the flood and the carriage accident and all."

He sat down in the wide chair by the fireplace and pulled her onto his lap. He told her about helping out when he had discovered the carriage mishap.

"How sad," Lauryn said, her voice sober. "And the poor little boy. Do you think he will be all right?"

"With careful nursing, he should be, and I'm sure his mother will see to that," he told her, tightening his arms about her.

For a few moments he simply sat there, allowing the feel of her in his arms to sink in, needing the physical reassurance. She was here, and had not somehow disappeared in the time he had been away. She had waited for him. She had met him with open arms.

The soft warmth of her body gradually dispelled the cold knot of fear that had been inside him, without him even knowing.

She put her arm about his neck and in a moment lifted one hand to stroke his hair, combing the dark strands with her fingers.

There was a look in her eyes he could not decipher, but just having her so close eased him, and other more purely physical feelings quickly rose. He took her free hand and raised it to his lips, kissing it gently, turning it and tracing the line of her palm, kissing it again and feeling her whole body quiver in response. The way she responded so intensely to him, to his touch, pleased him deeply.

"I've missed you," she told him, her voice low and tremulous. She leaned closer to kiss his ear, nibble lightly on its lobe. He felt his need intensify yet again.

"And I, you, more than I can tell you," he answered. His voice, too, had changed, grown husky. He put his hand up to cup her cheek, pulled her face down so he could kiss her lips, gently at first, then when she met him eagerly, with more force, allowing his hunger to surface. She answered with her own need.

Her lips were warm and smooth and luscious, and they opened willingly for him. His tongue slipped inside, and he thought he might happily submerge himself in the warm feminine depths of her mouth, a small reflection of the other warm and even more enticing depths yet to come.

And on that thought, he clasped both arms about her slender body, lifted her easily, and carried her across to the bed, placing her in the center and throwing himself over her—catching himself on his arms so that he didn't press his weight upon her too heavily—so that not one precious moment would be wasted.

Lauryn felt him lean over her, smelled the particular masculine aroma, touched his cheek and felt the subtle coarseness of male skin. He was intensely male, and it spoke to her on every level. When he kissed her, she reached up to pull him closer, kissed him back hungrily, wanted to merge with him, press her body closer, feel the strength of him, the firmness of his torso and the hardness of his muscled arms and legs when he pulled her even closer, as if their two bodies could become one.

He rolled onto his side and his arm pulled her into him. She slid easily into his grip, clinging to him, kissing him wildly until they were both breathless. Then they paused only to push his jacket aside and she helped him as he pulled off his neckcloth and twisted till it unwound, then stripped off his linen shirt.

Next came the fiddly buttons on the back of her dress. In his impatience Marcus tugged at the buttons, and she heard a few threads break; she didn't care. There were no words spoken and no need for words—only the need driving her, pushing him—the hunger that ached inside her and surely inside him as well. She pushed the skirt down and pulled at the bodice and then turned her back so he could make short work of her stays, and still there was more clothing to shed.

Oh, to be a savage, she thought, to return to Eden with fig leaves and animal skins and go straight to the primal state. But finally she was down to her shift and her drawers, and then she was free of it all, and Marcus had his strong hands on her, touching her skin, putting his lips on her breast. His lips seemed to burn into her skin, scorching her like a brand, and she jerked with the cold heat of them.

Then he was suckling at one breast, and she took the back of his head and stroked his dark hair, as his tongue surrounded her nipple and eased it into tense alertness. Her breasts ached for more; the other wanted the same delicious care, and she pushed his mouth to the other side, so he could repeat his caresses. Then he dropped his lips to her stomach, kissing the tender skin while she moaned and moved ceaselessly on the linen sheets— it felt too amazingly good to lie immobile. He sent currents of liquid need coursing through her body, and she could not seem to lie still.

And in the deepest part of her, there the great hunger still awaited his touch, and as always, Marcus knew. He slipped his hand down to cup her private place, where she was wet with need, and she arched, she was so ready for him. He traced his fingers there, the secret places—the special places—she gasped. It felt so achingly joyous it was almost edged with pain.

"I want you, Marcus," she whispered. "Now, my dear, now!"

And he positioned himself over her, lifting her hips so that he could thrust himself into her at just the right angle, and then he pushed hard, and she gasped again at the pleasure he gave her.

"Yes," she said, and she moved with him, in the rhythmic beat that was older than time, the dance that men and women had perfected when the dawn was barely born. And the joy was as deep as the first time, and as always, it seemed that this was the best time of all. He pushed deeper and deeper and harder and harder, and she wanted him to go on and on. She moved with him, and the pleasure of it circled in her and through her, winging past thought and mind, moving beyond emotion, bringing with it a primal joy that bound them together into one body, one soul, one being older than thought.

When at last he came with a spasm of wonderful force, she was floating so high, so wide, the joy blossoming into such ever-widening flares of shooting stars, that for once, she did not to her surprise come with him into a delightful spiral of completion, fading down to fall into his arms and drift into delightful exhaustion. Instead she continued to rise, higher and higher. She stared up at Marcus in a bewildered but joyous haze of passion.

"Don't try to stop, darling," he murmured. "You're past the moon—keep going, my love, keep going." He kissed her heartily, and as he pulled himself out below, pushed several fingers into her, slipping them in and out to keep the rhythm going so that she still floated, still arched herself against him, unable to believe that she was still experiencing the aching pleasure of greater and greater intensity, joy that rippled through her, over her, over her whole body, like ice and fire, till every inch of her skin seemed aflame. She was created anew by Marcus's tender handling, and every thing he touched felt exquisitely joyous.

How long she floated, flew, sailed, she had no idea, but she did not stop, and presently, he was leaning over her again, firm again, wonderfully hard as his shaft once more pushed just where it should be. Together they arched, rose and fell, came together in glorious and speechless ecstasy.

And somewhere at the top of the farthest star, this time they peaked together, and the bursting joy, like a bubble of golden light, gilded them both with the satiation of complete delight. Lauryn shut her eyes and lay back, cradled in the sanctuary of his arms, and wondered if she had the strength left to breathe.

Tendrils of her damp hair stuck to her cheek, but nothing mattered except lying close to the man she loved, feeling his breath warm against her cheek, his heart beating beneath her hand, and remembering how they had circled the heavens together.

He held her carefully, as if she were something precious to him, and she had never felt so totally loved, as if every strand of her body had been unwound and she floated on an ocean of joy. This must be what heaven felt like.

*The next morning Lauryn woke to see pale rays of sun*light slanting through the half-pulled draperies, which they had never shut. Marcus lay on his stomach, his head turned to one side, and he looked open and vulnerable as he slept.

She touched one lock of his dark hair, careful not to wake him. What an extraordinary night . . . they continued to find new heights to climb, new prospects to ascend to . . . Yet how long would she be allowed to spend with him?

It had been a long time since he had mentioned their agreement, the time limit he had imposed. He certainly seemed satisfied with her performance, just as she was continually joyfully surprised with his! But she knew, as much as she wanted to push the knowledge aside, that they could not live forever on this one golden isle, isolated from the rest of the world. At some point, Marcus would have to resume his real life, and so would she. Not matter how wonderful their love-making, she could not spend the rest of her life as a kept woman, living a life that was not really who she was, who she was supposed to be.

She had thought she could assume this identify for a few

days or a few weeks, but as deeply as she had tumbled into loving this amazing and complicated man, could she put aside her own identity to make him happy?

Almost, she could, Lauryn thought, her heart twisting. But to give up forever her status, more, her honor, her integrity. . . .

And why, of all times, after the most glorious lovemaking of her life, when she still basked in the glow of it, when her whole body felt easy and rested and complete, full of health and vigor, her spirits high, her heart happy, should she be thinking this now?

She loved him.

She had known it for days. She didn't want to give him up. But could she give herself up, even for Marcus, even for the exquisite joys he brought her, even when he often gazed at her with what she would have sworn was love in his eyes, despite the fact that he had declared the term itself forbidden?

She had never faced such a difficult choice.

Shutting her eyes against the sunlight, which shone stronger by the minute, Lauryn wondered how much longer it would be until she had to decide. Sighing, she leaned across the pillow to kiss his cheek very lightly, then turned and slipped out of bed. She went down the hall to the other bedroom, went in quietly to see the contessa still slept, washed, and, with the help of one of the maids who appeared shortly afterward, got herself ready for the day.

Somehow, Lauryn thought it might be a trying one.

When she went down to the dining room, the earl joined her soon after. When he came into the room, he walked across to the table, and, although he did not kiss her with the footman and maid in the room, bent to smile and say, "Good morning, Mrs. Smith."

"A particularly fine one," she agreed, with a private smile.

"After such a fine night, how could it not be?" he replied, even more quietly, then straightened and went to fill a plate from the sideboard while the maid poured his tea.

He sat down and applied himself to his breakfast with, she saw, a hearty appetite. Smiling down at her plate, she spread some very good peach jam onto her toast and took a bite.

They sat in companionable silence, almost like a real married couple, Lauryn thought with a pang, and it seemed so unremarkable and pleasant, sharing a breakfast table, that all her worries seemed silly and small.

And then she heard, distinctly, the sound of the brass knocker from the front door. The footman turned and went into the hallway, and the earl also lifted his head.

Frowning, he said, "Who on earth, at this hour?" He set down his teacup and turned to the maidservant. "Is my brother at home?"

The maid answered, a bit hesitantly, "I don't think his camp bed was slept in last night, me lord."

Marcus swore beneath his breath. "A fine hour to be returning from his adventures. The boy will never grow up."

Lauryn hoped the brothers would not quarrel again. She heard the sound of heavy footsteps in the hall—oh, dear, was Carter drunk? It did not sound like him at all. She looked toward the hall, waiting for him to emerge.

In a moment, in the doorway appeared the broad frame of her father-in-law, Squire Harris.

"Squire!" She gasped and dropped her piece of toast.

Fourteen

"*Lauryn!*" *Squire Harris exclaimed, his voice heavy.* "You are indeed here, and with such a man! I feared it would be so, but I can hardly credit it."

The earl turned his head and motioned to both servants; the footman had come back into the room behind the new arrival. "You may leave."

They filed out of the room, though the maid threw a glance back at them, looking distinctly curious. Then the footman shut the door behind them.

Lauryn half rose from her chair, then sank back into it, clutching the frame. Her knees had gone weak and she thought she might swoon, and she had never done such a thing in her life. "Why—how—"

"How did I find you? You may well ask, child. Going off without a word to your own family. Your sisters have been in a rare state, I may tell you!"

"But I left Ophelia a note!" Lauryn tried to interject.

"She had not a word, I promise you," he told her, his voice grim.

"But I did, I gave it to her daughter to give to her," Lauryn said, her voice trembling. "Oh, dear, it must have gone astray. I am so sorry you have all been worried about me. I should have written—I just didn't think. . . ."

She had had other things on her mind. She had been an inexcusably selfish wretch, Lauryn told herself.

"How did you realize that your daughter-in-law was here, then?" Marcus inquired, his voice even.

The squire turned his head, and his expression changed. "A chance encounter with a man who had played cards with us both, Sutton. Said he'd been at your estate later when you'd— ah—shown off a new favorite, a woman with pale skin, red gold hair, and striking beauty. That sounded much too familiar."

The older man drew a deep breath, as if holding on to his self-control only with great effort. He drew a packet of papers out of an inside pocket and tossed them onto the table, where they made a solid thud.

"And then when I received the deeds to my estate back from your man of business . . ." His frown was menacing. "I don't know what you take me for, Sutton, but I'm not a fool! Whatever diabolic bargain you convinced my innocent daughter-in-law to make, over a foolish mistake that was mine alone!"

"No, no," Lauryn interrupted. "It's not what you think!"

"Certainly not," Marcus said at almost the same time. They both paused, and the moment of silence allowed the squire to charge forward again, like a bull with only one thought in his head.

"I will not stand by and allow you to destroy her good name. I am here to remove her from your influence and return her to her invalid father, who has not the health to meet you on his own behalf, and for the sake of her honor, to call you out, Sutton!"

"No, no, you can't!" Lauryn thought she might die, here and now. It was all her fault. She had wanted to help her father-in-law, not destroy him totally! If he killed Marcus in a duel, he would go to prison, or hang, and Marcus—oh, dear heaven, Marcus would be dead. And if the squire were killed,

Marcus would be convicted, and she would have the squire's death on her conscience for as long as she existed. How could she live with that?

"Squire Harris, you must listen," Marcus said, meeting the older man's outraged gaze. "You are jumping to conclusions."

"When I see the two of you alone in a secluded hideaway, what other conclusion should I come to?" the squire thundered.

"But they are not alone! Who zaid they vere alone?" Someone spoke decisively from the doorway. "And who iz this rude and noizy man?"

Lauryn jumped. She had not heard the door open in the tenseness of the heated exchange, and now she turned, as did the two men, to see the contessa, dressed in her usual Continental elegance, standing in the doorway and looking at the newcomer as if he were a peasant tracking in straw from the barnyard. Lauryn felt hysterical peals of laughter rise inside her, but she pushed them back.

"Contessa, this is my father-in-law, Squire Harris." She looked back. "Squire, this is my friend, the Contessa d'Ellaye."

"And your-sweet daughter-in-the-law 'as not been alone, no. *Moi*—am I not 'ere? Am I no one? Am I not alvays the correct duenna? 'Ave I not alzo been at the earl's estate vith 'er? *C'est dommage* for listening to pernicious gozzip vhen, as zo often, it 'as no truth beneath its ugly head." The contessa looked down her long nose at the squire, who for once appeared confounded.

If the contessa's passionate entreaty did not have him totally convinced, it at least made him stop shouting. Lauryn threw the other woman a grateful glance.

Marcus took advantage of advantage of the pause in the older man's accusations to step in. "As I was trying to tell you, Squire, you have no cause for alarm, and you need not assume nefarious motives. I sent you back the deeds, which I never had any real interest in, because I can hardly accept your property when we are soon going to be, more or less, related."

"What?" Squire Harris turned to stare at him. Which was

just as well, as Lauryn had done the same, knowing that her eyes were very wide. Hopefully her father-in-law would not notice her shock.

"I am hoping to persuade Mrs. Harris to accept my proposal of marriage," Marcus finished, his voice level.

"You expect me to believe such nonsense?" the squire demanded, his face reddening once again. "I already told you I'm not a fool!"

Lauryn had jumped to her feet. "Oh, how can you!"

Rubbing his jaw, her father-in-law stopped and glanced at her.

"Yes, you muzt not inzult her in zuch a vay!" the contessa put in. "Why should Zutton not azk for 'er 'and in marriage? Why iz that zo impossible to believe?"

"I only meant, the difference in estate, in fortune, that's all. Of course Lauryn is lovely and sweet-natured, but—but—"

The contessa made a rude noise, and Lauryn herself had turned away, putting her hands to her face. She couldn't face any of them. She thought, wildly, she should tell both men to go to the devil!

"Lauryn . . ." the earl said.

She shook her head and walked across to stare out the window, though she was aware of seeing nothing.

"I think," she heard the earl say to Squire Harris, "that we should continue this conversation in my study."

The squire grunted. "Aye. I shall speak to you presently, my dear," he called to her, and she knew that he meant, in his bull in the china shop kind of way, to be reassuring. Oh, the fat was in the fire, now.

When she heard them walk out of the room and shut the door behind them, she drew a deep breath and at last turned. The contessa had sat down at the table and was eating a cold piece of ham.

"Shall I call for some hot tea?" she asked. "That was so good of you, Contessa. How can I thank you?"

"Ah, *non*," the other woman made a dismissive motion. "Vhat a loud man your father-in-the-law iz. Does he beat you?"

"No, no," Lauryn said, laughing a little hysterically and coming to sit down once more. Her knees felt suddenly weak. "He just—he's trying to do the right thing as he sees it. I didn't mean to worry everyone. I did leave a note. I wonder why it disappeared? And I should have written once I left. But I knew what would happen if they discovered where I really was."

And that was exactly what had occurred, she thought. And even though the contessa had tried to give her cover, and now the earl had offered another outrageous lie—how long did he think the squire would believe such an implausible story, and one which, moreover, made her ache inside, with its contrast between the real and the fairy tale.

She put one hand to her face.

"I believe I am to vish you 'appy?" the contessa was saying.

Lauryn looked across the table at her. Was she being funny? Surely she would not be cruel enough to offer sarcasm.

"I need to go upstairs," Lauryn murmured. "Please excuse me." And she fled the room.

In the study, the two men faced each other. They were still on their feet, as the squire had refused his host's offer to take a seat, and he still appeared grim faced. "If you expect me to believe that you have sudden and convenient thoughts of marriage—this from a man known to be one of London's most infamous rakes . . ."

Marcus drew a deep breath. He could not plant a facer on the squire's reddened countenance, as much as he longed to. The man was older and he had a legitimate grievance; he was trying to protect Lauryn, even if he did it with all the grace of a cross-eyed ox.

"Sometimes reputations become exaggerated," he said, his tone controlled. "But I will be a good husband, I give you my word. And I think you should allow Lauryn to have a say in her own destiny."

"As if you mean to make a serious offer," the squire snorted. "You shall not get off so easy, my lord. I meant what I said; I came here to call you out."

Once more, Marcus reminded himself to stay calm. The idea that he would lie about such an important proposal made his temper hard to control. And to think that he had been forced to blurt it out in front of Lauryn instead of presenting it carefully to her. Last night he'd thought about how to bring it up, and somehow, no moment, amid all the wondrous passion, had seemed quite the perfect time.

Perhaps he was simply afraid to put it to the test, afraid she would not accept him. . . . He pulled his thoughts back to the obviously still suspicious squire.

"You may call me anything you like," he told the other man. "I am simply not going to accept your challenge." He walked across and pulled open a drawer in his desk, taking out some papers.

"Here." He gestured to the squire to come closer and take a look.

Squire Harris approached the desk and bent over, squinting to read the print and the names written on the document. "But this–this—" he sputtered.

"Yes, this is a special license," Marcus agreed. "I obtained it when I traveled down to London, so that Lauryn and I can be married as soon as she agrees to my proposal. They are not cheap, and I would hardly have gone to this much trouble, applying to the bishop, simply for a bit of what you deem nonsense, don't you think?"

The squire, at last, seemed to have run out of accusations. He sat down heavily in the closest chair. "I find it—well, I am surprised to think I might be wrong."

"I am sorry my reputation is that bad," Marcus told him, going to the tray by the window and pouring out a glass of wine. "I suppose I should have taken a greater care before now about gossip and how it tends to become exaggerated. It simply never seemed worth the trouble."

"And now?" the squire asked, watching him with a surprisingly shrewd gaze.

"Now"—Marcus handed him a glass, and thank heavens the other man took it and seemed at last ready to make a tentative peace—"now, I will have a future family to think of, and I will certainly have to be more careful. That is assuming that she accepts me. If you will excuse me, sir, I think I need to make sure of that, first!"

He nodded to the squire, and then, as he had been wanting to do since they entered the room, went smartly out and back to the dining room.

But to his disappointment, only the contessa was there, finishing a leisurely breakfast. She raised a cup of tea to her lips and glanced at him over the rim.

"If you zeek your perhaps fiancée-to-be, look upstairs. And next time, Zutton, my dear, I should 'andle a proposal of marriage with a bit more élan."

He grimaced. Was Lauryn angry? Disappointed that he had not spoken to her first, in private? It really was a disgraceful way to tell her, in front of everyone.... Proposals were important to women, he had always been told. His heart beating fast, he took the steps in a rush, hurrying up the flight and to his bedroom. The door was shut, and he tapped on the panel.

He heard a murmured, "Come in," and he turned the knob and went inside.

She was sitting in the chair by the hearth, her feet tucked up beneath her. She had been looking into the fire, and she did not at once turn to face him.

If she were truly angry . . . his heart sank. He pulled up a low stool and sat, literally, at her feet, ready to abase himself if that was what she wanted. The only thing he wanted, now, was her.

"I'm sorry the way it came out," Marcus told her, reaching for her hand. "I should have had more forethought."

At least she let him take her hand, grip it in his, and raise it to kiss it lightly. "We didn't expect my father-in-law to come raging into the room," she pointed out, as if it had been only an inconvenience.

"Still, what I said, it must have been a shock."

"Yes, rather," she agreed, her tone hard to read, especially as she still refused to meet his eyes. "How is the squire? Were you able to appease him?"

"Yes, I think so."

"Good," she noted. "That was a clever thing to say, then."

He waited for her to finish, but she paused and did not go on. He pressed her hand and brought it to his cheek, wondering how he could make amends.

"Yes, it is a clever–clever ruse," she continued, clearing her throat. "But eventually, he is bound to notice—"

He suddenly understood what she was saying. "There is no ruse!" He reached to grip her chin and turn her face to his. For the first time he saw the tears sparkling at the edge of her lashes. "My darling Lauryn, do you think I would make sport of such an important subject, to appease anyone?"

She blinked but didn't answer.

"I have been wanting to ask you to marry me for days, but I've been afraid. . . ."

Her eyes widened.

"Yes, afraid, I blush to confess, to know what your answer would be." He forced himself to go on. "I was terrified you might not stay . . ."

She raised her brows. "Marcus, do be serious. How many women have ever turned you down, even on much less important questions?"

"None of them were you," he told her simply.

She caught her breath.

"But—" she began, than paused. "Before the squire came, you never spoke of it—"

"As I said, I was afraid to put it to the test." He closed his eyes for a moment, then looked back at her. "Shall I be forced, as I was with the squire, to take you down and show you the special license?"

"You have already obtained it?" Her eyes widened again.

"Of course. When I went to London," he told her. "It was one of the main reasons I traveled to town."

"Before the squire came," she repeated, almost to herself, and something lightened in her eyes. "So it is not just my honor . . ."

"Your honor is important, I have no doubt. But it is all of you I wish to hold on to, my darling Lauryn," he told her. "Surely, you must know that by now."

"I have had my own fears," she said, very low. "I could not be sure, either, Marcus. You have known many beautiful women, charming women, talented women . . ."

Shaking his head, he pulled her closer and repeated into her hair, "And sad to say, none of them were you."

They sat for a time, sharing the opportunity to be close. Lauryn was very quiet, laying her head against his chest. Then he kissed her once more and placed her upon her feet. "I regret to say we should likely go back downstairs."

"Oh, dear, yes," Lauryn said, blushing. "Squire Harris will think—well, heaven knows what he will think."

She stopped at the looking glass over the bureau to make sure that her gown was straight and her hair in place, then they walked back down the staircase. The squire sat in the dining room with the contessa, having a late breakfast and conversing in apparent harmony.

So they sat down again at the table and had fresh cups of tea, and the squire told Lauryn about her family.

"I understand Ophelia has another play going on. Can't imagine that her husband the vicar puts up with that nonsense." The old-fashioned squire shook his head. "I should think that she would have enough to keep her busy, especially now with the child, and all."

Lauryn raised her brows. "Giles understands how important Ophelia's writing is to her," she noted, her tone even. "Fortunately."

A knock sounded; was someone else at the front door? Good grief, what further unexpected guests could surprise them? Lauryn looked across at the earl. Marcus turned and waited for the footman to return. This time he came with a silver tray, bearing a letter upon it.

Nodding, the earl accepted the letter and uttering his excuses to his guests at the table, ripped it open at once.

He frowned.

"Is anything wrong?" Lauryn asked.

"It is from Colonel Swift," Marcus told them. "The Harbor Master has been killed. I think I should ride into town."

"I can go with you," the squire offered. "I need to find a hotel room, though I mean to start back for London, soon."

"I would prefer, if you don't mind, for you to remain with the ladies until I return. I would feel better with someone here." Marcus looked worried as he turned back to them. "We've had some strange occurrences of late. I would rather not leave them alone with only servants in the house."

"Of course," the older man said. "Happy to be of help."

"But where iz your brother?" the contessa said, as if she had just noticed that Carter was not at the table.

"That is my other concern," Marcus answered, his tone somewhat grim.

Lauryn looked at him, and he met her gaze with a worried frown. When he excused himself to the company, she followed him into the hall.

"May I not come with you?"

"I would really prefer that you do not," he said, keeping his voice low. "There seem to be violent men involved in whatever menace swirls around us. I just hope—"

She looked into his eyes and touched his arm gently. "You don't really think Carter is involved?"

"I don't know," he said honestly. "I hope not; I would not like to think he would be capable of this. But perhaps he became ensnared before he knew how deep he was going to be pulled in, or how evil the men he dealt with . . . I don't know. But I must find him."

She put her arms about him and hugged him, then with a sigh, let him go. "Be careful," she whispered.

He kissed her quickly, relishing the feel of her soft lips and the look of concern in her eyes.

"I will return as soon as I can," he told her. "And I am going to send a couple of Swift's men to stand guard here. I do not like this habit someone has of killing anyone who seems to get in his way!"

As soon as his horse was saddled, Marcus set out, and he

made good time into town, glad that the sky was clear and the road hard and dry. He went straight to Colonel Swift's residence.

Happily, the colonel was at home and waiting for him to arrive. Marcus was admitted at once and taken into the colonel's library.

"Glad that you're here, Sutton," the ex-military man said, standing up from behind his desk as Marcus entered. He looked grave. "Bad business, this."

"I was surprised to get your note. Is it clear that this is murder, then?" He took the chair that the colonel motioned him toward. "No question that it could have been an accident or a natural death?"

Swift poured them both drinks at the sideboard, and then brought the glasses balanced on a tray, offering one to Marcus, before returning to his chair. "Not unless you know how a man can strangle himself."

"Point taken," Marcus said dryly. He lifted his glass to the colonel, then sipped his whiskey.

"Were there signs of a struggle?"

"Almost none. A few papers scattered on his desk, but the lock on the door was not pried, and the body was found lying on the floor behind his desk. The Harbor Master did not seem to have made an excessive effort to try to get away."

"Which suggests he did not realize he was in danger until the last minute, and that he most likely knew his assailant, don't you think?" Marcus suggested.

"Yes, my thoughts, too," Swift agreed.

Marcus sipped the liquor, then said slowly, "I wonder if this killing could be connected in some way to the cargo recovered from my ship."

The colonel narrowed his eyes. "What do you mean?"

"I've found a problem there; someone was smuggling items in my ship that I had no knowledge of, until just recently. Now I'm trying to track down the miscreants involved. I wonder if the Harbor Master could have been taking bribes to look the other way—or even taking a percentage of the profit, perhaps."

"Wouldn't surprise me, I'm sorry to tell you," the colonel said, shaking his head. "This Harbor Master has not had the best reputation."

"What about our men watching the shop on Two Hen Street? Anything new, there?"

"One interesting thing, well, two. Are you aware that your brother has been seen going into the shop?"

Marcus gritted his teeth. "Yes, he told me. My brother can be a bit of a fool. I'm afraid he may have tipped them off to the fact that we have been tailing them, but all we can do is hope not. What else?"

Swift pursed his lips. "Second, they've made two trips to a ship recently docked in the harbor, the *Blue Dragon*. We checked discreetly and its ports of call include Hong Kong and Calcutta."

Marcus set up straighter. "Now, that is news, ports where most anything can be bought and sold."

They discussed how to continue the watch over the warehouse and agreed they must put the ship in the harbor under observation as well. Marcus also asked for two men to be sent out to the hunting lodge.

Then he set out to check the hotel and the bigger taverns, but none of them offered any sighting of his brother.

Where the hell was Carter?

Surely his brother was not involved with this gang of smugglers?

Feeling a prickling of unease, nonetheless, Marcus observed the sunset coloring the sky and decided he had been gone too long. He wanted to get back to the shooting box and check that all was well; he wanted to see Lauryn. He'd considered going by the jeweler's shop, but there were better stores in London, and there was no rush, he told himself. Better to get home just now. He needed Lauryn inside his arms once more, just to reassure himself—would he ever be able to take her presence for granted?

He urged his horse on and before the light had started to fade, he slid out of the saddle, threw his reins over the horse's neck, and rapped the knocker on the door. It seemed to take too long for the footman to come, and he felt the skin crawl on the back of his neck.

If something was wrong—but then the servant opened the door, and Marcus cursed himself for having an imagination that was entirely too active.

He left the servant to take his horse around to the stable and strode quickly inside. He ascended the stairs with equal speed and glanced into the sitting room. Only the contessa met his eyes, but she put out her hand.

"Marcus!"

Something in her tone alerted him.

"What is it?" he demanded, and this time, a cold finger of alarm did run down his back. "What's wrong? Where is Lauryn?"

She looked at him, and he feared the pity he saw in her eyes.

"Madame Lauryn iz gone."

Fifteen

$\mathcal{M}$arcus felt the room spin, and he had to put one hand on the doorframe to steady himself "What do you mean?" His voice sounded harsh even to his ears. "How can she be gone?"

The contessa gave a dainty shrug. "*Je ne sais pas*. I do not know, me. I had gone to 'ave a rest. When I came down, the lady was not 'ere. Nor 'er father-in-law."

He felt the blood in his veins turn to ice, and he could barely walk to the nearest chair. He fell into it. She had had second thoughts about the marriage. She did not love him, she could not bear to tell him so. She had asked the squire to take her home.

Oh, God, how could he bear it? He would be alone again.

Somehow, he had known, in that cold, far part of his heart, the part that had never warmed, that it was too good to be true. That long-buried fear that had survived from his childhood, the terror he had never acknowledged suddenly encased him with its hitherto unrecognized and paralyzing lethargy, and he felt as if he could not move, could not think.

Leaning forward, he dropped his face into his hands. His life was over.

"Marcuz!" the contessa admonished him. "You must not just zit there. Zomething is wrong, I know it muzt be."

He was too lost in his own despair to hear her. Lauryn could not love him. No woman could love him. Certainly not someone as good and beautiful in body and soul as she. How had he deceived himself—folly, it was all folly.

"Marcuz, she took no clothes. It iz all wrong."

But he had bought her new wardrobe, he thought dully. Lauryn had such pride, she had probably refused to take the new clothes with her. Although, God knew, he would have wanted her to have them. What would he do with them, except burn them to keep them from reminding him of her, her warm touch, her soft skin.

"Marcuz!"

To his shock, he felt a sharp slap on his cheek.

He looked up to see the contessa standing in front of him, her hands on her hips. "Are you mad? Listen to me!"

He blinked. Her voice was a distant buzzing. He tried to concentrate, tried to focus on the contessa instead of his increasing misery. "What did you say?"

"It iz not right, vhy vould she go now? You 'ad just made the proposal!"

"She does not love me," he said dully, as if explaining something so obvious as fire burns and rain falls. "She does not want to marry me. I suppose she asked the squire to take her home."

"You are being ze ninny, Marcuz!" The contessa shook her head. "Of courze the lady loves you. Do you not zee 'ow she looks at you? 'Ow she is pulled to you? Are you blind?"

A faint tremor of hope stirred inside him. He was afraid to allow it to take root. "But she never said yes. I thought she was happy, but now it occurs to me"—the words were like huge, jagged chunks of pure agony, and it pained him to pull them out, one by one—"It occurs to me that she never actually said yes. Worse, she has never said she loves me. . . ." The lump in his throat was big enough to choke his own horse. He tried to swallow and found that he could not.

"Did you forbid 'er to zay the vord?" The contessa gave him a shrewd look.

"What?" He stared at her.

"Oh, Marcuz," she shook her head at him and sighed. "I remember your tricks, my dear foolish man. When we began our tryst, you told me never to forget it was only for amuzement. You bade me not talk of love or commitment, never to think that we vould be together for the long time. Do you not recall? And what did you tell Miz. Smith of the changing names?"

Marcus groaned out loud. What a fool he was, indeed!

"But if she does love me, why would she leave?" He felt the first seed of hope put out tiny tendrils, and he was almost afraid to offer it encouragement. Did she really love him after all?

"That is vat ve muzt think of," the contessa suggested. "Because if Madame Lauryn did not go of 'er own volition, Marcuz—"

"My God!" He jumped to his feet. "If there is any chance of that!" He walked up and down, fear cold within him now, worse than even his despair had been. "You are sure she is not in the house?"

The contessa nodded. "*Oui*. I have zearched it all. Zent zervants to the outbuildingz, though why she vould go there— ve looked, but *c'est rien*. There iz not a zign of her."

His lips pressed together into a thin line, Marcus headed back toward the front doors. He walked outside, looking around the front of the house. The gravel drive was too hard packed to offer him any clues, but he walked out to the gates, and there he saw something he had not bothered to take note of in his haste to see his love when he had ridden in.

A carriage had recently stood here; he saw the indentations in the slightly muddy earth, and signs of the horses that had pulled it. And there, more signs of carriage wheels, and if anything—he felt the hair on the back of his neck prickle—the wheels seemed to leave slightly deeper lines in the soft earth, as if more weight might have been added to the carriage.

Had Lauryn been taken away in this unknown carriage?

The squire had come on the public stage and hired a smaller vehicle in the nearest town; these were not the marks of his gig, Marcus was certain. To be sure, however, he almost ran back to his stable.

Sure enough, the squire's hired gig still sat outside, and his two-horse team were still being tended by the earl's servants. No, Lauryn had not left with the squire, so they had two people unaccounted for, or three, if Marcus counted his brother.

Bloody hell.

His heart racing with fear for Lauryn, most of all, and concern for all of them, Marcus yelled at the nearest groom, "Saddle a fresh horse."

"Aye, yer lordship," the man answered, dropping the brush and hurrying toward the tack room.

Marcus ran back toward the house. Inside he told the contessa what he had found. "Send a note to Colonel Swift and tell him what we know, and what we fear," he said.

"Vhat vill you do?" Her voice was tight with concern.

"Follow the tracks as long as they last," he told her. "The drive is muddy, and the tracks will likely blend into other vehicles' treads on the road. But I must try."

After Marcus departed, the contessa went upstairs. She and the squire did not seem to get along; they had a fundamental difference of worldview, Lauryn thought, privately finding it a tiny bit amusing.

She offered to show the squire around the grounds; it was a bright sunny day after another night of rain, and getting some fresh air sounded appealing.

This turned out to be a good move, for when they had some private space, she discovered that the squire had more news to share.

"You may find this a surprise," he said, clearing his throat as they walked among the blooming wildflowers and artfully planted shrubs that adorned the rock garden. "That is, I know it has been a short time, but I got to know her after you left. She came up to see about me numerous times, asked if I had ordered dinner, even blessed me out once when I came back to the hotel one night having, ah, overindulged in the spirits a bit, but in a way that seemed to indicate a genuine interest."

"Really?" Lauryn lifted her brows. "Of whom are we speaking?"

"Oh." The squire looked a bit self-conscious. "Miss Mallard, the hotel owner's daughter. I know she's not precisely a lady, perhaps, with her father in trade, but she's a very ladylike girl, nice manners and very modest and well behaved."

Lauryn bit her lip to keep from smiling too widely. She thought she could see where this was going now, and she was delighted. "Oh yes, I thought so, too."

"And I had noticed her earlier. We'd chatted now and then, you know," he added. "So it's not all that sudden, in a way, but . . ."

"But?" she prompted, when he paused again and rubbed his boot against one the larger rocks, still seeming to find it hard to get all the words out. Was he afraid of what she would say? "I thought her very nice, myself."

"Yes, indeed." He brightened. "And it was so quiet, without you there, you know, so we began eating dinner together, and I got to know her better. Anyhow, I have proposed, and she has accepted," he blurted, all in a rush. "And I hope you will not mind. Of course, now, it will not be so bad. I was worried about you and Martha sharing the same house, and perhaps not being happy, but now—"

"I think it is a wonderful surprise," Lauryn told him, smiling and leaning to kiss her father-in-law's cheek. "I hope you both are very happy."

He would have a reason to live again, she thought. He could go back to Yorkshire and put the pieces of his life back together. As young as Martha was, and really—the squire was not an old man—there was even the chance of more children. No one could replace her late husband, but if a new son or daughter should be born, it would make the squire and his new wife most happy. She blinked hard for a moment, then smiled most sincerely at him. "I'm delighted for you!"

He looked both happy and relieved, and they continued to walk and chat.

Presently, the wind picked up, and the clouds overhead turned darker.

"It looks as if it might rain again," Lauryn observed, shivering. She had come outside without a shawl. "Perhaps we should go in."

She led the way back toward the house. As she headed for the corner of the building, going first on the narrow rock path, she lowered her head against the breeze and almost stepped into a dark form.

Gasping, she looked up in surprise.

Hardly an arm's length away stood the Asian man she had seen spying on the warehouse.

Before she could call out, he had one hand pressed hard against her mouth, the other pulling her to him. He smelled of garlic and other spices she did not recognize, exotic, pungent scents. She kicked, but her soft boots did little damage, and his arms had remarkable strength. She struggled against him, but she could not break his hold, and she couldn't even make enough noise to warn the squire.

From the corner of her eyes, she saw two other forms slip around them and heard an ominous grunt as the thud of a blow fell. There was the crumpling of a body falling.

Oh, dear Lord, she thought. Don't let him be dead, not now, when he is finally ready to start living again.

And what about her? Would they kill her here, too, when she was so full of love, also taking the first steps toward a heady new life, with a man she loved so desperately?

Oh, Marcus, she thought, where are you?

And then lack of air made her lungs ache and her insides go hollow. Stars blossomed before her eyes, and her own knees weakened. She slumped against her attacker, unable even to struggle any longer. Darkness descended.

She came to once, facedown on a hard seat, becoming dimly aware of the rumble of carriage wheels rolling and feeling herself jostled roughly. Desperate for air, she tried to get a breath, but she also felt instinctively that she must not show that she was awake, so even though her limbs cramped painfully, she did not move, and she kept her eyelids closed. She could feel ropes binding her arms, and something also bound her mouth.

Would she ever see Marcus again? Despair washed over her, and she almost sobbed aloud, but a memory of the comfort of his arms about her, the glory of their blissful unions, the simple pleasure of sharing a secret smile when they both found humor in someone's else's comment helped her hold onto a kernel of stubborn resolve. No, she must not give up!

She had found something so precious, so rare—a true kinship of mind and body and spirit—how dare these murderous criminals attempt to take that away from her just as she was about to grasp a whole wondrous new life?

"Oh, please, God, help me to survive," she prayed silently. "Pray keep the squire safe, too; he also has a new life before him. Show me the way out of this." She kept her eyes closed. If they were inside a carriage, she thought there would be little of merit to take note of, and she tried to have patience. It was not as if she had any choice! She had to bide her time.

It was as Marcus feared; before he had gone very far, it became impossible to follow the muddy trail of the carriage as it blended into other treads from other carriages that had crisscrossed the main road. When he had jumped off his horse for the dozenth time and knelt to try to make out which track might mark the vehicle he sought, he knew it was hopeless. And the sun was higher now, drying up the muddy trails.

Cursing, he remounted and pushed his heels into his horse's sides, urging him on. At least now that he was not watching every foot of the road, he could make better time. As he rode, he thought hard. He had two leads, the shop on Two Hen Street and the ship in the harbor. Which was the most likely?

The ship worried him the most simply because if Lauryn

were taken to the ship, and it were to set sail—his heart raced just thinking of the dangers! She could be taken to the other side of the world, or her throat cut and her body dropped into the ocean on the way, and he would never see her again, have no chance of saving her. He could not bear to contemplate such a fate!

He had to save her. She was his life now. He could not bear to even consider an existence without her.

He prodded his horse to an even faster gait. The universe could not be so cruel as to show him the possibility of such happiness and then snatch it away again. He would find her, he would get her back, or die trying.

Lauryn found that lying sprawled across the seat of a small carriage, closeted in such close quarters with several men who did not seem to wash often and who smelled of sweat and unfamiliar spices, while one bounced about on a bumpy road with eyes closed, was a good way to become rapidly nauseated. However, she had a surely dirty cloth bound about her mouth, to keep her from crying out when she awoke, she surmised, so she worked hard at not retching, because that would only make matters worse. She feared they must be riding forever, but at last the carriage pulled up to a stop, and the ride had likely not been as long as it seemed.

The kidnappers had been talking in low voices among themselves for the last part of the ride, but as they spoke in a strangely accented language that she had never heard before, their conversation was not helpful. Lauryn had no clue what they were about to do, or why they were doing it, which was most frustrating.

She didn't know if they were about to kill her—although in that case, why had they not done so back at the hunting lodge? Which brought back frightening questions about what they had done to the squire, but worrying did no good, so she pushed those thoughts away. She had to think of herself and a way to escape. She kept her eyelids resolutely shut, and now she heard her captors scrambling out of the carriage and the door shutting.

She waited several long minutes to be sure all of the men had climbed out, but when she heard nothing, she allowed herself to carefully open one eye just a slit. There was nothing to see: the curtains were pulled over the small windows. The carriage was small and dirty, likely a hired vehicle, she thought. She was lying sprawled across one of the seats, and she could not even change her position or they would know she was awake, and she thought it more prudent to put off "waking" for as long as she could.

She tried to hear what was outside the carriage; the door had been left just a little ajar. Where were they? Drawing a deep breath, she smelled dead fish and the scent of brine, and she could make out shouts and whistles that were faintly familiar. She felt herself go cold.

They were at the docks. Would they toss her into the water? She could swim a little. When she and her sisters were small, they had gone into one of the lakes near her home, and her father had taught them. But with her arms tied, she would sink at once. She shivered with fear. Watching the door, Lauryn struggled to lift her bound arms far enough to allow her fingertips to touch the cloth strip over her mouth. Could she move it a little?

She pushed it up so she could bring her teeth to bear on the ropes on her wrists. Gnawing at the ropes, she tried to loosen the knots. The ropes were tight, biting into her skin, and the knots seemed secure.

Oh, damn, damn, she thought.

Then the sound of footsteps near the door forced her to hastily pull the gag back into place and lie down as she had been, shutting her eyes quickly. She heard the door pulled open, and the chatter of more foreign words.

To her alarm, they were wrapping her in some heavy cloth, and then two of them grabbed her shoulders and feet and it was all she could do not to shriek against her gag as they lifted her with ungallant force out of the carriage.

She was carried like a roll of carpet quickly across the

docks. Lauryn thought of screaming for help, but she was now so muffled in fabric that she doubted anyone would hear her. And anyhow, the gag across her mouth prevented her from making any noticeable outcry.

Worse yet, the folds of cloth around her allowed very little air to reach her. She was gasping for breath—was this how they would kill her, instead of the watery grave she had feared? The enveloping folds were suffocating and she fought for breath, but a deeper darkness was descending once more.

*Marcus made up his mind as he approached the out-*skirts of town and rode straight for the docks. The image of that ship, poised to sail away, kept haunting him. The shop would be there, he told himself. The ship was too easily moved and should be checked out right away. As he rode toward the harbor, however, he had time to appreciate that the ship, sitting out in the water, would also present special challenges. One might find several ways to sneak into a building without being noticed, but trespassing onto a ship was another question altogether.

He stopped at the hotel and left his horse and then walked the last couple of blocks to the docks so he could approach quietly. His heart seemed to skip a beat when he saw to his intense relief that yes, the *Blue Dragon* still sat at anchor in the same spot.

Now, what to do?

He walked casually among the bustling sailors and dockworkers, at last finding a man with a wooden leg who was selling hot apple turnovers from a cart at the far side of the dock.

Waiting till the man had a lull in his trade, Marcus went up and bought a pastry, tipping him generously.

"Ta, gov," the man said, winking.

"Guess you get a good view of the goings-on from here," Marcus said, trying to make his tone light.

"You could say that, gov," the vendor agreed, wiping his hands on his greasy apron.

"You seen anything odd about that ship?" Marcus took the last bite of the turnover and pointed to the one he meant, licking his fingers.

"The China blokes? They don't talk much, 'cept to each other, and who can make that out." The man shook his head.

"What have they got on their ship?" Marcus persisted. "You seen what comes and goes?"

"Not much," the vendor told him. "They took some boxes off. Took a rug on today, sorta peculiar, I thought, but who knows about foreign blokes, you know?"

"I know," Marcus agreed, but he felt a icy shiver up his spine. A rolled up rug would hide a body, living or dead . . .

He had to work fast!

Could he get more information, even official help? Who had replaced the murdered Harbor Master? He proceeded to the office to find out that the replacement was a short man with a stutter who was still trying to figure out the ins and outs of his position.

"Ah, my lord, I'm n-not sure that we can go aboard a sh-ship of a foreign nationality and search without more cause—"

"But I have cause!" Marcus almost shouted. "They may have abducted my fiancée, you idiot!"

"But we have no real evidence, your l–lordship," the Harbor Master told him, without meeting his angry gaze. He glanced through a stack of papers. "I will have to check my regulations and get b-back to you."

"Regulations be damned," Marcus muttered. He strode out of the office, knowing only that he would have to find Lauryn himself, and fast.

But coming out of the building, he almost collided with Colonel Swift, and his spirits lifted at once.

"There you are!" the colonel said. "Thought you'd be here. I got the note from the contessa and I came at once, with some of my men."

"So you know about Mrs. Smith," Marcus told him.

The other man nodded. "Yes, damned worrying. At least, you'll be glad to hear that after you left, they found the squire in a heap outside the house."

"How is he?" Marcus asked quickly. "Is he alive?"

"Has a nasty knock on the head, but he's come around, though a bit dazed. Should be all right," the colonel told him. "But now, what about your lady?"

Marcus looked toward the harbor. "I tried to get the new Harbor Master to give me permission for a search party, but he hasn't found the correct regulation, or more important, the backbone, to order it done, so . . ."

"So?" the colonel prompted.

"So it looks as if I will have to go out on my own," Marcus told him.

Swift grinned. "I can give you a hand with that, if you wish."

Marcus smiled back. "If you don't mind breaking a law or two, in a good cause," he pointed out. "My biggest fear has been that they would sail out of here before I can get into the damned hold to make sure they don't have Lauryn aboard." He knew his expression was bleak as he stared out across the water. "I don't dare try to get out there before dark; there's no way to sneak up on a bloody ship."

The colonel nodded toward the water. "I'm no seaman, Sutton, but having lived in a seaport for years, I can relieve your mind on that score. The tide has turned; they won't be sailing this day."

"Ah." Marcus took a deep breath. "That is the best news I've had. Then I would say we'd best get busy; we have some preparations to make."

It was just as well he had something to keep him busy; otherwise, the hours remaining to sunset would have crawled painfully by. In the back of his mind, Marcus was tormented with thoughts of Lauryn. Where was she, what was happening to her? If she were in danger, being mistreated right now . . . it made his stomach turn, just considering it.

He had to take it step-by-step—rushing in precipitously could just get her killed, he reminded himself again and again. A hostage onboard a ship could be all too easily disposed of by dropping her body overboard, and that they must avoid at all cost. So he continued to gather his men and the boats they would need to slip out across the harbor as soon as it was dark enough. The day dragged on, and from now to the rest of his life, he felt sure he would never remember another day that stretched so slowly and painfully to its close.

After making final arrangements, he and the colonel and their men shared an ale and bread and cheese and meat pies at a tavern toward the last hours of the day. He heard the reports on the watches that had been kept on the shop, as well, during the time they had waited. Nothing that was very exciting, except more contacts between the shop and the ship. There were certainly packages being passed back and forth.

"So if they are bringing in merchandise, the shop could be where it is sold," the colonel said, keeping his voice low.

Taking a swallow of his bitter ale, Marcus nodded. "Yes, I think that must be how it is worked."

"And you think someone connected with your shipping company was using your ships to aid in the smuggling?"

Marcus grimaced. "It looks that way."

The colonel shook his head. "I'm sure that was a blow, to find one of your own men selling you out, so to speak. Do you know who it is?"

Marcus thought of his brother, still unaccounted for. "No, I have some suspicions, but I'm not sure, as yet." He glanced at the sky outside, deepening from gray to black. "I think we can go to the boats now, do you agree?"

The older man nodded and motioned to their men, who put down their thick mugs. They stood and headed toward the boats.

This time when Lauryn woke, her head throbbed with a dull ache and her chest still seemed tight from struggling to breathe inside the thick folds of the rug. Her arms remained tethered and were almost numb by now, but the gag on her mouth seemed to have worked a little loose. She was half lying, half sitting, as if she had been pitched onto the floor facing the wall and left there. She also seemed to be sitting partly in a puddle; her wet clinging clothes added to her discomfort.

She must still be dizzy, Lauryn thought, from all the shaking and tossing about. She felt as if she were moving, very subtly. The floor seemed to be shifting beneath her, moving back and forth in a slight motion.

Then she became aware that it was not just her dizziness—the floor *was* moving back and forth, back and forth.

She was on a boat, a ship. Oh, God, where were her unknown captors going to take her?

Or was her first thought true—would they simply convey her out to sea, drop her into the ocean, and allow her to sink?

Lauryn thought that drowning would not be a good way to die.

She had to get out of these bonds!

She struggled against the ropes that secured her wrists, but they were still firm and the knots were damnably tight and competently tied. The gag around her mouth seemed to be slipping a bit, however, and she was able with great effort, as her arms had become almost numb, to lift her hands again and this time pull the gag down to fall against her chest, and then to once more use her teeth to gnaw upon the ropes that restrained her wrists. Still, she was unable to make much leeway.

Desperate, she pushed herself up a little, intending to look around to see if there was anything in the room that she might use to try to cut the ropes. A row of boxes and straw hampers were stacked along one wall. She twisted to see over her shoulder and as she did, Lauryn gasped.

There was another body in the room.

Sixteen

Lauryn struggled to turn herself enough to get a proper view. It was a man, and he was wearing western attire, not the dark pajama-like outfits the Asians wore. It was—she twisted again, trying to get a view of his face—it was—

"Carter!"

"Eh?" came a drowsy but familiar voice.

"Carter, what are you doing here?" she demanded.

"The rats are doing a jig," he told her. "Not to worry. Too much cinnamon will spoil the pudding."

"Carter, wake up!" she insisted, keeping her voice low so that she would not be overheard outside their compartment. Now that she could see him better, she saw that he was not bound. "You must get these ropes off me. I don't know what they are going to do with us. Carter, wake up!"

He blinked again as if struggling to see her. "Ah, you came to the tea party? One lump or two?"

"We'll have more lumps than that if we don't get out of here," she told him grimly. "Carter, you must untie my hands."

"In a moment, so sleepy . . ."

To her horror, he shut his eyes again.

"Now, Carter, this is serious!" she hissed at him. "I don't want to die."

He struggled to open an eye, then the other. "What's dying?"

"Us, you ninny. Wake up, you must wake up, Carter!" She heard her voice break and swallowed hard. She couldn't lose control now.

But at least he seemed a bit more alert. "What's wrong? Don't want to see a lady cry, y'know."

"Sit up, Carter, that will help," she told him. "Come closer, you must untie my hands. I cannot do it alone. Please, Carter. You must sit up and help me. I don't want to die."

Pleading with him, talking to him and keeping him awake—he must have been drugged, she thought, whether against his will or of his own volition she had no idea—she coaxed him, one small step at a time, closer to her until she could hold out her arms and get him to peer at the ropes that bound her wrists.

But the fog that clouded his mind also made him clumsy. He pulled at the knots, but his fingers were slack, and he seemed to have little wit about him.

Lauryn was close to tears again. "Carter, you must do this! We may both die here, else," she pleaded.

"I can't," he told her simply. "Never good with knots, not a seaman, don't y'know."

He seemed about to step back, and she gazed at him in alarm. "No, don't leave," she begged him.

"Better to use my knife, don't you think?"

She almost laughed in her relief. "Yes, of course, try the knife."

It was only a small penknife, but the blade was sharp. The ropes would likely ruin the knife, but she promised herself silently she would see to it he received another of the best metal if only they both got out of this alive. He sawed at the coarse rope, and at first, her heart sinking, Lauryn thought the fiber was too tough. She urged him to keep trying, and, although he swayed, he put his lip between his teeth and kept at it.

And at last the rope showed signs of fraying.

Lauryn held her breath. "Yes, Carter, keep going!"

As the rope spilt more deeply, she pulled harder against it. But a sudden sound outside the compartment made her freeze. Oh, God, was someone coming?

"Carter," she whispered, "put your knife in your pocket and go back and lie down. Pretend to be asleep."

"Why?" He blinked at her.

"I think one of the Asians is coming to check on us, or worse," she told him. "Hurry."

He did as he was told, but his movements were still clumsy, and he dropped the small knife almost at her feet. Biting her lip, she reached down to scoop it up inside her palm, closing her fingers around it.

By the time Carter had lain down once more, closing his eyes, the door to their small compartment was indeed creaking open.

Lauryn had already shut her eyes and positioned herself back against the wall, half sitting, half lying, though facing out a bit more than before. She could only hope they would not remember exactly how she had been situated.

She allowed herself to peek out of one half-opened eye when she heard the newcomer grunt from a few feet away. He was bending over Carter. He poked him in the belly.

Carter hiccuped but only jerked a little. "Here now, that hurts!"

The Asian stood up and lifted a wicked-looking club, preparing to bring it down upon Carter's head.

She didn't think Carter was lucid enough to stop him. Pulling her legs beneath her and throwing herself toward the attacker, who had his side turned toward her, she thrust the small knife into his neck.

The result was very unexpected. It was, after all, quite a small knife. A spurt of blood emerged and continued to squirt out like a fountain, without seeming ready to stop at all.

The Asian gasped and put up a hand to try to slow the flow of blood, but his attempts seemed futile.

Lauryn felt sick; she had had no idea her attack would be

so successful. Backing away—she was already covered in the man's blood—she put one hand to her mouth, then saw that even her hand had blood on it. She thought she might be sick.

Circling the man, who had now fallen to his knees, the club dropping from his hands, she tried to get closer to Carter.

"Get up, Carter," she urged. "Others may come. We have to get out of here."

"What's—what's—" Carter had to be pulled to his feet. He, too, was now drenched in the would-be attacker's blood. Losing consciousness, the Asian slumped to the floor. He would-be dead soon, Lauryn thought. She did not think anything could stop the blood gushing out of his neck. She had killed a man; the realization made her dizzy.

She had not meant to do so much. She swallowed hard. She could do nothing to take it back, and the blow to the head might have killed Carter. Would she sacrifice Marcus's brother to save an unknown assailant?

The man lay unmoving, and the bleeding at last slowed. It was done. They had to go. She looked down at the blood soaking her light-colored day dress. Carter's clothes were not much better. If someone saw them, it would be obvious that they had assaulted a crewman. Was there anything in the boxes at the end of the compartment they could use to change into?

First, she had to get herself free. She took up the small knife and, leaning against the wall, put it between her knees. This time, desperate and determined, she attacked the ropes again, ripping the rest of the way until she could pull her wrists, now slippery with blood, free at last.

She went across to the boxes and hampers, searching rapidly through the ones she could pry open. She found a hamper full of apparently new and unworn clothing, the pajama-like dark outfits that the smugglers wore. It would make them less noticeable as she and Carter tried to slip off the ship, she thought. How they would make it across the water—well, one thing at a time, she told herself, her stomach tightening with fear.

She pulled some of the clothing out of the hamper and tugged off her soaked, sticky gown and petticoat, pulling on the loose-fitting outfit over her short shift and drawers. She took her bloody clothes and hid them in the hampers, sticking them deep beneath the other clothing.

In the next box, she found handfuls of small hard balls, paper-covered, with small bits of string emerging from them, rather like candles. They had a distinctive smell which she couldn't place at once, although she felt she should know it. What was this? On a impulse, she put a handful into the pocket of her tunic.

When she was done, she went to kneel beside Carter and shake him awake once more.

"Come, Carter, put on these clothes. We must try to escape."

"Is the pudding ready? Don't burn it again."

"Carter, you must wake up, or we will be killed," she told him.

With more shaking and nagging, she got him on his feet, and he shed his jacket and put on a top like the Asians wore. Then they went to the door of the compartment and eased it open. Lauryn still had the small knife, and she had also picked up the clumsy but lethal weapon that the dead Asian had been prepared to wield.

She led them out into a narrow passage that smelled of foreign odors. It was dark and hard to see.

"Hold my hand and try not to make any sounds," she whispered to Carter. "Now come along."

First they had to get up to the deck, she told herself. Then they would have to find a way to get to shore. Could they swim, if no other way else presented itself? How cold and how rough was the ocean? She felt her heart sink at the thought, and hoped it would not come to that.

She tiptoed along the passage, pulling Carter behind her. He tended to stumble, and she winced at every sound he made. Once he caught something with his foot, and the grating rumble seemed to echo all over the ship.

"Carter!"

Then, to her horror, a man stepped out into the passage ahead of them.

Had they been noticed?

"Shhh," she warned, and they pressed themselves back against the wall of the passageway, hardly daring to breathe. Her heart beat so loudly that Lauryn feared it must be heard all over the ship.

But whoever it was went the other way, and in the dimness did not appear to see them.

It took long moments before she felt she could breathe normally again, but then she unpeeled herself from the wall and tugged Carter, still unsteady on his feet, along with her.

When they reached the end of the passage, she found a narrow, steep flight of rungs, and saying a quick prayer that they met no one coming down as they went up, Lauryn climbed as rapidly as she could, urging Carter to follow behind her.

When she at last smelled fresh air above her, she put her head up cautiously.

She knew this was a dangerous moment, when someone on deck might spot her emerging. But she had to risk it sooner or later. So, waiting a moment, she listened hard. She heard waves slapping the side of the boat, and the cry of a seabird, but no sounds of human voices. Could they be this fortunate?

She had to take the chance. Trying to stay close to the deck and thus be less obvious to any chance observer, she crawled up and out of the hatch. Her strange outfit was at least suitable to clambering around like an insect on a vine, she thought ruefully, her heart beating fast as she tried to look about her.

Carter was not being as careful, and she pulled him down as he came out and started to stand.

"What—"

"Shush!" she commanded.

"Something wrong?" he asked.

"Carter, be silent," she warned him, "if you want to get out of this alive. I can't explain now."

He blinked at her, but she couldn't assume he would have the wits to understand until the drugs wore off.

On hands and knees, she crawled behind a piece of nautical equipment—in the dark, she had no idea what, and she might not have known in the daylight, Lauryn thought—as she tried to figure out what to do next.

Was the earl looking for her? He would be, Lauryn told herself. Surely he was out there, trying to find her, trying to find the men who had abducted her, turning out the local watch and the magistrates, the colonel and his men, and they might have some clues to where she would be, although she wasn't sure if they could have any idea she would be on this damned ship.

But what if he wasn't?

With a chill that ran right through her, Lauryn remembered the earl's mother, his fears about women who left and didn't return.

What if he thought that Lauryn had walked away?

Surely, he would not believe such a thing.

But . . . what if he did? Emotions were not rational, and she had seen the doubt in his eyes before now.

Fear rippled through her. Oh, heavens, she thought. Would she be trapped here because fear entrapped Marcus? She shut her eyes for a moment and tried not to panic. If he did not know by now that she loved him, would love him forever, when would he know?

Would they have any hope of a real life together?

They jolly well wouldn't if the smugglers fed her to the bloody fishes, she thought. And if Marcus didn't come, she had to find a way out for herself.

She looked over the canvas-covered mound in front of her and tried to decide which way they should go. There must be smaller boats about, if they could find one. But then it would have to be lowered, and she had no idea at all how one would do that, and without making noise enough to attract the attention of the crew.

Oh, dear lord, what were they going to do?

But she would not give up without making an effort!

Lauryn rose slightly, bending a little so that she still was barely a shadow on the dark deck. But before she could take more than a step, an arm reached from behind her to wrap about her neck.

Unable to move, she could barely even take a breath.

This was the end.

Seventeen

"Y ou are so anxious to find your way out?" someone spoke softly into her ear, with a heavy Asian accent. "Perhaps I can assist you, yes?"

She wanted to weep, to scream. To have come so far, only to fail.

Lauryn didn't answer. She would struggle, but he had his arm about her neck, and she barely had air to breathe.

Where the hell was Carter?

There seemed to be only one smuggler here. He pushed her out onto a clear area of the deck, closer to a lantern which flickered dimly, giving a small circle of light. But the man stood behind her, holding her stiffly, so she still could not see him.

"I recognize your ugly alien faces," he said, his voice soft. "You are the sister of the brainless one who was watching from the tavern." He addressed Carter. "And you have been to the shop, trying to find out more than you should. You spoke of the house when you were deepest in your drug dream. We had already followed you back to the house in the countryside where you all live. Is it not so?"

He tightened his hold on her neck, and she was too afraid to move. Her assailant seemed to take this as a yes, and she was not about to correct his assumptions about family ties and put Marcus in danger, too.

"We do not like to be followed; we do not like strangers to know about us or our business. Those who do have short lives," her unseen aggressor remarked, with his cold voice. "Our business thrives as long as others ignore us. What we do is easy enough. All we need in the ports is a greedy Englishman or two, and they are easy enough to find. We have important backers. Then there is the opium you locked away from us in the warehouse. You deserve to be punished for that, do you not?"

Lauryn felt as if she had been dipped in ice. Oh, dear God, how was she going to get out of this?

"But first, how did you escape from your compartment?" he demanded.

She didn't even try to answer. He jerked a little on her neck, which made her gag.

"You will respond to me." He repeated the question.

"I turned into a bird and flew," she said, not seeing that she had anything to lose, except a minute or two of time. She was fast losing hope. He held her tightly, and she could see no way to get past his grip.

"You are a witch, perhaps? I have heard the stories. Witches do not like water. Perhaps we should throw you into the ocean and we will be rid of your tricks, yes?"

She shuddered, and was sorry at once as she knew that he felt it.

She thought that he laughed, very low, and the sound made anger spark through her.

"Ah, you do not like this idea. Then it must be a good one. Unfortunately, I must consult with my superior before I toss you over like garbage," he said, his tone, she was sure, designed to be insulting. "He advised holding onto you for a time in case we should need a hostage."

He raised his voice and called out in his own language, and two more crew members appeared out of the darkness.

He removed his arm from her neck and pushed her, and she almost fell. But the two other men grabbed her and shoved her roughly. She fell to the wooden deck and sat there, rubbing her bruised arms.

They were to guard her, Lauryn guessed, while the first man went to get orders on what to do with her now.

But where had Carter disappeared to, and would they check their jail first and find the man she had murdered?

She shivered again. If so, the Asians might not settle for a simple drowning; they might torture her first. Or, heavens, who knew? She needed to get out of here, now!

But she couldn't leave Carter behind. Anyhow, she didn't know how to get away again, with two alert jailers now staring at her.

Then a wisp of movement behind the two men, who stood at the outer circle of the light, both watching her intently, made her blink.

Carter?

Had her two watchmen noticed? No, they didn't turn, and they seemed to have eyes only for her. She plunged her hands deep in to the pockets of her top, wondering if Carter had any ideas. He was still so dazed from the drugs, she rather doubted it. If he tried to attack one of the men, the other would overcome him in short order, even if the first one didn't.

She had his small knife, but with two guards, that seemed worthless, and anyhow, she remembered the blood pouring from the man she had killed and wasn't sure she could do that again, even if she had a hope of hitting the right spot.

Lauryn felt the balls in her pocket and realized she had forgotten she had them, although she still didn't know what they were for. She put one hand back to her nose, trying to identify the odor. And suddenly she knew—it was gunpowder.

These balls held gunpowder?

How could she use them?

If she could set them off—the lantern. She needed to get them inside one of the lanterns. But how, with the men watching?

She stared back at her two jailers, watching them as intently as they watched her. "Could I have a drink of water?" she asked, her tone civil.

They stared at her, not even blinking.

"Just a drink of water?"

Their expressions didn't change.

"Your mother is a pig," she said clearly.

No change.

"I don't think you understand English," she said.

"I think I must do my spell dance," she told them, standing up. "And if I eject circles of power, they must be put into the fire. If there is a spirit outside the circle, whose name is Carter, he must put them into the fire."

Bringing her hands out of her pockets, concealing what she gripped in each fist, she waved her arms into the air, back and forth, in a rhythmic pattern.

The two men still watched, but they glanced at each other, looking somewhat uneasy. She turned and twisted, singing anything that came into her head, snatches of folk song, old nursery rhymes, and always circling a little so she could make them turn with her, so that she edged into the darkness. Waving her arms back and forth, bending to the deck, she rose to the tip of her toes, then bent again, and when she spun the dark paper-covered balls across the deck, she saw the men blink, but she suspected they were not sure of what they saw because she immediately spun back the other way. The two guards turned back with her as if afraid of what she would do next.

They were muttering to each other now. Did they really believe she was a witch? If so, they had a surprise coming soon.

To her relief, she saw Carter behind the guards' backs, sneaking up and opening the lantern's door and slipping the small balls inside its glass guard, then he retreated rapidly.

Abruptly she ceased her singing, and dropped to the deck and covered her head with her arms.

Looking perplexed, the guards stared at her.

The lantern exploded.

One of the guards shouted with pain. A jagged piece of metal had sliced into his cheek. The other seemed more frightened than hurt. Shouting in his own language, he beat the flames out of his clothing.

Lauryn didn't wait to see what happened next. She ran for the dark end of the ship, hoping to find a place to hide, and some way off the damn boat. If necessary, they would have to swim for it. She heard the sound of footfalls and saw Carter pounding along beside her.

"Well done," she breathed.

"Good job to think of the fireworks," he muttered. He seemed to be getting his head in order, as if the drugs might be fading at last from his blood.

"Is that what they were?" she asked. "I should have brought more along. Quiet, now." She ducked under a sail and looked about for a decent hiding place.

Another dusky shadow rose up out of the darkness. She gasped as a hand rose to cover her mouth. Not again!

Then she almost fainted with joy.

She knew the touch and the smell. Not an Asian this time—it was Marcus!

He pulled her hard against him, then, when she clung to him, took his hand away from her mouth and gave her a swift, hard kiss instead.

"How did you get here?" she whispered.

He motioned to Carter for silence.

"We have boats below; we were waiting for some way to get up to the deck unnoticed when you created a splendid diversion," he replied, his voice very quiet. "This way."

He led her toward the side of the ship, and she followed, moving as carefully through the darkness as she could, when suddenly a small light appeared out of the blackness, illuminating a man's face.

Marcus stopped so suddenly that she walked into his back and grunted slightly, then she glanced around him. She started to speak, then bit her lip instead, not sure what was going on.

Behind her, Carter was less careful. He sauntered forward. "Here, Tweed, what're you doing here, ol' man? You get knocked on the head by these Chinese blokes, too?"

"Shut up, Carter," Marcus muttered.

The man holding the small torch smiled, but it was not a cordial expression.

"No, Carter. You have no room in your small brain for subtleties, do you? Did it never occur to you that I might be the one giving the Chinese crew orders instead of the other way around?"

"What?" Carter stared at him.

Eyes widening, Lauryn saw Marcus's shoulders tighten, but she felt his lack of surprise, as well.

"You don't seem to be shocked, 'partner,'" Tweed said. "Don't say you had already suspected me?"

"I didn't want to," Marcus said, his voice low. "But you did have every opportunity, eight years ago. You knew the shipping schedules; you knew the captain of the *Brave Lassie*. You could easily have handled getting the opium off the ships unchallenged. And you always had a hunger for advancement. But you were making money; you were already getting ahead, Tweed, so why?"

The silence seemed long. She could hear the waves hitting the side of the ship, and in the distance, the sound of Chinese voices. Oh, God, she thought. More crew were coming. Marcus and Carter and she would soon be overwhelmed by sheer numbers, and all would be lost.

"Not fast enough," Tweed said, his voice ugly. "Not fast enough, Sutton. You stand there, with your title, and your wealth, and your handsome face—how dare you fault me for wanting more?"

"But you have it now; you've got your title and your wealth against all the odds," Sutton pointed out quickly, his voice low and urgent.

Did he hear the sound of running feet, too? Lauryn felt a drop of perspiration run down the small of her back. The crew were coming, and the three of them would not have a prayer.

"And now you've found the girl you want—so why take such chances? Why stoop to murder again?" the earl demanded.

"It's not enough," Tweed said, sounding desperate. "You should see the damned diamond diadem she's picked out for her engagement present. She always wants more and anyhow, I know too much to stop. This is only a sideshow, pocket money. The important trade goes to big companies, English companies, trading Indian opium into China for big money. I just wanted a little piece of it." He was sweating, too.

It all sounded like nonsense to Lauryn. She knew only that he was going to hold them here until more Chinese arrived, and they would be lost—murdered—how on earth could they evade the man's gun? Daring a quick peek around the earl's shoulder, she saw the pistol pointed at them and felt Marcus's gathering tension. He was going to try to rush Tweed, and Marcus would be shot at close range—she could not let him sacrifice himself for the rest of them! Oh, heavens, what could she do?

She dug her hands into the pockets of her outfit—one last firework ball remained. She pulled it out. If she could hit the torch that he held, the open flame—make just enough of a blast to startle him . . .

She touched Marcus's back to warn him and felt him tense again, though he would not know why. Praying that her aim was good, she stepped a few inches to the side and threw.

The gunpowder exploded in their faces.

Marcus ducked and pulled her down with him.

Tweed instinctively jerked his head away from the fiery exploding powder as he pulled the trigger. But he had lost his careful aim. The ball went up and over them, and then Tweed sagged, cradling his face in his arms.

She wanted to ask Marcus if he was hurt, just to be sure, but he was dragging her with him toward the bow of the ship. "Come on, Carter," he called. "Hurry!"

Crew members were running toward them.

Marcus pulled his own gun from his waist. He fired toward the smuggler leading the rest, and the man fell. Then Marcus lifted her over the side, and she fitted her feet into the rope ladder that hung over the side of the ship.

At another time she would have sworn she'd never be able to climb down such a thing, but when one's life hangs on the need, unusual skills blossom. Lauryn scrambled down with more speed than grace, then gasped as she lost her footing and fell the last couple of feet. But hands reached out to catch her so she did not drop into the water.

Carter came next, while she waited with her heart in her throat, hearing sounds of blows and shouts above them on the deck. At last, there was Marcus, half climbing, half falling down the ladder.

One of the men pushed their boat away from the larger ship. Around her, the men bent to wield their oars with all their strength. Lauryn felt for Marcus in the darkness, even as they thrust themselves away from the blacker silhouette looming above them. He clasped her hand in reassurance.

Their boat rose and fell on the waves that tossed them about like a scrap of seaweed on the vast, trackless ocean. She heard a noise like a hornet zipping over them, and realized with a shiver that bullets were flying past their heads.

"Down!" Marcus pushed her toward the damp musty bottom of the boat. "They are shooting." To the men he called, "Row for your lives!"

Around them the men bent over the oars and plied them with grim energy. Lauren bent lower, too, but she was more interested in the earl's condition. She smelled fresh blood, even with the strong scent of brine on the wind that buffeted their faces and snatched away their voices. When she touched his face, she could feel traces of sticky moisture.

"Are you all right?" she yelled at him as sea spray stung their faces and drenched their clothes.

"Yes." He pressed her hand again and put one arm around her, gripping her, holding tight to the boat with the other as it rocked and swayed.

The moon came out from behind a cloud, and the smugglers on the ship sent more bullets flying their way, but they were almost out of range. She strained her eyes to see Marcus more clearly, but it was still too hard to make out details.

She clung to him as the small boat rose and fell, shifting as the waves lifted, then dropped them. Around them, his men plied the oars that took them away from the ship and back to safety.

When they reached the dock at last, they paused only long enough for Marcus to have a knife wound on one shoulder bound up. When she could see the blood that soaked one side of his shirt, her face paled.

"Don't fret," he told her. "The wound is shallow and not to be considered."

She had her own views about that, but at least the bandages seemed to stop the bleeding. The colonel stayed to inform the new Harbor Master of the night's events, and Marcus promised to return first thing in the morning to add his own information.

"I have a lady here, my fiancée," Marcus explained. "She was kidnapped by the smugglers and has had a harrowing ordeal. And then, too, her chaperone is back at the lodge and will be worried sick about her."

The Harbor Master looked shocked. "Of course, of course, dreadful experience for a lady. You must get her back as soon as may be!"

Lauryn wasn't sure which the man was most concerned about—her safety or her good name. It was a bit amusing to find herself put back on the side of proper ladies once more.

They accepted the loan of Colonel Swift's carriage, and she and Marcus and Carter traveled back to the hunting lodge. While they rode, she and Marcus sat side by side and discussed what would happen to Tweed and the Chinese gang.

"The smugglers will no longer be able to operate here, now that they have been found out," Marcus told them. "How long before they pop up somewhere else, it's hard to say."

"You don't think Tweed will travel back to China with his coconspirators, do you?" Lauryn asked.

"I doubt it," Marcus said, while Carter yawned in the other corner of the carriage. "He would be in an alien land, with no one whom he cared about. And really, I don't know if there is enough hard evidence here to convict him."

"He may get off?" Lauryn widened her eyes when she remembered how close she and Carter had come—and Marcus, too—to dying.

"Not really. Still, I think he will face his own worst nightmares," Marcus said, to her mystification.

"What do you mean?"

"That high-flying fiancée of his, who wanted so much, will not be pleased to have rumors flying about. I rather think she may not stay the course."

"Oh." Lauryn lifted her brows. "No, she doesn't sound the type given to unswerving devotion, does she?"

"So when gossip buzzes, he may find he has lost all the things he really wanted—an aristocratic wife and entry into the highest circles—at the first hint of scandal."

Lauryn sighed and rested her head on his healthy shoulder. She didn't care about scandals. At least Marcus was still relatively well and they had all come out in one piece.

When they entered the shooting box, they found the squire tucked up on Carter's camp bed in the study, his head wrapped in bandages like a turban, looking pale but apparently not too much the worse for wear.

"Lauryn!" he called when he saw her in her strange outfit. "I was coming after you myself, no matter what the damned doctor said, if you had not returned by the morrow—what sort of heathens would kidnap a lady? Thank God you are safe. And you as well, my lord." He looked at the bloodstained shirt and shook his head. "I am glad to see you on your feet."

"I had a bad time, too!" Carter pointed out, looking aggrieved. "The bloody opium smugglers pumped all sorts of noxious stuff into me, don't you know."

"Poor Carter," the contessa murmured, patting his arm. "Ve are zo glad to zee you zafe."

Carter said, "Just so," and didn't appear to notice the slight twinkle in her eyes.

"I am most thankful, *moi*, to zee you all," the contessa said. "Ve have been most disquieted zince you have gone."

"Thank you for looking after the squire," Lauryn told her. "I am so relieved you are all right, sir."

"Oh, I'm too old and tough to be so easily dispatched." Her father-in-law nodded, then winced and seemed to regret the motion. "Do you think you have stopped these blackguards, my lord?"

"Only for the time, I'm afraid. They will show up again in

another coastal town, when they think the fervor has died down. As long as there are fools who will buy opium, they will traffic in it and as for the corporations—we must push Parliament for intervention there." Marcus shook his head at the thought. "I suspect we have put the Englishman who dealt in this end of it out of business, however, so that is something. And the most important thing, of course, is that we have our two lost ones back safely."

"Yes," Carter agreed. "I was of no mind to be fish food!"

Lauryn shivered, and Marcus frowned at his brother.

"If you'll forgive me, I'd like to get out of these—um—this costume," Lauryn said. She headed for the staircase, asking the maid to bring warm water when she could.

When she entered the bedchamber, she was almost surprised at the emotions that rushed through her. How could this room feel so much like home? She had not been here that long, but it seemed like such a refuge already. She had to blink away tears. She was safe here; she had been so happy here.

Not long after she had entered and had, with a shudder, peeled off the foreign clothing and begun to scrub off the alien scents that had come with them, she heard the door open. Peering round the screen, she saw that the earl had entered.

"May I come in?" he asked, his tone formal.

"Of course," she said.

He pulled off his close-fitting jacket and started to shed the shirt that was stained with his blood, but paused; his wound must be tender.

"Let me help," she said.

Rubbing herself quickly dry with a linen towel, she pulled a robe around her and came out to assist. Pushing him gently down to the chair, she eased the shirt over his bandaged side and over his head.

"Wait," she told him. She returned to the dressing table, emptied the dirty water into the pail underneath, poured clean water out of the ewer, and readied soap and towels. "All right," she told him. "Now, come sit in the chair here."

Looking amused, he obeyed. "I'm not a babe."

"No, but I like to take care of you, anyhow," she said. And, she thought, you are weaker than you care to admit from loss of blood. So she bathed him very carefully, cleaning the other scrapes and cuts he had obtained, and he leaned back and seemed to enjoy her tender touch.

When she was done, she took away his soiled and blood-stained clothing and found him fresh nightclothes, then insisted that he lie down in the bed.

"I'll get you a glass of brandy if you like," she told him. "Or a cup of tea before bed."

"Yes," he said. "Anything. But what I want most is you, curled up beside me."

"That part I pledge," she told him. "With all my heart and soul." It sounded much like the wedding vows they would soon be exchanging, and the thought gave her goose bumps, making her skin prickle.

He held out his healthy arm, and she came to him so he could draw her close.

"For all my life, darling Lauryn," he said. She pressed herself close to him and reflected that never had she imagined that she might end up here, so happy, so blessed.

Marcus seemed to see some doubt in her face. He tightened his hold. "What is it?"

Lauryn did not try to dissemble. "You know there will be gossip. Someone is bound to recognize me—there were people who saw me at your estate, the house party . . ."

He grimaced. "Damn Carter and his bright ideas . . . but it doesn't matter, my love."

She raised her brows. "These things always matter."

He shook his head. "No. You are brave enough to stare them down, and we will be together. If there is gossip, it will die. You will be my countess, and even more important, the love of my life. That's what matters."

The last knot inside her seemed to loosen. She lay her head back down upon his chest.

"I love you, Marcus."

She heard him sigh deeply. "That's the first time you've told me so, darling Lauryn."

She punched his good arm lightly. "You forbade me to say it, you wretch. And I have not heard it from you, either!"

"I love you, I adore you, I worship you. I will spend the rest of my life showing you just how much." He raised his head and looked down at her. "How is that?"

She smiled into his dark eyes. "It will do for a start."

Epilogue

*O*phelia looked over to make sure that her husband, Giles, and the other men were occupied with their own talk and shook her head. "Really, Lauryn, I cannot believe you got married so quietly and without the support of your sisters!"

"I know, but under the circumstances . . ." Lauryn began.

"Such as having the honeymoon before the wedding?" Her younger sister's tone was low and teasing. She sipped her flute of champagne. "I never dreamed you could do anything so shocking, Lauryn. But you are safe, thank heavens. Such hair-raising adventures—you turn my blood into ice with your stories!" Ophelia gave a theatrical shiver, adding more thoughtfully, "Although I may borrow the plot for my next play—"

"Don't you dare!" Lauryn interrupted. "That would truly cause gossip."

Ophelia laughed. "But really, has anything been heard about your villain?"

Lauryn sighed. "Marcus got the news just as we were setting off for London. They found a body washed up on shore several towns to the south. It was hard to determine his identity, but he had a leather wallet on him with Tweed's initials embossed upon it, so it is thought to be him."

"Oh!" Ophelia shivered for real this time. "Did he do himself in, or was he murdered by his bloodthirsty cohorts, do you think?"

"That, we'll never know." Lauryn lowered her voice as a maid came by with another tray of delicious savories.

They were having an impromptu celebration at the earl's large house in London. As soon as they had gotten back into town, Lauryn had wasted no time in sending notes around to all available family members.

"At any rate," Ophelia told her, changing the subject quickly, "I am so happy for you, Lauryn. I have been wishing for years, since your first year of mourning ended, that you would find someone, although I did not expect your romance to be so, ah, dramatic."

Lauryn made a face. She had used to lecture her harum-scarum younger sisters often enough; she would hardly allow them to scold her about decorum now. "And you would know about dramatic."

Ophelia giggled. "True."

"And I understand, too," Cordelia, the other twin, suggested. "But we must throw a huge reception for you here, and then you can have another in Yorkshire, so Father and the rest of the family can be there, and we will all journey up and celebrate again. I am just so very happy for you! The earl seems a truly agreeable man."

"Oh, he is, and so much more besides." Lauryn grinned at them. "It will take me months to tell you how wonderful he is."

"We look forward to hearing it," Ophelia agreed, hugging her once more and almost spilling her bubbly on Lauryn's traveling costume. "Although, gracious, you had us so worried. When you have your own little ones, you will know better than to trust an important note to such small hands."

Laughing reluctantly, Lauryn turned to watch Juliette, just now crawling beneath a table, trying to catch up with her cousin Olivia. "Yes, I suppose so."

Her gaze traveled on to see Marcus—his wound was healing

well—speaking to Giles and to Cordelia's husband, Ransom, about the honeymoon trip they were planning. She felt love well up inside her like a golden fountain. "I look forward to that, as well," she said. She felt his answered glance, like an unspoken enticement.

"Come," she told them. "I'm missing Marcus." She cared not at all that her sisters giggled. So, with the little girls pattering behind them, they headed across the big room to rejoin their husbands.

Enter the rich world of
historical romance
with Berkley Books.

Lynn Kurland

Patricia Potter

Betina Krahn

Jodi Thomas

Anne Gracie

Love is timeless.
penguin.com

Discover Romance

berkleyjoveauthors.com
See what's coming
up next from your
favorite romance
authors and
explore all
the latest
Berkley,
Jove, and
Sensation
selections.

Fall in love

- See what's new
- Find author appearances
- Win fantastic prizes
- Get reading recommendations
- Chat with authors and other fans
- Read interviews with authors you love

berkleyjoveauthors.com

Penguin Group (USA) Online

What will you be reading tomorrow?

Tom Clancy, Patricia Cornwell, W.E.B. Griffin,
Nora Roberts, William Gibson, Robin Cook,
Brian Jacques, Catherine Coulter, Stephen King,
Dean Koontz, Ken Follett, Clive Cussler,
Eric Jerome Dickey, John Sandford,
Terry McMillan, Sue Monk Kidd, Amy Tan,
John Berendt…

You'll find them all at
penguin.com

*Read excerpts and newsletters,
find tour schedules and reading group guides,
and enter contests.*

Subscribe to Penguin Group (USA) newsletters
and get an exclusive inside look
at exciting new titles and the authors you love
long before everyone else does.

PENGUIN GROUP (USA)
us.penguingroup.com